Rachael Stewart ad[...]
heartwarmingly rom[...]
been writing since sl[...]
the stacks of scrawle[...]
to. A Welsh lass at heart, she now lives in Yorkshire,
with her very own hero and three awesome kids,
and if she's not tapping out a story she's wrapped
up in one or enjoying the great outdoors. Reach
her on Facebook, Twitter (@rach_b52) or at
rachaelstewartauthor.com.

Award-winning author of sensual, emotional
adventures of the heart, **Rebecca Hunter** writes sexy
stories about alpha men and spirited women set in
Australia for Dare. She lives with her family in the
San Francisco Bay Area.

If you liked *Mr Temptation* and *Baring It All*
why not try
Pleasure Payback by Zara Cox
Rescue Me by Faye Avalon

Discover more at millsandboon.co.uk

MR TEMPTATION

RACHAEL STEWART

BARING IT ALL

REBECCA HUNTER

MILLS & BOON

First Published in Great Britain 2019
by Mills & Boon, an imprint of HarperCollins*Publishers*
1 London Bridge Street, London, SE1 9GF

Mr Temptation © 2019 Rachael Stewart

Baring It All © 2019 Rebecca Hunter

ISBN: 978-0-263-27382-3

MIX
Paper from
responsible sources
FSC C007454

This book is produced from independently certified FSC™ paper
to ensure responsible forest management.
For more information visit www.harpercollins.co.uk/green.

Printed and bound in Spain
by CPI, Barcelona

MR TEMPTATION

RACHAEL STEWART

MILLS & BOON

To my grandparents,
for inspiring my love of Mills & Boon.

To Jenny, for all those weekend trips to the market,
scooping up secondhand Mills & Boons and writing
our own tales together;

And, of course, to my very own Mr Temptation, for
proving to me that love like this is real and worth
taking a chance on.

Yours always, R. xx

CHAPTER ONE

'*Fuckers.*'

Daniel raked his fingers through his hair and rose to sit at the edge of the bed, his body hunching over his mobile and its glaring news feed.

It was entirely expected, everything he'd envisaged the night before, so why was he so riled?

He'd asked for it. And the press had delivered. In fact, more than delivered—the article had to be the most scathing yet.

But where was the usual sense of fun, the thrill of living up to his name, of pissing on his mum's glory?

'Honey, whatever it is, let it go and come back to bed.'

The voice purred at him from behind, a set of nails down his bare back designed to add to the appeal, and yet he wasn't taking the bait. Not even a nibble. Both his cock and mind uninterested.

'You should go.' He twisted to take in the naked rear of the woman who was last night's fix. What was it? The third—fourth time they'd slept together.

She was beautiful, everything you'd expect an elite

model of her calibre to be. But he was bored, the spark already dying out; it had to be a record. He felt a pang of guilt and buried it. She wouldn't care, not really; he was careful who he chose to fill his bed. And she'd got what she came for. He always lived up to his rep.

'What time is it?' She rolled onto her back, stretching out and pulling the crisp white sheet down her front, her bared rose-tipped breasts pert and alert. His cock gave a twinge, a little interest after all...

But not enough.

It was gone eight. He was due at his sister's in less than an hour and the press were already gathering outside. The sooner they broke out, the better.

'Time you went,' he said, rising to his feet. 'I'm hitting the shower.'

'I'll come with.'

She moved to follow and he faced her off, unconcerned that the semi he was sporting gave a very different response to his, '*Nej*—don't.'

She gave a sultry pout and fell back onto her haunches. 'Party pooper.'

'Don't tell me you haven't got a rammed schedule for today.'

She rolled her eyes with a resigned sigh. 'Thanks for the reminder.'

She turned to reach across the bed and take up her mobile from the side table, her focus now on the screen while her pert little ass beckoned him.

Shower. Now.

Making himself turn away, he headed to the bathroom. He could get his fix later, find someone new perhaps. Hell, he could have his pick…maybe that was the problem…

'Annie, dahling,' he heard her coo down the phone, 'can you sort me an escape from The Shard? Seems we've caused a bit of a stir with the paparazzi…'

He set the jets of water running and drowned out the remainder of her conversation. He'd just finished with his hair when her naked body curved around the doorframe.

'Sure I can't change your mind?'

Ah, fuck it, another ten minutes isn't going to hurt…

'Zara, Shit-Bag is on line one—he's after a number for a contact, apparently.'

EJ, her PA and right hand, leant back over her office chair, her head appearing through the open doorway to Zara's private office. Not even her black-rimmed glasses were big enough to conceal her raised auburn brow and sparking blue gaze. She was as pissed at taking the call as Zara was to receive it.

'Tell him I have an appointment. I'll call him back.' It wasn't a lie, she did, and she needed to get moving if she wasn't going to be late. She had the whole day mapped out touring London with her latest client, Julia Larsson, showing her abodes that matched the property brief they'd mapped out together to a T.

'Righto,' EJ said, dropping back into her own space. Although it wasn't really as if the rest of her team had any designated space as such. Not yet.

Other than her office, the walls were only partially in place, the refit as per her design spec was halfway through completion and they were all living with a rather open workspace in the interim. Not that it really mattered. Zara only had a handful of employees currently, but it paid to have space for her expansion plans and, more importantly, it paid to have the right kind of space to entertain the right kind of clients.

The kind of space she'd had up until five months ago when Shit-Bag had left her no choice but to walk out of her former company. Six months of trying to work together following their break-up having taken their toll.

'Err, Zara, he says it's urgent.'

EJ walked her chair back into view and gave her an apologetic grimace, making a derogatory hand signal against the receiver at the same time. The latter succeeded in pulling out a smirk. How very different from the way EJ had reacted to him in the early days. How very different from every woman when first being caught in his charismatic web. She'd been no exception. Falling for his clean and slick appearance, a voice that rumbled with teasing provocation no matter what was being said and a body fit for a boxing ring.

Yeah, you fell for it, all right, but no more—you're older and wiser for it now.

'It's okay,' she assured her, 'let him through.'

Her tummy twisted, but her smile at EJ was solid. She wasn't going to upset her with her own discomfort. And she most definitely wasn't going to let *him* hear how much he could still hurt her.

She lifted the phone receiver and accepted the call. 'Charles, what is it?'

'Zara, be a good girl and send me Tristan Black's phone number, will you?'

His brash condescension had her teeth clenching, her anger flaring. *Did I really find that cockney arrogance sexy once?*

'I'm rather busy right now,' she said neutrally, using the anger to her advantage. Anger she could work with, it was so much easier to control than pain. 'I'll see if I can find it later and send it on.'

'Come on, Zara, darling, it's urgent and you know full well you have his number.' If she didn't know him better she'd think she caught the hint of panic, as though he could sense she was about to cut the call. Which she was. But panic? What could be so important that he needed to reach Tristan this second? 'Look, our blasted systems have gone down and I don't seem to have it on my mobile.'

'Perhaps that's because he was *my* client.' She couldn't help the barbed comment. But hell, he'd refused to let her take anyone, enforcing the restrictive contract clauses to the letter. She'd been lucky to set her new business up at all. Even luckier to take EJ with her.

It didn't matter that he was the reason she'd had to leave in the first place. That she'd been the one who had worked twenty-four-seven to make it the success it had become. The success it still was, only now it was his baby, he was the one reaping all the benefit.

'Very true,' he said smoothly, his composure back so swiftly she'd probably imagined the crack—it was too much to hope for after all. 'But, you know, my client now, of course.'

She clenched her fist around the phone, his smarmy tone and gibe making her want to hurl. The sooner she could have him off the line, the better. 'I'll dig it out and send it on, good—'

'Wait, there's something else…'

She halted midway through hanging up, the skin at the back of her neck prickling as her memory bank came alive. She knew that tone, knew it meant some big revelation or other. Wasn't it just how he'd sounded when he'd finally been forced to admit all his extra-curricular activities?

'What is it?' She asked the question even though every instinct told her she didn't want to know. The awkward cough he gave only confirming it. 'Charles, spit it out, I don't have all day.'

'I'm getting married.'

The air caught in her lungs, ice seeping through her veins. Of all the things she could have imagined it being, it certainly wasn't that.

The great bachelor, Charles Eddison, finally getting hitched. Five years and he'd failed to make an honest woman of her. She'd loved him with all of her being and yet it hadn't been enough. And now, one year after their break-up, someone had managed to do it, someone had been special enough…

It just hadn't been me.

* * *

'Easy, *liten syster*,' Daniel said into his mobile as he pressed the button for the lift to her floor. 'I'm here now.'

'Less of the little,' she snapped, her irritation making her London accent revert to her Swedish lilt and making him grin. 'Or I'll start calling you Danny.'

He gave a mock shudder. 'Quit the strop, then.'

Someone swept up behind him, a scent wrapping around him, vanilla twisted up in something so enticing he was damned if he could place it, and his eyes swerved of their own accord.

'Strop! You were supposed to be here half an…'

His sister's voice trailed away into the distance, his sight landing on the woman whose interesting scent had nothing on the visual. He felt his mouth quirk, his interest instant. She was beautiful, in an unusual, edgy kind of way. So not his type, a definite 'no' on paper, but when presented with the physical, she was all kinds of yes…

She faced the lift, waiting just as he was, one purple stiletto tapping impatiently, her body encased in a fitted black trouser suit, a leather-clad portfolio hooked under one arm, all quite usual but—

'Are you listening to me, *Dann-eee*?'

'Sure, I'll be right up,' he said distractedly, cutting the call and pocketing the device.

It was her hair that fascinated him: cropped to her ears, the reddish-brown mass was parted high to one side, windswept almost. And then there was her make-up, neutral save for the liner around her eyes and the bold lip colour—*was that purple?*

His gaze narrowed over it and she must have sensed his attention, her eyes flickering in his direction. 'You know, it's rude to stare.'

Her voice was husky, a crisp edge that rasped along his spine and sealed her appeal. He was hooked.

Her eyes were back on the doors, her lack of interest obvious. He should've taken it as a sign, but since when had he backed off from anything he fancied? In truth, her lack of interest only added to the appeal.

'Rude?' he said, raising his brow. 'I've been called many things before—arrogant, reckless, even an arsehole—but rude, not had that one yet.'

Her mouth twitched but she didn't turn to look at him, the ping of the lift arriving serving as a temporary interruption.

The doors opened and he gestured for her to precede him. 'See, I'm not *entirely* rude.'

She looked to him then, her silver-grey eyes sparkling and those bold-coloured lips lifting into a smile that momentarily gutted him. *Jesus,* she was hot. The bow-like shape stretching and still the lower lip was full—swollen, even—almost as though it had just been thoroughly devoured.

Maybe she'd had to reapply that colour after it had been rubbed clean away. *Oh, to be the cause of that little misdemeanour.*

'Thank you.'

It took a second to realise she had spoken, to realise

he was staring all over again, and then sanity returned. 'You're welcome—which floor?'

He pressed the number for his sister and her thick black lashes lowered to trace his move. 'The same.'

He nodded and came to stand beside her. The lift closed and together they stood, the silence heavy and loaded—*at least to him.*

Did she know who he was? Anyone with one eye on the media knew who he was: the sexy, Swedish billionaire who stuck one finger up to his celebrity roots and made it in the real world—the business world—the playboy who liked his women plentiful and hot, and always without strings.

That was pretty much how the article had summed him up that morning before really crucifying him.

Hell, maybe she knew exactly who he was and what he was like, hence her lack of interest.

If that was the case, she definitely wasn't his type.

Not at all.

Liar...

Okay, so maybe it was time to break with tradition.

Did he have to be heading to the same floor?

She'd had enough of arrogant arseholes for one day and here she was stuck in a lift with a self-professed one. She couldn't deny he'd amused her with his honesty and self-deprecating introduction though.

But he was trouble.

He wasn't like Charles. He wasn't smooth and perfect, clean-shaven and pristine.

No, this man was all about the stubble and the bed-head hair; a sun-kissed surfer plucked from the ocean, jazzed up and dumped in the city. The jeans and sweatshirt hugging his imposing frame looked laid-back but they screamed designer from top to toe. And the way he had her pulse tripping over itself, he was just as dangerous. On every level.

'Now you know so much about me,' he suddenly said, his accent thick and exciting her far more than was fair, 'how about you let me take you for a drink?'

She almost swallowed her tongue, the portfolio digging into her side as she turned rigid. 'I'm busy.'

'Not right this second,' he said, his amber eyes twinkling with amusement and holding her own. 'But at a mutually agreeable time, of course?'

Of course. She mentally rolled her eyes. *Would he just get the hint?*

Her resolve was good, but she wasn't immune. She could feel the temptation well enough and the sooner she got free of it, the better. She dragged her eyes away, forcing them on the intricate pattern twisting through the gold lift door ahead. 'I don't think that's a good idea.'

'Care to tell me why?'

Because I'm not a fool. 'I know you.'

The lift announced the arrival of their floor and he spoke over it. 'You do?'

'Obviously not you exactly,' she said, relief sweeping through her as the lift doors opened and she stepped out.

Purposeful, she turned left towards Julia's and hoped

he would take the hint or a different direction at least. He didn't.

'Obviously,' he reaffirmed, falling into step behind her. 'I'd remember if I'd met you before.'

Her tummy gave an annoying flutter and she squashed it. She was going to have to be more specific. Brutal even…

'What I mean is, I know your type.'

'My type?'

'Hell, yeah, great in the sack, perfect bedroom material…' she sent him a scathing look '…but beyond that…well, we don't go there, do we?'

His step faltered. 'Wow, hung, drawn *and* quartered.'

She could hear his surprise, feel his unease, and victory surged warm in her veins. Her harsh assessment had hit its mark, hopefully enough to send him running.

And if that didn't, the hint of her being the relationship kind should do it.

'You have quite the opinion of men.'

She gave a derisive laugh and turned a bend, the sanctity of Julia's hotel room now only a few strides away.

'So, you're either an anti-male lesbian—' it was her turn to falter mid-step '—or you've been burned before. Which is it to be?'

A lesbian…

She laughed with reignited vigour. It wasn't the first time she'd been mistaken as such. Ever since she'd opted for the cropped hairstyle—one of her many post-breakup actions—she'd been hit on by women and men alike, hoping she swung their way. But she wasn't about to tell him anything close to the truth.

'Typical arrogant male—just because I'm not interested in you *per se*, I have to be a lesbian.' She'd arrived at Julia's door and to emphasise her point, she faced it and rapped against it. 'Now, if you don't mind, I have work to do.'

He wasn't moving away. If anything, he was settling in right alongside her—*what the fuck?*

She didn't have time to ask what he was playing at; the door swung open to reveal her rather disgruntled-looking client—*shit.* 'I'm so sorry I'm late, Ms Larsson.'

The woman visibly cringed. 'Drop the Ms, makes me feel ancient, it's Julia…and so you should be,' she said, shrugging a tan leather jacket over a white T and looking from Zara to her unwanted companion. 'The pair of you.'

Pair of us?

Zara looked to him and he gave her a bemused shrug. 'Seems you can't get away from me that easily.'

'Oh, good God, Daniel, don't tell me you've hit on my estate agent already?' The woman's eyes flashed furiously, their colour strikingly similar to *his*.

Come to think of it, so was the golden hue to her shoulder-length hair…

'I wouldn't call it hitting on, exactly,' he said, with another one of those annoyingly casual shrugs. 'We were actually just discussing sexual tendencies.'

'You've got to be kidding me!' Julia looked at her,

cheeks flushing, eyes bright. 'Seems I owe you an apology too.'

'You do?' Zara's voice sounded faint, her brain rapidly piecing the situation together.

'This *animal*,' Julia said, gesturing to him in mock disdain, 'is my brother—well, half-brother, to be exact. But seriously, Daniel, *vad fan*?'

'Brother?' she repeated, her eyes sweeping to the man himself, the realisation that she wasn't going to evade him any time soon setting off a troubling dance in her chest.

'In my defence,' he said, a curious frown creasing his brow, 'she brought it out in me.'

'That's your excuse?' Julia said incredulously, delivering a playful shove that barely moved him, his eyes remaining fixed on Zara's every bit as curious and heated and very, very interested. 'If I didn't value your opinion so much, I'd tell you to just do one and leave us to it.'

'Seems that makes two of you today,' he said, his penetrating gaze reaching inside Zara's mind and triggering a replay of all that she had said with embarrassing clarity. 'It's a bloody good job my ego is big enough to take it.'

'No one's ego can be as big as yours, *storebror*,' Julia said. 'It's just lucky your heart is also as big.'

'And don't you forget it,' he said, looking to his sister with open affection now, freeing Zara at last, to breathe, to think, to get with it... 'So, are we going to take this show on the road? Or are we going to stand here and do more *Daniel-bashing*?'

Julia gave a giggle and, God help her, Zara smiled, the move easy. Too easy.

'For the record,' he added, 'my preference is definitely for the former.'

And then she laughed. Really laughed.

Charming. Good-looking. Dangerous.

No. No. *No.*

CHAPTER TWO

DANIEL WAS GRINDING his teeth. His arms folded across his front. His body rigid as he leant back against the door that housed what Zara had referred to as an *ample* bathroom for *this size* of apartment, in *this desirable* an area.

He'd say this: desirable or not, you could certainly save time going for your morning constitution while brushing your teeth over the sink. And the shower-over-the-bath—you had to be some kind of contortionist to use it. Why was he the only one seeing these issues?

At least this third property was an improvement on the previous two. It had natural daylight for starters, and no pounding pub or store adjoining.

He watched them cooing over the open-plan living space now—*the strategically placed sofa that permitted the perfect view of the park across the road and the minute television that was as big as it could ever be in the space available*—and bit into his tongue.

He wasn't sure what was more painful: The fact he'd been forced to take the estate agency's car—albeit a classic chauffeur-driven number, but when his state-of-the-art limo was at the ready, seriously, what sense did that make? Absolutely none. Or the fact that his opinion, when he chose to voice one, was counting for nothing, despite what his sister had said to the contrary earlier.

Or was it the fact that any fleeting look or touch from Ms Agent herself and his body stirred.

Yet she'd made it ever so clear it wasn't happening, not in a million years.

He was now at the point where he was convincing himself his attractive little sister *was* far more the agent's cup of tea. Or indeed, her choice of cocktail, the drink suiting her fire so much better. The attention she was lavishing over Julia, totally OTT in his opinion, and yet his sister was lapping it up.

'So, come on, what do you think?' came Julia's on-the-spot question.

They both turned to him expectantly, his sister's skin annoyingly aglow and happy—*she liked it...really liked it.* Ah, *skit.*

He cleared his throat and pushed away from the door, heading to stand between them, careful to keep his eye on the window and the view beyond. 'It's…nice.'

He had *tried* to sound enthused, but the reality was his comment stank, its tone utterly tepid. Funny enough, just how he was feeling.

'Nice?' she pressed.

'The view is good; the location is convenient and—' he shrugged '—nice.'

'What about the actual apartment?'

He turned and let his gaze sweep the living area, the

dining table for two and the kitchenette; he didn't even want to think on the bathroom.

She could do better.

Her sleaze of an ex-husband should be picking up the brunt of the cost and if not him, she should be letting Daniel help. But he'd had this argument a thousand times over and she wasn't having any of it.

'You need to stop frowning so much,' she piped up. 'Gives you wrinkles, you know.'

'You're clearly not impressed,' Zara remarked and guilt nagged at him. It wasn't down to her ability, or lack thereof, to sell the place; she was doing her job plenty well enough.

'It's not your fault,' he assured her. 'My sister is being stubborn, and, rather than accept other people's money to afford the kind of place she has grown up with, she is determined to do this alone.'

Julia rolled her eyes, her arms folding across her chest as she pinned him with that pig-headed stare he was accustomed to. 'Don't start that again. Dad's trust fund is already helping me out enough. I'm not taking your charity too.'

'If not mine, then you should bloody well take Edward's money. The guy deserves to be coughing up for all he did.'

'Do you honestly think I want any ties to that man?' she said fiercely. 'It's bad enough that he did the rounds with my so-called friends. The sooner the divorce is final and I can cut all ties, the better.'

He could sense Zara backing away, could feel the

personal nature of their conversation putting her on edge. 'Okay, okay,' he said, reining it back in. 'I'm sorry to have mentioned him. I just want what's best for you, and this isn't it.'

'Why?'

'It's impractical.'

'Why?'

'*Kristus*, Julia, you're a tall woman—care to explain how you're going to use *that bathroom*?' He threw his hand in its godforsaken direction and she frowned, his point failing to register. 'Allow me to demonstrate...'

He strode for the bathroom and pulled open the door. Doing his damnedest to ignore the sickly pink decor and vanity ware. He waited for them to appear before climbing into the bathtub, contorting his body to fit between the glass shower screen and the sloping wall.

He straightened as far as he could, his head slightly bowed as the shower head met with his shoulder— '*See?*'

They saw, all right. Their eyes glittered, their lips quivered and then they had the audacity to erupt in almighty belly laughs—*for fuck's sake.*

He dropped his gaze, dislodging himself from the enclosure with as much dignity as he could muster. 'You think it's so easy? You try it.'

'I'd rather not,' Julia blurted, her hand over her mouth as her eyes still danced.

'Okay.' He looked to Zara pointedly, ignoring how her amused gaze lit him up inside. *If she thought the apartment was so good, she could bloody well demon-strate.* 'Why don't *you* do the honours?'

His demand appeared to sober her up, her eyes flick-ing between the pair of them and her professionalism winning out as she said, 'Sure, could you just hold this?'

She thrust the portfolio into his chest and stepped inside the room. He realised the error of his sugges-tion immediately. He should have first left the confined space before goading her to enter, to get up close.

Head out of your pants, head out of your pants, head out of your pants.

'It's like this,' she said, eyes flashing defiantly, their bodies chest to chest—she could tell him anything now and he'd fall for it, but, to his surprise, she raised her hand and pulled at the shower screen, the damn thing moving towards him as she stepped away.

'Just back up a little,' she ordered.

Back up? He was pressed into the edge of the toilet as it was. He spread his legs, the position oddly vul-nerable and erotically acquiescing. He watched, fasci-nated, as the access opened up, creating space to permit her entry, all graceful and easy as she climbed inside.

But, ha, the shower head still looked ridiculous as it brushed the tip of her head.

'And you can remove this for more height, like so,' she said, reading his mind and slipping it out of its rest. 'Which also makes it great for cleaning the bath.'

She gave a sweep of the area but in truth all he could think about now was her wet and naked and all soapedup—not even the sickly pink backdrop could dampen the heat spreading below his waist.

'Perfectly demonstrated, thank you, Zara.' His sister gave him a smug grin. 'See, big bro, that's how it's done.'

'You're welcome,' came Zara's response, his eye swiftly returning to her and the imaginings he shouldn't be having. She slotted the shower head back in place and slipped him a sidelong glance through the glass screen. Her fingers froze over the contraption, her eyes widening ever so slightly, her pupils following suit—did she know where his head was at?

And then the moment was gone, a shutter falling over her expression as she gave a small cough, her eyes snapping away.

'Right, well, I think we're done with this one,' she said, unceremoniously shoving the shower screen in his face and almost sending him to his ass on the pink porcelain.

'Shall we move on?' she said, already heading out.

'Yup.' Julia nodded, smirking right at him.

He screwed his face up in a childish gesture—*whatever*.

'If you both go on down,' Zara said, expertly ignoring their little exchange—*thank fuck!* The pair of them were doing his ego and renowned charm no favours at all.

'I'll join you shortly,' she continued. 'I just have to take care of an errand for the owner.'

'Great,' Julia said, moving for the front door. 'I have a quick call to make so I'll meet you downstairs.'

'I'll catch you up,' he called after her, pushing the glass door back into place and wondering why the hell he hadn't thought of that.

Perhaps because you've never had to endure one before?

He shook his head, brushing the entire incident off as he followed in Zara's direction.

'Can I have a quick word?' he asked, entering the kitchenette hot on her tail. His intention had been to talk budget with Julia out of earshot but as Zara turned in the small space, hemmed in as they were by the cupboards and the breakfast bar, all thoughts of conversation evaporated.

'Yes,' she said, her eyes wary as they lifted to his, her hands coming to rest on the countertop either side of her as she backed up against it. 'But first you need to stop looking at me like that.'

'Like what?' He knew the answer well enough, but how would she describe it, what she saw in him? She was good with words—she'd demonstrated it repeatedly throughout the day, when eloquently describing the features of each potential abode. And in truth, he could listen to her talk and talk and talk. Perhaps that was why he was so keen to criticise: he wasn't ready for her job to come to an end; he wasn't ready for her to complete a sale for his sister and vacate his life.

He watched her eyelids flutter, her tongue flicking out to moisten that bottom lip he was so fascinated with. *Was she nervous?*

'You know what.' Her eyes dropped to his mouth,

their depths revealing in their helpless nature, and his lips curled upwards. So she wasn't as unaffected by him as she'd have him believe.

Power surged, his ego with it. 'What if I said I can't help it?'

Her eyes snapped back to his. 'Then make yourself help it because this—' she wagged a finger between them '—isn't happening.'

'No?' He stepped forward and her eyes widened, her lips parting on a ragged breath.

'No.' She gave a small shake of her head, the move sending a lock across her forehead and he itched to push it back. 'I don't date clients.'

'Technically,' he said, his voice gruff even to his own ears, 'I'm not a client.'

'You're as good as.'

'I disagree.'

'Whether you disagree or not, I don't care,' she rushed out. 'I'm not falling into this trap.'

His brow knitted together; she'd flummoxed him now. 'Trap?'

She paled, her words seeming to surprise even her, and then she visibly recovered, her chin rising, to say, 'The kind of trap where I let this get in the way of my business.'

He studied her face, her sincerity. 'You sound like you're speaking from experience.' He didn't like the idea one bit. *Oh, the irony.* 'I take it you've not always been so averse to dating clients?'

She hesitated, her teeth worrying over her lower lip

and teasing at his concentration. Was she going to evade giving him an answer? Or should he just kiss her and be done with the whole conversation? He was veering towards the latter when she spoke.

'Not my clients, no, my ex-business partner...we...we were together.'

'You dated Charles Eddison?'

She exhaled sharply. 'We more than dated, we lived together for five years.'

Five years, Kristus*!*

He felt sick at the very idea.

And then she squinted up at him, her eyes suddenly curious. 'How did you know it was him? Do you know him?'

'Not personally,' he admitted, not liking the way her admission griped with his gut and keen to get back to more enjoyable conversation. But five years, *Jesus*. 'I know enough of him, considering we looked at using his services initially.'

'You looked at using him?' She frowned. 'Julia didn't mention it.'

'Why would she? She met him and took an instant dislike.' Had he met the guy too, he was sure he would have felt the same, even more so now. 'Someone on his team recommended you.'

'They did?' Her frown grew. 'I had no idea.'

'Well, now you do, can we move on?'

She didn't acknowledge him; instead her eyes became distant, their sadness unmistakable. As was her vulnerability. No doubt Charles had done this to her. Left her like this.

'When our relationship ended so did our business partnership, hence why I'm working from the ground up all over again.' She dragged in a breath and straightened, her focus coming back as her confidence fell into place. 'And hence why *this* just isn't happening.'

He faltered, his brain telling him to agree, to move past the pull that was driving him to distraction.

She's so not your type. She's a bag of emotion. She's not safe in your hands.

Instead he found himself saying, 'You're overthinking it. As much as Julia loves me, she's already bought into your skills as an estate agent, as have I, for that matter. Nothing between us will sway her to go elsewhere.'

You idiot, why pursue her? She doesn't fit with your no-strings rule. This woman goes in for attachment. Worse still, she's been burned by it already and still suffering.

But then, if that's the case, maybe she's ready for the no-strings alternative.

Maybe she's ready to become your type.

'You have my word,' he pressed gently.

You bastard.

She lifted her eyes at his soft declaration and immediately regretted it.

He hovered just above her, his wolf-like gaze burning into her own, the rush of warmth it inspired sending her toes curling inside her Louboutins. His confidence in her ability to fulfil her job beating back the negative words Charles had thrown at her on her way out of the door all those months ago—*'You'll never make it on your own.'*

Ha, well, they chose me, not you...at the recommendation of someone on your team, no less.

It felt good to know she still held favour there after walking out.

As for Daniel's word, she held his eye; was he for real? 'Your word?'

He made an affirmative noise deep in his throat, almost enticing a reciprocal one from her as it strummed at the heat swelling down low.

'I'm willing to bet you're just as caught up in this attraction as me,' he said huskily. 'And if that's the case, you'll realise this is about a bit of fun; no harm, no foul, no jeopardised business arrangement.'

'You reckon?' She sounded breathless, out of control.

No, no, don't let this happen.

He nodded and raised his hand, her breath catching as she anticipated his touch, wanting and dreading it all the same, knowing that when it came she would lose herself in it, in him.

'I'm not very good at...*fun.*' She threw his description back at him, desperately clinging to what she knew to be true even as the heat of his hand brushed beneath her jaw, his touch so light it was barely there. And she wanted it there. Wanted every one of those fingers pressed into her skin as he kissed her.

'Fun?' he questioned softly, his hand following the contours of her neck as her head lolled back into his palm of its own mutinous accord.

'Not this sort of fun.' She trembled; fear, excitement, all manner of urges melting away the need to break free.

'You're going to have to clarify, because I'm talking about sex, nothing more, nothing less.'

Sex. Even hearing him say it had her tummy contracting over the ferocity of her need as her confession burst from her lips. 'And so am I.'

His brow became a fierce V, his eyes sparking with something akin to surprise, disbelief, something more... but then it hooded over as he asked, 'You're afraid of keeping it casual?'

She shook her head. *If only that were her problem.*

'I'm not very good at *it*.' She stressed the *it*, praying it would be clear enough, even as her contracted tummy now squirmed in shame.

Why admit that? Why admit something buried so deep inside?

Because it wasn't so deep.

Hadn't Charles brought it all to the surface when he'd called her that morning?

Hadn't the revelation of Julia's relationship troubles kicked up her own storm?

His expression softened, a strange sense of relief shining through. 'I don't believe that.'

'It's the truth,' she breathed, her chin lifting defiantly.

She needed to convince him, to get him to back

away. She hadn't been able to let anyone near her since Charles. Her revamped image was all part of her great big *back-the-hell-off-I'm-not-interested* persona. She didn't want anyone to get close enough to risk Charles's words being reaffirmed by anybody else—*'You're cold...so frigid in the sack...it's such hard work.'*

Daniel wasn't getting the message though, his intent searing her as his head lowered, his mouth brushing against hers to say, 'Why don't you let me be the judge of that?'

'I'm not...' Her words trailed away, his lips coaxing her to silence, to oblige, to move beneath the hypnotic pressure of his. She lowered her lashes, a small noise quivering at the back of her throat.

Did that really come from me?

She tightened her grip over the counter edge, trying desperately to regain control. 'We shouldn't do this.'

He closed what little gap remained, his hardness pressing up against her belly and replacing all sane thought with sensation, the pang between her legs instant and desperate. She clenched her thighs tight, nursing it, wanting it to grow and not wanting it to all the same.

His tongue flicked out to tease her mouth apart, his free hand joining the other to hook around her neck and hold her in place. 'Then tell me to stop.'

He took her lower lip in his teeth and tugged, the effect ripping a moan from her and sending streaks of heat straight to her neglected clit—*Christ*. She wanted him. Badly.

'I didn't think so,' he murmured against her, his tongue seeking entry as her own dared to taste him. He was so musky and male, gentle yet demanding. He teased around her mouth, testing every curve, stoking the fire inside.

And then he growled, the sound fierce as his tempo changed, his desperation breaking through his control and she ignited with it. Like a switch being flicked on, she came alive to match him, move for move, her own mouth hungry for more. Her hands seeking out the crazy flop of blond, and loving that he let her. That he didn't care. Not like Charles. Charles would have told her to watch it, be careful...

He broke his mouth away, pinning his forehead against her own, his ragged breath sweeping down her front, down the channel of her V-cut blouse. 'I think you're very good at this.'

'Is that so?' Wow, was that really her? So heated, so flirtatious?

She looked to him from beneath her lashes, every nerve-ending alert as it craved the hardness ever-swelling against her.

Yes, this was her. And this man wasn't Charles, he was as lost to the moment as she... *Or was he?*

Doubt sparked. What was she doing? She had no interest in opening herself up again. Especially with a man she didn't know. Couldn't trust.

His mouth closed over hers once more, ravenous and urgent, his hand dropping to lift her against him. She moulded into him, her neck arching under the pressure of his continued kiss, her muddied thoughts warring with the passion racing through her veins. It felt so good to feel this rush again.

Again? Who are you kidding? No one has made you feel this crazy, this hungry, this desired.

And she could trust him enough to give in to this—*couldn't she?*

He had heart enough; he wore it on his sleeve for Julia, his sister—*her client. Shit!*

She stilled beneath him, her eyes flying open.

You're meant to be working, not getting cosy with your client's brother!

She pushed him away, ignoring his widened gaze and the hard expanse of muscle that flexed beneath her touch. What the hell was he playing at, pretending to have something to discuss, only to seduce her? 'That was a dirty trick.'

'What was?'

She forced her breathing to steady, shifting her eyes away from the seductive fire in his. 'Coming in here, under the pretence of a conversation, only to make a move.'

She stepped around him and headed to the sink, amazed that she could make her jelly-like body do her bidding. She took up a plastic jug from the drainer and turned on the tap, throwing her focus into what she was supposed to be doing.

'I wasn't pretending anything,' he said, his voice still so near in the closed-in space. 'I wanted to speak to you without my sister listening in.'

'Really?' She raised a sardonic brow at him over her shoulder and regretted even looking. He was ruffled, the evidence of her touch in the state of his hair, his puffed-up lips, the heat to his cheeks. He was too hot before, now he just taunted her with what she knew to be real. What she knew she could have if she chose it.

He grinned. 'Yes, *really*. It was your provocation that made me forget it.'

'*My provocation?*' Water overflowed the jug in her hand but she couldn't care.

'Yes, *you*.' He reached out and cupped her chin, scanning her face with that same curious look he'd been sporting half the morning. 'There's just something about you, and I can't seem to control my reaction to it.'

She couldn't speak. Wasn't it how she felt too? Hadn't he broken through the layers she'd effectively held in place for months, all in the space of a look, a touch...?

But hell, it was hardly surprising when she'd been celibate for so long.

'Need a hand with that?' he said, reaching around her to twist the tap off and his proximity made her heart skitter anew.

'Thank you,' she said, backing away enough to escape the kitchen, jug in hand, the spark of an idea creeping up on her that she just knew she should quash before it took hold. It wasn't wise, it wasn't rational...but still, it was there...

Would one night do it?

One night—*with him?*

She walked around the flat, watering the plants that

adorned it, all the while feeling his eyes on her, penetrating her, lighting her up from top to toe. He'd resumed the position he'd been in earlier, his brooding silhouette resting up against the bathroom door. And just as he had then, he clouded her judgement, her mind struggling to function under the effect of his gaze.

Would one night release her from this? Clear her mind and rid her body of this insane need so that normal service could resume?

'I think you've given that one enough.'

'What?' She frowned and followed his line of sight to the spider plant she was tending to, seeing the water pooling at the pot rim, a trickle commencing down the side. She cursed, her cheeks warming as she righted the jug. Seemed she couldn't even cope with the simple task of watering plants in his presence—*unbelievable*.

'Can you pass me some kitchen towel?' she snapped and then cringed, realising she was projecting her frustration onto him and making herself add a guilt-ridden, 'Please?'

She wished she hadn't softened her request when she saw how his eyes danced, how amused he was at her fluster, knowing it was because he understood the cause.

'Sure.' He pushed away from the door and headed into the kitchen area.

She forced her eyes away. She couldn't carry on like this. For however long it took to find his sister a home, she needed to get this under control. Christ, she needed his sister to spread a good word. Not tell every Tom,

Dick and Harry that she was an airhead... Or, worse, that she couldn't stop lusting after her brother long enough to concentrate.

'Here,' he said, coming up alongside her and offering out the paper towel.

'Thank you.'

She didn't quite meet his eye as she took it and bent forward to clean up the mess.

Now was the time, she realised; if she wanted to put the idea to him, she needed to do it now. 'One date.'

He stilled in the periphery of her vision. 'A date?'

'Yes,' she said, ignoring the bemusement in his tone.

Hell, you'd be bemused if someone had just burst out with those two words.

Straightening up and smoothing her wrist over her hair to right it while avoiding the damp kitchen towel clutched in her hand, she nodded. 'Let's go on one date together.'

'You *want* to do that?'

Yes... No... Yes.

The words whirled through her mind as their gazes locked and she lost herself in his warm, amber depths, a wedge forming in her throat.

Are you crazy? Do you really know what you're letting yourself in for?

She headed for the kitchen, praying he hadn't spied her hesitation. She prided herself on knowing her own mind, for heaven's sake—why was he making that so hard?

'Yes, I do,' she said, placing the jug back on the

drainer, grateful that her voice gave away none of her internal wrangling and feeling her resolve swell.

You've put the idea out there, you can bloody well follow it through.

Turning to look at him, she leisurely travelled his entirety, taking in his sheer beauty, his continued silence and bemusement, and her tummy gave the smallest little flutter. Was he going to turn her down?

Hell, no.

'Unless, of course…' she said the words softly, teasingly, her legs moving of their own volition to close the distance between them '…you don't want to?'

He didn't budge, his body seemingly fixed in place as he watched her approach, a telltale pulse ticing in his jaw as he no doubt worked to gauge her intent.

He didn't have to wait long, not in this confined space.

Once she was within touching distance she reached out, her fingers hooking over his belt buckle with daring provocation. The move bold and quite unlike her. Yet it felt completely natural, instinctive with him, as did the words that slipped from her lips. 'Unless, of course, you don't fancy a bit of fun together?'

CHAPTER THREE

A DATE?

She wasn't simply asking for a date.

She was asking for a whole lot more.

So why wasn't he straight on it? Why was okay suddenly so hard to say?

He narrowed his gaze, searching her face, looking at those steely grey eyes, all smoky with suggestion, her head tilted to one side.

Had he imagined her earlier vulnerability? Had she been playing him with that unexpected confession? But to what end? It was hardly the greatest come-on—*Hey, I'm shit in bed*—but then, perhaps that had been her game, to put him off. Only it had failed. Their chemistry was off the charts and she screamed of a woman in need of some fun. He suspected she'd not indulged since Charles had done away with her.

She toyed with his buckle, her eyes locked with his. 'One date.'

And then he watched her lashes lower, her eyes travelling down his chest as her free hand came up to rest over his thundering heart, the heat of her palm perme-

ating through his sweatshirt and rendering him speech-
less, utterly captivated. What would she do next?

'One…' she lifted her gaze, her eyes almost black as
the pupils drowned out the grey, her enunciation bold
as she leaned closer '…night.'

*A night—for fuck's sake, grow a pair: you want her,
she's offering.*

But he didn't do emotion.

Not in his bed.

Not now.

Not ever.

And she blazed with emotion.

And didn't that make her appeal all the more? Make
her different. Make her special. Make her interesting.

She lifted onto tiptoes, her lips coming up to caress
against his own as she said, 'Let me know when you've
made up your mind.'

And then she turned and headed for the door so
quickly he was left in a shroud of her vanilla scent,
and so confidently he was left seriously doubting the
emotion he'd read in her earlier.

This woman—*vulnerable?*

He looked to the teasing sway of her hips snug beneath the trouser suit, the sureness of that walk on those
steep stilettos, the entire motion purposefully provoca-
tive on her part, and he realised hc had to have been an
idiot. There was no way.

Ja, he'd been played, all right, and he didn't care
what her intent had been, only what effect her luscious
body was having on him right that second.

'You're on,' he said, striding after her, his hand reaching on impulse to settle in the small of her back and making his palm tingle with the possessive contact. His eyes narrowed on the touch—*how strange.*

'It'll be the perfect opportunity for us to discuss what I need to without Julia in earshot,' he said, drawing back his senses, telling himself the reason he'd given her made the perfect excuse to keep such a get-together platonic. If that was what he needed to do, what he had to do, to protect himself, to protect her.

'So, it wasn't just a ruse, you do have something you want to discuss?' she asked, her surprise evident and making him grin.

'I never lie,' he assured her, 'no matter how much I want something…or someone.'

'Glad to hear it.' She returned his smile as she pulled open the front door and gestured for him to precede her out. 'Are you free this evening?'

'This evening?' He let his hand fall away from her back, ignoring how it itched to return as he stepped into the hallway and turned to watch her follow suit. 'So soon?'

'Why—you busy?'

'No.'

'Complaining?' she pushed, her smile becoming one of teasing as she closed the door and turned the key in the lock.

'Hell, no.' He wasn't. Not really. But her earlier behaviour had left its mark, still bothering him in the aftermath of their kiss, devoid of her lips so close to his.

But did he really want that worry to get in the way of the night they could potentially share?

Fuck, no, he wasn't an idiot. And he wasn't sentimental.

One night, and then he could go back to his usual careful selection.

'Good.' She flipped open her portfolio and extracted a card, passing it to him, her eyes confident, almost hard as she said, 'My office, eight p.m.'

Definitely played. She's as sure as you are turned on—so why is that wavering doubt still clinging on?

'I'm easy on what we do from there.'

He raised his brow, unable to help himself, his thoughts going down a far more pleasing route. 'Easy?'

She sent him a smile that made him want to pin her to the wall, his unease obliterated by the rising desire, and then she turned and headed for the stairwell, leaving him to follow close behind, his mind alight with the varying degrees to which she could be deemed easy...

By the time eight p.m. rolled around, Zara was fizzing over with nerves and pent-up need.

Spending the afternoon fulfilling the requirements of her job, knowing full well what the evening held, had been a real challenge. And she'd been flat out, right up until that second, the pressures of her start-up venture not waning. But now it was time for fun.

She looked to the clock, reaffirming what she already knew, having glanced at it several times over. It had just gone eight and there was no sign of him as yet.

Had he changed his mind?

Was she about to get a call loaded with excuses? A text even?

Shit.

Disappointment sank deep in her belly, the familiar taste of rejection sitting bitter in her throat.

'What did you expect?' she muttered under her breath just as movement in the outer office caught her eye.

Daniel!

'How did you...?' She stepped out of her office, trying to calm her pulse now tripping out and dancing over the disappointment.

'Security let me up.'

'They're paid to vet visitors.'

'You can't blame them,' he drawled. 'Not when they're faced with someone as charming as me.'

'Charming?' she scoffed, her hand hooking over EJ's chair back, the move casual but in reality serving to hold her up, her knees already turning weak over the sight of him.

He'd changed, she hadn't—*crap.* She drank him in, even as her own feeling of inadequacy swelled. He wore a white shirt open at the collar, accentuating the golden hue to his skin, a dark suit that fitted his frame oh-so-beautifully and all she wanted was to strip it all away. A year of sexual abstinence and it was coming back to hound her unforgivably.

He paused two strides away, his eyes raking over her, their effect as tangible as his fingers, and she felt her nipples prickle against her blouse, her jacket still slung over her office chair offering no concealing protection as he rested there. Her braless state clearly evident. But she had no need of bras, not when she was so small, so 'boy-like', according to darling Charles.

'Happy to see me?'

The heat to his voice, to his gaze, made it clear he wasn't bothered by her teeny assets and had her hunger swelling thick and fast in return, any inadequacy on her part promptly and joyously forgotten.

How could he do that so easily? Make her forget the insecurities that plagued her?

She tried to respond but her throat had closed tight, leaving only the ability to nod, and as she did she wet her lips. His eyes rose in tune with the move, something incoherent escaping under his breath, and then he strode forward, reaching out to crush her to him as his mouth claimed hers, ravenous and brutal, and everything she wanted.

'The feeling's mutual,' he rasped against her lips before devouring her whole, his tongue fencing with her own, his hands shifting to fork through her hair, his body walking her back until she hit the wall.

He tore his mouth away, his fingers smoothing around one side of her neck as his mouth attacked the other, a crazy mix of swirling pressure, nips and sucks that had her going out of her mind. Her head pressing into the hardness of the wall as she arched for him, her breasts desperate and aching as they thrust upwards.

'This afternoon was torture,' he grumbled against

her skin, his hot breath tormenting the dampness he'd created. 'Had I known you'd been braless it would've been even more so.'

His fingers dropped with his words to stroke over one pleading peak and the electricity that ripped through her made her cry out, her body arching further.

'Fuck, yes.'

He repeated the move and she positively writhed. She couldn't remember a touch so potent, so thrilling. Her breasts ached with maddening intent, desperate to be bare, desperate to have him pinch, flick, suckle, anything and everything. Charles hadn't done this to her, driven her to the edge of reason. They were in the office, for fuck's sake, not a private room, not a bedroom.

He leant back, his gaze burning down into her. *'Kristus*, baby, I could take you right here, right now, to hell with dinner.'

She couldn't respond, she just wanted him back, crushing away every thought, every sense with the all-consuming lust curling its way through her, knowing the crescendo would be worth every debauched second.

She drove her hands through his hair, pulling him back to her hungry mouth, telling him with her move that the only dinner she craved was him. But then the sound of gossipy chatter in the outer corridor invaded her senses, a semblance of clarity with it—*the cleaners.*

She swallowed a curse and edged along the wall, taking him with her.

'My office,' she managed to get out, shoving the

door further ajar and stumbling through it. She hit the lights off as he spun her back against the wall, kicking the door closed.

'The lock,' she blurted, reaching for it and twisting it in place. Her hands returning to him, twice as hungry, twice as confident. She slipped them beneath his jacket, uncaring of its obvious expense as she shoved it from his shoulders. He let it fall to the floor as she pulled at his shirt, tugging it out of his trousers while his hands reached for her blouse, doing the same.

As the cool air swept over her exposed torso, she froze, a second's hesitation as Charles came back to haunt her anew, the evening light illuminating her boyish body in all its glory. It was one thing to find her clothed and sexy, but would he feel the same when he saw...

Her blouse swept over her head and she dared to look up at him. All hesitation evaporated as lustful heat bore down into her, etched in every taut line of his face, the thin amber rim of his dilated gaze burning fierce.

'I want to worship every last bit of you.' His palms now gentle as they cupped each small mound, her sensitised peaks nesting at their heart, his thumbs caressingly soft. 'You are beautiful.'

Sounds from the outer office had his gaze flicking to the doorway, beyond which the cleaners were going about their job.

'You think you can keep quiet while I drive you crazy?'

The undulating ache in her lower belly swelled with

glee, her head nodding, her eyelids fluttering as she struggled to breathe.

'Good girl.'

She clenched her tummy tight as he dipped his head to nuzzle into her neck, picking up on her pulse point and toying with it. 'I'm going to make you wish you could cry out.'

She pressed her palms into the wall either side of her, not knowing where to put them, wanting to rake them all over his body, through his hair, but feeling immobilised, caught in a web of his creation.

He rolled each nub with his thumb, making her pant as they swelled obediently. 'You're going to come so hard.'

She whimpered. She knew it. She could feel its promise already building.

The rolling caress became a tweak and she bucked, a cry she couldn't suppress erupting as she realised she could come from this attention alone. She was that desperate, that deprived, that wanton...

'You'll need to do better than that.'

Better?

She tried to focus through the haze and he looked to the door pointedly—*Christ*, there was no way she could do this quietly.

'You need me to help,' he said softly.

How? She frowned.

He raised one hand, his fingers brushing over her lips, her plump and swollen flesh moving helplessly beneath his touch and relishing every teasing bit of it.

'Use me,' he said. 'I'll make you forget Charles ever existed.'

Forget fucking Charles, God, yes!

An exciting tremor rippled through her as she nodded against the wall and manoeuvred her head to nip into his palm, getting him where she wanted him. And then his head dropped, his mouth sucking in one desperate peak before releasing it from his teeth, and she cried into his hand, her nails scraping into the wall as she clawed at it.

'So responsive,' he muttered against her, his teeth grazing her swollen flesh as he spoke. 'So addictive.'

His free hand joined in the attentions, his touch wild with his own mounting need.

'More,' she pleaded softly.

He gave a muffled growl in response, dropping to his knees, his tongue gliding over her navel as he dropped both hands to her trouser fastening. He popped it undone, the zipper following suit, the fabric dropping to the floor, cold air hot on its tail, and then came his hands brushing up her bare legs, their palms hot, fingers caressing. He locked his teeth around the small bow at the centre of her thong's waistband, plucking at it, the elastic stinging her skin as her eyes dropped to his.

'Fuck...' she whimpered.

He was too hot, too seductive; her head was dizzy on it, intoxicated even.

He slid his fingers beneath the waistband and she bit her lip in anticipation, watching as he pulled it down, pushing it to join her trousers at her ankles. She was about to step out of them all when his head dropped, his tongue sweeping inside her seam and making her cry out. She clamped her jaw shut, her knees buckling, and he gave a deep chuckle.

'Seems you can't keep quiet.'

She looked down at him, his head cocked back, his chin resting teasingly above her strip of hair and her need took over, driving out the order, 'Rather than criticise me, put your mouth to better use.'

His eyes flashed and she rammed her fingers through his hair drawing him against her, absorbing his appreciative growl in the cluster of chaos between her legs. She was losing it in every way possible, her knees turning to jelly as she opened herself up to him, and rode his tongue, his teeth, every bit of friction he could give her.

She grabbed at his shirt, felt his muscles rippling wildly as he worked her. She reached for his hand, tugging it back to where she needed it, across her mouth. He pressed her head back into the wall with it, his hold tight, her breaths rasping over his fingers as she struggled to take in enough air to fuel the crazy spiralling tension.

She clawed at the wall again, her legs buckling further, and he used his shoulders to hold her steady and open, hungrily devouring her, sucking up her wetness, flicking wildly over her clit and layering it up with the bite of his teeth.

The tension grew with punishing force and just as the handle to her office door shifted, she exploded, her entire body convulsing with an orgasm like no other.

She bucked over him, her head falling forward, her muscles rippling wildly, and he held her to him, his head moving to press against her belly as he kept her upright through the waves.

In her post-orgasm daze, she could hear the voices on the other side… 'If it's locked leave it'… 'Thought I heard something though'… 'Not for us to worry about.'

The footsteps retreated, and she felt shyness creeping in.

What the hell have you just let happen? In your office, of all places?

And then he leant back on his haunches and met her eye, pinning her with the unrestrained heat of his need, and she knew exactly what she'd let happen and why, because, even in her sated state, her body was already on the up, her pulse kick-starting over its impulsive desire to please him. To strip him as bare as she and enjoy every last bit.

For a split second he sensed that same vulnerability, that same inkling that she wasn't the feisty, controlled diva her exterior made her out to be. And then it was gone, her fingers pushing him back so that he had to splay his palms out, pressing them into the floor to stop himself back-planting completely.

'My turn,' she said, slipping one heeled foot out of her pooled clothing and then the other.

Leaving her shoes on, she stalked towards him. All statuesque, confident and sexy as fuck. His blood rang in his ears, surging to the head of his dick.

'Easy, tiger,' he warned, not that it was aimed at her, but to his raging erection that was fit to explode any second.

'Lose the shirt.' She jutted her chin towards him, her silver-grey eyes as wild as her hair, her lips lifting in a one-sided smile.

He'd never witnessed anything so sexy. Never been more turned on. He did as she asked, undoing each button while his eyes raked over her, devouring every last inch. The way her breasts were still pert, her breathing still hitched, the apex of her thighs still slick, her entire body begging him for more.

Slipping the shirt from his arms, he heard the faint catch in her breath, saw her drag her lower lip inside and keep it there, her eyes lost somewhere between his pecks and his groin.

She nudged his thigh with one heeled foot. 'The rest.'

His hands moved to his trouser fastenings of their own accord. He was torn between the pull of her mouth and the pull of her pussy—both wet, both slick, and everything his straining cock needed.

Fuck, you can't lose it like some out-of-control teen!

He'd never had to worry about performing before. Why the hell was he having to now? He needed to get himself under control. He needed the situation under *his* control.

Retracting his legs from beneath her, he stood and shoved off the remainder of his clothing.

'I didn't say stand.'

It was a complaint that carried no force, her eyes now fixed below the waist, her mouth parted and hungry.

'Needs must, angel.' He bent for his jacket and retrieved his wallet, flipping it open. 'I'll make it up to you.'

He extracted a condom and tossed the rest aside, trying to stop his eyes feasting on her but doing so all the same. She was exquisite and he was imprinting every curve into his mind for later perusal. 'Turn around,' he said automatically. He wanted the whole of her.

She met his gaze, eyes wavering, and then she did as he asked, turning away slowly. He tore the packet open and sheathed himself, his eyes drinking her in. The crazy state of her cropped hair. The delicate frame to her shoulders as they undulated softly with her breathing. Her milk-like skin so pale and alluring. Right down to her narrow waist, softly flaring hips and that delicious bare ass, so pert and inviting. His cock leapt and he took a ragged breath, trying to rein it back.

Get in control.

He closed the gap between them and felt her jump a little as his cock nudged against her back.

'You are exquisite,' he whispered alongside her ear, his hands stroking at her arms by her side. She shivered, her skin prickling beneath his touch.

'I want to fuck you over your desk,' he murmured, his head dropping to the curve of her neck as he stroked down her belly, feeling it draw tight beneath his caress, her anticipation palpable as his destination became clear.

'I want to fuck you there,' he continued, his fingers finding her nest of curls and dipping inside, teasing the silky wetness apart, 'so that every day you're in here, you can remember it.'

He found her beaded clit and she bucked wildly on a moan, her head arching into his shoulder, and he clamped his jaw shut as his cock pulsed wildly into her back. *Kristus*, he'd never known someone so responsive, so genuinely lost.

Her hands flung back to grip at his thighs, her pelvis tilting into his touch.

He stroked her, lapping up every little whimper, every escape of air. He gazed down her front, between her small, tantalising tits to where he worked her, and let his free hand trail along her collarbone, his touch barely there as it teased a path to one taut peak. He brushed across it and her head writhed against him, her whimpers increasing. He did the same to the other and her nails bit into his skin.

She was close, her rocking becoming jagged, full of tension. Grabbing her by the hips, he swung her before the desk. Disregarding the orderly array of paperwork, writing implements and whatever else as he palmed her back. He stroked from the base of her spine up, encouraging her to bend forward with his exploration. By the time his fingers caught in her hair, she'd stretched herself over the desk, her body the perfect addition to the orderly state, her milky skin contrasting with the glass top, her breath creating steam like patterns across it.

Beads of perspiration broke across his back; his

jaw ached with the effort to stave off the heat surging through him.

Steady, steady...

He bent his knees and cupped her hips, teasing her ass higher into the air. Taking hold of his cock, he brushed it down the valley of her smooth, round mounds.

God, how you'd like to claim her there too.

'Please, Daniel, now.'

Her ass nudged upwards with her words, his swollen head slipping just inside her entrance, too inviting to take pause, and he thrust inside her, hard and deep. Through the whirring in his ears he heard her cry out and her body clenched around him, tight and hot. He stilled, wanting her to adjust, to be comfortable, but she wasn't having it. She wriggled over him, her hands reaching beyond her head to grip at the desk edge.

'*Steady,*' he ground out—to himself, to her, to them both.

He wanted to savour it, to enjoy every mounting second. But she felt so good, so wet, so inviting. Her sounds wanton and as desperate as he.

He slid one hand between her legs, seeking her out once more, loving how it made her still, her building tension palpable in every taut muscle. He rocked into her, his thighs slapping against her own, his own pleasure-filled tension working its way through every limb and taking over, ramping up his tempo.

He tightened his grip in her hair, pulling her head back, making her arch to him. He wanted his hands everywhere: on her clit, her pretty little tits, everywhere.

He caught movement ahead, saw their faint outline reflected in the window before him—*so fucking carnal*. He would take that image everywhere with him. She panted her impending climax; he watched it take hold of her body in the glass before him and it tipped him over the edge. He exploded into her, the force winding him, the cries of her orgasm breaking their way into his consciousness and compounding his own.

He dragged her up against his chest, holding her tight, the waves racking their bodies as they rode them together. He held her like that until the very last aftershock rippled through them and he could trust his voice to work. 'You are so fucking hot, you know that?'

She gave a sound that was more of a scoff than a giggle.

She had no idea. None at all. How was that possible?

She turned her head into his chest, nudging at his chin with a soft sigh. 'You're not so bad yourself.'

'Not so bad?' He squeezed his arms around her in mock offence and she rewarded him with a melodic giggle, one that rippled through his very core. 'We're not heading for more Daniel-bashing, are we?'

She gave a proper laugh. 'I wouldn't dare without your sister to hand.'

'Well, thank fuck she isn't.' He bowed his head, resting his chin upon her shoulder and wanting nothing more than to go round two, three, maybe even four as soon as he was able. 'What say we stay here and order takeout?'

'Hmm.' She stretched out against him, finding

her feet, and he felt his cock protest as it slipped free. 'Sounds good.'

He hadn't realised he'd been holding his breath until it escaped with her reply, and now he grinned, pressing a kiss to her shoulder before straightening to release her. 'I take it I have to brave the outer realm to get cleaned up.'

She turned her head to give him a sheepish look. 'Afraid so.'

'Fair enough, you sort the takeaway and I'll try not to expose myself to the cleaners.'

'You're on.' She chuckled. 'Chinese, Indian, Thai…'

He deliberately chose her line from earlier that day. 'I'm easy.'

'I know.' Her eyes sparked into his and his cock bucked with it. Round two couldn't come soon enough.

'So long as I have you for dessert.'

She turned into him, her fingers tracing a path over his chest and setting off goosebumps in their wake. 'Oh, I think that can be arranged.'

A tremor rippled through his body, it was already gearing up, and then came a flash of sanity.

Don't forget your other purpose.

He almost wanted to forget. Didn't want any part of reality eating into their time together, but he still had a duty to perform and the sooner he did…

He looked down into her heavy-lidded gaze, its pull drawing him in, and forced himself to stay in check. 'I also need to have that talk with you about Julia too.'

She tensed, her fingers dropping away along with her

eyes, desire giving way to professionalism, and totally at odds with her naked and entirely distracting form.

'Of course,' she said softly, her body easing back, and he wrapped his arms around her, pulling her up against him again. He wasn't about to lose her over it.

'It won't take long,' he assured her, his head bowing to caress her lips with his own as he added, 'then we can get back to more pleasurable pursuits.'

Her contented sigh filled his ears and warmed his blood, his lips curving up even as he kissed her—*much better.*

CHAPTER FOUR

'HEY, I THOUGHT you weren't going to be in this morning.'

Zara was currently bent over her desk doing her damnedest not to think on last night's escapades and concentrate on the printed schedule for the day ahead. She looked up at EJ's remark, watching as the woman threw her coat over the back of her chair and headed through Zara's open doorway. 'Morning to you too.'

EJ gave her a mock grimace. 'Good morning, boss.'

'I wasn't supposed to be in,' she acknowledged, her eyes dropping once more to the page, 'but it turns out our client's brother is now on the scene and he insists his car do the driving. He's picking me up shortly.'

'Oh.'

She caught the rise to EJ's voice and flicked her a look. It wasn't just her voice on the up, the woman's brow had hit the roof. What had got into her?

'Oh?'

A smile teased at EJ's lips. 'Well, did he happen to be involved yesterday?'

'Yes.' She frowned. Where was this going?

'And is he good-looking, by any chance?'

'*EJ,*' she burst out. 'That's entirely inappropriate.'

As was everything we'd done together.

Her cheeks flooded, her eyes dropping to burn a hole through her desk. 'He's the brother of a client.'

'And?' The woman's innocent tone couldn't have been more forced. 'I'm only saying that when you returned yesterday there was a definite air about you. Considering Shit-Bag had done such a fabulous job of ruining the morn, I was hardly expecting you to come back in such good spirits.'

'Good spirits?' Zara snorted. 'Hardly.'

'Whatever…you're just changing the subject now.'

'I'm not changing anything.'

'In that case—good-looking, was he?'

Her phone rescued her, buzzing with an incoming text message. She checked the screen and her heart skipped over.

It was him.

She let go of a slow breath, trying for outward calm even as her insides went on a crazy dance. 'He's here.'

'You going to send him up?'

'Absolutely not.' She slipped the schedule into her bag, her eyes off EJ and her overly assertive radar. 'I should be back around three.'

'Great,' EJ declared, 'and if he offers to take you out in the meantime, just—'

Zara sent her a warning look, cutting her off, and got a pouting grimace in return.

'You're incorrigible, EJ.'

The woman just grinned at her. 'Not in the slightest. I'm just keen to see you back out in the field.'

'The *field*.' She rolled her eyes and lifted her jacket off the chair back, shrugging it on. 'We're not in school any more.'

'True, but you know the age-old adage—*all work and no play...*'

She shook her head but couldn't help the smile that crept in. 'I'll see you later.'

She threw her bag over her shoulder and made for the doorway.

'Yup, and then you can fill me in over coffee,' EJ called after her.

She shook her head further, her smile stretching wider.

Hell, EJ was right, all work had made for a pretty rough year. Whereas last night, on the other hand...

She was still smiling when she got outside, her pulse rocketing as she spotted him on the pavement, casually leaning back against the rear of a blacked-out limo. His stare collided with her own and the heady thrill she'd spent the morning trying to suppress came back with relentless force. As did EJ's words: *all work and no play.*

Perhaps it was time for a bit of both?

She headed for him, her smile warm and loaded with a multitude of memories. If his sister was in the car watching her, heaven knew what she would think. But she couldn't help it. He had this power over her, and since he'd left her place of work at two that morning, barely a second had passed without her thoughts being on him.

He straightened as she neared, his grin making clear his mind was keeping hers company in the gutter. Did he find the attraction impossible to resist too? Was he already on for a repeat? Despite their—*her*—one-night agreement?

Whatever the case, you still have a job to perform, said her reality-checking conscience.

'Morning.' She paused before him and tore her eyes away long enough to flip open her bag and pull out the addresses for the day—*work, focus on work*. 'Do you want to give this to your driver?'

She passed him the sheet, not that he even looked at it as he took it from her, his golden eyes mesmerisingly intent as he asked, 'How did you sleep?'

'Like a baby,' she lied. She'd tossed and turned, her body craving the presence of his. But such an admission was hardly the way to start a professional road trip. 'You?'

'Same.' He nodded and the tilt to his grin told her he'd caught her lie and was working right along with it. His eyes searched hers. Was he looking for the answer to the same question as her—*on for a repeat?*

A sharp rap on the car window invaded the moment, jarring them both to their senses.

'That'll be Julia,' he said, shaking his head ruefully. 'Did I tell you she was an impatient minx?'

She laughed. 'You can hardly blame her when we're finding her a new home. It's exciting.'

'That's one word for it.' He sighed. 'Did you think about what I asked you?'

'I did.' And she had. In between the restless thoughts of him, she'd taken on board his request to speak to Julia about her budget. To see if she could get her to accept his financial aid and get a home that he deemed more suitable.

Initially, she'd balked at the idea, her own affinity with the woman's situation making her understand why she wanted to go it alone and be indebted to no one.

But she'd also sensed Daniel's feeling of responsibility towards his sister, admired it even, and he clearly had the money to back it. Not to mention it would increase her commission.

Still, no matter the benefit to her business and his admirable reasoning, the idea of convincing another woman to do what she would not didn't sit well, and her face must have said so as his shoulders sagged. 'You won't do it, will you?'

'It's not that I don't agree with your motivation for doing it,' she reasoned gently. 'I think it's lovely that you want to give her the means to purchase a more expensive home.'

'But?'

She gave a sigh and looked away from his earnest expression, needing to guard her own rising emotion as their conversation struck a more personal chord. 'I understand why she wants to do it on her own. She's a grown woman and, after everything she's been through, she doesn't want to be beholden to anyone.'

'Even her big brother?'

She looked to him then, facing off against the exasperation clear in his amber gaze. 'Even you.'

'But she's all I have,' he stressed. 'All I care about in this world, and from the moment she was born she's had it rough.'

'I'd hardly call being a trust-fund child rough.' The flippant remark was out before she could stop it and she watched his face harden, her tummy twisting with guilt. 'I'm sorry, that wasn't fair of me.'

'No, it wasn't,' he ground out. 'Money isn't everything.'

Money isn't everything. Did he not see the irony in that?

'No, it isn't,' she agreed. 'And that's exactly why you should let her go it alone. She's happy with what she can get.'

'But I'm not.'

He said it so fiercely her eyes widened in surprise and Zara had to wonder, was this purely about him wanting to share his own wealth or was there more to it?

'Look…' He broke off and ran a frustrated hand through his hair, scanning their surroundings as though struggling for the right words. 'It's hard to explain.'

'Try me.'

His eyes returned to her, hesitant and probing.

'You can trust me,' she said, guessing at what he needed to hear.

'I know that.'

His simple admission warmed her through, giving her the confidence to press. 'So?'

'It's just hard to talk about the past. You never know when it's going to be thrown back in your face again.'

She pondered his words, kind of understanding where he was coming from, but he needn't have worried. 'I'm not going to raise it again, unless you want to, but it may help me to at least understand, to help fight your corner.'

She smiled a little on the last, hoping to reassure, and he returned the gesture, his hand rising to cup her chin gently as he looked into her eyes, that same curiosity from the previous day shining through. 'You're right.'

And then he released her, his hand falling to his pocket, his eyes to the ground as he kicked aside a stone. 'She was abandoned as a baby,' he said bluntly. 'Her mum literally dropped her on our doorstep and legged it.'

She gasped, she couldn't help it, the image he painted so tragic, his expression suddenly so empty.

'As you can imagine, my mother lost it, having my father's betrayal thrust upon her in such a permanent way. She insisted Julia be sent away, spending her entire childhood in boarding schools and under the care of people employed by my parents.

'She never had a real home.' He looked back to her. 'She never had it easy.'

Her words came back to hound her, and she shook her head. 'I'm sorry.'

'You don't need to apologise,' he said. 'Just understand. It wasn't until I became an adult myself that I learned of her existence. When I found out what had happened, I tracked her down. She was going off the rails by then and it took me years to bring her back from the brink, to make her realise she wasn't alone any more.'

'You'd never guess at any of it. She seems so grounded, so happy in spite of her recent break-up.'

'Yes, she's quite the character.' His smile didn't quite reach his eyes. 'So you see, my efforts saved her then and they can do so again.'

Zara frowned up at him, admiration making her heart swell, even as she saw the error in his reasoning. 'You love her, that's effort enough.'

'Is it? Surely if I'd looked out for her more she never would have married that jerk. I would have seen him for what he was.' His hand was back in his hair, his stress and guilt ringing through his every movement. 'That's the reason for this mess, that's the reason I have to make it up to her again. She went through hell with him and I should've been there to prevent it.'

'You can't be held responsible for her mistakes.'

'Can't I?'

She reached a hand out instinctively, resting it over his arm. 'No, she's lucky to have a brother who loves her. You could have followed in your parents' footsteps but you didn't.'

He looked to her touch upon his arm, and covered it with his own hand. 'No, and I won't let her down now either.'

She shook her head slightly. 'Letting her do this by herself isn't letting her down.'

'No, but helping her will go some way to ease how I feel.' He met her eye. 'You have to understand that?'

She nodded. *She did.* And her heart swelled with just how much she got it. But her emotions were at war with one another. Her need to ease his suffering colliding with the woman's need for independence. But ultimately, it couldn't hurt to do as he asked, to at least talk to her. 'I will speak to her, but I'm making no promises.'

His expression brightened, taking her own mood with it. 'Great.'

'Don't get your hopes up,' she said swiftly. 'I'll talk to her, perhaps over lunch, and if she says she's not interested, she's my client—what she says goes.'

'I have no doubt you'll convince her,' he said, his attention pulled away by the gentle whir of the window rolling down behind him.

'Come on, people,' Julia exclaimed over it. 'I'm dying of excitement here.'

'Keep your hair on,' he teased, his good humour coming to the fore as he reached through the window to roughly caress his sister's head.

'Touch my hair again, Daniel, and you'll lose a finger.'

'Which one? I'm particularly fond of—'

The window started back up, her face creased into a severe scowl. He started to laugh, his eyes dancing as they returned to Zara and she lost sight of everything, including how to breathe. His laughter kicking up a frenzy as it reached into her belly, his eyes so alive, so sexy, so captivating. She trapped the sensation in her gut, trying to douse the sudden ache.

And he read her reaction, his amusement trailing off, his eyes heating, regret creasing at his brow. 'There are so many things I'd rather be doing right now, but duty calls.'

'Really?'

'Yes, really…you, for one.'

She gave a sharp intake of breath, her body tightening over the thrill of his blatant remark. 'And what of work?' she blustered. 'Don't you have more pressing matters that you should be tending to there?'

'Not until she's sorted.'

'Uh-huh.' She nodded, but she was barely aware of what they were discussing now, her body still dancing over his, *'You, for one.'*

He stepped past her and headed to the front of the vehicle, leaving her eyes to trail after him, helplessly devouring the way his dark jeans and charcoal sweater fitted him to perfection. Surely this burning anticipation should've been well snuffed out by last night's antics, not rising ever higher. It should've been setting off alarm bells too. Instead she was getting high on it, thriving on the mutual desire coursing between them.

EJ's words seared her mind—*'Get back in the field.'*

Hell, she was already there, naked and waiting as far as he was concerned.

The driver's door swung open before he reached it, a chauffeur in full-on livery stepping out. 'Sir,' he greeted, nodding respectfully in her direction too.

She gave him a smile and hugged her bag to her chest, regulating her breathing and trying to remember, no matter how high she wished to put *Sexy Big Brother* on her priority list, work still came first.

'Ms Anders has kindly pulled this schedule together for you, Peters.' He flicked her a glance and her breath caught mid-regulation, hanging in her throat until his eyes released her and the air with it.

'Very well, sir.' Peters took the sheet from him and made to move off. 'I'll just get the door for—'

'No need.' Daniel stopped him with a grin and raised palm. 'I can let us in.'

'Of course, sir.' His driver nodded and as he climbed back inside, Daniel headed back towards her.

'Shall we?' he said, his hand closing over the door handle. 'That's if I can remember how to use one of these…'

She laughed. 'Doors can be quite complicated, by all accounts.'

He pulled it open. 'You're telling me. Wait until I introduce you to my Vantage.'

'Your Vantage?' she repeated softly—she knew what a Vantage was, had hankered after one herself, but that wasn't what had a question mark hanging on the end of her words. No, it was what he'd meant by it. Was it his way of saying that he expected there to be future outings together, alone, outside business? Outside their arrangement?

Even though neither of them had confirmed it out loud, was it a done deal? Were they now—*dating?*

Excitement swelled. The fear that had stopped her from wanting more initially now taking a back seat as hope bloomed. Hope that, despite her first impressions, he really could be the perfect package. Nothing like Charles at all. The way he'd worshipped her body from head to toe, he'd made her feel like a goddess, not like a boy dressed up, not as Charles had made her feel, when he'd tried gifting her bigger boobs every Christmas and birthday they'd spent as a couple.

She shuddered with the unwelcome memory and honed her focus on the warm amber depths now staring down into her expectantly.

'You really do need to get in,' he said, 'before my sister threatens another, far more important part of my anatomy.'

Whatever had got to her faded. The lines creasing her brow softened, her eyes once again bright, her smile once again teasingly subtle, the hint of promise making Daniel ache to add some alone time into the schedule she'd mapped out.

She lowered herself into the car and he followed suit, his mind preoccupied as it had been since he'd unwillingly left her that morning, fighting the urge to insist she leave with him. He hadn't been ready to go, not without her accompanying him. Which was crazy. That didn't happen to him. He could only think it was down to her insistence, up-front, for a one-time-only deal. That when it was over, it was over, and it was that rationing that had him so eager for more.

Not that she seemed to be sticking to that rule. Yes, she'd kicked him out of her office at two, but she was giving every sign she was up for more this morning. And that sure as hell worked for him.

'Did I hear you trying to impress the lady with your car, Daniel?' his sister chided as they pulled away from the kerb.

He grinned. 'Maybe.'

'Ooh, you're honoured,' she said in that same teasing tone, eyes narrowing on Zara with speculative interest.

Oh, no, here we go.

'He never *tries* to impress the ladies, Zara, they just seem to fall at his feet. He must think you're different.'

Zara smiled, no trace of discomfort, unless one caught the brief tic to her jaw and the subtle flush to her skin, as he did, sitting so close. 'Please excuse my sister, she just loves to mock me.'

'No apology necessary,' she said, head turning, her gaze flicking to his, both confident and amused. 'But for the record, if you were trying to impress me, cars would be the way to go.'

'You like cars?'

She nodded. 'An obsession passed down by my father. We have a family race day at least once a year.'

His mind rushed with imagery; taking her around his track in Italy, testing out his fleet, seeing how she handled the stick, the wheel, the speed… Adrenaline pumped wildly through his system. 'I like your father already.'

She gave a small laugh and he clamped his jaw closed.

Where the hell had that come from?

He didn't talk family with women. And yet that morning alone he'd already done so twice. And that was twice too much.

'Ew…get a room, you pair,' his sister drawled, saving him from his own discomfort. 'Do I have to remind you that this is supposed to be about me? Me and my new home? Not you guys getting your rocks off.'

Now Zara squirmed, her eyes snapping away, her spine straightening and accentuating the teasing length to her neck that was far too close for comfort.

'Of course, I apologise, Julia,' she said, the flush to her cheeks becoming obvious now, making her all the more appealing with it as she concentrated on flipping open her bag. 'Take a look at this. It's our first destination for today.'

She extracted her tablet, launching the property file as she passed it to Julia. Daniel feigned interest in it across the back seat, but really his attention was on the line of Zara's body, almost within brushing distance. Her scent, that same vanilla smell that had drugged him yesterday, subtly invading his senses.

Suddenly he wished the car to be smaller, the back seat more compact, then she would be forced up against him and…

And then what?

He would kick his sister out and have an entirely different day.

Not a dick move at all.

He gave a heavy sigh and both women looked to him. 'Problem?' Zara asked.

'Don't you start being negative already,' came his sister's add-on. 'Else I'll steal Peters for the day and you can get out now. Your opinion is starting to hinder rather than help, *storebror*.'

He forced himself to grin. If only they knew it wasn't the property that had driven his reaction. 'Better?'

She laughed and Zara smiled, her eyes resting too long on his mouth, and a ripple moved through his groin. It was going to be a long morning, unless... What were the chances of sneaking in some one-on-one time mid-viewing?

Turned out the chances were slim to none.

And he'd tried.

Even telling Julia to go and have a conversation with a neighbour doing her laundry in the communal area to get rid of her briefly. Didn't matter that the woman looked like an axe-murderer in the making. Julia just needed to be gone long enough for him to have a conversation with Zara that told him where they stood. Maybe even get a date lined up. Hell, maybe even squeeze in a quickie. He'd take what he could get.

But no joy.

Zara stayed glued to her side. The perfect agent, the perfect attentive professional doting on the most important person in the room. And he, well, he was jealous, following them around with a grump on that only earned him their amusement.

'You're getting wrinkles again,' Julia teased, heading out of property two as he held the door open for them both. 'Tell him, Zara. I think he'll listen to you more than me.'

Zara sent him an amused look. 'She's right, you know.' She passed him by, turning just long enough to say under her breath, 'You needing me to kiss them away?'

His mouth dropped open, his cock perked up.

Hell, yeah.

He let the door swing shut and fell into step beside her. 'Are you toying with me?'

'Maybe.'

She said it just as quiet, just as discreetly. Julia, completely oblivious, piped up from ahead, 'So, I'm starved—where are we doing lunch?'

'Johansson's.'

His sister froze. 'No, we're bloody well not.'

'Come on, Jules, give the guy a break. He's busted his ass this past year getting that place off the ground.' He buried the tiny shred of guilt at making his sister do something she didn't want to, but hell, it was about time the pair talked. And that talk would give him ample opportunity to have his own chat with Zara. 'It's good for publicity, us being spotted rocking up there.'

She exhaled on a ragged breath, her head shaking. 'You mean, *you* rocking up there.'

'Okay, me,' he admitted, only a little sheepish. He felt Zara's eyes narrow on him.

She really has no idea who you are.

'It's a dirty move using that on me,' his sister grumbled.

'Ah, get over it. The food is sublime. You're going to love it.'

She spun on her heel and strode ahead towards the car.

'Was that some kind of payback?' Zara asked.

'Let's just say, her and Johansson have a bit of history, but it'll take her mind off that ex-husband for a bit, and, seriously, the food is great. You'll both love it.'

Thankfully the drive was short, the awkward silence filling the car only compounding the pent-up frustration coming from another part of him.

He'd secured a private table in the outer corner of the establishment, far enough away to be out of hearing distance of the other diners. Perfect for their conversation. Only first he had to leave to give Zara the opportunity to talk to his sister about letting him help.

He used his lack of a sweet tooth as an excuse and left them over pudding to catch up with Johansson. The guy's commanding boom reached him as soon as he entered the bustling kitchen. As if he sensed something out of place in his domain, he looked straight to Daniel, his face breaking into a wide grin. *'Hej!'* he bellowed, rubbing his hands into his apron and heading over. 'Was it good?'

Daniel returned his smile. 'As if you need ask that.'

Johansson nodded eagerly. 'But did *she* like it?'

'Why don't you ask her yourself?'

His grin became a grimace. 'I don't think that's wise—a public showdown wouldn't be great for business. How's she doing?'

'She's okay.'

He nodded, his jaw pulsing. 'If I ever get my hands on him...'

'Hell, you and me both,' Daniel agreed, 'but that definitely wouldn't be good for publicity.'

Johansson gave a bark of a laugh. 'Since when have you cared about your public image?'

'Fair point.' He grinned. 'Let me do the killing, then, and why don't you see about making her all happy again?'

His friend's expression turned wistful, at total odds with the manic kitchen around them. 'I tried that once.' He shook his head. 'But it's not meant to be. She deserves better.'

'What? Like Edward?' Daniel scoffed, unable to help himself, and Johansson visibly blanched.

Skit, *great going, reminding him that Edward stole her away in the first place.*

'Look, just talk to her.'

His hesitant gaze swept the kitchen. 'I guess it wouldn't hurt.' He rubbed his hand over his face. 'Hell, I'm not even supposed to be in here any more, but it's hard letting go.'

'Of the girl, or the kitchen?'

'Funny, Daniel, very funny.' He sighed and piped up with reignited vigour, 'Come on, then, before I change my mind.'

Daniel raised his hand to his friend's chest. 'Whoa, just give them five. They're having a chat.'

'Ah, her and the mystery lady…' His friend raised a brow. 'So, who is she?'

'She's Julia's estate agent.'

'*Just* her estate agent?'

'Don't you start ribbing me.' He grimaced. 'Julia's been at it all morning.'

'From the talk in the kitchen, the pair of them have stirred up enough excitement among the male waiting staff to tell me she's no plain Jane.'

'And?'

'And you're never one to pass up an opportunity.'

He shoved his hands into his jeans and shook his head. 'Whatever.'

'Is that all you're giving me?'

He shrugged. 'Nothing to tell.'

What was wrong with him? He wasn't one to *over* share for sure, but he was never one to avoid the truth either. Yet telling Johansson about Zara felt wrong, debasing even.

'If you say so,' Johansson said, clearly not believing him. 'So, how is the hunt for a new home going?'

'It's going.'

'Going?' He chuckled. 'Sounds awesome.'

'It could be the death of me. Or Edward even, if Zara doesn't make her see sense.'

His eyes narrowed. 'Zara?'

'The estate agent.'

'Ah.' He nodded, his grin wide and all-knowing. 'Yes, of course, *Zara, just the agent.*'

'Johansson, put a lid on it.'

'Come on,' he said, pounding Daniel on the back. 'Let me grab a couple of beers and you can chew my ear off while they finish up out there.'

CHAPTER FIVE

'OKAY, I'LL CONSIDER IT.'

Phew. Zara breathed a sigh of relief at Julia's concession. It wasn't just the fact that it would make Daniel happy that his sister might relent, it also meant the conversation was done with. Zara hadn't gone in with the intention of talking about her own past experience with Charles, but as Julia had opened up it had come out naturally. And together they had commiserated, had a mutual bitch and bonded over it. But now she was ready to put him back in the past and move on. As was Julia. And the excitement of house-hunting was the perfect fix.

'Your brother will be pleased,' she said. 'You can't blame him, after everything you've gone through, to want to see you happy.'

'But I don't need a big house for that.'

'No,' Zara agreed, 'but maybe we can go a little better and make you both happy.'

'A compromise position, I like it.' Julia grinned, raising her water glass in salute. 'You're an excellent saleswoman.'

Zara returned her smile. 'I try.'

'And I know he just wants the best for me.' She took a sip of her drink, her eyes suddenly sombre. 'But I wish he'd stop trying to make up for the past. None of it was his fault—he doesn't owe me.'

'I think you'll struggle to convince him of that.'

'Don't I know it?' She sighed and leaned back in her seat. 'He really is a good guy, no matter what the press say about him.'

Zara shook her head confused. 'The press?'

What did that mean? It was the second time his public status had come up and now she was burning to ask. *Who was he?*

'Yes, but then the press are never really happy unless you're screwing in their faces,' she said dismissively, unaware that Zara was on high alert now.

Seriously, who the hell was he?

Daniel Larsson didn't ring a bell. But then if they were only half-siblings it didn't necessarily mean they'd share the same surname. Maybe Larsson was Julia's married name?

Suddenly she wished she were more in the know, had kept abreast of the news, or was it more the gossip columns if Julia's remark was anything to go on?

She sipped at her coffee. Could she probe? And how exactly?

She was considering her exact phrasing when Julia's expression froze, her eyes flashing wildly as she looked past her in the direction of where Daniel had disappeared off to half an hour ago.

Zara turned to follow her gaze and, sure enough,

there was the man himself, only this time he was tailed by another—*Johansson*; she'd put her money on it judging by Julia's reaction and the apprehensive look on the other man's face.

He was even taller than Daniel, dark and fair-skinned—no sun time for this guy. His eyes were as blue as the ocean and bright with appreciation as they fixed on Julia and remained.

So it was that kind of history. Daniel had played that well.

'You ladies done?' He looked to her pointedly and her heart skipped over, drying up her words.

Julia got stuck in instead. 'If by done, you mean, has Zara convinced me to be more open to your idea, then yes, you can consider us done.' She softened her bluntness with a smile and then her gaze swept to their new guest and her cheeks flushed. 'Niklas.'

'It's good to see you, Jules.' He swept forward, leaning across the table to kiss her proffered cheek and anyone could catch the moment hanging in the air, sweeping them up in the sizzle.

'You too.' Julia looked up into his face as he straightened. 'It's a lovely place you have here.'

'I would've liked you to come sooner.'

'I would have if…' She shrugged, her eyes lowering. 'Well, things are different now.'

'Too right, they are,' Daniel said, stamping out the sudden lull and easing himself into the seat alongside Zara, near enough to breathe in his aftershave and leave her needing a whole lot more. None of which were appropriate in that moment, and she kept her eyes averted. On safer ground. 'Why don't you make up for lost time and show her around, Johansson, now that Julia has come around to my—?'

Julia's eyes snapped to his. 'I've not *agreed* to anything yet, *storebror*. I've said I'll consider it.'

'Okay—okay, now you've agreed to at least *consider* my proposition I have things I'd like to discuss with Zara.'

Julia eyed them all, nervously shifting in her seat, seeming flustered. 'Right, fine, but remember, this is *my* home—what I say goes, Daniel.'

'Sure thing.'

'I'm depending on you, Zara, to help keep him in line.'

His sister's trust in her had Zara smiling, her head momentarily off the distraction to her left as she nodded her assurance. It felt good that the woman trusted her to keep her corner. She wouldn't let her down.

Julia gave her a smile and then rose from the table, her eyes cautiously on Johansson before she moved away. Zara watched them go, watched how Johansson's hand swept into the curve of her back, the move more telling than either of them probably realised, and then they were gone, and the atmosphere shifted with a very different electricity.

Or not so different, if she dared think on it properly.

She looked to Daniel, hands folding in her lap as she fought the need to reach out for him. This was a restaurant, hardly a place to re-establish the intimacy they'd shared the previous night, but the urge was there, making her pulse race and her tummy draw tight.

'Alone, finally,' he said under his breath, his gaze sweeping the discreet arrangement of tables before coming back to her. 'Thank you for talking to her.'

She took up her glass of water for a drink, needing its chilling quality to loosen up her vocal cords. 'You're welcome.'

'You're becoming fast friends, by all accounts.'

She let her eyes drift to the other diners, trying to douse the effect his nearness inspired, but, just as it had in the car, his warmth radiated down her side, luring her in whether her eyes were on him or not. 'Well, she's my client. I'm looking out for her best interests.'

'And me?' he said, all husky and pulling her resistant gaze back to his own, imprisoning her with his heat. 'Are you simply looking out for mine too?'

Her throat closed over completely, her heart rapping against her tonsils. His sexual interests, she was all over.

But isn't he a potential client now too, investing in the same property?

The warning bells chimed but her body wasn't listening. 'It would seem so.'

'Aren't I the lucky one?' He reached up, his fingers sweeping back a lock of hair, brushing it behind her ear, the gesture intimate and barely there, yet its effect working through her system like an electric current. 'Can I take it our one-date arrangement can become two?'

She smiled shyly, the fact he'd read her so well, had hit on the question that had been burning through her all morning, making her suddenly coy. 'Is that what you want?'

But you shouldn't want it, her conscience screamed. *Not now he's potentially crossed the line...not now he's in client territory.*

His hand slipped to her thigh, his fingers stroking through the fabric of her trousers and making her breath catch. 'I daren't tell you everything I want right now.'

'No?'

'No,' he repeated, his head ducking to close the distance between them, his eyes flashing darkly. 'It's agony, keeping my hands off you.'

She swallowed, her belly on fire with his words. 'Agony?'

He nodded, his fingers creating a crazy trail of excited nerve-endings over her thighs, edging ever closer to her nested hub that now throbbed and begged for more.

'Yes, agony.'

He dropped his gaze to his water glass, taking it up with his free hand and sipping at it, a look of deliberation on his face as he scanned the room. He appeared detached, a dizzying contrast to the hand under the table, which certainly wasn't. He nudged at her thighs and excitement swelled, her legs parting ever so slightly to grant him greater access.

'You know, everyone is enjoying their meals.' His hand curved over the very top of her thigh and smoothed inwards, the move coaxing out a small whimper as she narrowed her sights on him and mentally pleaded for him not to stop. Even though he must, because they shouldn't. Not here.

'And what I want to enjoy this second,' he continued, 'is making you come.'

She gave a small gasp, her torso contracting on a rush.

'Right now?' She swallowed.

He couldn't mean it.

But, Christ, if he did…she couldn't imagine anything hotter, anything more thrilling, the intense pang taking over her clit, over her mind, driving her to accept. She licked nervously at her lips, her eyes sweeping over the other diners again, the waiting staff…and then she saw them, Julia and Johansson, heading back towards their table. Julia, flushed to high heaven, and Johansson, awkward as fuck.

'They're coming back,' she said on a shaky breath, moving her hand to brush his away before smoothing her fingers over her cheek.

Christ, it was hot.

'Her timing's as impeccable as ever,' he grumbled, his hand returning to the tabletop, his disgruntled remark making her smile.

She gave a soft, 'Hush,' and looked to their approaching guests, hoping she didn't look as red as she felt. As red as Julia did.

'Are you guys good to get going?' Julia blurted when she was within earshot.

Johansson thrust a hand through his hair, looking to Daniel as if he could either murder him or beg him for a rescue.

'Sure,' Zara said, rising out of her seat and smoothing her trousers straight. 'I'm going to make a quick call and see if we can swap this afternoon's viewing now that we have a potential budget uplift. There's a property I'm really keen for you to see.'

The interplay between Daniel and his friend continued and she hooked her arm through Julia's, encouraging her away. 'Let's go down to the car while your brother takes care of the bill.'

She looked to him apologetically, not liking that she was lumping him with that errand but hoping he understood.

He nodded and rose out of his seat too. 'Of course.'

'I can take you through the property details while we wait,' she said to Julia, feeling the tension radiating from the woman, her arm rigid beneath her own—maybe she'd misread the cause of the woman's high colour after all. She felt like liquid after her little escapade; Julia was anything but.

'I'd like that.' Julia nodded, her eyes wavering to Johansson's, a mixture of regret, sorrow, anger, Zara couldn't tell, but the woman was far from happy. 'It was…good to see you again.'

No one could miss the words sticking in her throat and Johansson gave an awkward nod. 'You too.' He looked to Zara. 'Make sure you find her the best.'

'Of course,' she said. 'The meal was truly lovely, thank you.'

'You're welcome.'

She pulled Julia in the direction of the exit and

left the men to commiserate, pay their dues, come to blows—*whatever*. It was none of her business and her priority was to ensure her client was happy again.

But something told her they were leaving happy well behind.

It wasn't just Daniel that Zara had wrapped around her little finger.

When he joined them in the car, she already had Julia revved up on the next house viewing. He was impressed. Johansson was still ready to murder him. He had no doubt his sister harboured a similar desire, but she was all gushy over this new property now, thankfully.

And yes, he felt shit about being the cause of his sister's and his best friend's displeasure, but when were the two of them going to realise there was a chance for them?

In the end, he'd left his friend on the proviso that they'd have drinks that evening. The guy needed to unwind. It scuppered his hopes of a repeat of last night but at least he knew now that Zara wasn't cutting him off.

He grinned. The extra time gave him more time to plan too. He wasn't ready to share her with the world just yet or, more specifically, the press. It was fine house-hunting with his sister; that could be deemed innocent enough. But as soon as it became just the two of them...

He looked out of the window, to the passing neighbourhood, the scathing words of that last article spearing him. What if it had been her photo splashed alongside it? Zara, all innocent and unaware...

His teeth gritted, his fingers biting into his knee—
hell, no.

He had to open her eyes sooner or later to who he
was. Sooner, if he was to do right by her, but his gut
sank with the realisation. He wasn't ready for it.

No matter how refreshing it was to have her like him
for what she'd seen with her own eyes, it wasn't fair to
keep her in the dark and he needed to get there before
the press did. Hell, maybe Julia had already done it for
him. They'd been chatting enough. But he doubted it; he
knew by the way she still looked at him that she had no
clue. And suddenly he hated it with a passion, his well-
cultivated public image that kept all women at arm's
length. Where they belonged—*where she belonged...*

He looked to her alongside him, felt her presence reverberating through him and the certainty of his men-
tal spiel wavered.

Did he *really* want to keep *her* at arm's length?

And what was the alternative? A relationship? A *real*
relationship?

Scorn heated him through. *Don't be an ass. Relationships don't work. Look at your parents.* Kristus, *look
at Julia and Johansson—they're made for one another
and even they can't make it work.*

But sex—he could enjoy the sex. And she wanted
that just as much as he did. Hopefully his reputation
wouldn't kill that off.

She chose that exact moment to slip him a look beneath her lashes, her sultry eyes transporting him back
to their table at lunch, back to what he'd wanted to do,

what she would have let him do, he was sure, and his cock twitched.

Fuck, no, nothing could kill this thing between them.

He brought his fingers to his lips and her eyes followed the movement, her nose flaring as she inhaled softly.

'How many other properties do you think you can line up now that I've agreed to the *potential* budget uplift?' he heard his sister ask, her stress over the word *potential* totally for his benefit, he knew, and Zara's gaze swept away to give his sister her full attention once more—*damn it*.

'To be honest,' she said, 'I've not had a chance to look much, but, trust me, there will be many, so let's take this one as a start, get a feel for what you think and then I'll use that to shortlist more.'

All he heard was *many*, and *many* definitely worked for him. He would make his schedule work around the *many viewings* so long as they came with Zara.

'Don't worry, Daniel, you don't need to attend them all,' his sister said. 'I know how rammed your schedule is since you hit the UK.'

'Have you only recently flown in?' Zara looked to him, brow raised in open curiosity. She really didn't read the papers. They needed that talk, and soon. It was nagging at him more and more with every passing second. The uneasy feeling that he'd kept it from her on purpose, which he hadn't, not in the beginning, but now…

Goddamn it.

'Hmm?' she pressed into his silence and he came alive with a nod.

'Flew in last week.'

'Yes, you see, my brother thinks I'm a delicate flower in need of his protection,' Julia mocked, but her eyes were warm. She appreciated his presence even if she didn't come right out and say it.

'I wouldn't say delicate, and, besides, it's not all about you. I have business to conduct too.'

'And that's why I'm saying you don't need to accompany us on every visit. I can fill you in later.'

He couldn't stop his eyes flitting to Zara's. 'I want to.'

Her lips lifted in a small smile. 'It's nice that you want to see your sister settled.'

'I am nice,' he said with a grin, spying Julia's eyes rolling in her head as she turned to look out of the window.

'Here we go again,' his sister muttered under her breath and Zara's smile became a grimace, Julia adding louder, 'Are we nearly there yet?'

The childlike question had him biting his cheek not to laugh and Zara's eyes flashed at him in warning. He really wasn't making her job easy.

'Ten minutes, tops.'

Zara combed a hand through her hair, the move sending her scent over him, her neck arching invitingly, and he had to fight to hold himself still—their next private moment couldn't come soon enough.

And he would tell her all. He really would.

But maybe after...

CHAPTER SIX

THE VIEWING HAD gone well. Julia had oohed and ahhed over practically everything. Daniel, on the other hand... She just couldn't read him.

Or maybe she was reading him too well and that was the problem.

She looked to him across the back seat of the car and worried over her bottom lip. He was talking business down his mobile, his Swedish dialect washing over her and teasing her to distraction. Between them, Julia sat poring over the property files, acting oblivious to the chemistry thickening the air. Or if she wasn't oblivious, she was content that her position at least separated them both and made her feel less gooseberry-like.

Christ, gooseberry-like—way to go in making your client feel valued, Zara.

She really needed to get the entire affair under her control before she truly pissed the woman off. It wasn't fair on her and it certainly wasn't professional.

What the hell's got into you?

His eyes flicked to hers, his lips quirking mid-sentence and her body jolted with excitement.

Him. That's what.

She snapped her eyes away. She needed to get this house-hunt done and dusted like yesterday. Before she committed career suicide, this time at her own hand. No matter how much her body wanted to smash her work ethic to pieces, no amount of fun was worth going through all that again. Work and her client's satisfaction had to be her priority. Speaking of which, she dialled EJ and asked her to pull together a list of new properties for Julia to go over tonight. There, that was work-focused! Then she threw herself into her emails, anything to keep her attention off him until the car pulled up outside her office building.

Daniel was still engrossed in his conversation so she looked to Julia as she undid her seat belt. 'I'll get those new properties emailed across to you later today.'

'Thanks, Zara.'

She went to open her door and Daniel started, dismissing his caller and pocketing the device in one swift motion. 'I'll see you up.'

'There's really no need.'

But he was already opening his door.

Julia turned to her. 'I'd say I'd come too, but I don't think he wants me to.'

He leant back to send her a brotherly look. 'Very astute of you, *liten syster.*'

She dug him playfully in the ribs. 'Just don't be long. I have somewhere I need to be.'

He chuckled and stepped out, ducking his head back in long enough to say, 'Sure thing.'

Zara watched him close the door, disbelief and a far more worrying emotion warming her through and making her smile softly.

She looked to Julia, all set to bid her farewell, and her intent died at the grave expression on the woman's face—*what was wrong?*

'I like you, Zara, I really do.' She worried nervously over her lip, her eyes tracing her brother's movement around the back of the car before coming back to pin Zara with their uneasy quality. 'And I sure as hell love my brother, but…just be careful. Don't get carried away with him.'

Zara's eyes narrowed, the hairs pricking at the back of her neck with a sudden chill. 'Why would you—?'

She was silenced by Daniel opening her door, his voice breaking through the cabin. 'Come on, she may be smaller than me but don't be fooled. Julia is capable of kicking both our asses.'

Julia gave her a smile and a shrug that bordered on apologetic. 'He's not wrong.'

Not even their shared humour could ease the effect of her warning.

What did she mean?

'Let's talk when I've been through those files,' Julia continued, clearly understanding her hesitation. 'I'll call you.'

'Of course, whenever you're ready,' Zara replied, injecting an enthusiasm into her words she didn't feel, and climbed out of the car. She couldn't even look at him, her apprehension keeping her eyes fixed on the office building as she headed straight for it.

The car door slammed shut, his hurried footsteps on the asphalt coming up behind her. 'Hey, I didn't mean to scare you quite so completely.'

She sent him a swift look. 'I have an appointment shortly,' she lied. 'You really don't need to walk me up.'

'I wanted to speak to you alone.'

She frowned, yanking open the heavy glass door and heading into the bustling foyer, his sister's words resonating and distracting her as she asked on auto-pilot, 'What about?'

'I wondered if you were free—' He broke off, narrowly missing the door closing in on him as he leapt through it and swept her a questioning look.

She avoided his eye and continued on.

Yes, I'd normally hold the door open, but right now, I don't feel anywhere near normal.

'Like I was saying,' he tried again, beating her to the lift button and pressing it. 'I wondered if you were free tomorrow night?'

'By "night", I'm guessing you mean another date,' she said, ignoring the excited thrum of her body.

Think on his sister's warning. If anything, it means you should give an outright no.

'It's not a good idea.'

A few people joined them in the queue and she could see him re-evaluating his next words, his grin speaking volumes. 'I beg to differ.'

'You do?' she said, striving for neutral and fixing her sights on the lift doors.

Come on, come on, come on...

'I do,' he said confidently, his gaze still on her.

She could feel the heat of it teasing at her resolve—thank God they were in company.

The lift arrived and they stepped inside. The small space was rammed with other people and she let go of a relieved breath.

He ducked to speak against her ear. 'Feeling safe?'

His hot breath tickled, his words burning up her core.

Safe? With him?

It was a ludicrous question, one that conjured up answers at both ends of the spectrum. She was inexplicably drawn to him, her body craving every millimetre of his, and she loved that he cared so much for his sister that he wanted to help her. She loved that he could make her laugh. She loved how well they worked together, how he knew how to drive her crazy, how he made her feel beautiful and desired. She could go on and on.

But did she feel safe?

No.

She felt all kinds of vulnerable and his sister's words had a rage of emotion whirling up within her. Too many memories. Too much heartache.

As the lift slid into position on her floor, she stepped out and strode across the office, straight for EJ.

The woman was busy sifting through a document but as she spied them her jaw fell open, her eyes flitting past Zara to the man following close behind.

Of course they would. He was Charles all over again...

She sent her warning look—*snap out of it.* 'Have you sorted that shortlist for me?'

EJ came alive, flustered but alive. 'Sure, I'll email it across now.'

'Thank you.'

EJ's gaze flitted pointedly between them.

Introductions?

She let go of a small breath and gestured to him. 'Elizabeth, meet Daniel, Ms Larsson's brother. Daniel, meet Elizabeth, my personal assistant.'

'It's a pleasure to meet you,' EJ cooed, colour spreading in her cheeks and exacerbating Zara's nerves.

Yes, definitely Charles all over again.

'And you, Elizabeth,' he said smoothly.

Her PA let out a small ripple of laughter that seemed to surprise even herself. 'Is there anything else you need from me?'

To keep your head on, Zara wanted to reply but, hell, who was she to talk? 'No, that's great, thank you.'

She turned to face him. 'I'll go through the shortlist and send it on now. Please tell Julia I look forward to hearing from her.'

His eyes wavered over her face, working to understand her shift in mood, she was sure. 'And as for tomorrow?'

She looked to EJ briefly, not wanting to give the woman any more ammunition. She already sensed the grilling that was coming. 'Let's discuss that later.'

He nodded. 'I'll send you my number.'

'Great.'

Like hell it was great.

She had to stop herself from saying, *You can go,* but her eyes must have done the job for her as he said, 'I'll leave you ladies to it, then.'

With that he turned and walked away, relief flooding her even as her eyes feasted on his seriously sexy exiting rear. Confusion, frustration, fear—they all swamped her and she fisted her hands, forcing herself to turn and head for the sanctity of her office.

She was about to swing her door closed when EJ's hand hit the frame. 'What the actual fuck, Zara?'

She said it under her breath so that the outer office couldn't hear but the force of her reaction was clear and Zara turned to her, baffled. 'What?'

'I can't believe you kept it from me,' she said, wide-eyed.

'Kept what?'

'His chuffing identity!'

'His identity?' Zara frowned, dropping her things onto her desk and rolling her head on her shoulders. Her lack of sleep the previous night was catching up with her, and muscles she hadn't known she possessed were starting to ache like crazy.

'You don't know who he is, do you?'

She looked to EJ's narrowed gaze and gave a tired laugh. 'Who he is? Lord, you make him sound infa-mous.' And then she remembered: his reference to publicity, his sister's mention of the press, the growing sense that he wasn't just anyone…

'You *really* don't know, do you?' EJ let go of a flustered breath and raced back to her desk, pulling out her magazine stash and slipping the one from the top—her most recent, Zara would guess. She strode back towards her, swinging the door closed as she went.

'He's not just any Daniel,' she blurted, slapping the well-known gossip mag onto Zara's desk and pinning its cover man in place with an over-zealous finger. 'He's *the* Daniel Lazenby.'

'Right, what did you say?'

Daniel slammed the car door closed and pinned his sister with a glare.

She looked to him, blinked and then turned to the window on a small sigh. 'Nothing of substance.'

'Nothing of substance?' He shook his head in disbelief. 'She couldn't get me out of there quick enough.'

'I just gave her some advice.' Her eyes came back to him and the cloud-like quality to her amber gaze dampened his anger. 'Woman to woman.'

He frowned. 'What's that supposed to mean?'

'That I told her she should be careful around you.'

He thrust his fingers through his hair with a frustrated breath.

There's no coming back from such a damning declaration, not when it comes from your very own sister.

'*Kristus*, Julia, it's great to know you have such a high opinion of me.'

Her eyes widened. 'Really, you want to go there?'

They fixed one another silently, the sound of the ignition filling the cabin and their bodies rocking softly as the car pulled away from the kerb.

Hell, she's right. What can you say to that? Deny her words of caution? Act like they're unfounded?

Still, he should have been given the opportunity to speak to Zara first.

And say what, exactly? Hey, I'm a publicly proclaimed and self-confessed playboy whose family notoriety means you should stay the fuck away, but fancy a repeat?

'No, I didn't think you would.' She looked away, her attention once more on the passing streets. 'Look, she's not like the other women you go around with, and I'm not judging you, Daniel—seriously. With parents like ours it's no surprise you don't want to hold down a relationship, but she's not like that.'

'How would you know?'

'Because we've talked, our history with men is not too dissimilar and, I'm telling you, she's relationship material and you...you're still too busy avoiding anything close to a relationship, playing the role Dad did to the press and pissing your mum the hell off. You have no idea what's best for you.'

'I don't know what you mean.' He did, but he was in no mood to discuss his dear old parents. Not when his mind was on more important things—like getting Zara back on side.

Slowly, she turned to face him. 'Yes, you do. And that

image you paint, the whole heartless playboy act, it'll catch up with you eventually. It'll be you that suffers.'

Something in her words caught at him. Her honesty, her emotion, her love. Whatever it was it had him on edge. 'You don't need to stress over me. I'm a big boy, I can take care of myself.'

'I don't doubt it, but while you're playing at being the big boy, you can stay away from her.'

'I can't. I'm helping you house-hunt.'

'Not any more.'

He swallowed heavily. 'Come on, Julia, don't let this get in the way of finding you the home you deserve.'

'Women seem to lose their judgement when they're around you and I won't have that on my conscience,' she said forcibly. 'You're off the hunt.'

Kristus. *Now what...?*

'Okay,' he said eventually, a new plan starting to form that wouldn't put his sister in the middle. 'I'll back out of the legwork, so long as you'll still consider my financial assistance.'

'You will?' She didn't look convinced and he couldn't really blame her with the ideas now taking shape.

'Yes, consider yourself in the clear.'

She beamed then, leaning in to peck him on the cheek. 'One day, you'll grow up and realise a relationship is what you need too, but until you do, I'm having no involvement in finding you a match.'

'Such a thoughtful sister, aren't you?' he teased, mentally rejecting her suggestion of what he needed…and then the doubt set in. Hadn't he already spent enough time debating their 'just sex' status? Was he changing? Was he wanting more?

Unease settled in the pit of his stomach, as images of his childhood, his parents entwined with others, swirled in his mind. The goading from the press, the public and now his mother's media-hyped and utterly false marriage… His jaw pulsed, his stomach twisted.

Yeah, you want a relationship like a goddamn hole in the head.

He shook it all off, focusing on what he did know, what felt right.

Zara. In my bed.

He wasn't ready to let her go. Not yet. He would be at some point, of course he would, but right now…

CHAPTER SEVEN

EJ's DISBELIEVING RANT was still spinning around her head hours later.

'You must know who he is. His family are the Swedish version of the Kardashians—the chuffing Osbournes, even. And he's like their black sheep: the hunky, successful, don't-trust-him-with-your-sister kind of sheep. Come on, Zara, you must know? He's a billionaire businessman, for Christ's sake, and since hitting the UK the press have been all over it, all over him.'

And still Zara had stared at her blankly—dumbly, even. How could she have been so clueless?

Now everything made sense. The comments about the press, the public image... In fact, it made more than just sense, it reaffirmed all the reasons she should have stayed the hell away and not crossed that line.

'He's not the kind to get serious with,' EJ had eventually said, and then she'd given her a tentative smile, 'but you could still have some fun.'

Like hell.

It was late, the office deserted, and she was taking advantage of the solitude to smack her head with her stupidity, quite literally, the magazine clutched in her hand making a damn fine implement.

She'd lost count of the number of times she'd read the blasted article after EJ had left it with her. And then she'd scoured the Internet for more.

She knew it couldn't all be true, that the press would have embellished or twisted the truth to work for them, but there was never smoke without fire. And there was enough smoke to know he wasn't a man to get involved with.

She'd known his parents to be questionable—his honesty regarding their treatment of Julia had told her that. But now they were on another plane. His father a rock star, his mother a beauty queen, their marriage infamously fraught. His father dying notoriously in the bed of another woman and his mother marrying the band manager swiftly after his death.

And then had come the TV show—*a reality TV show, for fuck's sake!*

Not that he'd gone in for it. He'd famously stormed off the show a decade ago, turning his back on his mother and having nothing to do with his two brothers.

But it would appear he'd only changed the TV cameras for those of the press. Flaunting his extreme sexual antics and by all accounts following in his father's playboy footsteps. And she couldn't get her head round it. Couldn't pair the man she was getting to know with the man splashed all over the media, his own mother disowning him at every turn with outspoken disgust at his behaviour. As if she had any right to judge after all she had done.

They were a mess, through and through. And here she was, getting far too close for comfort.

Her breath shuddered out of her as she turned to her computer screen and the *Forbes* article covering the great success that was Lazenby Enterprises. Now appreciation swelled, appreciation for the man that had done it all alone, achieved billionaire status without any of his family's wealth. And she had to admire him for that, just as she could admire his open affection for his sister, but the rest…

Argh—she was a fool.

She tossed the magazine onto the desk, the pages sweeping open to *that* page, having been well-fingered by now.

She stared at the photos. A series of different women, hanging off his arm or worse, and then the main image, of him pressing some blonde up against the glass entrance to The Shard, of all places. She cringed—did the man have no decency? And then her entire body mocked her, wanting to be that woman, wanting to be the one he'd pinned up against it. Jealousy, desire, self-loathing, all manner of crap pushing her to the brink, and she rubbed at her face in frustration, shoving herself out of her seat.

Don't let another man get to you!

It was time to go home and forget him. She'd done it with Charles. She could sure as hell do it with this brief fling. Even if he had made her climax harder than she'd ever imagined possible, numerous times over. Even if he did make her feel so desirable, so alive—*stop it!*

She cut the flashbacks threatening her sanity and moved to lift her mobile just as its screen lit up, a number she didn't recognise calling.

She frowned, checking the time. *Cold callers? This late?* They were clearly sinking to a new all-time low.

She cut the call and started packing up, shoving her laptop into her bag and lifting her mobile to go the same way. The thing came alive again, its chassis vibrating into her palm and that same number burning into her, unease creeping up her spine. It couldn't be…he wouldn't…and yet, the feeling was there, as if he were in the room with her.

Don't bloody answer it, said her sanity as her thumb hovered over the acceptance button.

She looked to the creased-up article, to his body engulfing blondie, and her anger trampled all over her sanity.

Fuck that, she thought, *he deserves my wrath.*

She answered the call and raised the phone to her ear, forcing calm into her tone.

There was a chance it wasn't him.

'Hello, Zara Anders.'

'Zara, it's Daniel.'

Fuck, fuck, fuck.

Her brain screamed over him, his voice instantly recognisable and sending fire through her veins. And not of the kind that she needed. She was struggling to think straight, her words coming out automatically as her brain tried to articulate exactly what she wanted to throw at him. 'What can I do for you, Mr Lazenby?'

'Please don't call me that.'

'Why?' she said simply. 'Would you prefer one of the names the press are so willing to dish out for you? They make excellent use of alliteration.'

He gave a heavy sigh down the phone. 'If it's going to make you feel better...'

She cracked a little. 'Do you honestly think me slinging their abuse at you is going to fix how I feel?'

'It's better than your professional front,' he said. 'Your anger I can deal with, you shutting me out I can't. And you have every right to be angry. My sister shouldn't have said what she did. It wasn't her place.'

'No, it was yours,' she bit out. 'Not that she really told me anything, she simply warned me off you.'

'And she shouldn't have done.' She could hear his frustration down the phone.

Poor rich playboy, pissed off that his little sister had ruined his plans to get laid again.

She would have thrown that at him if he hadn't added, 'She should've given me chance to explain.'

'Which bit exactly?' she blurted. 'Your infamous family, your business stature or the best thing of all, your renowned status as a *male slut*?'

'*Kristus.*'

'What? You can't take the truth?'

'I didn't purposefully keep anything from you,' he argued. 'It's not like I go around introducing myself based on my status in life. I mean, *skit*, how would that go down? Hey, my family are media whores, my business makes me billions and I like sex, fancy a fuck?'

She inhaled sharply, his words hitting more than a nerve; they hit a truckload sitting right at her apex.

'It would've beaten being made a fool of,' she said through her teeth. 'To have known who I was getting into bed with.'

'I get that, but you're no fool,' he rasped, 'and I hate that you think I made you one.'

In the call background, she could make out a door opening, wind buzzing down the phone as he carried on. 'I didn't tell you because it was refreshing, meeting you, knowing you didn't know who I was. Surely you can forgive me for relishing in that.'

She spun on her heel, her anger wobbling. She could understand that. It had to be a bitch dating when you were a walking advert for money and status. But hell, it didn't make yo-yoing from blondie's knickers into hers acceptable—not on any level.

'Poor rich billionaire, can't go on a real date because the girls are only after one thing. I feel so sad for you.' Her voice dripped with sarcasm, her eyes dropping to the desk, to the open magazine. 'The girls you're used to clearly don't mind being one of many, or the reputation that comes along with that, but I have no interest whatsoever.'

'No interest?' She sensed his smirk and her anger rallied, along with the defiant nub of nerve-endings that tripped out over the memory of that smile. 'I think that's not the whole truth.'

Bastard. He knew what he did to her.

But not any more.

He was bad news. Her instincts, the press—hell, even his own sister made that clear. She covered the receiver and let go of a pent-up breath.

Just be professional and leave it at that. You still have a business relationship to maintain.

'Now that I know who you are,' she said, her voice surprisingly smooth, 'I can assure you I have absolutely no interest.'

He chuckled, the sound teasing her down the phone and making her hand clutch it tighter.

Don't turn me on, don't...

'Shall we put that to the test?'

What?

'No, Mr Lazenby,' she said, her voice pitched on panic, and something else—blasted *excitement.* 'We shall not put it to the test.'

Her eyes darted around her office, too many memories triggering feelings that told her very much where that test would end up.

The background noise down the line fell away, as though he'd entered a quiet building, and he said softly, 'You sure about that?'

A thrill trickled through her spine.

Are you sure about that?

She was in trouble. She pinned her sights on the images. The one taken just yesterday morning as the couple left the hotel together, the look of satisfaction on his face and the haughty one on blondie. 'Positive,' she thrust out. 'I will associate with you as a client but that's as far as this goes.'

'Really?' She heard a familiar ping down the phone—a lift? *Her* lift?

No, he wouldn't be...

She strode to her office door, swinging it open and spearing the lift. 'Where are you?'

The phone cut off and she knew the answer, even before the lit display above the lift started to announce its movement.

Oh, fuck.

Daniel pocketed his phone and ignored the weird rate of his pulse. He never got excited about anything. Hell, he got turned on, had great sex, but genuinely getting excited about something, it just wasn't him. Not even the buzz of a successful deal could trump this.

But he was excited to see her.

Or was it actually nerves?

He had to be honest, he'd never failed in getting what he wanted before. Yes, they were on rocky ground but they worked too well together to let this get in the way. Surely she'd see that.

He ran a finger through the collar of his shirt and watched the lift count its ascent.

He'd known she'd be the type to still be at work; his instinct hadn't let him down there. He just hoped he hadn't got the strength of her attraction wrong too.

The doors opened and there she was, arms crossed over her middle, face like thunder, and he couldn't help the grin that formed, or the flutter that happened some-where deep inside. She was damn sexy when she was mad.

'This place needs new security,' she blurted. 'We're closed.'

'You're still here,' he said, stepping out of the lift.

'Not for long.' She spun on her heel and strode for her office, her entire body swaying provocatively and tugging at his groin. *Kristus*, she killed him.

'Can we talk, please?' He moved after her. 'Just let me apologise?'

She sent him a look over her shoulder. 'I'd rather you left.'

She reached her desk and grabbed up her jacket, rounding on him to shrug it on, the move parting her blouse far more than his body could take. 'An apology isn't going to change anything.'

'It'll make me feel better.'

'Consider your apology delivered, now go.'

She swung her bag over her shoulder and bent to switch off the lamp upon her desk. His gaze fell to the glass tabletop and with it came a flood of memories, a rush of blood directly south.

'I'll call your sister tomorrow, once I've arranged the next set of viewings.'

He barely heard her; his need to have her accept his apology and get to where they'd been less than twenty-four hours ago had his mind racing with words, none of which seemed good enough.

She strode for the door, her hand closing around its

edge, and then she looked to him pointedly. 'Now if you'll…'

Piss off, her eyes silently finished, their spark making him grin all over again as he rounded to face her. 'You know, you're sexy when you're angry.'

He saw her throat bob, her eyelids flickering as her gaze fell to his mouth, the move fleeting but enough.

'Don't say things like that.'

Her voice had lost its force, and its whisper-like quality was urging him on. 'Why?'

'It's not appropriate.' She looked away, fixating on the exit. 'Now please, can we leave? I don't need you here, dragging the whole paparazzi on your tail and stirring up trouble that my business could do without.'

His shoulders relaxed, their previous tension surprising him. 'Is that what has you so worried?'

'One of many things.'

'Well, let me put your mind at rest,' he assured her. 'I'm alone, no one's followed me, not tonight.'

'I find that hard to believe,' she said, her eyes coming back to him and flashing with something akin to pain. 'If I didn't know better, I'd think you loved nothing more than creating scenes for them to exploit.'

'They can be relentless.'

'But not tonight, hey?' She looked hurt as she threw the accusation at him. 'Can't say I blame them. I'm hardly your type.'

Her words pierced him, resonating with the same argument he'd had a thousand times over, and then her eyes flicked to the desk and for the first time he saw the magazine laid out there.

'Judging by that double-page spread, you have quite the rep,' she continued, 'and I don't want that anywhere near me.'

She wasn't worried about her business. If she truly knew all there was to know about him, she would know her association with him would bring people flocking.

No, this was personal, and it was time he set the record straight. Time she understood who he was, accepted it and came to bed with him, her eyes open.

'You'd be happy never to see me again?'

She flicked her hair back, her hand flexing around the door edge still determined, but it was her eyes that gave her away, even as she spoke. 'That's exactly what I'm saying.'

'Really?' He stepped forward, his hand reaching out to stroke along her jaw, his thumb tracing over her lower lip.

She made a small noise in her throat—almost a whimper, almost a moan—her eyes falling to his mouth, her teeth drawing back the lip he'd just traced.

'Can you honestly deny this chemistry?' he pressed.

Her head shook, the move so slight. But it wasn't enough. He wanted—no, *craved*—her verbal denial. 'No?'

'No,' she breathed, her head shaking that little bit more. 'I can't deny it.'

Yes. His restraint snapped and he propelled forward, his desire taking her to the wall, his hands thrusting into her hair as her bag hit the floor. She gazed up at him, eyes wide, and then her hands were in his hair dragging him down, their lips colliding in a fierce kiss, tongues plundering desperately.

Heat exploded through him, her essence flooding his taste buds, her hunger rivalling his own, their hands travelling everywhere all at once, wild and crazed.

'I need to have you,' he rasped over her, the force of his desire shaking him up inside; he was like a man starved.

'But you'll ruin me.'

He pinned her forehead with his own, staring down into her blazing gaze and seeing fear in the depths of her eyes.

Kristus, *take a pause, reassure her.*

'I won't, I promise,' he assured her. 'I court the press, not the other way around.'

He felt her brow furrow beneath his. 'You *court* the press?'

'Yes, I control what they see. It's on my terms, most of the time.'

'Your *terms*?'

He took a deep breath, his hands loosening their hold in her hair, his eyes closing. He didn't like where the conversation was heading; it gave too much away, went too deep. And there was no way she'd understand. Fuck, even he was starting to struggle. 'It's complicated.'

She palmed his chest, pushing him away, the heat of her touch searing through his shirt even as she parted their bodies and the cold air seeped between them. He opened his eyes and immediately regretted it, the disgust in hers tearing through him.

'You *want* them to splash you all over the media,' she said incredulously, her frown furrowing further, her body righting as her own strength seemed to build at the disappearance of his. 'You *want* to feed this hideous persona.'

'It is what it is,' he said simply, although inside he hurt, actually hurt.

What the hell is wrong with you?

He looked into her eyes, to the disgust still burning bright, and something inside him died. An irrational anger surging. 'I am what I am.'

'But why?' She shook her head. 'Why be like that at all?'

Why? He had a thousand reasons why, although, in truth, it really came down to two. His parents. They'd taught him all he needed to know. But that was none of her business. He didn't need to indulge this conversation. He could sooner be gone and get himself back to how things were, in company where he could be at ease with who he was. Johansson was waiting on him after all. 'I have to go.'

'Can't you at least try and explain it to me?'

Explain? Kristus, *she was at it again.*

Pressing into his past, forcing it to the surface, making him talk. She really wasn't his type. He never should have come here. Never should have pushed to indulge this crazy obsession he had developed over her.

'Why?' He threw his panic-driven anger at her,

not caring that it was misdirected, not caring that she wrapped her arms around her middle in a gesture that smacked of her own pain. 'You want me to convince you that you're not just another notch in my headboard?'

Her cheeks paled, and he knew he'd hit his mark, but the joke was on him. He was the one that needed convincing of that fact, not her.

He thrust his fingers through his hair and moved past her. 'Just call my sister when you're ready to sort the arrangements.' He didn't look back as he headed for the lift, couldn't bear to see the way her eyes glistened and body shook.

This is for the best. If she's this upset already, just think what it would be like a few weeks down the line.

'You'll be pleased to learn that, following your little chat this afternoon, she's ensuring we have no more need to see one another going forward.'

'So that's it, you've delivered your apology, attempted to seduce me when I'm in the know and, now that I've questioned your behaviour, you're leaving?' She stormed up behind him, the heat of her wrath penetrating his back, her words hitting so many nerves he could barely think straight.

'It's not like that.'

'No?'

He paused at the lift and he sensed her stop too, but he didn't dare look at her. He needed to be gone. Now. Before he backed up and kissed it all away, the pain, the disgust, and sank them both deeper into this mess.

'I'm sure you'll agree, it's for the best.' He ignored

her question and pressed the button for the lift, grateful when the doors promptly opened. 'Now you don't have to see me, unless you choose to.'

He didn't know why he'd added the latter.

Liar. You still hope she'll look past your reputation to your bed. Well, fuck hope. You're leaving this one well alone and moving on...

'Goodnight, Ms Anders.'

He stepped into the waiting lift and pressed 'Ground', his eyes finding hers of their own volition. His insides clenched, her bright gaze holding his own, and then the doors came to his rescue, shutting out her penetrative stare and calming him the fuck down.

It's okay, some space, some time away, and life can go back to how it was.

Pre-Zara.

Pre-all-this-weird-feeling-shit.

What the fuck just happened?

Dazed, Zara rubbed at the back of her neck, trying to coax away the unease that prickled there. How could the mood have changed so suddenly? So dramatically? One minute he wanted her and the next, he couldn't move away fast enough. And all because she'd probed.

She turned away from the lift and forced her legs to return to her office, her limbs still shaky with the thrill of him. Not even the chill of his departure had stamped that out.

And what the hell was that about?

All that she knew of him, of what was wise and sensible to her sanity, and still she wanted him.

She scooped her bag up off the floor and tossed it onto her desk, dropping into her swivel chair and letting it spin with the force of her fall— *Now what?*

Something didn't sit right.

As the chair came to a rest, she looked to the magazine still spread open, the words bouncing off the page even though she was too far away to read it. Not that it mattered—she knew it by heart.

The man on the page and the man she'd met yesterday, though they looked the same, they weren't. He was a contradiction, a dangerous contradiction at that. And although her sanity told her to leave well alone, to keep him painted bad, she couldn't.

Something had called to her, something she'd glimpsed when she'd thrown her insults at him. A pain, an anger even, that went far deeper than what she'd said had warranted, and for all her self-preservation, she didn't want to believe the article. She didn't want to believe the press. She wanted to believe in him. To gain an understanding of him.

Don't be a fool. You're playing with fire.

She laid her head over the back of her chair and stared up at the ceiling, her thoughts turning to the very real fire he'd stoked up low in her gut.

Yes, to pursue him would be foolish. No matter that her body ached for him. No matter that she knew somewhere beneath that cocky exterior was a pain she wanted to understand, to fix. He wasn't for her.

She should be relieved that his sister had stepped in, that her eyes had been opened to this side of him, the side that very much mirrored Charles.

So why did she have the irrational urge to run after him?

Because you're a glutton for punishment.

Two beers in and the heavy weight in Daniel's gut hadn't shifted. He was slumped in Johansson's deep leather sofa, head back over the curve, eyes unseeing on the ceiling. All he could see was Zara's face, her eyes as she'd expressed her disgust over him, his life.

'If I'd known you'd be in such great spirits, I would have said to hell with the press and let's go out-out.'

He sent his friend a look.

'Jeez, don't give me the puppy-dog eyes,' Johansson said, taking a swig from his bottle and pushing off the sofa. 'Another?'

Daniel tilted his bottle back and fore, eyeing the drop left. 'Sure.'

'God, you even sound broken,' he said. 'I thought this was supposed to be a *let's cheer Johansson up* evening, not the other way around.'

'Ah, hell, I'm sorry.' He dropped forward to rest his elbows on his knees, his eyes on his bottle, his mind still on her disdain-filled face. 'It's just the way she looked at me. I can't get it out of my head.'

'Yeah, you've said that, at least three times already.' The guy actually had the audacity to grin as he strode across the open living space and into the kitchen. 'She's really got under your skin.'

'You don't have to sound so pleased about it.'

'Don't I?' Johansson said, dropping his empty on the side and pulling open the sleek black fridge. He extracted two bottles, the glass chinking together, and swung the door closed again, his eyes coming back to Daniel, alive with amusement. 'You've been giving women the run-around for years—feels like payback to me.'

Daniel scoffed. 'Nice to have you onside, *old friend*.'

Johansson laughed as he popped open each bottle and headed back towards him. 'Hey, I'm just speaking the truth. I love you, man, but seriously, it's time you were treated to your own medicine.'

'Right, fuck it, we're going out.' He chucked back the remnants of his current drink and stood with new-found determination. 'I'm not listening to this *skit*.'

'Sit,' his friend said, thrusting the fresh bottle at him. 'I was kidding. Going out is the last thing either of us need.'

'You reckon? Because I could sure as hell do with burying this unpleasantness in a woman far less concerned with my reputation and all about the fun I can deliver.'

Johansson shook his head, inhaling slowly as he considered him. 'I'll make you a deal—you're still like this after this drink, then we'll head out.'

Still like it. Hell, Daniel was still like it several bottles and two bars later.

Nothing could dissuade him from her, no amount

of blonde, brunette, short or tall, nothing was working for him.

'Come, Danny,' the redhead purred as she curved her body into his side, 'I think your friend and mine look too at home to have us cramping their fun.'

He sipped his drink and disengaged his fingers from between the bar edge and her over-zealous hip bone, flexing them to regain some feeling. He should've discouraged her by now, done something to get rid, but he hadn't had the inclination to do that either. He didn't like this sudden obsession with one woman. It wasn't him. And it sure as hell wasn't convenient.

She shifted into his eyeline, pouting up at him. 'So, Danny, what say we head back to mine?'

He grated his teeth together—her *Danny* was doing overtime on his nerves. He looked to Johansson and met the guy's desperately pleading *'Help me'* gaze over the honey-blonde seemingly intent on devouring his entire neck. It would have been funny if the cause of their discomfort weren't so troubling.

Troubling for Daniel. Not so troubling for Johansson. It was good to see him out of place in surroundings and company such as this. This had been their norm for years, when they weren't working their asses off, that was. And it was still Daniel's go-to on a night off. But he couldn't settle. Neither of them could. His friend's reasoning was solid: he'd met the right woman for him, and the sooner his sister and Johansson could get past whatever nonsense kept them apart, the better.

But for Daniel, his reasoning made no sense. He barely knew the woman, and he'd been ordered out of her life for good. Maybe that was the problem. He didn't take orders from anyone, least of all his *liten syster* who, as much as he loved her, had no hold over him.

And he got Zara's upset over his past, he really did, but he also knew she wanted him and he wasn't letting go of that. He just needed to come up with a plan that ensured she couldn't escape him so easily.

He necked his bottle and gestured to Johansson— *time to break out*. He had a plan brewing and he wanted a clear head when he put it in motion.

Tomorrow couldn't come soon enough.

CHAPTER EIGHT

'How'd it go?'

EJ asked the question from under her desk, head and fingers buried in a nest of cables.

'It was okay,' Zara said, slipping off her jacket and rubbing away the tension in her neck. The tension that had taken up permanent residence since Daniel had walked out the previous night. 'What exactly are you doing?'

'Trying to make sense of this mess,' EJ muttered. 'The IT dude may be a dreamboat to look at, but his technical abilities I'm less than sure of.' She gave a har-rumph and tossed the stuff aside to clamber up, brushing off her summer dress as she went. 'Just okay, huh? Doesn't sound good.'

'No, no, it was fine,' Zara assured her, knowing full well her less than enthusiastic response was down to a very different cause.

'Fine?' EJ raised her brow. 'So, what's the problem?'

Zara rubbed at her neck again. 'Blasted men.'

'Amen to that,' EJ said on a laugh. 'I'm getting some water on ice—you fancy one?'

'Please.'

She left EJ to sort the drinks and headed into her office, swinging open the window and letting in a fresh breeze. They were having a surprising heatwave and, no matter that the office was air-conditioned, nothing beat the real thing. She took a breath, taking in the distant view of the city as she evaluated the day's viewings.

It had started out well enough. She'd got through one viewing with praise aplenty from Julia, and then the woman's phone had pinged on the threshold of property two and giddy, excited Julia had become a woman intent on murder. She'd apologised profusely, saying she just had to make a call and, thinking to give her privacy, Zara had stepped back outside. But she'd have to have been in another neighbourhood to miss the eruption that had then ensued as Julia had delivered her brother—the man Zara was doing her damnedest not to think on— the ear-bashing of a lifetime.

'So come on, give us the low-down,' EJ said, coming in behind her and kicking the door too. 'I'm all ears.' She passed a chilled glass Zara's way and promptly sat down on the visitor chair. 'And don't skimp on the detail.'

In spite of her stress, Zara laughed. 'I wouldn't dare.'

'By men, are we referring to Mr Swedish Sexy-Pants?'

Her laugh erupted twice over, EJ's way with words working some magic. 'In part. It seems Mr Swedish Sexy-Pants took an old flame of Julia's out on a bender last night and managed to get himself papped by the tabloids with some women.'

'So by old flame, not really all that old, then?'

'No, I'd say it still burns strong enough.'

'Enough to put a dampener on the remaining viewings?'

'No, she seemed happy enough.' She took a sip of her drink, her mind backtracking over the viewing and Julia's parting words. 'She's actually considering making an offer on the second.'

'An offer? Well, that's fantastic.' And then her eyes narrowed on Zara, her lips turning down. 'But you're not acting like it's fantastic.'

'It is, you're totally right.' But she couldn't inject the enthusiasm into her tone. Truth was, the first thing she'd done when she'd left Julia's company was google Mr Swedish Sexy-Pants and been confronted with the very same image Julia had likely been sent. And it had stung, the burn of jealousy wholly out of her control.

'So I take it the problem is nothing to do with Julia and everything to do with Mr—' A tap at the door saved Zara from the remainder of EJ's damning statement and she pushed up out of her seat. 'Hold that thought.'

Zara turned back to the window and EJ headed to the door, pulling it open.

'Someone's here to see Zara,' she could hear Russell, one of her trainee agents, say.

'Well, she doesn't have any appoint—' EJ's voice broke on a strange little sound. 'Right—good—yes, I'll be out in just a sec.'

She promptly closed the door and leant back against it as Zara turned to eye her curiously. 'Who is it?'

'Er… Mr Swedish Sexy-Pants.'

Zara's tummy somersaulted. *'Fuck.'*

EJ's brows hit the sky. 'Do you want me to get rid?'

What the hell could he want?

He'd made it clear he was backing off, that day's scoop only serving to re-emphasise the fact she was old news. But here he was on her doorstep and, God help her, her body loved it.

Do I want rid? No.

Should I get rid? Yes.

'Zara?'

She forced herself to calm down; there was still her business with Julia to protect. 'Can you see what he wants, please?'

It was hardly the seeing-off she wanted to deliver, but it maintained her professional front and that was what mattered.

'Sure thing.' EJ swept out, door closing behind her, and Zara took several deep breaths. He could be here for any number of reasons. Any number that didn't involve getting their rocks off. Hell, he'd had his fill with some redhead last night, he could hardly be looking for another hook-up.

And if he was…

She clenched her fists and reeled her mind back.

Don't be a fool.

The door shifted open and in walked EJ, her own colour considerably higher than a moment ago.

'So, looks as if we have a new client,' she said as the door clicked shut behind her.

'We what?'

'He wants to sign up.'

She had to be joking; she *was* joking—there was no way...

'I'm not having you on. He wants a place on the out-skirts and one in the city—he wants *two* homes.'

Two—Jesus, the commission...

Forget the commission. He's only doing it to get in your knickers...again... Can you really let him do that? Let him buy you?

But if he buys two properties then it's money for the business...

And what about you, your sanity, your dignity...? You can't do this.

Her mind spiralled out of control, the personal war-ring with the professional.

'Can you imagine the fees on that?' EJ said, nar-rowing her focus on what really mattered—*the busi-ness*. And if he needed the residences and she needed the business, then maybe there was a win-win situation to be gleaned...

If she delegated...

'Get one of the team to sit him down, go through his requirements—'

EJ was already shaking her head.

'What?'

'He's specifically requested you.'

Of course, he has.

'And, let's face it, you're the best and a guy like that,

he needs to be given the best. Just think what it'll do for business.'

Just think what it'll do to you.

She let go of a flustered breath—what choice did she have? Her business was in its infancy. Having him as a client was too big an opportunity to pass up. It was a risk she had to take and endure.

Endure?

Her insides laughed at her.

You can't wait to be around him again. You crave the rush, the way he makes you feel, the way he desires you, the way you lose yourself in him...

Her racing thoughts were leaving her well behind. She needed to put the brakes on and fast. 'Give me two minutes and send him in.'

'Fabulous,' EJ blurted, spinning on her heel to pull open the door and disappear through it, thankfully shutting it before Zara could get a glimpse of the man himself.

Two minutes. Two minutes to compose herself and perform the job she was a pro at.

Not be a swooning mess itching to be ravished.

She could do this. She bit into her lower lip hard. She *would* do this.

'Ms Anders will see you now.'

Her PA smiled at him politely as she opened the door to Zara's office and gestured for him to go in. His heart did a weird skip, which he promptly buried, and he strode forward, giving her a smile of gratitude as he passed by.

Zara was before the window, her white shirt-style dress casting a glow around it in the sunshine and hinting at the curves beneath. The weird skip went off again, falling over itself as he tried to maintain his calm, to play it cool.

'Mr Lazenby,' she said, her tone crisp and professional, and everything he didn't want. She crossed the room towards him, her white dress swaying distractingly above the knee as she offered her hand. He eyed it, a small smile playing about his lips. Okay, so that was how this was going to go. He could work with that. It beat her turning him away.

He slipped his hand around hers, his fingers reaching as far as the pulse point of her wrist, and he let his fingers rest there, enjoying the play of emotion in her face. Her colour rising, her lips parting at their contact, the move so minute it could have been missed if he hadn't been watching her so closely.

'If you're going to be working for me, I would prefer you called me Daniel.'

Her tongue flicked out swiftly, teasing him with every want, before she nodded, removing her hand from his. 'If that is what you wish, why don't you take a seat and we can go through your requirements?'

She gestured at the visitor's chair and he had to fight the urge to suggest they go somewhere else. Somewhere private. It wouldn't do though. First and foremost, he had to convince her that he was there to employ her services, not to fulfil the multitudes of desires raging through his brain. Especially after how things had been left between them.

He looked to the chair, to the desk to which it clung, and memories collided with new imaginings and he stilled.

'Perhaps I can get you a drink, while you get settled? Tea, coffee, water?'

He knew she'd read his mind in that second, could hear the tension in her voice. 'A water—please.'

She swept past him, clouding him with her scent, his tummy drawing tight as he felt his sanity crumble.

What is she doing to you?

It didn't matter what she was doing to him, he was there to burn it out.

Get her onside, get the properties that made perfect sense for him to own—real, honest sense, none of it purely to get his kicks—and fuck her until he could get past it. Get back in control.

He scanned her office, forcing out the distracting memories only too willing to surface, and waited for her to return. He didn't need to wait long. She walked back in, one sandal-heeled foot kicking the door closed as she made for him, eyes steadily averted.

She set his glass down on the desk in front of him and moved behind it, settling into the chair before taking a sip of her drink and lifting her eyes to his.

'Before we get started, I think we should set some ground rules,' she began. 'If I am to do this for you, there is to be no crossing of lines. I am excellent at what I do, and I'll find you the right homes, but that's where our connection ends.'

He nodded as he listened, his hands folding into his lap as he sat back in his chair, giving the impression of being completely at ease. 'I understand your need to lay it all out there in black and white.'

'Good.'

'But let me also be clear, I am employing your services *because* I know you to be great at what you do. My decision to set up a home for myself here is about being closer to my sister and my growing business interests. It's not some made-up ploy to make you spend time with me.' She gave a satisfied smile and he added, 'Not entirely.'

Her eyes widened, her sharp intake of breath barely discernible. 'I—'

He held up his hand to interject, his smile cocksure. 'Make no mistake, I will purchase two homes through you, but also know this: I *want* you and I intend on having what I want.'

'Well, really…' she blustered, her cheeks flushing, her tongue flicking out to nervously wet her lower lip, teasing his restraint.

'You can relax, Zara,' he assured her softly. 'I'll wait for you. You can decide when this line you have drawn is safe to cross and when you do, I'll be ready.'

Her eyes wavered, her jaw clenched tight and he had the feeling she was grinding her teeth as she worked for an answer. He took pity and bent forward, releasing her gaze to lift up his glass for a drink.

'Now we've got that covered,' he said, settling back, 'shall we begin?'

* * *

Forty-five minutes later, she'd worked through her standard Q & A—something she knew by heart and could do in her sleep, which was lucky because her brain was still clawing its way back from his 'I *want* you and I intend on having what I want' declaration.

Having what I want. Of all the cocky, arrogant, self-assured, pig-headed things to say. And what had she done to dissuade him? A big, fat nothing. If her body hadn't been so on fire at the prospect, she would have thrown back his behaviour the previous night and lain all the anger at his door. Instead she was annoyed at herself. For being so easy where he was concerned.

She looked at him now as he scanned the document she had filled in and waited for his affirmation that all was in order. She used the time to calm the nerves that were mounting by the second now the Q & A was done, their business for the day complete. Would he leave quietly? Or would he push again? And if he did, was she ready for it?

He flipped the pages back in order and his amber eyes lifted to her, their depths searing her across the desk and thickening the air around them.

You're far from ready.

'Anything amiss?' She sounded cool and professional, everything her body was not.

'It's perfect,' he said, holding her eye as he passed the document back to her. 'When can we begin?'

'I believe I can get something in the diary for later this week—if that fits with you?'

'Also perfect.' He pushed up out of his seat, his sudden movement jarring her into the same. 'I'm assuming that's all you need for now.'

'It is,' she said simply.

Was that it? Was he leaving so easily?

Disappointment landed deep in her gut and she smoothed a hand through her hair as she rationalised it away—*you don't want more.*

'In that case, I won't keep you any longer.' He gave her a grin that reached all the way to her toes, heat whipping through her. 'Call me when you have something.'

'I will.' It was all she could manage, afraid that any more would give too much away.

She watched him turn and walk to the door, her breath hanging in her lungs.

And then he stopped, his head turning to look at her over his shoulder. 'Oh, and congratulations, by the way.'

Her breath escaped. 'Congratulations?'

'On Julia—she rang me earlier to say she's placing an offer.'

'Oh, right, yes.' She nodded, her brain catching up. 'She's happy, then?'

'More than—you've done a great job.' Open admiration fuelled his words and a delicious warmth encased her. He meant it.

'Thank you. I'm glad she's happy.'

He gave a small smile. 'Me too.'

'And does she know you've asked me to source these homes for you?'

His smile turned sheepish. 'It may have come up.'

She shouldn't ask how it went. Not after the warning Julia had delivered. And yet she asked anyway. 'How did that go?'

He shrugged. 'I'm looking to make a home for myself close to her and there's no one she'd rather got the commission than you, so…'

The commission. The money. It was all that mattered ultimately. Her business.

Yeah, and what about that redhead he got into bed with last night? Are you going to be able to keep your jealousy in check, or lose it like Julia did over Johansson at the viewing?

He frowned and turned to face her head-on. 'What's wrong?'

Christ, did I have to be so transparent?

'Nothing.'

He stepped forward, his frown deepening. 'That's not what your face is telling me.'

'It doesn't matter.'

'It does to me.' He said it so earnestly she could almost believe his feelings were capable of running deeper than sex.

'I was there when Julia spoke to you today,' she admitted. 'I didn't mean to eavesdrop, but she was making it impossible.'

His jaw twitched, his voice tight. 'You know about the article.'

'Yes.'

'Nothing happened.'

Get off the topic.

'It's none of my business.'

'I'm making it your business,' he said, his eyes boring into her own. 'The truth is, I went out looking to forget this thing between us and failed.'

'That's how you forget?' She gave a harsh laugh. 'Falling into bed with the next willing woman? I shouldn't really be surprised.'

'It's all I know.' He rammed his fingers through his hair. 'Hell, if you'd lived through my upbringing you'd understand.'

'I asked you to help me understand last night, and you refused.'

He looked to the door, his eyes wavering between it and her, his hesitation clear. 'I'm not used to talking, least of all with the women I sleep with. In truth, they don't ask, and I don't tell.'

'And I threaten that status quo?'

His lip quirked up at the corner. 'Something like that.'

'Well, for what it's worth…' She raised her chin in forced confidence, acknowledging the vulnerability of what she was about to say and saying it anyway. 'I think you're better than the press would have people believe.'

'Better?' he scoffed gently. 'Have you read those articles?'

She nodded. 'You know I have. But they're not the same person as the one stood before me just now, the one that loves his sister so openly and cares what I think.'

'No?'

She shook her head, fighting the desire to close the

distance between them and kiss an agreement out of him. 'You just told me that nothing happened last night. If you didn't care what I thought, you wouldn't be telling me that.'

Her deduction hung in the air between them, their gazes locked in some silent exchange, and then he blinked, a shutter falling over his expression. 'Regardless, it's still me, it's how I've always been, and you need to either accept it or keep that line in place.'

And then he was gone, heading out of the door and leaving her mentally slapping herself.

What are you playing at?

She fell back into her seat and thrust both hands through her hair, gripping the back of her head in disbelief. *Way to go focusing on the professional. You can't even do it for five minutes.*

EJ found her in the exact same position when she bustled in moments later.

'Wowzers!' she exclaimed, pushing the door closed, and waving an exaggerated hand at Zara's miserable form. 'If I had that man following *me* around with that puppy-dog-lost look I'd be dancing, not looking like the world was coming to an end.'

Puppy-dog-lost. She came alive at that, shaking her head with a small laugh. A puppy was not the animal she'd associate with Daniel…

'What?' EJ said, her brow raised in mock innocence. 'I'm only saying that it seems to me you've just won us a mega-contract and a bit of selfish fun in the process— what's the problem?'

'You make it sound so simple.'

'Isn't it? It's not like you'd be looking for anything serious with a man like him, but why not grab a little fun while you can?'

Fun. Oh, yes, he can deliver on the fun. But how will you feel when the fun fizzles out? When he flip-flops between you and some other woman? When he gets bored?

Hell, you could be bored by then too...

It was a feisty retort and one that she could cling to. Not that she believed it possible, not for a second, but if she went in with her eyes open...well, that made it okay, right?

CHAPTER NINE

IT WAS FRIDAY and the weather was holding out, glorious sunshine, temperatures worthy of a day at the beach, not work. But she'd lined up an out-of-city viewing, keen to get out of the smog and into the open countryside.

She was looking forward to it. Far more than was healthy. But she didn't care. She had a real energy that she hadn't felt in years. And this was the first time she'd seen him in two days, unless you counted the numerous occasions in her head where she relived each and every encounter.

But nothing could compare to seeing him in the flesh. Or his car...

No way.

She should have known he would turn up in it, after his comment earlier in the week, but as she watched the deep blue Vantage pull up at the kerb outside her office building, she had to swallow the lump in her throat and work to control the thrill rushing through her veins.

She should have known it would be no ordinary Aston too. Not when the man driving it was Daniel. It bore race livery, the kind that inspired a heady reaction in her blood, and her palms dampened against the tablet clutched to her chest.

The man himself stepped out of the driver's side, his black T-shirt clinging to every honed muscle of his chest, and she forced her eyes up to meet with his over the roof.

'Morning.' He grinned and her insides bubbled over, making it hard to speak. Instead she smiled and closed the distance, meeting him at the passenger side and trying not to devour him from top to toe, lapping up his fitted T that gathered midway over his crotch and the stonewashed jeans that hugged his hips with mouth-watering intent. He pressed down the handle and opened the door for her. 'Are you well?'

She nodded and smiled up at him, wishing her voice normal. 'Nice wheels.'

'I thought you'd appreciate it.' His eyes raked over her, his pupils eclipsing the burning amber that seemed to strip her of her clothing and make her wet for him in one. Maybe she shouldn't have opted for the delicate red dress, its flimsy fabric offering up no resistance to her nipples now prickling to the fore. 'It was worth it to see your reaction.'

Which one?

She sucked the inside of her lip, forcing her body to relax as she lowered herself into the seat and let him close the door for her, cocooning her in all that was luxury. She feasted on every alluring detail, using it to distract from the race inside. She brushed her fingertips over the exquisite leather, tracing the lines in the embroidered trim, the curve to the centre console and dashboard—*sweet*.

He pulled open the door on his side and she brought her hands onto her lap, placing them atop the tablet and telling herself to behave.

He dropped into his seat, his grin building anew, and set the engine going. 'I'm glad you approve. You can take her for a spin later.'

Her eyes snapped to his, excitement urging her to say yes, but, 'I wouldn't want to risk pranging it.'

'I trust you.'

His simple statement warmed her through. He made her feel too good, too easily.

'Do you want to plug the postcode into the satnav while I get us out of the city?'

'Sure.' That gave her something to do, something to concentrate on other than the confusing dance going on inside her.

One hand on the wheel, he used his other to launch the system and all she could do was watch the hypnotic ripple across the back of his hand, his fingers moving deftly over the joystick and reminding her of the other talents they possessed. Talents that involved working her to the brink, regardless of their surroundings. Like in the restaurant when she'd wanted him to go a whole load further than the tip of her thigh—

'She's all yours.'

'Huh?' She almost leapt; if not for her fiercely pinned hands on her lap, she was sure she would have done.

He raised his brow, his eyes laughing at her. 'The satnav...'

'Oh, yes, sure.' She could feel the heat spread through her cheeks, an outward reflection of her inner fire, she was sure, and pinned her sights on the equipment and very much off him.

She fumbled over the postcode, both fingers and eyes refusing to do as she bid. She blamed it on his proximity, on his scent. So close, his aftershave engulfed her senses, so near, the heat of his body called to her.

'It takes some getting used to,' he remarked.

'Huh?'

God, do you have to keep making that noise?

'The controls.'

'Yeah, sure, almost done,' she mumbled, finally getting it and settling back into her seat, her hands back in her lap as a woman's voice invaded the cabin with its first instruction. She checked the display—eighty-two minutes to destination.

They were going to be the longest, most teasing eighty-two minutes of her life.

'So, you get your love of cars from your father?' He looked across at her briefly, his eyes colliding with hers as her pulse skidded off.

He remembered!

Don't go all soft. It wasn't that long ago you told him.

She smoothed a steadying hand through her hair and nodded, thinking on the familiar and the calming territory his words had inspired.

'I do, he's race-mad, it's high-speed motor racing all the way for him.'

She smiled as she remembered the numerous arguments her parents had had over family holidays. Her mother pushing for the Caribbean, her father insisting on Monaco, and the compromise position they always got to: a nice family holiday abroad that didn't quite get them all the way to the Caribbean but kept them all happy, and the British Grand Prix at Silverstone.

Still, she'd give Dad his dream one of these days and get him to Monaco. She would, of course, have to go too, just to make sure it lived up to expectations.

'Why the smile?' He was looking at her, a peculiar glint to his eye, and then his attention was back on the road and leaving no indication as to what he was thinking.

'My dream is to take him to Monaco, do the whole thing properly, you know? I almost had it all arranged for last year.'

She stopped. The direction in which she was heading too personal and bringing back memories she really wanted to do without.

He frowned across at her. 'What happened?'

She shrugged with forced nonchalance and set her sights out of the passenger window.

If he couldn't see her, he couldn't read her.

'It just wasn't meant to be.'

'What about this year? It's just over a month away. I know people that can sort you a nice VIP package.'

She gave a laugh that sounded far more bitter than

she intended. 'Thanks, but it's going to be a pipe dream for a while, just until I get my business up and away.'

He studied her for a moment and she wondered if he would press further but then he looked away and she breathed a small sigh of relief.

'I read up on your previous company,' he said, cutting her relief short, and she clamped her jaw shut. 'It was very lucrative...still is, from all I can gather.'

Her pulse twitched in her cheek, the tablet biting into her fingers as she sensed his continuing attention on her, split between her and the road.

'Seems strange that you would give all that up because your relationship with Charles broke down.'

She loosened her jaw, letting out a small breath to say, 'It wasn't straightforward.'

'No?'

What would it hurt to be honest with him? Just get it out and be done with it.

She hated voicing it though. Made her worst fears feel more real. That she wasn't good enough. Still wasn't.

'I couldn't remain in business with him after we broke up.'

'I take it that was his decision?'

'Yes.'

'After five years?'

Christ, he remembered that too.

'Yep, five years.'

Five years, and every one of them wasted.

He flexed his fingers around the wheel, his gaze unreadable on the road. 'It's a long time to be together. What happened?'

She turned to look at him.

Why all the questions? The interest?

'It turned out I wasn't enough woman for him.'

His eyes snapped to her, narrowed and intent, and then he blinked and looked back to the road, but they'd left their mark, searing her with a passion she couldn't quite decipher.

Was it anger? Desire?

'He was unfaithful?'

'Repeatedly.'

She watched his fists flex around the wheel again, the tension rippling through his body.

'How did you find out?' It was then she understood the cause, the distant tone to his voice giving away the internal reflection going on beneath. He was thinking on his own parents. He was angry at them. Just as he'd been the night in her office—

'You don't need to tell me.'

His prompt pulled her up and she looked to the road, trying to ignore the way the memory of that night chilled her. Or was it just the memory of what Charles had done?

No, it wasn't that. Charles no longer seemed to carry the same weight, which would be a good thing, if not for the cause of that switch being sat right alongside her.

'No, it's fine,' she said. 'To be honest, it became impossible to miss in the end. There's only so much lipstick on the collar, weird credit-card purchases and mistaken text messages a woman can take before she has to open her eyes to it.'

'He didn't come right out and tell you.'

'Hell no, I had to yell it out of him.' She grimaced as she remembered that particular fight, but not with the familiar ache of loss, more with shame over the foolish way she had ranted. She never should have given him the satisfaction of seeing how much it had hurt.

'I'm sorry, I shouldn't have pressed,' he said gently, his hand moving from the wheel to rest upon her leg and making her flinch with the bolt it sent through her. He lifted it away immediately, misreading her reaction and apologising again.

'It's okay,' she said, pushing back the ache to have his hand return. 'It's a relief really. At least it happened before we ended up married, or, worse, had children.'

She sensed the air tighten and immediately realised her faux pas—*shit*. 'I'm sorry.'

He flicked her a look, his eyes strangely dark and haunted, and her heart ached inside her chest—he suffered, no matter how strong he appeared. 'Why?'

'Your parents, your…your…'

Words failed her. It didn't feel right to discuss something that she had gleaned from sources other than him, and unpleasant sources at that.

'You can say it,' he said. 'Believe me, I've had years to get used to it.'

She swallowed. 'I'm sorry, I don't like the gossip columns at the best of times and stuff like that shouldn't be splashed around for the amusement of others. I wish I could un-see it all.'

He surprised her with a smile, his eyes softening to look at her and taking her breath away. 'You and me both.'

Emotion welled, their budding connection encouraging her to try for more. 'It must have been hard growing up like that. I know you said Julia had it rough, but for you and your brothers it can't have been much better.'

He gave a small shrug. 'We had some good times. Dad was home six months of the year and during that time we would make the most of it.'

'When did it change?'

'In my teens. My brothers and I were getting older and liked having our own space. There was less need for them to be with us and they seemed less and less interested in each other. Of course, the rumours in the press didn't help with that.'

'No,' she said quietly, easily filling in the blanks. 'I can imagine.'

'And then one day, he left. The next thing we knew he'd been found dead and his mistress made clear whose bed he'd been in when it happened.'

She watched his knuckles whiten around the wheel, the intensity of his stare through the windscreen clawing its way through her gut, and she couldn't stop herself reaching for him. Her fingers resting over his thigh.

'Do you really have nothing to do with your family now?' She knew what she'd read but she just couldn't get her head round it. His closeness to Julia. His obvious love. Could they really be so bad that he'd turned his back on them?

He was quiet and still. He didn't even seem aware of her hand upon his leg. And then he turned to her, his eyes scanning her face. 'You say it like you can't believe it possible.'

He looked back to the road. Should she drop it? Did he want her to?

But she knew she was close to understanding him, and she wanted that, no matter the risk that posed to her *just-in-it-for-the-fun* stance.

'They're still your family.'

'They *were* my family,' he said. 'If we had weathered the storm together and then tried to make a normal life of it maybe things would have been different. But when the cameras arrived, everything became an act, a farce. *I* couldn't even tell you what was true and what was fake, put on for publicity's sake.

'My brothers thought it was great, going along for the ride, but it changed them,' he said tightly. 'And I couldn't stand it, I had to get out—that's when I found Julia and decided to go it alone.'

'But it wasn't your brothers' fault. Don't you miss them?'

His throat bobbed. 'While they still perform for the cameras I want nothing to do with them.'

It was a question of trust. She could see it so clearly now. She'd hazard it was the same for his mother too. But still, time had moved on; a lot could happen in ten years, a lot could change. His brothers certainly had, from all she had read, and she wanted him to see that.

'But your younger brother is hardly part of the show any more. He's away studying engineering at university.' She watched him tense up but refused to back down; he had to realise things were different now. 'And your eldest brother is happily married, by all accounts, and now expecting his first baby. You're going to be an uncle in a few months.'

His head turned back to her, his eyes narrowed and hard. 'You really have been doing your research.'

'Sorry.' Heat launched into her cheeks. She really had read up on him, far more than her determination to keep her feelings wrapped up should have permitted, but she couldn't help it. 'I guess I figured no more surprises was the best way to move forward.'

He looked back to the road, his tone as dead as his body was still. 'No more surprises.'

He said it as if he agreed with her reasoning. He said it as if it was fine that she would have read all there was to read. That all the horrible things the press had said were above board and solid. She wanted him to deny some of it, to pick apart the untruths, anything to paint him as less than bad. And why? So that she could see this as more than it was: a simple fling and two sales.

That he would suddenly morph into her Prince Charming and whisk her off her feet.

That's not who he is. He never will be. Get back on track. Focus on the sale and the sex. That way you're safe.

She could almost hear her conscience laughing at her.

* * *

Daniel's body throbbed with tension. And not from dragging up his past, but from the worry she would soon run a mile.

She knew the worst of it all. And there he was adding to it, telling her things about his past he didn't even discuss with Julia. Johansson occasionally got a flippant comment, but never anything that ran so deep as all he had told her. And then she'd brought up his brothers, facts he'd been more than aware of and, if he was honest, in denial over. His worry they held his departure against him preventing him from trying to make amends.

He looked to her fingers upon his leg and felt her reassuring heat seep into his jeans.

She's not running, she's trying to bring you comfort. After all she's learned, she's offering her understanding...

Was it possible that if she could maybe his brothers would too, given the time, given the chance?

'I worry they won't forgive me,' he said, his voice quiet as he fixed his sight ahead. Out of the corner of his eye he saw her turn to face him, her fingers flexing into his thigh.

'I think, given all you've been through, it wouldn't take much for them to understand why you did what you did.'

He raised his brow in disbelief. 'How can you be so sure?'

'Because I do,' she said, her voice so earnest he wanted to pull the car over and pull her into him. How could she understand him? How could she be so generous with her affections when he'd been so restrained with his own? *Affections*—did he really think she held such for him? And if she did, then he should be running, doing everything he could to put her at arm's length, and yet he couldn't contemplate anything worse. 'Because I understand why you did it, and they will too.'

A rush of emotion swamped him. She was incredible. How he wished he could be different. How he wished he could open up his heart and pursue the kind of happiness his brother appeared to have found. The happiness he was so sure Johansson and Julia had on the horizon.

The kind of happiness she'd once thought she'd shared with Charles. Fucking Charles—how could the man have had her for five fucking years and done what he did?

Anger rushed his veins. 'For what it's worth,' he said darkly, 'Charles was a fool. He had it all in you.'

Her eyes shot to his, their sudden brightness screaming volumes, and his gut twisted up. *What the fuck are you doing?* Saying something so sweeping, so dramatic and so…fucking soft. It screamed of emotions he didn't feel. Of a desire to commit that absolutely wasn't there. And yet, out the words had come, from a place he couldn't control, where his thoughts were on exactly that. How could that man have had her as his own, made a home with her and then played away? It made no sense.

And then it made total sense. It was the way his parents had been, the way Julia's ex had been. The way…

No, he stopped himself short—it *wasn't* how he was. He never committed, never gave false hope, never offered a relationship. He had no interest in monogamy. It wasn't in his nature.

So why the hell say it?

Because she has you captivated. Because she makes you want to talk, to open up. Because she makes you want to be the better person.

And isn't that part of her appeal? What makes you want her?

Something stirred deep inside and he frowned at the road. It didn't matter the reasoning, he wanted her, and he didn't back away from what he wanted. The consequences, whatever they might be, could come later.

She retracted her hand, folding it into her lap. 'Thank you for saying that.'

Her voice was so soft, so thoughtful. He slipped her a look beneath his lashes and his stress evaporated. She looked so goddamn delicious. His comment had brought out a glow in her cheeks, her eyes still shone, and all he wanted was to roll back the seat and reacquaint himself with every stretch of her perfect skin. Bury his own unease in the ecstasy they could so easily conjure.

But she hadn't agreed to cross that line…not yet.

He forced his attention onto the road. Off her smoky grey eyes that he wanted to lose himself in; off her lips, so full and appealing as they glistened in soft pink today; off her dress, and the way the red fabric fell over the gentle swell of her breasts, hinting at the perfect rose-tipped nubs; off her delicate waist and her legs, bare from the mid-thigh down, and definitely off her cute red-tipped toes that peeked from her heeled sandals.

Hell, summer could bring torture in itself.

'Maybe I will drive after all.'

His eyes shot to hers.

Caught gawping while driving could easily be a new traffic offence.

He gave a lopsided grin and shook his head, as much at her as himself. 'You shouldn't have worn that dress if you expected me to focus.'

'I may have had an ulterior motive.'

His heart raced.

Was she saying...? Was it possible?

'An ulterior motive, you say?'

Her fingers dropped to toy with the hem of her dress, teasing him with little glimpses of more. 'Perhaps...'

'Care to share?'

'I think it's more fun for you to find out,' she said, and the sultry heat to her gaze almost had him pulling the car over anew. 'But for now, I think it will serve us well for you to concentrate on the road.'

She turned away, her hands shifting back to grasp her tablet, and telling him the moment had passed. For her. He was still in the thick of it. And with it came a weird sense of panic. Now convinced the line was about to expire, that he could have her, was it right?

He wanted her. She wanted him. But was she looking for more? Was he letting his desire drown out all the warning signals? The signals that had kept him free of emotional baggage, free of this...

And what was this?

He'd never wanted a woman as he wanted her.

So who was he really trying to protect: her or him?

His chest tightened, and he tried to forget it, to think on less troubling things, like the curve of her legs outstretched beside him, but it was no good. The woman to which they belonged didn't just trigger desire any more, she had set off an emotional torrent within him that he couldn't understand.

He was still trying to rationalise it away over an hour later, the journey having been spent in a strange silence, broken only as often as was polite to engage in the odd remark, mainly from her.

'You'd love living in Hertfordshire. It's beautiful out this way—a real getaway from the city. You know, the house we're viewing already has a lot of interest; I'm hoping you'll like it, but it's a bit of a risk based on the info I've gleaned from you.'

And so on. All of it tame and professional, and way off the elephant filling the intimate cabin with a thrumming tension.

He didn't know where concern over his own confused feelings ended, and his concern that she would want more began.

'This is it,' she piped up, her sudden excitement palpable, and he looked to her, to all that was happy and alive in her face, and realised his concern for her far outweighed his own. Julia's warning struck home, as did his own. She wasn't right for him.

'Take the next left.'

He looked to where she indicated, to a private drive lined with trees, and he nodded to it. 'Through there?'

'Yes.'

He swung the car onto the gravel, taking it slow as the tyres crunched over the loose road surface, and he grimaced. 'It's pretty, but I wouldn't say it's bodywork friendly.'

'That can be easily remedied.'

'True,' he acknowledged, although his tone was distracted, a heavy feeling swelling in his chest.

'I'm glad you agree.' He felt her smile at him and his determination wavered, his weakness where she was concerned never more pronounced.

When had he become so weak, so driven by emotion?

'Just keep that in mind when you see the rest.'

He eyed her warily. Just what was that supposed to mean?

'Like I said earlier, this one is a little bit of a risk, but it will help me gauge where you're truly at,' she said, still with that pulse-invigorating smile. 'I like to start with something like this just to ensure we don't miss any real opportunities.'

'Fair enough.'

He continued down the drive, the trees concealing the house from view until he rounded a corner onto an open courtyard and drew the car to a stop.

'Isn't she beautiful?' came her soft-spoken remark.

He looked to her, to the flush in her skin and the brightness of her eyes, and lost himself, his response coming easily. 'Very.'

She met his eye, the hint of a smile in her glossy lips. 'You're not even looking.'

No, he wasn't.

Kristus, *get with it!*

He gave a grin, masking his wayward thoughts, and leant over the steering wheel to sweep his gaze up and over the house. It was appealing and there was something homely about it despite its imposing size. Probably due to the vine that crept over the walls, softening the large expanse of soft yellow stone.

'It's a repossession,' she said, dropping her gaze to the door and seeking the handle to get out.

'Here,' he said, leaning across her, and she gave a sharp intake of breath, her tummy drawing in where his arm brushed across her. He looked to her face, only millimetres away, and his mouth dried up, the air too thick to take in as he stilled.

Her eyes dropped to his mouth and she tugged on her lower lip with her teeth, releasing it slick and inviting— lust exploded within him, his mind buried in the onslaught. He swivelled his body, his hand reaching up to clasp her neck, drawing her lips to his, desperate and demanding.

God, she was sweet, minty, with a hint of whatever flavour the gloss brought with. His brain clouded over, the warmth spreading like wildfire through his gut. He couldn't draw breath, couldn't think of anything but the taste and feel of her; of her delicate tongue as it slipped and teased against his own; of the little whimpers breaking free in the back of her throat; of her pulse beating wildly beneath his fingers hooked around her neck.

'Is this what you meant by ulterior motive?' He spoke against her lips, refusing to part for more than the words needed.

'Uh-huh,' she hurried out, her hands coming up to thrust through his hair, just as hungry, just as caught up. He was doing her a service, fuck being honourable.

Don't be a dick.

It was his sister's voice that pierced his brain and he released her, taking in deep, sanity-bringing breaths. 'We shouldn't do this. You were right,' he said between pants, risking a glance and seeing all that was sexy, alluring but also vulnerable in her exquisite face.

She shook her head, a dazed frown forming. 'No, I wasn't.'

'I don't do relationships.'

The crease between her brow deepened and he had to fight not to kiss it away. 'I know you don't.'

'Then this...'

'This is just sex, pure and simple.' Her frown eased, her words so matter-of-fact.

He eyed her, disbelief giving way to far more base urges. 'Are you sure?'

She nodded. 'Do I really have to convince you?'

Before he could answer, she fisted her hand in his shirt, yanking him in, her mouth crushing his with such force, such need, the fire exploded, the strain against his jeans so fierce it made him wince but still his cock thrust, desperation sending him bucking against the constriction. Her hand dropped to seek him out, her fingers brazen over the fastening of his trousers, working it undone.

Skit, *they were out of control.*

He opened his eyes, peered through the glass; the house looked deserted, but was it? He was about to ask when her hand slipped inside his clothing, her fingers wrapping around him— *'Fuck.'*

He dropped his gaze to where she held him, her hand fighting with the restricted space to move over him, and he pulsed in her grasp, pre-cum slipping through her fist.

He wanted more. Needed more. He shimmied his jeans lower and swept a hand to her thigh, loving her soft heat beneath his palm. He brushed upwards, his intent turning hazy as she started to pump over his cock.

He screwed his eyes tight and pressed his head against hers, the muscles of his thighs rigid with his need to stave it off. 'I'm going to make a mess of my car if you keep this up.'

'No, you won't,' she breathed, brushing his hand away.

He opened his eyes to look at her. 'I want to touch you.'

'And I want to taste you,' she said, her head lowering as his cock all but exploded in her fist, and likely would have done if she hadn't let go that second to use her hands to reposition herself.

She clambered up, her knees pressing into the side of the centre console as she angled over him, encouraging his own body to fall back into his seat, his hand reaching out to brush through her hair as he lost himself in the hunger of her gaze. Then she dropped her lashes, her focus on his dick as her fingers slipped gloriously around the throbbing heart of him. He clamped his jaw tight, heat streaking through his thighs, through his gut, the blood congregating at his head painfully acute and then she wrapped her tongue around him, lapping every drop of pre-cum and sending his mind dizzy with lack of oxygen.

Breathe, goddamn it.

He was losing it, so wholly and completely, he bucked upwards, pushing for more, and she treated him to a peck at his tip. 'Patience.'

'*Fuck.*' He was trying, he was always steady in the sack, always in control, right till the very end, but she was making it impossible. Just as she was in life.

Her mouth came down over him. Once, twice, and then she drew him deeper in, hard and deep. Fireworks went off behind his lids, his head thrown back against the seat. Up and down she milked him, sweet little sounds erupting deep within her throat. Her own excitement calling his hand to her as he reached under her curved form, under the floaty fabric of her dress, seeking out the wetness he knew he'd find. It was there before he even reached the trim of her underwear, its slickness over her thighs almost pushing him to the edge, and he seethed between his teeth, forcing down the ache, his free hand gripping the arm rest in the door.

And then he slipped beneath the lace, his fingers surrounded by her wetness, her neatly trimmed pussy offering up no protection from the fact that she dripped for him.

Hell, yeah.

He bowed his head, his eyes taking in her head bobbing over his cock; he'd never wanted to draw a moment out so bad in his life. 'You feel so good,' he said, his fingers sliding within her seam, her slickened warmth welcoming him in, and she bucked against his hand, a moan reverberating around his cock.

'You like that?' He swirled over her pea-like nub and she writhed, her murmurs fervent and urgent. He was using her need, focusing on it, to slow himself down, but it was turning into his undoing. His tempo ratcheting as her breathing turned ragged around him, her fist pumping wild and tight beneath her mouth.

Their sounds filled the cabin: her sucking lips, the slapping of her wetness around his fingers, the moans neither could suppress. And he lost it, the force of his orgasm sending his butt off his seat, his cock smacking the back of her throat, his cum with it.

She clenched around him, her own body racked with waves as her climax took hold, and still she took his all, drinking him down, her satisfied moans so erotic, her movement captivating. He watched her intently, his fingers cupping against her as she rode it out, and then gently he slipped his hand away, out from beneath her pants and to his lips, tasting her as her head lifted.

'You taste as good as you look.'

Her cheeks were flushed, her smile sultry, her hair

as wild as her eyes as she looked to him and his chest contracted, his lungs winded.

'You too,' she said, licking her lips as she dropped back into her seat and righted her hair, her composure falling back into place and stunning him still. 'You ready to see what this baby has to offer?'

She gestured to the house and it took a moment for him to recover, a moment for his hands to obey his bidding and right his jeans.

She was ruining him, not the other way around.

CHAPTER TEN

'You're trying to get me to disengage your services, aren't you?'

Zara smiled to herself. Daniel had just followed her into the final room of the house, the orangery, or at least it would have been an orangery in its heyday. Now it was a nest of weeds with grand ornamental features being drowned out by a variety of foliage. But it was still beautiful and telling of a history that she would love to know.

She turned and smiled at him, the glorious sun warming her through the glass. 'Not at all. I'm gauging your reaction to a little bit of work.'

'A little?' His eyes opened wide, his hands stuffed into his pockets as they had been most of the way around the house; she'd hazard a guess that he was scared of catching something. 'This is more than a little.'

'Well, it's not like you'd be getting your own hands dirty,' she reasoned. 'And besides, a man like you needs to make his mark. What's the point in buying something finished when you're only going to want to change it anyway?'

She walked to the double doors that led outside and turned the key that rested in the lock, pushing them open and stepping out. Her eyes swept the landscaped garden, taking in its original form, the beautiful arrangements of flowers, shrubs and, at its heart, a water feature that probably hadn't seen a drop in at least a decade. It was utterly charming. Or at least it could be.

He came up alongside her and she sent him a sidelong glance. 'At least buying something like this you won't be paying over the odds and tearing it apart to make it yours. You'll be able to start afresh and not waste a penny.'

He studied her for a moment, and she turned to face him properly, her head cocking with a smile. 'See, you know it makes sense.'

His own smile grew with hers and he shook his head, looking back at the building and turning to take in the grounds. 'I can see your point.'

'Good.'

'But I wonder if it's wasted on me, these extensive grounds and no children to terrorise them.'

He said it with a trace of humour in his voice. But all she heard was no children and the simple statement clutched at her chest. Which was madness. There was no future with him. There never would be. Why couldn't her body get the message and stop the emotional singsong in her blood at everything he did or said?

Just do your job...

'Granted it's a fabulous home for a family, but the grounds are adaptable—maybe you could consider doing something with them. Your own race track, perhaps?'

She said it suggestively, flirtatiously even, her professional front sliding perfectly in place, and she watched his eyes come alive. It was an encouraging sign, on the house-selling front. So why did her belly feel as if a brick had settled in?

'Have I told you already how good you are at your job?'

'You have...' she forced her voice to keep its flirtatious tilt '...but you can always tell me again.'

The heat of his gaze, of his appreciation, held her captive, the air around them falling silent save for the wildlife. Her momentary sadness fading away.

'You are so good in many ways.'

He wasn't thinking on her expertise, the house, the grounds, the purchase, not any more, of that she was certain.

'Are you asking for another demonstration?'

His eyes flashed. 'Are you offering?'

She nibbled on her lower lip, a startling spread of heat kick-starting in her gut.

How can you need him so bad, so soon?

'Perhaps.'

His gaze swept over her front, his depths dark and hungry. 'It's cruel not to wear a bra, you know?'

She daredn't look; she could already feel the hardening peaks pressing into the fabric of her dress, doing their own job of pleading. 'It is?'

He lifted his palm to cup one small mound and she

whimpered over the lightness of his touch, the ache blooming just beneath.

'Yes.'

His other hand mimicked the move, palming her other softly, and then he rolled his thumb over the stiffened peaks and her breath caught, her body swaying with the power of his caress.

'So responsive,' he murmured.

Her head started to spin over the dizzying sensation, her lids fluttering closed as carnal heat flooded her body from top to toe. 'God, that feels good.'

'Hmm…turn around,' he drawled, and she floated into doing his bidding, her body lying back against his for support as his hands kneaded her breasts through the thin fabric of her dress. He lowered his head, his mouth brushing against her ear. 'Open your eyes, take in the great outdoors, the freedom to feel, to let go in the open.'

She did as he asked, the sun beating down on her flushed skin, the birds singing in the trees, the rolling gardens stretching out as far as the eye could see… It was salacious, it was risky, and it was everything she craved.

'Come.' He nudged her forward to the walled edge of the overgrown pond and stilled, one hand slipping from her breast to trail down her front. 'Take off your underwear.'

A thrill ran through her blood as she bent forward, shimmying them down, a breeze mixing with her wetness and taking her to another level. She lifted the skimpy lace and he took it from her, slipping it into his pocket. 'Raise your skirt.'

The throb between her legs was a full-on punching beat now. It hurt so much she wanted to service her own need there and then, but doing as he asked was pushing her to the edge, was too good to let it stop.

She gathered up the fabric, bringing it to her hips as his fingers stroked up the backs of her thighs, over the curve of her bottom. 'So perfect.'

She gave a small sound. It wasn't outright dismissal, but it wasn't agreement either.

'You are,' he whispered against her ear. 'Don't doubt it.'

His fingers hooked around her front, one hand separating her folds, parting her to the air, to his touch, as his other hand dipped within, gathering up her wetness and bringing it back over her clit. A spasm shot through her and she rocked against him, a flurry of heat spreading out from where he stroked her, sending her hands clawing at his thighs behind her for support.

'That's it, baby.' His erection pressed into her back, his breath rasping as he dropped his mouth to her neck, nipping at the sensitised skin and driving her crazy. But she needed more, she needed him, she didn't want to lose it without him.

'Please,' she begged.

His caress over her clit slowed. 'What is it, baby?'

He was teasing her, coaxing out sounds that she barely recognised as herself. 'I want you.'

'Right here?'

'Now.'

He gave a low chuckle and nudged her legs apart with his feet. 'Drop forward.'

Excitement swelled, the ache intense as she bent over the wall and he fisted the fabric of her dress above her back, his free hand working his fly undone.

'Do you have…protection?' she asked over her shoulder, a moment of clarity hitting as she pleaded with him to say yes. She couldn't imagine hitting the rewind button. Not now.

'Of course.' He slid his hand into his back pocket, pulling one out and using his teeth to open it.

Of course—he knows you're a sure thing.

'So sure of yourself, aren't you?' she teased, ignoring the spark of hurt that came with that acknowledgment and watching as he extracted the condom, his smile one of boyish arrogance, making her tummy flip-flop.

Be grateful he is prepared and you're not having to back-pedal, that you get to have your fill.

Still, it wouldn't hurt to goad him for it…

'If I wasn't bent before you half-naked,' she said softly, 'I'd put you in your place.'

'You're the one being put in her place,' he said, slipping the empty packet back into his pocket and spanking her playfully.

Or at least it should have been playful but instead it made her bite her lip, a whole other fantasy taking over.

And he read her, his expression turning dark, his eyes dropping to where his cock rested against her behind, his free hand caressing the spot he'd just tapped. 'If I wasn't so far gone already, believe me, I'd go there.'

His eyes burned into where their bodies met and she swore she'd come just looking at the desire etched in the lines of his face. He grasped at his cock, sheathing himself before sliding between her legs, rocking forward against her pussy, slickening himself on her wetness, rubbing against the tip of her ache, feeding it, coaxing it higher.

She moaned, her body writhing to manoeuvre him to her entrance, her head flying back as her fingers bit into the stone of the wall.

'Fuck me,' she begged.

But he slipped away, his fingers returning to delve inside her, coating himself with her wetness, testing her readiness. And then he withdrew, slipping them upwards, between the crease of her bum, finding the cluster of sensitised nerve-endings around the tiny, puckered opening—*fuck*.

Her legs quivered beneath her, the startling caress new to her and intense. He pressed inside and she moaned frantically, barely comprehending the wicked sensation firing through her, ricocheting through her walls. And then his cock was at her pussy, thrusting deep, his free hand coming around to her front, finding her clit, rolling over her. Every bit of her came alive, teased by his expert attentions, too much to focus on a single one. Pleasure worked its way through her entirety, tensing up her muscles, and she couldn't rein it back; it was out of her control, her climax tearing through her, shattering her apart in seconds.

His hands flew to her hips, holding her steady, gripping tightly as he rocked into her with his own cry of completion, the sound mingling with the birdsong and so carnal she wanted to fix it in her mind.

She straightened against him, her hands reaching behind her to cup his head to her neck, clasping him to her. His breath rasped into her shoulder, his body shuddering with his extended release, and she revelled in it, her prowess, her hold over him.

'If that's how you put a woman in her place,' she whispered into his ear, 'you can definitely do it more often.'

He chuckled against her, the sound stilted by his winded state.

'To be honest…' he wrapped his arms around her middle, holding her tight '…I think you had me in my place.'

She laughed her approval. 'I could get used to doing that.'

And then she stilled, a chill sweeping through her body.

There will be no getting used to anything. It's a short-term deal, remember?

'What's wrong?' He raised his head, angling in to get a better look at her face, but she avoided his eye, moving away to right her clothing and allow him the freedom to sort himself out.

'Nothing,' she managed to say squarely. 'But we'd

best get moving if we want to get to property two in good time.'

She started back inside, feeling bad that she'd left him cleaning up, but she didn't want to ruin the moment any more than she already had.

You're in this for short-term fun. Remember that.

Him getting wind of any longevity she had in mind would certainly put an end to any future fun.

And she wanted more. A whole lot more. As much fun as he was willing to give.

'Can you clear my schedule for Friday, Diane?'

Daniel gave the instruction to his PA and ignored the twitch to one brow that said *again*.

'Of course,' she said smoothly. 'What would you like me to block it out with?'

He pulled at his collar, suddenly hot. 'House-hunting.'

Up went the other brow, but her eyes returned to her monitor. 'What would you like me to do about Mr Lee? I have him flying in from Singapore Thursday in preparation for the meeting you had scheduled.'

'Ah, *skit*, was that for Friday?'

How could he have forgotten?

They were negotiating a takeover bid. It was a big deal and should have been top of his list. 'What time is the meeting?'

'Nine.'

'Okay… Okay, keep it in, but clear me for the remainder.'

She nodded and tapped away, freeing him to head to his office and deal with his blunder in private.

Two weeks and he hadn't been able to concentrate properly. Two weeks since Zara had come into his life and every waking moment had become about her. Property viewing taking over half his schedule, although fucking was the predominant use of that time. Every viewing, it didn't matter how many times they'd been at it, they'd screw. There was just something that came over her when she got all enthused about some little feature, regardless of how small, and he would crack, unable to keep his hands off her.

And as far as the houses went, truth was he'd seen plenty that he liked already and was willing to offer on. What he wasn't ready for was the end of their working relationship. Without property viewings, their relationship didn't exist. No relationship meant the end to their sex life and the idea left him cold.

He wasn't bored, he wasn't sated, if anything his need had got stronger, his desire to be with her an uncontrollable force that had him doing crazy-ass things like almost shafting his next big takeover.

He raked his fingers through his hair and dropped into his seat, his head arching over its back as he tried to make sense of it. And promptly gave up. Going deep was never his thing. He didn't dwell on the peculiarities of emotion; it was a wasted effort. He only acted on them. And acting on this right now meant keeping her very much tied to him for as long as he desired.

He took out his mobile and dialled her number.

She answered in two and he smiled.

She'd been waiting for him.

'That was quick.'

'I was sending someone a message when it rang.'

'Oh, yeah.'

Her laugh rippled down the phone, teasing a smile from his own lips. God, she made him feel light.

Light? What the fuck did that even mean?

'So, a bit of bad news,' he said—and it was; he didn't want to delay seeing her another second. 'I can't do all day Friday. I have a meeting first thing that can't be moved.'

'Oh.' Her disappointment nagged at him down the phone, mirroring his own, and then she was back to being all professional. 'Well, it's no problem. I can re-schedule for another day.'

'Can you just push it to midday? I'll be done by then.'

'Leave it with me. I'll rethink the viewings, stick to the city and that way we can still get two in.'

He grinned. 'I like your thinking. And why don't I take you to dinner in the evening to apologise for messing you around.'

'Dinner?' He heard her breath rush and his own surprise sparked—*an evening dinner? A date?* It was hardly inside the perimeter of what they'd shared so far. But it would spark interest. Press interest at that.

'Sure, why not?' he said. If she was happy to risk it, he sure was.

Only, she hadn't answered; in fact he wasn't even sure she was still there. 'Zara?'

'You mean, like the dinner we were supposed to have that first night?'

He laughed. She was right—they'd never left her office, so caught up in one another as they'd been then. And still were. More so even. And what was that about? 'Yes, an actual dinner out this time, or we could stay in, again?'

It was her turn to laugh. 'I'd love to, but I can't.'

His gut sank and he straightened against it, his hand taking up the soft basketball he kept by his desk, squeezing it as he asked levelly, 'Can't?'

'I'm busy.'

Busy—doing what?

He wanted to press, but really what business was it of his?

'Okay,' he said, and an awkward silence extended. If not for the subtle sound of her breathing he'd think she was no longer there.

'You could always…' she began and broke off.

His hand stilled around the ball. 'I could always?'

'Well…you could come with me?'

Not another guy, then.

Relief swamped him even as he tried to rationalise it away—it made sense he wouldn't want her seeing someone else while they were sleeping together. Perfect, rational sense. It didn't mean anything more.

Since when have you been jealous of anyone though?

'Daniel?' It was her turn to bring him back to the call.

'Would you like me to?' he asked, parking his unease and focusing on what he wanted in the here and now.

'Only if you want to. It's an awards thing. I'm not up for any, the business is too new, but it's good to show your face among the people in the industry and the reporters.'

'The reporters?' So there were going to be press? Did she realise the potential consequences of that, especially after she'd made it clear how she felt about him—no, not him, his public image?

'Yes, a few.'

'And you're okay with that?'

'If you are.'

'Excellent.' He was so frigging relieved she wasn't going out with another guy, so happy that she was willing to be seen on his arm in public, he'd take anything. And what the hell was that about? The question erupting again and coming far too frequently of late. 'It's a date, then.'

'A date,' she said softly.

He bit into his bottom lip, a weird excitement rippling in his blood. 'See you Friday.'

'Friday.'

'Bye.'

'Bye.'

Hang the damn phone up.

'Looking forward to it.'

'Me too. Goodbye, Daniel.'

She cut him off and he lowered the phone from his ear, staring at it as if it were the crazy thing. Not him.

CHAPTER ELEVEN

ZARA SCANNED THE road outside her office and smoothed out her dress for the umpteenth time, her tummy fluttering with anticipation, nerves, excitement, the works…

He was due to collect her any minute, Peters doing the driving as per his usual request. But now she wasn't sure whether it was because of the higher class of vehicle or because he wanted the freedom to *fully* enjoy the ride. Either way, she wasn't complaining.

She'd seen him Monday, Tuesday, spoken to him Wednesday and yet she felt as if she'd been starved of his presence. She'd even left her phone on charge in the living room the previous night to avoid texting him from bed. Her inability to get him out of her head, particularly when she got beneath her quilt, making the temptation too much. And she didn't want to appear needy, the fear of sending him running never quitting.

But you are needy…permanently.

She let out a shaky breath, a familiar sense of panic welling. She knew it wasn't a good sign, that she was getting in too deep.

He was still the Swedish billionaire and sworn bachelor that no woman could tie down. Even if he had spent every spare moment of the day outside work with her the last two weeks, including weekends, her viewing schedule as heavy as his calendar would permit. She was surprised he'd afforded her as much time as he had. Julia herself had even made the same remark when she'd called by with flowers to thank her for her help.

In fact, his sister had even gone as far as to comment on how different he seemed in general. How good it was to see him out of the press. And then she'd lain the blame at Zara's door and not so subtly suggested that maybe she'd been wrong to warn her off him. That maybe she was good for him after all.

But nothing had changed. Not really.

No matter how much she hoped it to be the case, he still wasn't asking for more. Their desire still burned strong and it was that which kept him hooked, out of the public eye and with her. And it was also that which meant she wasn't getting anywhere with the property hunt. She wasn't pushing him into a decision and, although he seemed amicable enough to all the properties, he didn't seem close to offering. He seemed far too interested in prolonging their time together and, as much as she wanted that too, she couldn't put her business in jeopardy for it. She needed to secure some sales and if not with him, with other clients, else what was she even doing?

She gave a sigh and checked her watch. He was late. She pondered texting him—no, too desperate. And, if she was honest, she'd give any ordinary client at least fifteen minutes before chasing, so fifteen it would be, maybe even twenty.

Twenty-two came and went; she frowned, the fluttering in her belly taking a dive.

He's probably just held up.

She opened her bag to take out her mobile as a glossy black Sprinter pulled up in front of her, the kind you expected to pull up just before a grand bank job, and she looked at it curiously, watching as its doors opened seemingly of their own accord.

Daniel!

Her lips lifted, happiness swelling as he stepped down onto the kerb, and she had to stop herself racing to him, keeping her stride slow and steady as the fluttering became an exploding bubble inside.

'You look too good to waste on house viewings,' he whispered against her ear when she paused before him, his eyes scanning the surroundings. She was used to that manoeuvre now, knew he was assessing their company, gauging friend or foe. They'd not appeared in any article yet, despite their growing intimacy in public. But tonight, tonight was a whole other story. Tonight there were sure to be press and they had both accepted that risk.

She felt the nervous bubble reach her throat and she swallowed, smiling up at him. 'And this vehicle looks wasted on it too. I was expecting alarms to go off and a group of bank robbers to appear.'

He laughed. 'You sound far too excited by that prospect.'

'What can I say? I like to live dangerously.'

'Don't I know it?' His eyes flashed with some unknown thought and her pulse leapt. 'You good to go?'

She nodded and looked inside the vehicle for the first time, her lips parting as she took in the magnitude of what she was seeing—it was more akin to a private jet than a jazzed-up van, Mercedes or not.

'Wow.' She stepped inside, scooping up the skirt of her black dress to maintain her modesty as she went and dropping into one of the leather reclining chairs housed inside.

'Wait until you see the back,' he said, climbing in behind her and magically setting the door to close. The cabin was entirely private, a large flat-screen TV positioned behind the two leather recliners that faced her, a table splitting the middle. It was the height of luxury, the plush furnishing brandishing various sockets, holders, buttons. Windows with full-on blinds, a glass roof that extended the entirety and absolutely not what she would expect.

'This is incredible.'

'If I'd known you'd love it this much I would have used it sooner,' he said. 'As it happens I'm only using it now because I've come straight from an on-the-road meeting.'

'An on-the-road meeting? People actually have those?'

'It comes in useful when we're having to visit prospects and need to discuss things in private. It also minimises the downtime due to travel.'

'Makes total sense.' And then, curiosity getting the better of her, 'So what's in the back?'

'A bed.'

'No.'

'No, you're right, it's just a toilet.' He grinned, his amber depths flashing brightly. 'But now I'm wishing it was a bed.'

His killer smile went to her head, his words making her want, and the mood shifted instantly, the tension palpable. She licked her lips and his eyes dropped to the move, coming back to her dark and loaded, his voice tight. 'Have you eaten?'

'Eaten?' she said dumbly. She didn't want to think about food. Not now. Not when his white shirt hung tantalisingly open at the collar, his tie loose about his neck and pleading with her to reach out and slip it off entirely.

'Yes, you know, food?' he said, killer smile still teasing, eyes still burning. 'I can't have you going hungry.'

She smiled, her fingers wanting to reach out and pull him in. Yes, the seats were great, plush and comfortable, but they were separate and right now she wanted to be pushed up against him in one inviting seat. 'I'm good, thank you.'

'A drink—champagne?'

'I shouldn't, I'm working.' Not once had she succumbed to alcohol in his presence. Heaven knew where her lowered inhibitions would take her, where her loosened tongue would end up…

'But I'm the client and if I say it's fine…' He raised

his brow in enthusiastic encouragement and laughter erupted through her.

'You're incorrigible.'

'Nonsense, I'm about to secure you two massive sales—you deserve a celebratory drink.'

About to... He'd chosen.

Back came the panic, her insides quivering, and she tried to suppress it.

It's good for the business, it's good news, focus on that.

'Does this mean we don't need to have these viewings this afternoon?' she asked, trying to keep her voice level.

'No,' he said, pressing a button in the panel alongside him and causing the table to retract, unveiling a fridge beside her. He bent and opened it, his arm brushing her lower leg and sparking a frisson of excitement, but it died as it hit the chill she couldn't stop from spreading.

What did he mean by no?

If he was done, then they were done?

She watched him, her emotions holding her silent and still. He extracted two glasses and a bottle of champagne with a stopper in place.

He's already opened it—he's already planned this. They really were done and he wants to celebrate it.

So what? You still have tonight—that's not a property viewing, that's a date.

That has to count as something of a future after this viewing is all done with.

She was clutching at straws, but she had to, the alternative something she couldn't bear to think on…

He settled into the seat opposite her and offered her a glass. 'We definitely need those viewings.'

Okay, so he hasn't decided.

Or has he?

Christ, she was a confused mess.

She took the glass and waited for him to pour it, the bubbles taking an age to die back so he could top it up, and once he had she didn't wait for a toast, she took a swig and prayed the alcohol would do something to sort her out. 'So why the celebrating now?'

He shrugged. 'I'm trying to give you a rational reason for enjoying a drink that works to your professionalism.'

Thank Christ for that.

Her head swam, her lips wrapping around the glass once more as she took another healthy sip. 'What I'm really wanting to do is enjoy a drink with you, spend an afternoon viewing, an evening schmoozing, and then take you home to my bed.'

Her pulse rocketed. 'Your bed?'

He met her gaze head-on, his darkened depths penetrating her own. 'Yes.'

Her heart soared—they'd done many a thing, but sharing the night wasn't one. 'Sounds perfect.'

She took a sip, smaller this time now that the panic had subsided, and he mimicked her, their eyes locking above their glasses, the air turning hot and thick.

How are you ever going to let this go?

She let the liquid soothe, its chilling effect sliding down her throat, her thoughts calming with it.

It's okay, you can handle this. You've gone in with your eyes open; you can let go when the time comes. You can.

'So, Mayfair?' he prompted.

'Yes, Mayfair first,' she said, 'and then I have an outsider to follow.'

'Another of your risky ones?'

She grinned. 'It's good to mix it up a little.'

'And where is it? This outsider?'

Her grin grew; she was already anticipating his reaction as she said, 'We're going south of the river.'

He almost spluttered on his drink. 'I may be relatively new to living in London, but even I know one doesn't live south of the river on my budget.'

'You didn't seem to mind being south of the river a couple of weeks back.'

He frowned over her comment and she bit the inside of her cheek, hating the jealousy that erupted over the brain-imprinted image of him at The Shard, pressed up against that blonde.

You're a fool to take him there.

You're an even bigger fool if you don't.

The inner battle that had raged since she'd secured the viewing came back with force and she shot it down. She had a job to do above all and the property demanded a viewing; it was something else. And as for her feelings, they could just do one.

'So where's the harm?' she asked lightly, keen to get back to comfortable ground.

'You tell me.'

Her pulse skipped—*shit.*

He wasn't referring to the property; she could tell it in the softness of his tone, in the pinched look to his brow. He'd read her jealousy in the force of her response and was wanting her confirmation. Was it a test? Was he gauging just how much she'd crossed the line and let her feelings get personal?

You idiot!

'There is none,' she said, her recovery delayed but firm enough—*you've got this.* She stroked a hand over her hair, her smile turning suggestive as she added, 'And I'll prove it to you, if you let me take you there.'

He was quiet, his eyes scanning her face, and then his mood lifted, his own lips quirking. 'In that case, I can't wait.'

'I'm really not sure we need to see the property south of the river,' he said truthfully, scanning her tablet and the details of the property they'd just left.

They were back in the Sprinter, his attention split between the impressive house he'd just seen, and the allure of the woman sitting before him. Legs crossed, the black skirt to her dress giving away far too much for the desire-filled fog to vacate his brain. It wasn't so much the perfection in the house they had just seen wanting him to end their viewings for the day, but his desire not to waste another second with her.

Somewhere a clock of his own making was ticking, ramping up a desperation that he could barely comprehend, let alone quash. He knew their relationship had shifted into unknown territory, that it wasn't just sex any more. And if it wasn't just sex, then what was it?

She turned to him now, eyes and lips smiling as she sipped at a fresh glass of champagne. 'You liked it, then?'

'What's not to like? It has the space, the roof terrace, the parking, a gym, swimming pool, sauna, lift…' He was just reeling off the brochure now, but truth was, it fitted the bill. There was no denying it. 'And best of all, no hassle of a chain, so why bother with the next?'

'Because you should weigh up your options, especially when they come with such a hefty price tag.'

He shrugged. 'It's what I'd expect.'

'I know, and I'm glad you liked it. It means I'm doing a good job.'

'Oh, you're doing an excellent job.'

'Why do I get the feeling you're not wholly talking about the property hunt?'

He held up his hands. 'I'm not dismissing your abilities as an estate agent whatsoever. You've found Julia a home already and this, well, this is spot on,' he said, placing the tablet onto the table. 'So what say you to sacking off the next viewing and filling our time in other, more pleasing ways?'

She considered him, rolling the stem of her champagne glass between her fingers. 'I want you to see the next one.'

'You do?'

She nodded.

'You really do?'

She nodded again and he spied that same spark in her eye, the one that she got when something about a property got to her. *Kristus*, there was no denying her, not when she looked at him like that.

'Fair enough,' he said, sitting back in his seat and telling himself to behave. He'd have her soon. Plenty of times over. They had the whole night ahead.

But then what?

His gut twisted. He couldn't string her along for ever. She had commission to earn and, hell, he'd seen half of London already—or he might as well have. But it was the properties that were keeping them together. No properties, no agent. No agent, no Zara.

It doesn't have to be that way, you idiot.

He looked across at her—every perfect angle to her face; the hair that had fascinated him from day one; those soft, full lips that even now glistened with traces of champagne and gloss; her eyes that sparkled with her own private joke—and he felt his heart squeeze even as his gut twisted tighter. Fear, confusion and an alien desire that had nothing to do with sex, and everything to do with wanting to be in her company, always.

He now lived every day to see that perfect exterior break with a smile, a laugh, an orgasm that he had driven… What would every day look like when that was no longer possible?

'You okay?' she asked, her smile turning into a frown, her eyes warm with concern as she leant towards him.

'Of course,' he said, too quickly, sending his eyes back to the window and his thoughts to the gutter.

It's just great sex; she's addled your brain with it.

Because what was the alternative? Feeling something for her? Loving her?

It wasn't possible, surely? He'd spent his life avoiding the strings that had seen his family torn apart. Could she really have changed him that much in so little time?

And what if she hadn't? What if it was just some weird emotion driven by the finite time frame they'd given themselves? And once that was lifted, he hurt her, just as his parents had done to one another? Just as Edward had done to Julia? *Kristus*, even Charles had done it to her.

He couldn't run that risk. Not with her.

But could he walk away?

He knew the answer in his gut and it terrified him.

She didn't care that he wasn't keen; she wanted to show him this place. She'd not seen it herself yet. It was an empty shell ready for someone to make their mark. And she'd busted a gut to gain access.

They passed the main foyer in silence, her doing her damnedest to ignore the physical reminder of that photograph taken against the very same glass. She nodded to the staff as they greeted them both and headed straight for the residential access, using the key card she had obtained earlier that morning to gain entry and open the awaiting lift.

'How did you manage to arrange this?' He was standing directly behind her, his awe evident, and she smiled. 'When you said south of the river, I hadn't thought you meant here. I heard the place was in some weird lockdown, impossible to view, even more impossible to buy.'

Her smile grew. She knew the intrigue would appeal, had known her ability to get him in would impress. The boost to her ego contended with the champagne in her blood and she entered the lift, her footing light. 'That's for me to know,' she said secretively, directing the lift to the penthouse and sending him a look beneath her lashes as the lift doors closed behind them. 'And you *not* to find out.'

He grinned down at her, his hand coming to rest in the crook of her back and sending heat radiating through her. 'You sure about that?'

'Hmm.' The delicate scent of flowers filled the air and she inhaled softly. 'Isn't the smell beautiful?'

He bowed his head close to hers. 'All I can smell is you, laced with champagne.'

A shiver rippled through her, excitement surging as the lift ascended, the effect dizzying as she felt herself arch instinctively over his palm, her head angling up to him. 'Concentrate.'

It was all she could manage to get out. She wanted him to enjoy this viewing, not her, not yet. Despite every screaming nerve wanting the latter.

He chuckled, the sound resonating through her core, a low ache kick-starting deep within.

'I am concentrating,' he said thickly, his head dropping to draw her lower lip into his mouth, his tongue sweeping tantalisingly across before he released her.

'And I like what I see…' His hands came around her front. 'What I feel…' He smoothed a palm over her thigh, gathering up the skirt of her dress, his other brushed up her torso. Blood rushed through her body, the ache swelling in her belly, her breasts, her nipples perking in anticipation of his touch.

She leant back into him, feeling him press against her, his solid girth making the throb between her legs fierce. 'I like what I feel too,' she whispered up to him as he stroked beneath her breast and the top of her thigh in unison, each caress designed to tease, to provoke, sending her body into a sensitised mass as she shuddered against him.

'I love how responsive you are.' As he said it his fingers trailed over one pleading nipple. 'I could lose my mind just watching you come.'

He swirled around the hardened peak, his caress maddeningly light. Her eyelids fluttered as her head fell back against his shoulder, and then she saw it, the camera—*shit!*

She had no idea whether they were functioning, no idea who was monitoring them. As far as she was aware these apartments were uninhabited, but it wasn't worth the risk to her reputation, to her relationship with the Qatari owners.

She righted against him, turning to face him. 'Big brother could be watching.'

Her eyes flitted up and to the right, gesturing to the camera behind her, and he followed her move. 'Thought you liked living dangerously.'

She laughed. 'There's living dangerously and then there's committing career suicide.'

He shook his head, his disappointment clear as his hands dropped to discreetly adjust himself, and hunger gnawed at her, his obvious hardness threatening her resolve. She averted her gaze—*behave.*

The lift came to her aid, the ground shifting beneath them to announce its arrival and the doors sliding smoothly open. She stepped out and stopped, the awe-inspiring sight freezing her to the spot. Even she wasn't prepared for this.

'Now that's something,' he said behind her, reminding her of her place, her role.

'Isn't it just?' she murmured, making herself move, leading him through the sparse room straight to the glass-walled edge. 'We're seven hundred and fifty-three feet up, making it the highest home in London, the highest in Eastern Europe in fact.' She trailed her fingers along the glass as she followed it round, losing herself in the breathtaking view, London's famous landmarks and the sea beyond. 'Can you imagine it at night?'

'It's pretty spectacular right now.'

'It's certainly a blank canvas to do with what you will,' she said, reaching a glass door that opened out onto what would be garden, a sunken plunge pool ready to be filled, a viewing platform.

He came up behind her, his body brushing against her back. 'There's something exhilarating about being so high up, don't you think?'

She nodded against him, a slight pressure buzzing

in her head, her blood pumping that bit faster. Was it the height? Or was it because his erection was back at her hip?

'Especially when desire is rushing through your veins.' He reached around her, turning her into him. 'I see no cameras now.'

Desire wedged in her throat, the sun beating down into her back adding to the heat raging through her system. 'No, no audience.'

He walked her back against the glass, pressing her up against it, and the photo speared her mind, the pain crushing her with the reminder of who he'd been, who he still claimed to be. But that was before he'd proposed a date. Before they had spent so much time together. Before even her own feelings had changed.

He frowned down at her, his eyes reading far too much. 'What is it?'

She looked into his soft amber gaze, his concern so evident, and hope flared. It was time to take work out of the equation.

Nerves twisted in her belly but she held his eye. 'We can't carry on like this, you know. I have a business that needs my time.'

He curved his hands around her waist, his eyes falling to her lips and back up. 'You are doing business.'

She laughed softly. 'Not *that* kind of business.' She hooked her hands around his neck. 'You're going to have to make a decision.'

He raised his brow. 'You mean, place an offer?'

'If you've seen a place you like, which you clearly

have, then yes,' she said. 'I have a business to think about and while I'm off with you, I'm not bringing in commission with other clients.'

'Okay, I'll place an offer. Perhaps Mayfair, perhaps here.'

'That decisive, hey?'

'Uh-huh.' He kissed her gently. 'But that makes one property. I still need the second.'

'One is better than none.' He leant in to kiss her again, but she pressed him away, forcing herself to stay focused and her voice serious. 'But you will need to commit to a second soon or...'

She couldn't bring herself to say it and his grip on her waist tightened. Not a lot but enough to make her aware of the tension rippling through him. 'Or what?'

'I'll be forced to move on to other clients,' she said resolutely. 'There are only so many properties in London to show you.'

'And what if I decide to extend my requirements? What if I want somewhere in another city, another country even—will you come to my aid then?'

She shook her head at him. 'Why are you so determined to employ me?'

His eyes raked over her face, his hesitation palpable.

Please say the right thing...please give me something to cling to, something more...

'Because I'm not ready to let you go.'

Her heart sank in her chest. 'And you think employing me is the only way to keep me?' Did he not realise how it sounded? How cheap it made her feel?

She extracted herself from his hold, creating some much-needed space between them. She couldn't think straight when he was so close.

'It's the one way I know how,' he said to her back.

His words clashed with the emotions welling inside— he *needed* there to be a reason. He would always need a reason.

And it would never be love.

Love. Why was she even thinking on it? He'd made his attitude towards relationships abundantly clear. And she had been a fool. Going in with her eyes open and not keeping her heart from wanting more. She'd done exactly what she'd told herself she wouldn't.

'We should go. I promised the owners we wouldn't stop long and I have the awards ceremony to prepare for.' She headed for the lift, not caring if he followed or what he made of her reaction. The situation was impossible. He was impossible.

Then why go ahead with this evening? Why let it go on at all?

Because the alternative hurt too much...

Daniel watched her go, the chilling effect of her departure leaving him stock-still.

He knew exactly how he'd sounded, every goddamn word colliding with the emotional turmoil within. He hadn't wanted to hurt her. He'd just wanted a superficial reason to keep her tied to him, one that didn't expose him and the feelings he'd sworn he'd never develop. He'd wanted the pretence of an excuse to avoid spelling out how he felt, to avoid laying his heart on the line, because once he did there was no going back—she would have the power to hurt him and it terrified him.

But as he looked to her standing before the lift, her back turned to him in total rejection, his lungs constricted with the pain. It was one thing to live his life in fear, but when that fear had already been realised, surely his only option was to dive right in and hope she would join him.

He moved to go after her, his mind set on what he needed to do when his phone started to ring. He headed for her, retrieving his phone from his pocket and eyeing the screen as he went.

His step faltered—*vad fan?*

It was his mother. She never called. Would never dare…unless…

He hesitated, not knowing what to do. Zara looked to him over her shoulder, her eyes narrowing. 'What is it?'

'My mother…'

She turned to face him slowly, her features softening, her voice whisper-like. 'Does she ever call?'

'No.'

She stepped forward, her hand curving over his arm. 'You'd best take it. I'll wait.'

CHAPTER TWELVE

'ARE YOU READY for this?'

Daniel turned to look at her across the back seat of his limo as he posed the question, his eyes drinking in every exquisite detail, and something inside him swelled, his collar suddenly too tight for the weird constriction taking up camp.

'Yes,' she said softly, her focus on the passing outside world, her body poised elegantly.

He'd seen her professional, casual, naked even, but tonight, tonight he got to see her glammed up. The sparkling silver dress with its shoestring straps accentuated the delicate curve to her shoulders and collarbone, the low-dipped V at the front framed her slight curves to perfection and it glided effortlessly to the floor where her silver stilettos left her dainty toes on display.

And yes, he desired her, but, more than that, there was a sense of pride, a feeling of excitement that soon the world would know to whom he was attached and this time he would welcome it. Not because of the negativity it would spark, but because he wanted them to know she was his.

And he hoped that after tonight, after he got her back to his place and spilled his all, she would agree to be just that.

She chose that moment to meet his eye, a nervous little glimmer in her dusky greys as they shone out amidst the smoky halo of her make-up, and his heart pulsed in his chest, his feelings for her blooming out of his control.

She wet her soft pink lips and looked back to the window, her hand dropping to rest on the black leather seat between them and he reached out, lacing his fingers through hers. Was she nervous about the event, the press or him? No matter, she had him. He gave her a gentle squeeze of encouragement and she mimicked his move, her mutual response warming him through. This felt so right, so perfect.

She turned to him again, her eyes hesitant. 'You can tell me to mind my own business, but did you catch up with your brother after your mother called about his wife?'

His heart stilled in his chest, the tension instinctive and short-lived as he remembered just how things had been left that day. How much better they'd been left.

'Briefly, she's been rushed into hospital with severe preeclampsia. They're going to have to deliver the baby early.'

'I don't know much about pregnancy, but that doesn't sound good.'

'He didn't sound good either, but both her and the baby are in the best place with the best medical team they can get.'

'You sound like you know that for a fact.'

'I made sure of it.'

She gave a soft laugh. 'I am so glad you spoke to them.'

He met her eye, his heart constricting in his chest. 'Me too.'

He wanted to tell her it was thanks to her. Wanted to lay all manner of things at her feet but they were out of time. The car nudged to a gentle stop, outside people milled, but he was barely aware of anyone save her. He gave her hand another squeeze and looked to the door as Peters arrived to open it.

There was a smattering of reporters and photographers, not the kind he was used to, but as soon as they spied him stepping out the clicks started up anyway, a hushed frenzy rippling down the pavement as they no doubt spied their unintentional jackpot. No one yelled at him, though. There was no abuse, and no one quizzed, *Who's the lucky lady this time?* or *How long do you give this one?* and so on. For that he had to be grateful, but still his hand left hers to sweep around her waist as she stood, drawing her close.

Possession warmed his core, compounded by the smile she sent up at him. 'Are you ready for this?'

She'd returned his question, but it felt loaded with meaning and his response came easy. 'Never been more so.'

She made a small sound in the back of her throat, her head turning to sweep the pavement and he found his eyes fixed on her, unable to move. She was stunning, all graceful and calm, and he thought his ribs might crack with the ballooning force deep inside. 'You look stunning tonight,' he murmured, pressing a kiss to her brow and ignoring the distant clicks.

'So do you,' she said softly, a warmth in her returning gaze.

Together they crossed the small pavement and headed through the entrance where a welcoming party greeted them, their fascination with his presence more than evident. But he took a back seat, playing the perfect date. Following her cue, talking to guests she chose to speak to and relaxing into it, a sense of calm befalling him, a sense of belonging at her side.

They were now chatting to an elderly man, Matthew, who'd been introduced as Zara's mentor back when she'd first started out, their conversation flowing easily. Daniel rested his fingers in the small of her back, toying with her above the thin fabric of her dress, his attention only half on the conversation, and then he felt her spine straighten, her words fall away with a sudden breath—*vad fan?*

He looked down at her, watched her swiftly recover, but not soon enough, not for him. She was talking again now but he wasn't listening; his eyes followed her line of sight from a second before. There were three men standing together talking, one with a blonde hooked over his arm.

Was it…?

Matthew started speaking. 'Yes, I heard, it's wonderful, I was just talking—'

'Excuse me one moment,' Daniel interrupted with

an apologetic smile, lifting his empty glass. 'Can I get you both a drink?'

Matthew looked to his almost empty glass. 'That's very kind, thank you.'

He nodded and looked to Zara, his blood racing with growing unease.

'Please,' she said.

'Won't be long.' He swept away, towards the bar, towards the group that had unsettled her, his curiosity and another, far more fierce emotion mounting. He had his suspicions, but he wanted to know for sure; he *needed* to know.

As he approached the blonde's gaze landed on him, her mouth parting as she *subtly* pulled on her partner's arm. He didn't need to hear to know what was being said, was used to people trying to be subtle and failing miserably. What he didn't anticipate was the man accompanying her to step into his path, almost causing them to collide.

Daniel backed up a step, his brow raised in question. 'Can I help you?'

'Charles Eddison,' he said, holding out his hand. 'And I think it's I that can help you.'

It was him— His jaw pulsed with the confirmation, his eyes searing into the man's proffered hand and tracing it right back to his face. He cocked his head to the side. 'Is that so?'

Charles cleared his throat as his woman sidled around him to offer up a smile. He was sure she intended it to be seductive; instead all he could see were surgically puffed lips, eyelashes that looked as if they weighed more than the hair on her head, and as for her age, she had to have only just hit the legal age to drink. 'Aren't you going to introduce me, Charles?'

'Sure…erm…' The man shifted nervously on his feet.

How did one introduce someone when they hadn't been introduced themselves?

Daniel wanted to laugh; he probably would've done if it weren't taking his all to hold back.

'This is…' the guy squirmed, looking to her and back to Daniel '…Claudia—er—my assistant.'

'And his fiancée,' the girl admonished with a giggle, her elbow digging into the guy's ribs.

Kristus, he felt sick, he could barely give her a nod in recognition, but it was hardly her fault she was associated with the man who'd broken Zara's heart. Jealous anger consumed him, clouding his brain. He could feel it ringing in his ears, turning over his stomach.

'So, as I was saying, Mr Lazenby,' Charles continued, his voice suddenly steady, his recovery poking at Daniel's anger. 'I believe you are in the city looking for a home yourself.'

'News travels fast,' he clipped out, his hands slipping into his pockets, the move outwardly casual, but in reality he needed to lock them away; the urge to swipe the smarmy look off the guy's face was burning into his fists.

'My firm, Eddison Associates, is the best there is.' He waved a flourish of a hand and Daniel felt his eyes glitter, his rage bloom—he knew where this was going. 'You'll see the evidence tonight in all the awards we scoop up.'

Charles paused, waiting for Daniel to say something, anything, to acknowledge his sweeping statement. A stony silence ensued. Daniel spied Charles' throat bob, his girl toyed with her drink, and he relished their discomfort, saying nothing.

'Anyway,' Charles blurted, first to snap, a hand rummaging into the internal pocket of his jacket, 'please allow me to give you my card and we can arrange—'

'You can keep your card.'

Charles stilled, a small cough erupting.

'I'm not int—'

'Daniel, is everything okay?' Zara's calming voice washed over him, her arrival radiating down his back and cutting his rebuke short. He turned into her, his smile warm but not enough to fool her as she frowned back at him.

'Absolutely, darling, come here.' He drew his arm around her, pulling her close, bringing her in to face Charles off together. 'Mr Eddison here was just offering me his services.'

He felt her tense beneath his palm and he stroked at her. 'But as you can see, Mr Eddison, I already have the best there is.'

He smiled down at her, his words sinking deep into his soul. He really did, and he wanted this fool of a man to know it, to recognise his mistake and rub salt in the wound. She met his eye, her gaze clouding over with some unguarded emotion, and it held him captive as he tried to read it—to read *her*.

Charles coughed uncomfortably, pulling his attention annoyingly away and, smile still in place, Daniel gave him a cold look. 'Thanks to the talents of Anders Estates, I'm about to make two significant purchases.'

'Two?' Charles practically squeaked, his brow raised.

'Yes, two, and rest assured the whole industry will learn just how good *this* firm is.' Daniel's smile grew. 'So enjoy the evening and the awards, Mr Eddison. Something tells me next year will be a whole other ballgame.'

He didn't wait for the man to recover, not this time. 'Shall we?' he said, gesturing to Zara to move off to the bar. 'I think we have some champagne with your name on it.'

'Of course,' she said. 'You go ahead. I just need to have a private word.'

He hesitated, his eyes flitting between her and a squirming Charles.

Hell, she has him by the balls. She doesn't need you.

He headed to the bar, not looking back until he'd placed their order. Then he turned to find Zara walking elegantly towards him, the dress casting a mystical light around her and drawing the eye of many males and females alike. *Kristus*, she was stunning. The scene topped off only by the sight of Charles gawping after her. Whatever she'd said, he looked like a man about to be strung up.

Go, baby.

Pride flooded his chest, and a new, more powerful emotion took hold, warming his grin as she approached.

And then his eyes met hers, and he chilled. She didn't look like the cat that had got the cream; she looked as if she was ready to commit murder and it was directed at him.

'What is it?' He took up the glasses that had just arrived and offered one out to her.

She took it but didn't smile, didn't thank him. Anxiety fizzled in his blood, his frown heavy as he contemplated her over his glass.

She took a sip, her gaze leaving him to scan their nearby neighbours before speaking in a tone low enough for only him to hear. 'I don't need you to fight my battles for me.'

'What?' He couldn't keep the surprise out of his tone. She had to be kidding. 'The man was being a smarmy twat. I gave him what he deserved.'

'You gave him the impression I only got the job for what I do for you in the bedroom.' She sent him a look and then her eyes were back on the room, their solemn depths haunting him. 'And he would be right.'

Daniel had to strain to hear but there was no mistaking it. And now he'd given Charles the ammunition to believe it too—*fuck*.

'It's not true.'

'No.' She sent him a bitter look, her eyes glittering. 'Didn't you pretty much tell me the same today when you asked to extend my services? Or have you conveniently forgotten that?'

'I know what I said, and I shouldn't have.' He shook his head. Now wasn't the time or the place for this discussion.

'No, you shouldn't have,' she agreed icily. 'But then, I shouldn't have been stupid enough to invite you. I only have myself to blame.'

Her words were crushing him. 'Don't say that.'

'Why? It's the truth.'

'It's not.' He reached for her and shrank back as she sidestepped his move, her eyes staring daggers at his outstretched hand.

'Please, Zara, it will all be forgotten about soon enough, yesterday's news.'

'For you, maybe.' Her words trembled, the sound making his throat ache. 'But I wanted to do this on my own, I wanted to show that bastard that I didn't need a man, that I didn't need *anyone* to make the business a success. Instead I've shown him the exact opposite.'

'No, you haven't.'

'Haven't I?' She looked at him then, the self-hatred in her gaze tearing right through him. 'I might as well have prostituted myself to save my company for all I've done with you.'

'*Kristus*, Zara, stop this.' He grabbed at her chin as she would have looked away. 'Please,' he urged into her eyes.

'Stop what? Telling you the truth?' She held her chin high in his hold. 'Didn't you tell me yourself that you would extend your requirements to keep employing me, to keep *paying* me so that we could continue to *fuck*?'

He felt the blood drain from his face, his hand falling away. Her vulgar dismissal of the time they'd shared crushing him.

'Oh, come on, Daniel,' she scoffed. 'Don't look so horrified. It was always just about the sex—you were always so quick to remind me of that.'

Around them people stirred, their argument drawing attention despite their lowered tones. He needed them out of there so that they could talk properly, so he could tell her how he felt.

And how do you feel, exactly?

It was one thing to second-guess, but another to know, and what experience did he have to base that knowledge on?

Hell, just be honest with her. It's a start. It's better than this.

'I wanted to talk—'

'Oh, save it,' she said, polishing off her drink and placing the glass back on the side. 'There's no need, I'm not backing you into a corner. We've both had our fun and I'm grateful to you for helping me see past Charles' negativity in the bedroom department. I mean, Christ, if I can keep the infamous Swedish bachelor hooked for as long as I have, there has to be something about me—right?'

She gave a harsh laugh, the hardness reflected in her eyes as they came back to him with force. 'But now I'm all about the future, something you're not, so if you'd be so kind as to deal with my assistant from now on, I'll bid you goodbye.'

He reached out, his hand on her arm to stop her when she would've moved away. 'You're leaving?'

'Yes.'

She tried to peel away his hand but he wouldn't—*couldn't*—let her go. 'Don't do this, Zara.'

'What?' She flared then, her composure cracking. 'What do you *want* from me?'

His hand fell away at the anguish in her face. She was angry, but it was pain that rode above it. And he'd done that to her.

'I want you,' he said softly, pleading with her to understand.

'Want isn't enough, Daniel.' She raised her head, her eyes locked with his. 'And I don't want you any more.'

He was struck dumb. The truth in her words hitting home and taking the very life out of him.

You're too late.

And then she came alive, her lashes fluttering as she gave a gentle shake of her head and turned away. 'Goodbye, Daniel.'

He watched her go, the room closing in behind her and his future with it.

Zara pinned her sights on the exit.

Don't look back. Don't look back. Don't look back.

The tears were building hard and fast, the wedge in her throat threatening to come unstuck. She needed to escape before anyone caught her, before she truly made a fool of herself.

She made it out into the foyer, halfway to the exit, she was almost—

'Leaving so soon?'

'Fuck,' she swore under her breath, stilling mid-stride.

'You know, I took you for many things, Zara, darling, but never a whore.'

A whore?

Her blood boiled, her sadness drowned out on a wave of rage as she turned to face a red-tinged Charles, her palm itching to swing for him. 'I have nothing to say to you.'

She made for the exit. He wasn't worth creating a scene for; he wasn't worth anything to her any more. He was just a sad little man who no longer had any hold over her. She thrust open the door and strode out into the evening, realising too late that he was hot on her tail, his hand reaching for her arm and pulling her to the wall.

'Let go of me, Charles.'

'You never used to mind me touching you,' he said, his face so close that she could smell his alcohol-tainted breath, could see a wildness to his eyes.

Christ, was he drunk? He hadn't seemed drunk inside.

She shook her head. 'If you don't back away, I'm going to make a scene.'

She eyed the pavement, the few people hovering, the odd journalist out taking a break.

He stepped towards her, forcing her back against the hotel wall. His eyes raked over her, their depths blazing. Fear clenched her throat tight and she raised her palms to his chest, pushing against his unrelenting form. 'Please, Charles, stop.'

Suddenly he shifted, his eyes widening momentarily before he flew away from her, his feet struggling to remain grounded on the pavement.

'The lady said to back off.'

Zara focused through the fear-filled daze, a raging Daniel consuming her vision, his expression unrecognisable as his eyes flashed dangerously on Charles.

'What is it, *playboy*?' Charles challenged, all drunken arrogance now that he'd recovered his stance. 'You going to fight her corner? Your latest slapper going to draw you into a fight? I don't think so.'

He laughed at his own joke, rolling his shoulders as he moved to step past them and then Daniel moved, so swiftly she couldn't judge his intent until it was too late, his fist making cracking contact with Charles' jaw. He flew back to the ground his hand coming up, his face slackened and distorted with pain, with anger, with humiliation.

Daniel stood over him, his shoulders heaving, his rage palpable and all Zara could do was watch, her body quivering, the same realisation she'd had inside, when he'd faced Charles off, flooding her anew and bringing terror rushing with.

She loved him.

And for a silly deluded second, when he'd come to her defence, she'd believed he loved her too. Had got caught up in the moment. Had believed she wasn't just another girl. It wasn't just sex.

And then reality hit and she realised she needed to

escape. To get away from him. From Charles. From everything that tore her heart in two.

And yet, here they both were, refusing to let her go.

Well, fuck that.

She turned and started walking, ignoring the curious looks of passers-by, the calls from Daniel as he took up chase. She walked as fast as her heels would permit.

'Zara, wait up, please, we need to talk.'

He came up behind her, his hands reaching out for her shoulder, and she ducked him. She couldn't risk his touch, knowing how it would make her feel, how it would crush her resolve so easily. 'No amount of talking is going to change my mind. I can't do this any more.'

'But—'

'Please, Daniel,' she begged into his wavering gaze, his confusion beating down into her. 'I just want to go home.'

'At least let me take you—let Peters take you?' he said, his hands thrusting into his pockets. 'I need to know you get home safely.'

Behind them, she could hear Charles' raised voice, the mutterings of several others that had joined him and the scene that was building.

Christ, what a night.

It wasn't just her that needed out, it was Daniel too. The press were going to be on this imminently. Her need to protect him had her nodding. 'Call Peters, get him to meet us at Victoria Bus Station.'

He looked over his shoulder, to the swelling group outside the hotel, and understood her meaning. With a nod, he placed a hand in the small of her back to usher her forward and, again, she stepped out of his hold. Moving with him but pretending he didn't exist. She just needed to get home. Then she could let go. Let it all out and deal with the mess she had made of her life. Again.

She'd rebuilt it before, she could do it this time too. *Couldn't she?*

Her heart squeezed tight in her chest, pain like nothing she'd ever experienced piercing her and sending her step faltering.

He reached out, steadying her, the warmth of his hand permeating her skin, her belly, her heart. 'Steady, baby.'

Baby—the endearment taunted her.

It wasn't her life that needed rebuilding, it was her heart, and it was in tatters.

She'd thought she'd been in love with Charles. The very idea was now laughable in light of how she felt for the man beside her. The man who'd made it clear he could never give her what her heart now craved.

Well, you only have yourself to blame, said her inner conscience, and she wrapped her arms tighter around her middle, her pace picking up to increase the distance between them.

The sooner she got away from him, the better.

They sat in silence in the back of the car, each hugging their own side, the cabin filled with the heavy strain of the scene they had left behind. He'd tried to speak to her, but she'd refused. And he got that she didn't want to talk but, hell, he had so many burning questions, the biggest of all he couldn't even bring himself to ask. Fear of what she might say keeping it trapped inside.

But he couldn't stand it any more and he found himself apologising. 'I'm sorry I hit him.'

'He deserved it,' she said quietly, her eyes still on the window, her tear-streaked face illuminated intermittently under the passing street lights.

Fuck, this was killing him.

He needed to know.

Was she upset with him? Or was it really Charles? Had she loved the man that much? Was she still in love with him?

Bile rose to the back of his throat and he forced it down, courage failing him.

'I'm sorry if it ends up front-page news tomorrow.'

'I couldn't give a fuck what the press make of it,' he retorted, emotion getting the better of him. 'The bastard did deserve that punch and I'll make sure any reporter that listens knows it.'

She looked to him then, properly for the first time since it had all gone south, her sad smile a thousand times more poignant with the water welling once more beneath her eyelids. His heart ached and he reached for her on instinct, but she recoiled into her seat, her face and body turning away, everything rejecting him.

The nausea swelled in his gut; he was losing her.

Hell, you've already lost her.

He leant back into his seat, his own eyes turning un-

seeingly on his own window, confusion raining thick
and heavy on his senses.

*Is this what life will feel like without her in it? As if
something's missing?*

Was this what it felt like to truly care for someone?
To actually love someone…

He looked across at her, broken and curled into her
seat, and inside he cracked, his fists clenching in his
lap.

*Ja, you love her, and just look where that's got her.
Not so good at escaping your parents' example now,
are you?*

Kristus—he was no better than Charles. And she'd
actually loved him. The lucky bastard had had it all
and thrown it away.

Whereas he'd never even given them a chance. How
could he convince her he had changed, that she had
changed him?

'Zara?' He barely recognised his own voice, its strangled quality alien even to him.

Slowly, she turned to look at him, the trail of tears
upon her cheeks wrenching him in two.

He swallowed, the words catching in his throat. He'd
never done this before. He didn't even know where to
begin.

'I wanted to talk to you tonight, after the party. It
had always been my intention,' he began and took an
unsteady breath, looking for courage that he didn't feel.
Somehow voicing it made it feel ever more real and the
vulnerability that came with it terrified him. He'd never

been more scared, or so desperate. 'I know we've not had the best start to a relationship and I know I've said and done a lot of things that I'm not proud of.'

Her lower lip trembled and she clutched her arms around her tighter, but she didn't stop him.

'And I know nothing of this, not really, but I think I'm falling in love with you and if you—'

'You think?' She gave a tremulous little laugh. 'Please, Daniel, don't go there.'

Of all the reactions he'd envisaged, her laughing wasn't one. 'I'm trying to be honest with you.'

She shook her head. 'You're trying to keep me any way you can.'

She sounded tired, done in, and then her gaze swept back to the window as her words echoed around the cabin. 'You're confusing desire with love.'

He swept towards her, one arm hooking around her waist to draw her in and she came willingly, her body falling into his.

It was a start.

'Desire is something I know plenty about, and this is more than that.'

Gently he nudged her chin up and their gazes locked, her voice whisper-like. 'I wish I could believe it.'

'You can.'

Beneath them the car nudged gently to a stop and he realised they were here, at her place, and any moment she would be gone.

'Don't go,' he rasped, his arms tightening around her. 'Give me the chance to prove it.'

'I have to go,' she said softly. 'I can't do this with you.'

He could see the truth of her words in her face, knew that any argument he could give would fall on deaf ears. He'd spent so long convincing her—hell, the world, even—that he wasn't capable of love, that she couldn't see past the facade.

Behind her, Peters opened the door and he slipped his arm from around her, letting her go, his words doing anything but. 'I'm not giving up on us.'

She dropped her gaze, her breath shaky as she slid away. 'Goodbye, Daniel… I mean it this time.'

And then she was gone, and his life emptied out, his insides carved hollow. In that second, he'd never been more convinced or more scared of something in his life: his love for her.

CHAPTER THIRTEEN

'I THINK WE need to change the office number,' EJ muttered as she brushed through her office doorway, two coffees in hand.

Zara looked up from the property details she'd been poring over for the last hour, nothing making sense. It was a one-bed studio, not some mansion, and yet it might as well have been Buckingham Palace for the amount of time it was taking. 'They're still calling?'

'Yup.' EJ set the coffee down and grimaced. 'Brings a new meaning to not taking no for an answer.'

She felt a pang of guilt. It was enough that she was being hounded, tailed on an almost daily basis, the intrigue her brief outing with Daniel had sparked still burning strong after three weeks of no contact. Not from her at any rate.

She sat back in her seat and took in the fresh bouquet that had arrived that morning. She hadn't had chance to share this one out among the staff yet.

'The press aren't the only ones,' EJ mused, spying her focus and bringing Zara's gaze back to her.

'He's just not used to dealing with the word.'

'You think that's all it is?' EJ arched a brow over her coffee cup, taking a sip as she watched her, concern softening her penetrative blues. It wasn't as if Zara looked a mess, but there was only so much make-up could do to hide the bags under her eyes, the reddened rims, not to mention the fact that she was sporting an ice-cream-fuelled swell.

'Of course it is.'

'I don't know,' EJ said, looking back to the flowers and letting out a contemplative breath. 'Seems to me the whole reason the press are on it so bad is because he's so quiet, not a story in sight, not since he decked Shit-Bag and, let's face it, the man had that coming.'

A bittersweet smile touched Zara's lips, the memory of Daniel's defence of her warming her through, and then the tide of pain hit, as it always did.

It doesn't mean he loves you, no matter what he says to the contrary.

'Sorry,' EJ said, pulling her out of the abyss she spent far too much time in these days. 'I didn't mean to upset you, I just—I don't know, maybe there's more to how he feels for you too. Maybe you should, you know, just talk to him.'

Zara took up her mug and sipped at it. It was the same conversation they'd had every day this past week, and every day she said the same. She couldn't trust herself to speak to him and not cave, dive in wholeheartedly and come out broken when he eventually decided he'd had enough.

It was better to have ended it now, before she fooled

herself into believing they had a future, before she got so wrapped up in their life together... She didn't think she could survive that level of heartache.

'He's coming in today.'

'What?' Zara's eyes snapped to hers. 'When?'

'In about an hour,' EJ said, a hesitant smile curving her lips, her brow raised in hope.

Zara's heart hit her throat, tension throbbing through every muscle. 'Why?'

'He's collecting the keys for the Mayfair place.'

'That was quick.'

EJ shrugged. 'What can I say? When you have a dedicated legal team and you're working with us, what's to delay it?'

'Still, you could have warned me, like yesterday, this morning even?'

She sighed. 'I was tempted not to tell you at all.'

'EJ...'

'What?' she blurted, a hand waving dismissively around her. 'Honestly, Zara, when Shit-Bag did his thing, it was hell watching you suffer, but that? That was nothing compared to what you're going through now.'

That was an understatement. But it didn't mean she should risk more pain, more heartache.

'He should've sent one of his assistants.'

'Yes, well, I'm sure he would've done in any normal situation, but this at least gives him a chance at seeing you,' she stated the obvious. 'I mean, the man has spent the last three weeks trying to reach you, flowers every other day, phone calls, I bet he's even been emailing, texting…'

EJ looked at her pointedly for confirmation and Zara gave a small nod. Not that his emails or texts ever gave much away. His apology dominating heavily and signing off with his desire to talk. The last one, arriving seven days ago, had simply said, You know where I am when you're ready, and then he'd gone quiet. Save for the flowers. They still came and, although they saddened her, she couldn't quite tell him to stop sending them. Even though she split them among her team, even though the happiness at seeing them was bittersweet, they were a reminder that he was still thinking of her, as she was him. And that, in some way, he suffered too.

Hell, maybe EJ was right: maybe she owed him a chance to talk, to explain.

And then what? You crumble at his protestations of 'possible' love and it all kicks off again, only to end up back here a few weeks down the line.

No, she just couldn't do it. She'd gone three weeks without any contact, without even a glimpse of him in the paper—and, boy, had she looked. Anticipating him to go on the rebound, to hook up with the next exquisite model, actress, figurehead, you name it. Anyone to confirm her suspicions that he was still a billionaire playboy regardless of his actions towards her.

But nothing.

And she wondered, really wondered, had she been different for him too?

That small spark of hope lit anew and fear rose to

swamp it, coffee sticking in her closed-up throat, and she forced it down. She needed to get out of there.

'I'm going to take an early lunch.' She rose out of her seat. 'Can you message when he's gone?'

EJ started, 'Come on, Zara, just one conversation?'

'Please, EJ—leave it alone.'

Her PA's gaze wavered, and Zara wondered whether she would push again, but then she gave a resigned nod.

'Okay, boss.'

Daniel had known she wouldn't be there, had felt it in his bones, but it didn't help the disappointment that slugged him when Elizabeth confirmed it. 'She had to go out,' she'd said, but he'd read the silent reason well enough.

She knew you were coming.

And he got it. He knew he'd screwed up. But it was driving him crazy. How could he prove he loved her if she wouldn't let him anywhere near her?

He looked to the envelope weighing heavy in his hand—it was his last hope. It had to work. He flew to Sweden imminently and he had to make sure she had this before he left.

'Can you give her this when she returns, please?' he asked, passing it to Elizabeth.

'Of course.' She gave him a small smile that smacked of sympathy and he wondered at just how much she knew, just how much Zara had told her—did she know how Zara felt about him?

'How is she?' He asked the question before he

thought better of it. Prying while standing in front of the entire office staff was not a great move, but he had to know.

'She's been better.'

He could sense the ears in the office pricking, the eyes being cast discreetly their way, and reined himself in. It wasn't the time or the place. But Elizabeth had said enough—Zara wasn't in a good place and, as much as it hurt that she wasn't happy, it gave him hope.

It was that hope that had him drawing out his stride as he left, taking a phone call in the lobby that could have waited until he was in the car, praying she might return before he left and he'd finally get to speak to her.

But she didn't.

And he left, hope still there, no matter how small.

He still wasn't giving up.

Not yet.

Zara waited another twenty minutes after EJ's 'all clear' message before risking her return, and by that point she was an emotional wreck. Just knowing he had been here, in her space, only moments before had her throat choking up. She could barely acknowledge EJ as she passed by her desk and headed into her office, knowing that words alone would break the seal.

'Sorry, Zara,' EJ said, coming into the office behind her, 'but he left this for you.'

Zara turned to see an envelope in EJ's outstretched hand. She swallowed hard, her hand reaching to take it, almost fearful. 'What is it?'

'No idea, he didn't say.'

Her fingers shook as she lifted the letter opener off her desk and slit it open. She tapped out the contents and the air escaped her lungs in a rush—*no way.*

EJ bent forward and gave a low whistle. 'Flight tickets?'

Fingers quaking ever more, she sifted through the papers: three tickets, to Nice.

Three? Nice? What's he playing at?

And then she saw the dates—next week…the Monaco Grand Prix. She was transported back to their car journey, to the moment when she'd told him of her plans for her father and had accidentally led onto her history with Charles. He'd remembered it all. He'd listened and…

Oh, my God.

The ache inside swelled, the tears with it. Had she been wrong? Could he actually…?

'There's a note,' EJ said, prodding a bit of paper out from underneath.

Zara lifted it up, the handwritten words blurring as the tears trickled over.

Please accept this gift for you and your parents.
You deserve it. You will be met at the airport in
Nice. Everything is taken care of.
    I want you to have a good time.
    I want you to be happy.
Daniel x

She stared at it dumbly, his words leaping off the page.

I want you to be happy.

'You can't tell me that man doesn't have feelings for you.'

She felt her head shake, her heart fluttering like crazy in her chest. 'I don't believe it.'

'Well, I do.' EJ plucked the documents off the desk and thrust them into her hand. 'And it's time you believed it too.'

'I need to speak to him.'

'Finally, the voice of reason.' EJ beamed. 'I'm going before you change your mind.'

She watched EJ leave, the world spinning, her head turning dizzy as adrenaline flooded her system. She had to go to him. Now.

But she didn't even know where to find him.

She didn't want to ring him, she didn't want this conversation over the phone, but it was better than the delay.

She raced to grab up her mobile, her trembling fingers taking far too long to dial his number, and her stomach sank as it went straight to voicemail.

She dialled his office number and his PA answered.

'Hello, is Mr Lazenby available? It's Zara—Ms Anders from Anders Estates.' She felt her cheeks heat over her flustered request.

'I'm afraid he is unavailable for the next few days, Ms Anders. Can I take a message?'

'No… Not really… Do you know where I can find him?'

There was a pause; she was probably wondering why Zara sounded so desperate and unprofessional. 'He's taking some annual leave, but, if it's urgent, I can get a message sent to him?'

'No—no, it's fine. It can wait. Thank you.'

She cut the call. Annual leave? It didn't sound like him, unless…

She dialled Julia and the woman answered in two rings—thank goodness.

She had her answer pretty swiftly. He was going to Sweden; he was going to meet his new nephew; he really was making amends. She pressed a hand to her mouth, a fresh wave of tears threatening as a multitude of emotions swamped her all at once.

'Is there a problem with the house purchase?' Julia asked. 'If so, I'm sure we can get a message to him?'

'No, no problem,' Zara assured her. 'Nothing that should interfere with his personal trip.'

'Well, I believe he is due in Monaco at the end of the week. Why don't you try him again then?'

Her heart soared.

Monaco. He would be there too?

CHAPTER FOURTEEN

'*THIS IS UNBELIEVABLE. This is unbelievable. This is unbelievable.*'

The same words had left her parents' lips a hundred times over. But it was. The whole thing. From the first-class flights to Nice and the helicopter ride to Monaco to the limousine service, all accompanied by champagne, all with no expense spared.

And here she now stood. Not in a hotel room, but in the master quarters of a yacht, the magnitude of which she could scarcely believe.

Her parents were up top with the captain, soaking up the qualifying sessions currently tearing along the track. The sound of the engines thrumming through the air, they were that close, the track residing just the other side of the dock. It was the perfect position, a dream come true for her father.

But her dream was still hanging in the balance. She'd been crushed when a chauffeur had greeted them at the airport. Even though Daniel had made clear she would be met, she'd still hoped that it would have been by him.

Should she have texted him? Told him that she

wanted to talk? That she wanted him to be here too? Or had she guessed wrongly? Maybe him being in Monaco hadn't meant what she thought? Maybe he had no intention of actually calling on her?

No. No. No.

She strode across the vast room, straight to the bedside table where her phone was charging, and grabbed it up. She couldn't debate his intent any longer; she needed to know; she needed to speak to him; she needed him here.

She launched her contact list and a tap at the door stalled her. She looked to it, her belly starting to flutter.

Would it be? Could it be?

Trance-like, she headed towards it. Not daring to let her excitement swell.

It swung open before she reached it and she froze to the spot, her knees weakening beneath her. Shock, surprise, joy, all overwhelming as Daniel filled the doorway.

'Zara.'

Daniel's entire world stood still; the sound of the ocean, the crew, the engines, all falling away, drowned out by the wild rush of blood in his ears, his heart slamming in his chest. He devoured the sight, her colourful presence calling to him among the backdrop of clean white and stealing his breath away.

She stepped towards him, her lips parting, her eyes glistening in the sunlight. 'You *are* here?'

His lips quirked at the wonder in her soft-spoken

observation. 'I would have met you at the airport but I didn't trust myself to keep it all in check in front of your parents.'

She smiled then, a gentle curve of her lips that filled him with warmth. 'Keep what in check?'

'My love for you.'

The words were so hushed he wondered if she'd heard him but then she suddenly came alive, sweeping across the room, her arms encasing him.

Kristus, *yes.*

He buried his head in her hair, breathing in her familiar scent as his arms wrapped tight around her.

'I'm so happy to see you,' she whispered, her cheek pressed against his chest.

'And I you.' He kissed the top of her hair, reality starting to sink in and in the best way possible. Did this mean she was starting to believe...? That she could also feel the same...?

He unhooked his arm from around her and sought out her chin, coaxing her to look up at him, the emotion in her gaze momentarily winding him.

He'd swear it was love that he saw. *Please let it be love.*

'I'm sorry I got things so wrong with us,' he began, and her brow crinkled, her eyes wavering over his face. 'What I mean is, I was a fool not to have seen it sooner... I love you, Zara. I loved you before I even realised what it was.'

Her smile bloomed, her welling gaze stripping him bare as the truth of his words sank in. 'You really do.'

His fingers flexed around her chin. Was she making a statement or posing a question? He couldn't tell. 'Is it still so hard to believe that I can love you?'

She shook her head, the move infinitesimally small. 'I'm just trying to convince myself this is really happening.'

'Let me help you with that.'

He smoothed his palm along her jaw, his thumb brushing over her cheekbone and filling him with awe at the softness beneath—how he'd missed this.

'I never want to be without you in my life,' he said thickly, his eyes locked with hers, urging her to believe. 'These past few weeks have been torture, not knowing how to get you back, how to make you see how I feel. This was my last hope. I figured if you realised how much I'd listened, how much I wanted you to be happy, you would see it for what it was—my love for you.'

She turned into his hand, her lashes lowering, a tear escaping over one lid as she pressed a kiss inside his hand. 'I couldn't believe it when I saw the tickets.'

Her eyes lifted to his on the last word, wet and blazing, and his heart exploded in his chest.

'I wanted to come after you that very second,' she continued. 'When I realised you truly cared, that you'd listened and remembered something so small from our conversations so early on.'

'It's not small, not to you, not to your family.'

She smiled up at him. 'No, it's not, you're right. But to you it would have been. And yet, you'd remembered and understood how much it means to us.'

'Then why didn't you hunt me down?'

'I did,' she admitted, her cheeks flushing slightly with her admission. 'But when I discovered you'd gone to see your family, I knew I couldn't intrude.'

'Intrude?' He tightened his arm around her. 'If not for you I might never have gone in the first place. I might never have reconciled with them.'

'Me?'

He smiled. 'Don't look so surprised.'

He brushed his thumb across her lower lip, the memory of which had haunted him the past three weeks, and his body stirred, the object of his fascination holding his eye. 'You made me realise that if I could change then they could too. I was barely a man when I left them—a lot has happened since then. I only wished I could have taken you with me. I missed you so much. Seeing my nephew and the joy he's brought to his parents, to see their happiness and wanting it for myself, for us...' He shook his head. He was getting ahead of himself, but he couldn't help it. The gates were open and there was no holding back. 'I'm sorry, I just—'

'Oh, Daniel.' She bobbed up on tiptoes, her lips finding his in joy, a sudden kiss of happiness that was over before he'd had his fill. 'I'm so hap—'

His hunger snapped, three weeks without her coming to the fore, and he groaned, crushing her against his chest, his lips silencing hers with such passion, such need. He was scared he'd hurt her but he couldn't stop, and the way she clung to him, the way she moaned, he didn't need to worry.

She curved into him, pressing up against his swelling hardness, granting him all that he needed physically. But there was something else he burned for more. He had to hear her say it.

He ripped his mouth away, his breathing ragged as he cupped her chin in both hands now. She opened her lust-filled eyes, wide and questioning. How did he ask? He'd never asked for those three words from anyone. He'd never needed to hear them before. But he needed them now more than life itself.

And then her expression eased, her head tilting to one side as she brought her own hands up to caress his jawline. 'EJ was right.'

'EJ?'

Who the hell is EJ?

'Elizabeth, my PA, she said you had a puppy-dog-lost look about you.' She smiled. 'Of course, at the time, I saw you more as a lion.'

'A lion?' He chuckled, the sound strained in his pent-up throat.

Tell me you love me, that you can at least learn to love me...

'An insatiable one at that.'

'I don't think I can ever get enough of you.'

She smiled and pressed a gentle kiss to his lips.

'You don't have to,' she said, dropping back. 'I'm not going anywhere.'

Her assurance was enough. It would do for now. Be satisfied. He squeezed her to him, love swelling in his veins. 'I love you, so very much.'

'I love you too.'

He stilled. The words resonating through him, each and every syllable chiming with his heart, his head turning dizzy with it. 'You do?'

She pushed back to stare up at him. 'Christ, yes.'

And then she was kissing him, her hunger, her emotion filling him. Tears welled behind his lids, making further words impossible; he threw them all into his kiss and he knew she was doing the same. They were both duelling for what they wanted: each other. Life had never been more perfect, more complete. And for the very first time, he felt like he'd come home.

EPILOGUE

THREE MONTHS TOGETHER and it felt like for ever. In the best way possible.

It was her birthday and Daniel had insisted on a surprise. What kind of surprise she had no clue. But they were travelling north from London and she'd been blindfolded for the last twenty minutes.

'You okay in there?' he rumbled close to her ear, his fingers squeezing her leg over her jeans and making her smile.

'I have to say, being sat in a moving vehicle while blindfolded isn't top of my list of fun.'

'Well, I'd hoped our antics last night might have meant you fell asleep.'

She laughed at that. 'Ah, so that explains your extreme virility.'

'Hey, I'm always virile.' His mock hurt had her cracking up further, her hand reaching blindly for his leg, his upper thigh, his—

'Behave!'

'Spoilsport,' she complained as she heard the tick of the indicator and the car start to slow.

'Not really,' he said. 'It's only because we're here.'

'Ooh, great.' Excited, she moved to take off the blind-fold.

'No, not yet.' She let her hands fall away, turning her head to face him even though she couldn't see. 'I'll do it when the time is right.'

Her body swayed as the car turned, the sound of gravel crunching beneath the tyres reaching her.

Where were they?

She waited patiently for the car to come to a stop. 'Now can I take it off?'

'Nope.'

She heard him open his door, felt the car shift with his weight as he stepped out and then it closed shut. She nibbled nervously over her lip, ears straining for his approach. She could hear his feet over the gravel, the latch go on her door as he swung it open and then his hand closed around hers, encouraging her out.

Awkwardly, she straightened and he cupped her upper arms.

'Okay, now turn a little.' She did as he asked, his hands guiding her. 'Now stop.'

He released her, his fingers moving to untie her blindfold. 'Ready?'

She nodded, every sense on high alert as he slipped the fabric away.

No way.

Before her, in all its picture-postcard glory, was property number one, the house of her dreams. 'But— But it was sold?'

'Let's just say the new owner was very reasonable when I explained how much the love of my life adored the house,' he said smoothly. 'He couldn't help but sell it to me—*to us.*'

She laughed, her head shaking in disbelief. 'How much?'

He blew through his lips on a *pfft*. 'So much for trying to be romantic. There's no pulling the wool over your eyes, is there?'

'Absolutely not,' she said, sending him a quick grin and looking back to the house, her jaw slackening in awe—he'd really bought it? For her?

'I knew you loved it,' he said softly. 'Watching you that first viewing, I think I spent all of it looking at you, rather than it. But when I came back last month—'

'You came back?'

'Well, yes, I had to be sure it wasn't some death trap waiting to happen and that I wasn't being blinded by some crazy romantic notion.'

She laughed again. 'Oh, I definitely think it's crazy.'

She could sense him frown. 'You do?'

'Totally.' She waved her hands at its magnitude. 'Who buys their girlfriend a house for her birthday?'

He came up behind her, his arms wrapping around her middle and drawing her close. She leant back into his inviting warmth, her arms coming up to overlay his own.

'No, perhaps you're right.' He dropped his head into the crook of her shoulder and nuzzled into her neck, a small contented sound rumbling low in his throat resonating right along her spine. 'But I would buy it for my wife.'

What? She stilled. *He couldn't mean?*

She turned in his arms, her gaze wide-eyed and welling. 'Are you…?'

He grinned, his face so full of love he stole her words away.

'Will you marry me, Zara Anders?'

He slipped his hand into the pocket of his jeans and she dropped her gaze, watching as he lifted it back up to her. There, in his upturned palm, rested a diamond ring, its single solitaire sparkling in the sunlight. Her heart swelled so big, she could scarce draw breath, the word 'Yes' slipping from her lips barely audible.

She watched as he took it up and slipped it over her proffered finger.

'I feel like I'm dreaming,' she whispered.

He interlaced his fingers through her engaged hand, his other tilting her chin up to face him. 'Do you need me to prove you're not? Because I can think of some very effective ways to show you that…and I quite fancy reliving the pond moment.'

He wiggled his brow, all hopeful, and she erupted in a giggle, the swing from romantic to horny sending her giddy. 'You're insatiable.'

'And you're a permanent tease on my senses. I say we're even.'

'Even, you say?' She nodded, giving mock-consideration to his words, her love for him swelling hard and fast.

'Uh-huh.'

She beamed. 'I love you.'

'And I love you, Mrs Lazenby-to-be.'

He dropped his head to claim her, his mouth gentle and coaxing over hers. She lost herself in his surprising softness, her body turning to liquid, and then he dropped forward, one arm hooking beneath her legs and swinging her up, forcing out a startled squeal.

'Pond. Now!'

* * * * *

BARING IT ALL

REBECCA HUNTER

MILLS & BOON

To my parents, who took our family on a trip to Green Island long ago.

And to Adam Summers (the Fish Guy) and Mike O'Donnell, who both generously offered marine biology insight. Among other helpful pointers, Adam made sure Natasha wore a dive suit over her bikini, saving her from harm by painful stingers, which I might have otherwise subjected her to.

Of course, all mistakes are my own.

CHAPTER ONE

IF THERE WAS anything Max Jensen hated more than thinking with his schlong, it was doing it in front of an audience. Natasha was late coming home, and instead of focusing on her sister, Alya, who happened to be Max's assignment, all he could think about was Natasha and what kind of trouble she was getting herself into. Alya's curvy younger sibling was a powerful distraction… but that wasn't the only reason his mind kept wandering back to her. Max was in security, for fuck's sake. Of course he was worried when she didn't show up on time. He just also happened to want to get in her pants.

Max glanced at his watch, then back at his client. "Shouldn't Natasha be home by now?"

Alya looked up from the papers she was reading and shrugged. "She probably walked."

Alone? It was none of his business. His business was laid out on the table in front of him—going over the schedule for Alya's weekend photoshoot on the Great Barrier Reef. He'd been the fashion model's bodyguard for years now and had gotten to know both sisters in the process.

"It's getting dark," he said, keeping his voice businesslike, as if he was talking about any other client. "And you said she sounded upset."

Alya leaned back in her chair and met his gaze. "If she doesn't come home soon, I'll call."

She set down her pen, and it rolled across the sleek table, echoing in the silence of the enormous kitchen of her downtown Sydney apartment. She was eyeing Max carefully, like she had read into his question and was coming to her own conclusions, so he looked right back. He had mastered this easygoing I-have-nothing-to-hide expression back in high school after a few years of practice on his hard-edged father.

Preparing me for life, my ass. Sure, Max had learned to dodge trouble—he even got paid to use those skills with the elite private security firm Blackmore Inc. But nothing about Max's life was what his father had intended.

He and Alya exchanged another silent moment, and then she gave a little nod.

"Natasha and Wayne were supposed to be celebrating her new research grant. All she said was that he wasn't quite as positive about it as she had hoped." Alya rolled her eyes and added, "Probably because she'll have less time for helping with his articles."

Natasha's boyfriend was a real wanker. He was much older than she was and self-important as hell. Max had crossed paths with him once in this very kitchen, and the asshole had droned on like the future of the world depended on his research. Natasha couldn't be serious about this guy, could she?

"She didn't sound happy on the phone?" he asked.

Alya shook her head and returned to the documents, and Max's shoulders came down a bit. Maybe they broke up. Goddamn, he hoped so. It was selfish, and under any other circumstances, hearing that Natasha was upset would be a punch in the gut. But his mind was moving in a totally different direction. *Yeah, thinking with your schlong.* He went right back to that night a few months ago when they had come so, so close to stepping over the line.

Since then Max had been looking for a chance to test the sexual buzz between them. Before it was too late. Because too late would be coming soon—specifically, at the end of next week, when his father would announce that he was stepping down as head of the Jensen Family Foundation and Max would become president. So, in addition to the photographers who followed him onto the beaches when he surfed or when he took a woman to dinner, Max's life would also include planned public appearances and board meetings. It was a path he had worked to avoid. And the last thing he wanted to think about tonight.

Thinking about quirky, witty, oh-so-hot Natasha Petrova was a hell of a lot more fun. She was the only woman he knew who could use convoluted biology theories about the rules of attraction to shut him down. Of course, it only made him want her more, though he didn't understand a damn word half the time. Maybe it was because he had just scraped by in biology class. More likely it was because he was concentrating on her lips. Luscious red lips. Which, all things considered, was better than staring at her breasts.

Over the years, he'd thrown dozens of propositions her way, each one wilder than the last, just to hear her response. Just to see her eyes light up as she laughed. Okay, also on the off chance that she'd forget about Max's family's name and his…reputation…and say yes to a little fun.

Max met Alya's gaze again and raised his eyebrows, daring her to speak her suspicions aloud. He wouldn't be surprised if Alya had caught on to his semi-obsession with her sister, but he still couldn't get a read on what Alya thought about it.

His client gave nothing away. Instead, she gathered the papers on the table in front of her and took one more glance at their schedule. "With all these precautions, you'd think I was royalty. But it's a relief." She gave him a quick smile. "Stewart should be here soon." Alya's boyfriend was picking her up to go back to his place for the night, which meant Max should probably head out…

Keys rattled in the front hall of the apartment as the door creaked open and slammed shut.

"Natasha?" Alya called.

"Yep, it's me." Natasha's voice echoed down the hall.

"Did Wayne properly celebrate your fabulousness at dinner?"

Max froze. He was a selfish enough bastard to hope the answer was no.

"Not even close," she called.

Max blew out a breath. She didn't sound upset. Or maybe that was wishful thinking on his part.

Natasha's keys clanged on the front hall table, and her shoes thumped to the floor, one by one. "Instead, he suggested we see other people. I'm officially free to have a little fun. His words."

Alya choked on her water, midsip. "What?"

Holy shit.

A better man would make himself known before Natasha spilled any more of the intimate details about her evening. But there was no way in hell Max was taking the high road here.

Natasha's footsteps clunked down the hall.

"We're taking a break. So I can have all the time I need for my career." The last sentence was filled with sarcasm.

The bathroom door closed. Alya stared at the empty doorway to the hall, her attention completely focused on her sister. All the better if she forgot about Max. The toilet flushed, and Natasha's footsteps came closer.

"This all started when I tried to wake him up with a blow—"

Natasha rounded the corner and froze, her eyes fixed on Max. Oh, fuck, she looked hot. But then again, she always did. The dress was white, classy, and it didn't show cleavage, but there was no hiding those natural wonders. Her black-rimmed glasses gave her a sexy librarian vibe, a visual he'd come back to later that night.

Natasha watched him from the doorway. Max kept his expression neutral while searching her face for lingering hurt or sadness. He couldn't find any traces. Just a hint of challenge. Good. If she'd come home in tears, Wayne might have needed a late-night talking-to. The thought was a mild surprise. As it turned out, even in this situation Max couldn't stand the idea of her getting hurt.

"Why the hell didn't you tell me Max was here?" Natasha muttered to her sister, her eyes still fixed on him.

Alya wrinkled her brow. "Sorry. I was stuck on what you were saying."

Natasha stared at Max for another beat. Then she let out a sigh. "I suppose I'll care more about this tomorrow, but right now, I don't give a shit. Everyone is welcome to hear about my fabulous evening."

Natasha brushed long, blond wisps of hair off her face and plopped down into the chair next to Max. She gave him another quick glance, as if she was still registering his presence. Her eyes lingered on his biceps for an extra beat before she turned to her sister. He hid a smile behind his hand. A nice guy would stand up and excuse himself, leaving the two sisters alone for a private conversation. Too bad he wasn't that guy. If Natasha wasn't kicking him out, he was staying for the rest of the show.

Alya was still shaking her head. "You okay?"

"I can't believe this happened again. I thought Wayne would understand, that with his own crazy schedule, he'd respect my work." Natasha gave a huff of frustration. "Dinner a few times a week, sex, support for each other's work and an occasional holiday—is that too much to ask? Why does dating always lead to other crap expectations?"

Alya snorted. "He didn't ask you to pick up his dry cleaning again, did he?"

Natasha shook her head. "I think I made my answer clear the last time he asked. Now it's his department's barbeque. But, seriously, why is he asking *me* to make a plate for it?" She turned to Max and pointed her finger at him. "And Wayne already mansplained all the ways medical research is different from other biology research, why his job is so much more important."

"You think I'd talk down your work?" he asked with an almost straight face. "Not a chance in hell."

Her complete absorption with saving the marine world was an appeal, not a drawback. Instead, Max had been thinking about the last time he'd witnessed one of her breakups. She'd been devastated. So if she wanted to direct some of her manfrustration at him, that was fine. Anything that steered her away from hurt.

"Maybe I should lower my standards. Just sex. No relationship at all." Natasha massaged her temples. "I think I'm getting a headache."

Max's rational brain stuttered to a stop at the words *just sex*, starting him down that thinking-with-his-dick road, which was paved with justifications.

She just wants sex. Hey—that's what I want, too.

Yeah, that wasn't a particularly nuanced or eloquent path.

Alya's heels clicked on the tile as she crossed the kitchen floor to the white cupboards. She grabbed a glass and filled it with water, dropped in a Berocca tablet, then set it in front of Natasha. All three of them watched it fizz.

"You're going to need this." Alya tapped the glass. "I don't get it. He actually took you to a beautiful restaurant with water views just to dump you?"

"Technically, I broke up with him, but that was after he suggested a more 'open' relationship. Oh, and he also backed out of the Hawaii trip. Wayne said the hospital was short-staffed so it was better for him not to take a holiday right now. And since I'll be putting in long hours soon, he didn't want to 'hold me back.' Nice of him, right?" Natasha blew more strands of hair out of her face and took a gulp from the glass. "This was before the waitress even stopped by. Of course, that helped me decide on my order. The caviar is pretty damn expensive, as Wayne now knows."

Max smiled a little. Natasha definitely sounded more frustrated than sad about the situation, and she still had her sense of humor. All good signs.

"I still don't get it. You and Wayne have always had tight schedules. What changed?" asked Alya.

Natasha glanced at Max, a flush creeping up her neck. She eyed him. "Promise not to bring this up after tonight?"

"I'll do *whatever* makes you happy, sweetheart," he said, slowing on *whatever*.

His words had the effect he was hoping for. Her eyes widened, and the flush racing to her cheeks deepened. She usually tried to hide it a little better. That forbidden surge of attraction. Except now it wasn't forbidden. She was single.

But he really meant it, and not just sexually. He had tried to stay away, despite the tsunami of hot tension that hit every time he found himself alone with Natasha, because he came with something Natasha despised: media scrutiny. In his case, it mostly took the form of speculations about his sex life and judgments about his general morality. And when he took the position his father had groomed him for next week, the attention would step up. His father's coverage had gotten personal at some point, at the expense of his mother. When Max took his place at the head of the Jensen Family Foundation, he had no doubt Natasha would steer as far away from him as she could.

Alya cleared her throat. "You were saying?"

Natasha was watching him, her lips parted a little, but she snapped her mouth shut at her sister's voice. "Right. The reason for the time apart." She drummed her fingers on the table and glanced over at Max. "Since you're here, and you're a guy—with a dick, I'm assuming—I want your opinion on something."

Max wrinkled his brow. "My opinion on Wayne?"

"Sort of."

Max frowned. He had met enough of the Waynes of the world to know they'd never take the time to make sure Natasha was happy. Still, she'd clearly had a rough evening, so maybe it was time to soften his assessment a little? Nah.

His opinion of Wayne could be summed up in two

words: pretentious asshole. The handful of times they'd met in person, Wayne had found a way to mention his super-important medical degree and how he was irreplaceable. Max had resisted a sarcastic retort about his own days at Princeton for Natasha's sake. And because the douche probably wouldn't have recognized sarcasm if it bit him in the crotch.

Natasha took a deep breath. "Okay, here's the question. What are some of the reasons you might not be interested in…sex with a girlfriend? And then you set her free for a bit."

Whoa. Not what he was expecting. And the thing that came to mind immediately would hurt. It was exactly what she didn't want to hear right now, so he searched for something that might make her feel better, instead.

"Um, maybe if you have surgery on your love stick, and it's in recovery?" He rubbed the back of his neck. "Or maybe you're doing some experiment with getting your girlfriend super horny before talking her into a sexy scenario involving—"

"Stop," said Natasha, putting her hand up to cut him off. "Wrong person to ask. Alya?"

Alya furrowed her brow. "You want me to say it?"

Natasha nodded.

"Okay. He wants to shag other women," said Alya softly.

Natasha glanced at Max for confirmation, but he said nothing.

Her mouth tugged down at the corners. "You were thinking it, too, weren't you?"

That had been his first guess, followed by the possibility that Wayne was gay. There was no way to give her an honest answer without hurting her.

"What reason did he give?" asked Max.

Natasha shrugged. "Too tired. Too busy. And he really is tired and busy."

Max raised an eyebrow. "What kind of blow job can you be too tired for? I'm curious."

Her face flushed a deep red. "You heard that?"

"I heard it, but I'm having trouble understanding it."

Natasha smiled a little, but it faded quickly. She bit her lip. Had Wayne, the self-important wanker, made her feel like *she* had done something wrong? Hell no.

"And he suggested you take some time off to have sex with other guys?" asked Alya.

"He didn't say those words exactly, but he implied it."

"Did he want you to report back to him?" asked Max. "Is this a kink thing?"

Both Natasha and Alya burst into laughter.

"I'm pretty sure Wayne is kink-free," Natasha said with a snort. "He doesn't seem to be into sex much at all."

What the hell kind of man wasn't into sex? A list of all the things he'd be into with Natasha came to Max's mind, but it definitely wasn't for her sister's ears.

Natasha's expression grew serious. And a little sad. Damn. She took a couple of gulps of fizzy water and glanced at Max as she set down the glass. "I'm really going to regret telling you all this tomorrow, aren't I?"

He gave her a soft smile. "I'll be sure to use it against you."

Natasha met his gaze and smiled back, just a little at first, but then her lips curved up into a full smile. *Goddamn*. After three years of watching these dickheads come in and out of her life, she deserved so much better than this. A crease had formed on Alya's brow, and Max was almost sure she was searching for a way to brighten up her sister's disastrous evening.

Then Alya sat up in her chair. "Hey, this means you can come to Green Island with me now."

Natasha's gaze flitted away from his, and a new flush rushed to her cheeks.

"What about Hawaii?" she asked her sister.

"Is going to Hawaii alone really better than a tropical island with your sister?" Alya flashed Natasha a photo spread–ready grin.

Max's heart pumped faster as he watched this exchange. Natasha on Green Island with them this weekend? Hell, yeah.

"But I had some potential field sites to check out," Natasha protested.

Alya waved her off. "Don't angelfish also live on the Great Barrier Reef? I'll pay for your plane ticket, and my room at the resort has a king-sized bed."

"I don't know," mumbled Natasha, but she was smiling a little now.

"Come on, Nat," said Alya. "Don't go on vacation by yourself right after a breakup. Besides, you know I'd feel a lot better if you were there with me."

Max raised his eyebrows at Alya, and she frowned at him and shook her head. Was Alya trying to guilt her sister into coming based on her own problems with men? If so, the tactic was effective. Natasha's brow crinkled up, and she sighed.

"I've never been to Green Island," she said slowly. "It's epaulette shark territory."

Alya jumped out of her chair. "That's a yes?"

"I guess so…" Natasha twisted her hair around a finger.

Alya tapped the schedule for the *Tropical Bliss* magazine shoot before her sister could protest further. "We're doing an early morning shoot and an evening shoot both days, when the tourists aren't flooding the island. So when the rest of us are working, you'll get the reef to yourself for a few hours. Other than that, I'll have time off. The whole trip should be fun."

Alya typed something into her phone.

"I'm going to get you booked right now, on my way to Stewart's, before you can change your mind," she said then smiled up at Natasha. "He'll be here in a minute. It's your last chance to back out."

Natasha looked from Alya to Max. She bit her lip. "Okay, I'm in."

Alya's phone dinged, and she grabbed it and waved. "You won't be sorry, Natasha. And can you see Max out?"

CHAPTER TWO

THE FRONT DOOR slammed shut, leaving Natasha alone with Max. Damn, this evening was taking yet another crazy turn. Max, of course, exuded his usual easygoing charm, as if he regularly talked with women about failed blow job attempts and great sex. He probably did.

The man was so sexy, so tempting…and soooo not a good idea, though sometimes it was hard to remember why. Sure, he'd do dinner and sex without hints about picking up his dry cleaning. But everything she'd heard suggested that he specialized in one-and-done nights, and she really didn't. Even if she made an exception to that rule, this was Max Jensen.

The Australian press loved nothing better than to speculate on the latest conquests of the reckless black sheep from an old-money ranching family, the country's version of royalty. As the "ugly duckling" daughter of Illana Petrova, as one American newspaper had called her at the tender age of thirteen, Natasha knew better than to go near a walking scandal maker like Max. She'd had enough of those in her life, having a famous Russian supermodel turned actress for a mother. Natasha had plenty of hard-earned academic achievements to her name, but they weren't the kind the media valued. The last thing she'd want was to put herself through another round of public comparisons, all superficial and all finding her lacking.

Max rested his forearms on the table, all tanned and corded with muscles, covered in dark blond hair. A bit of her resolve gave up and tiptoed out of the quiet kitchen.

She cleared her throat and looked up at Max. "You probably think I'm an idiot, not telling off Wayne."

"Not even close." Max shook his head.

"Then what are you thinking?"

"I'm thinking this is my lucky day," he said, his voice lower, a little husky.

Her eyes widened. "Not that kind of lucky."

Max leaned back in his chair and gave a loud bark of laughter. He shook his head and took a deep breath. "I thought I was the one with the dirty mind," he said. "I mean, our stars seem to be lining up tonight."

"I'm sensing a pickup line coming on." Natasha rolled her eyes, but heat crept up her neck. Max's grin suggested he was enjoying every minute of this exchange, and his eyes sparked with mischief and heat. Another chunk of her resolve snuck out the door, leaving her alone with her neglected libido.

"Maybe I need to step up my game with you," he continued, leaning forward, his arms resting on the table only inches from hers. "Maybe I should focus on your interest in animal mating. If that turns you on, we could watch some videos where the male comes up to the female from behind and bites her in the neck while—"

"Nope." Natasha shoved his biceps to cut him off, trying to ignore his hard, thick muscles under her fingers. "Animal mating is *not* the thing that turns me on. I just study the reproductive behaviors of angelfish, so of course mating patterns are something I think about."

Max stifled a laugh. "Sure."

Natasha gave him a hard stare. "You're belittling my career right now," she said. "Would you say the same thing to a guy who studies fish mating?"

His smile broke through, and he winked at her. "Of course not. The discussion would be much raunchier."

Natasha pressed her lips together. Did he really think she was turned on by this topic, or was he just messing with her? That was yet another problem: he was never serious. From that very first comment three years ago, when he'd given her a suggestive smile and spouted that cliché about getting over her latest dating disaster by getting under someone better, she couldn't decide if he was coming on to her or teasing her. Or both. Truthfully, Max's deep voice could make just about anything sound possible.

The very biggest problem with entertaining Max's flirtation was that she hung on to every word of it. Despite the fact that she knew better. Despite the disaster this kind of smooth-talking charmer had wreaked on her mother's life—and hers. She had been so very careful to avoid the trap of men who loved women, the more the better.

He was watching her, waiting for her comeback. His eyes were alive, as if he wanted nothing more than to hear the next thing that came out of her mouth. But one of them had to insert some common sense into this discussion, and it sure as hell wasn't going to be Max.

Natasha sighed, gesturing between the two of them. "There are a lot of reasons we should stay away from this. Why...?" She searched for a way to finish her question. Why did he want to start something with her? But everything that came to mind sounded too self-deprecating.

He hesitated, and for once the easy amusement faded from his expression. And in that moment, Natasha had to wonder how many careful calculations went into his seemingly careless attitude. Then his smile grew, and he leaned closer.

"Because you're sexy as fuck, and I've had a hard-on for you for years," he whispered.

Her mouth dropped a little, and she closed it quickly. There was no calculation in his expression, just unfiltered sexual interest. Could that be the whole truth? Probably not. Still, maybe it could be that simple.

Just like it had seemed the one night he'd looked at her like that before. Natasha had tagged along at one of Alya's events, and both of them had had more than their share to drink as the night went on. Later, after Max followed them back to the apartment, with Alya passed out in her bed, Natasha had led him to the door.

She had felt his gaze on her in the car, and she'd felt it again in their hallway, hotter, more intense.

When Natasha had reached the door to let him out, she'd turned around, and Max's half-lidded eyes had been so hungry. Like he'd wanted a taste, even though he shouldn't. She had worn a red dress that showed plenty of cleavage and smiled as his eyes dipped for a close-up view. Oh, God, she had been tempted.

I'm all for indulging with you, sweetheart, but you've had waaaayyy too much to drink to go down that road tonight.

His words had been soft, maybe even regretful, but they'd been enough to yank her out of her lusty stupor. Yeah, he had turned her down for good reasons, but the next time she saw him, it was as if that almost kiss had never happened. Like he had lost interest and moved on. Apparently not.

Was she really entertaining a hookup with Max again? *Come on, brain. Don't give up on me now.* His dates had a tendency to wind up on the pages of gossip rags…though there wasn't much chance of that with one little hookup, right? Or two or three, if they were spending a couple days together on a tiny island in the Great Barrier Reef…

Time for a last-ditch attempt to approach this rationally. She tilted her head and tried for a skeptical tone. "It just doesn't seem to fit into your rules for women."

"Is that what you think?" He smiled. "Interesting. What are my rules?"

She quirked a brow at him. "Number one, the woman

must show her wares on the market, preferably tall, with long hair and big breasts. Number two, she must love red carpet events." With each number she ticked off on her fingers, his smile fell a little. "Number three, she must have zero expectations the next day because you don't do repeat performances. You want me to keep going?"

He was silent for a moment, almost as if he were at a loss for words. No way. Not possible.

She gave him a mock-serious, wide-eyed look. "Did I manage to offend Max Jensen, the world's most laid-back guy?"

His face broke into his signature smile. "I'm flattered that you're paying so much attention to my sex life."

Heat crept up her neck. Of course he'd see it from that angle. And clearly he was right. "It's hard to ignore when it's on the front page of a magazine," she said, her voice a little short. Okay, maybe she had felt tiny twinges of jealousy seeing him with all those other women, but that wasn't why she had brought up the topic. Natasha twisted a strand of her hair around her finger, searching for a way to explain her hesitancy.

"A few years ago, Alya bought me one of those ridiculous dating advice books as a gag gift, but I read it anyway. You know why?" she asked. Max shook his head. "Because the book promised to help me find The Three S's. And two of the three are what I wanted the most—safety and stability."

Max raised an eyebrow. "Is the third one sex?"

Humor tugged at her lips once again. It was impossible to stay serious around him. "Nope. Status."

That answer earned a frown from him. "How did it work out for you?"

"I tried their methods and got bored." She gave him a wry smile, adding, "And tired of ending up on dates in pubs, pretending to like rugby."

Max didn't smile back. He just watched her with an expression she couldn't read. Then he sighed.

Leaning forward, he rested his arms on the table. He gave her his most serious gaze, and his voice did that sexy rumble when he spoke. "Rugby is a great sport, Natasha."

She bit her lip, but she couldn't resist smiling. Her eyes went to his arms, inches from hers, the muscles, the scars. Okay, maybe she liked one thing about rugby. The marks of Max's own years in the sport definitely added to his appeal.

The point was that despite not needing to follow those rules of dating to a T, they'd solidified for her what she was after in a relationship—The Three S's led to the exact *opposite* of the explosive, short-lived flings her mother had.

He reached for her, his fingertips brushing over her cheek. He was so close, and for a moment she was almost sure he was going to kiss her. But then his hand fell away, and he cleared his throat.

"Maybe it's time to set those S's aside for a bit… for a few days on Green Island…and let me help you focus on *my* favorite S, which is much more fun," he said softly. "Maybe you're into me because I *don't* follow any of that dating advice rubbish."

Her face heated, but she leveled her gaze at him. "Who says I'm into you?"

Max threw back his head and laughed. "*I* say you're into me. But I'm very into you, too."

He watched her closely for her reaction as he said those last words. Hell, yes, she was really considering his proposition. The longer the silence drew out, the more the charge between them built. His entire body ached for this woman; he'd wanted this for so long, but there was no way in hell he was going to push it. He had to get this right and she needed to be fully on board.

The heat in her eyes was unmistakable, but lines of uncertainty still creased her forehead. Finally, she sat up in her chair. "I'm not into animal mating videos."

He put up his hands in mock surrender. "Hey, I'm not judging. Everyone's got their thing."

She rolled her eyes, but the worry in her expression was melting.

"I have my things, too," he added, his voice huskier.

Sitting so close, the urge to kiss her was building. Just a taste. Not to sway her, just to test this attraction crackling between them. Slowly, he lifted his hand to trace the line of her jaw, the slope of her neck. Soft, warm breath came faster from her parted lips. She didn't move. Just stared at him with unguarded curiosity. And heat.

Max slid his chair up to hers, and when he got close

enough, he opened his legs around hers. Natasha's gaze moved slowly down his body, openly studying him, chest, biceps, stomach…her eyes flicked down between his legs, and he smiled. She was definitely considering her options.

But none of this would happen tonight. Nothing that could get mixed up in the vulnerability that her disastrous date could have left. Just a hint of what they could have on Green Island. Even if his dick was already ten steps ahead, the eager bastard.

He rested his hand around the back of her neck and leaned forward. His lips brushed against hers. Her breath hitched, and she stilled, so he waited, barely touching. Her mouth was soft and sweet, and goddamn, she smelled good. Like chocolate and strawberries and temptation.

Then she rested a hand on his thigh and shifted forward so their bodies were even closer. She licked her lips, her tongue tracing the seam of her mouth. His dick responded as if that was a handwritten invitation to the party. Still, Max waited. Slowly, she leaned in. Her wet, warm mouth pressed against his, parting a little, catching his top lip first, then his bottom. So he kissed her, tasting more this time, letting his mouth linger on the tangy, seductive flavor of dessert and desire on her lips. So much desire.

A sigh. A ragged breath. Her breasts brushed against his chest, and her hand tightened on his thigh. If she slid it a little higher—no. Not tonight.

Instead Max focused on the kiss. She tilted her head

for a slow, sensual dance with her mouth. He answered, using each stroke of his tongue to show her all the things he could do to her, all the ways he could please her. Then her kisses turned greedy, full of pure, unleashed want, and he groaned and went for more. Plans, even thoughts, faded, and all that was left was Natasha. His hand was tangled in her hair, pulling her closer as he devoured the taste of her. Nothing else existed, just the hot strokes and nips of her kisses.

Her hand moved up his leg, and she took hold of his shirt. His cock was begging to get in on the action. He wanted her up on his lap, straddling him so he could slide his hands under that dress, up her thighs until—no.

Max pulled back, breaking off the kiss. He took a steadying breath. Whoa. That was…intense. She looked a little dazed, and he was feeling about the same.

"I want you, Natasha. Just a couple days in paradise, no strings attached," he whispered. Okay, he wanted more than a couple of days, but that wasn't in the cards for them. Her body had already told him *hell, yes*. Now he just had to convince her mind to listen for once.

Max pressed on. "What do you think? Maybe the rules don't apply in Queensland?"

CHAPTER THREE

OH. MY. GOD.

How had she gone all these years without know-ing the way good kissing made her feel? She had al-ways thought kissing was a bit mundane, but that one had been…different. The experience shouldn't even be called kissing. It was so much more intimate. There had been a moment when the constant commentary in her mind had stopped. Time had stopped. It was…

Ugh, was she waxing poetic about the kisses of Australia's favorite player? Natasha resisted an eye roll. Of course Max was amazing at it. The rumors about him had to be based on some kernel of truth. And if his kisses were that all-consuming, he was definitely a good bet for a few days of relaxation and naked fun.

Maybe he was right; the rules shouldn't apply in the state of Queensland. A few days of no-strings sex with Max Jensen on a secluded tropical island, away from inquiring minds. Yep, she was really consider-ing this fling.

Natasha bit her lip. "What am I agreeing to?"

"You want a preview?"

"You're not going to flash me, are you?" she asked dryly.

Max chuckled. His laugh was infectious. She was trying to keep a straight face, but it was a losing battle. So she smiled, watching him. Damn, she was in so much trouble. But what a relief it would be to stop resisting all that charm, to stop thinking about all the ways it could go wrong and just enjoy Max for a few days. By the end of those few days, perennial playboy Max would be ready to move on, and she would be sexed up enough to get back to real life.

Max's gaze had shifted from amused toward hot.

"I'll be working during the travel portions of the trip, but on the island I'm just there to make sure Alya's not walking around alone. The magazine has its own security measures in place, so I'm mostly just backup support for your sister," he said. "A couple days on an isolated island, and we'll have time alone while Alya is working," said Max in his deep, obscenely sexy voice. Then he waggled his eyebrows. "Plenty of time to look for your favorite kinds of fish sex."

Natasha groaned. "I really think you have the wrong impression about—"

"Sex?" He cut her off, making the word sound obscenely hot with his deep voice. "I doubt it."

His smile faded and his lips parted, the way they had when he was about to kiss her. Damn, she wanted to kiss him again. The kitchen was silent again, the air thick and electric. She played with the half-empty glass on the table in front of her. She could totally do this. A couple days wasn't enough to turn her into a needy, crazy mess, à la her mother, no matter how potent his charm was…right?

She glanced over at Max, who was covering an amused smile with his hand. Like he was already three steps ahead of her, thinking about much dirtier ideas. Like he was planning.

Natasha stood up, and Max's eyes moved slowly up her body like a long, hot lick. The effect echoed in warm rushes of pleasure. And the man wasn't even touching her yet. Somewhere her brain was making its last-ditch warning efforts, but she buried those thoughts. Just a few days. Nothing more.

Max stood up right in front of her, the heat radiating from his body. She had never just stared at him like this. His nose was a little crooked, no doubt from his rugby days, and his eyes had flecks of gray in all that blue. His dark blond hair was tousled and his smile was dark and hungry.

"Hmm… It's worth considering…" she conceded with a little smile.

"No one has to know," he whispered, his words rasping in her ears. "Just you and me and all the dirty things you're dying to try. Is that what you want?"

She bit her lip. He wanted her in a way Wayne never had. And if she were completely honest with herself, which tended not to be a good idea when it came to the topic of men, she was hot for Max in a way she never had been about Wayne.

"There are definitely things I'd want to try with you," she said, her voice coming out husky.

His lips brushed against her neck. "I can think of all kinds of things you might like."

God, so could she. Natasha had actively resisted thoughts about naked Max, but once she let her guard down, the images were right there in X-rated detail. She flashed to the image of him over her, his eyes hungry, his biceps flexing, his thick, hard cock nudging her.

Natasha let out a soft moan and pressed herself flush against him.

"Damn, sweetheart," he groaned, his teeth grazing over her skin. "Tell me what you're thinking about."

She shook her head slowly. No way in hell was she going to describe that scene aloud. It was so…average, so *typical*. She needed to go for something a little more creative than that. Or maybe she needed a new approach to making out with Max.

Natasha smiled a little. "Actually, I'm ready to stop thinking."

She took off her glasses and set them on the table. Then she reached around his neck and coaxed his mouth down to hers. A soft brush of her lips, then another. Oh, my, she was kissing him again, and he tasted good. She dragged her tongue over his bottom lip and bit down. Max froze, and she pulled back. Was that too much?

Then he swore under his breath, and they went from zero to overdrive in an instant. Their mouths collided, his tongue found hers, matching her need, her hunger, stroke by stroke. Natasha gasped in breaths, giving in to the surge of pleasure coursing through her. His mouth teased hers with hungry promises, tempting suggestions of what would come next, if she just let go. So she did it. She let go, losing herself in the warmth of his big, hard body, taking everything she wanted. He backed her up until she was pressed against the heavy kitchen table. She wove her hands into his hair, tugging him closer, searching for that same bliss of their kiss moments before. Oh, yes. She couldn't get enough of him. His hands explored her waist, her hips, as his lips pressed against hers, so hungry.

But now she wanted more than a kiss. She squirmed closer, moving against his hard body, his erection growing and pulsing against her. His fingers flexed on her rear, and she ground her hips into his.

"Goddamn," he muttered. One hand moved lower, slipping under the hem of her dress, a hot, rough caress. His mouth traveled down her jaw, onto the tender skin of her neck, the scrape of his stubble sending erotic jolts through her. His fingers teased higher, higher on the inside of her thigh until he brushed against the silk of her panties.

"*Max.*"

The sound of his name stopped everything in the quiet kitchen. He sucked in a breath and shifted back. Natasha furrowed her brow and looked up at him. Max's eyes were half-closed, clouded with lust. She reached for him again, but he caught her hands and held her back. Another spike of desire burst through her, and her breath caught in the back of her throat. Max's smile was dark and amused.

"Hold on, sweetheart," he said, his breaths unsteady. "I'm way too close to fucking you right here on this table, hard and dirty."

The words—*just words*—made her gasp. Natasha let out a shaky sigh. "I'm not against that idea."

"No way are we starting tonight, when you're coming off an evening with another guy." He brought her hands behind her, so her back arched up toward him. She was heaving in breaths, and Max's gaze drifted down to her chest. His eyes were hot, desperate, and he gave a low laugh. "I am really fucking tempted right now, Natasha. But no test runs. If we're doing this, it can't be anything you could call a mistake."

"I wouldn't regret it, if that's what you're worried about," she said quickly.

Max smiled and shook his head slowly. "I'm nothing like Wayne or any of those other jerkers. I'll make sure you love it."

Just not too much. Just enough to get a little break from the pressures of grant applications, publications and jockeying for coveted academic faculty positions. Natasha was very aware of how fortunate she was, with fewer financial pressures than most researchers since Alya paid for various extravagances that came with a fashion model's life. Still, marine biology was *her* passion, and success in this male-dominated field was short-lived. But to step off that endless cycle of projects, just for a few days of luxurious indulgence on a tropical island with Max…

"Sounds like the holiday of a lifetime," she whispered, pushing away all other thoughts, concentrating on the man in front of her.

Max's breath hitched, and he brushed a soft kiss over her mouth. "I can't wait."

He let her go and straightened out her not-celebration-dinner dress. No way was she going to let Max single-handedly decide how their night ended. If he was going to leave her all hot and bothered, she wasn't going to make it easy for him. Though the enormous bulge in his pants suggested he wasn't any more comfortable than she was. Natasha took a deep breath.

"You drove here, didn't you?" she asked.

"Yes."

She licked her lips and turned to get a glimpse of his expression. "Park outside my window and wait for me."

His eyes widened, and his hands drifted down over her hips. Then he grinned, his lips brushing against hers one more time.

"Wow, when you indulge, you don't just take a bite. You eat the whole goddamn cake."

CHAPTER FOUR

NATASHA LISTENED FOR the front door and headed to her bedroom. Slowly, she walked to the side window. The blinds were half-closed. She lifted one slat to peek at the view. Across from her building was a high-rise of offices, now dark, and most of the cars on the street below were gone. Alya had chosen the apartment building for its central Sydney location and the fact that it had a doorman. Natasha would never be able to afford this flat on the soft money funding for her research and a part-time university lecturer's salary. Her sister, on the other hand, pulled in nice sums based solely on her good looks. But Natasha had long ago stopped expecting the world to be fair.

She lifted another row of the blinds and found Max immediately. The streetlight shone through the window of his black SUV, and from the second floor she could make out his face. He was smiling up at her.

Her phone beeped from across the room, and she grabbed it.

Max: This will be a lot more fun if I can see you.

Oh, right. He could only see bits of her through the tiny rows of blinds. And of course he'd tease her about it.

She took a step back, bumping into her desk. Her well-ordered desk, with only a pen and a blank notepad on top. Her eyes moved over the plain green bedspread of her neatly made bed and her bookshelves, contents organized by size. Not one thing was out of place.

What would it feel like to take a break from being this Natasha for a few days? Logical, orderly Natasha. Max was waiting for her to follow through, and she had two choices: back out or dive face-first into that cake. She smiled.

Natasha: I was just checking to see if you were naked. Didn't want to be the only one.

She sent the message and waited, watching him through the blinds. Max's head turned from his phone to her window, then back to his phone.

Max: I'm calling you out on that one. Don't believe you're naked for a second.

She chuckled.

Natasha: What happens if I really am?

Max's shoulders shook a little. Was he laughing? When he looked up again, he was definitely smiling.

Max: Then I take off my pants and keep them off until I get home.

Natasha: Home = parking space? Or will you walk into your building naked?

Max: Stalling...

He was right. Natasha scanned the view from her window again. Only two lights were on in the office building across from her. No pedestrians in sight. Was she going to expose herself to this Sydney street, just to prove to both Max and herself that she could have a little fun? Yes, she was.

Nothing *typical* about this. Creative? Yes. Though she wasn't sure if the real-life version of this little game of undress would be a turn-on or just nerve-racking. There was only one way to find out.

Natasha kicked off her flats and took a deep breath. She was even dressed for a strip show, with matching bra and panties. Coordinated for the possibility of post-celebration sex. Hmm...a possibility, not a sure thing? That was a little messed up.

How the hell had the evening gotten to this point so quickly? Only a few hours ago, she was sitting on the patio of La Capannina, contemplating getting a jump on her January schedule. Now she was single, on holiday and considering a few days of sexploration on a tropical island. Oh, and she would have had sex with Max right on the kitchen table minutes ago if he hadn't stopped them. Definitely not where she thought tonight was going.

But it was certainly sexier than the night she had planned.

Even Alya, who knew every little detail of her relationship with Wayne, knew nothing about that night she'd almost kissed Max…while her sister slept in the other room. These last moments in the kitchen together were a reminder of why she had been tempted.

Natasha was stalling again. She grabbed the cord to the blinds.

Well, here goes nothing.

Hell, yes. She was actually doing this. She was really going to take off her clothes for him.

Max's cock was already hard as a goalpost. Earlier, he'd been way too close to whipping out the magic wand. This little game she had started was going to push him over the edge soon. And despite having reservations earlier, if she was offering to strip for him on her terms, he wouldn't say no to that.

Natasha turned around, her hands searching for the zipper of the dress. Slowly, she lowered it, down her back and over her beautiful ass. Her dress gaped open, exposing all that warm, soft skin he had wanted to touch back in her kitchen. Max was going to personally thank the architect who had chosen full-length windows in her building. Natasha let her sleeves fall off as she glanced over her shoulder. And smiled. Oh, that smile, just for him. She inched the dress down, shimmying it over her hips until it fell. Leaving her in a see-through bra and panties.

Then she turned around.

Max stared up at Natasha's window as his cock pulsed hard in his pants. His invitation for a few days of fun had been a long shot, and her response had been straight out of his late-night, snake-spanking fantasies. He could still hear her uneven breaths, feel her teeth sink into his lip. His body was alive with the memory of the heat of her skin, the weight of her body against his. And when he'd kissed her back in the kitchen, she had finally let go, like she'd also waited for this moment for years.

Now, she was standing in front of her window in a barely there bra and panties, and those glasses of hers were the perfect addition. Innocent but naughty at the same time, which only made him harder.

Natasha certainly had two sides to her—though she tried hard to hide the second one. Most of the time she was a funny, quirky, confident scientist who chose her path based on logic and careful decision-making to make sure her life stayed in her control. Hell, Max loved this side of her. It was what had made him pay attention that first day she so thoroughly and insightfully turned him down. But it was this side that had kept her with that tosser Wayne. Because the fucker kept everything nice and orderly despite not actually caring for her.

Wayne was probably too self-centered to notice Natasha's other side, the one she seemed to be wary of. One that was curious, tempted. She rarely let anyone see it, but Max was going to give her the chance to explore that part of herself on Green Island. Maybe if he showed her what it felt like to have a man worship her for a few days, she'd avoid assholes like Wayne. And the hurt that came with them.

This peep show was the perfect balance, teetering between both sides of her. Would she go any further? It was questions like this that made his cock ache.

Natasha: You still have your pants on.

Max chuckled.

Max: Bra and panties = naked? Or are you ready to go all the way?

Natasha: Stalling…

Max laughed and looked up at her window. She had her hands on her hips, and her smile was wide. So far, so good. As long as he kept her smiling, she'd play along. He'd have plenty of time to get to the dirtier stuff next week.

Max set his phone in the docking station on his dashboard. He tipped his seat back a bit and unfastened the button of his jeans. Carefully, he lowered the straining zipper. His cowboy leaped out, stretching the material of his boxers, ready for a ride. He slipped the jeans over his hips and pulled them off, along with his socks and shoes. Then he tugged his boxers down, giving him plenty of room for the rodeo.

He looked back up at the window as his hand moved down over his cock. He cupped his balls and moved his hand up again, slowly, over his length, his gaze fixed on Natasha. Her arms fell to her sides as she stared down at him, her mouth parting. How much could she see? Had she ever watched a man get off in front of her? Another idea to file under Things to Try on Green Island.

She raised her hands to her breasts. He closed his fist around his cock and gave himself a hard squeeze. Would she get off in front of him, too?

But no. She was holding up her phone, probably texting him. Max grinned as his phone pinged.

Natasha: I can't see enough. Not a fair exchange.

Before he could think through the idea, he reached for his dashboard to type.

Max: You can come closer.

Silence. Was she considering it? She was still staring down at him.

His imagination kicked into overdrive. His hand was back on his cock as he pictured her walking out the front door of her apartment building and climbing into the seat next to him. She'd still be wearing just a bra and panties and those glasses, because, hey, this was his fantasy. *Can I get a closer look?* she'd say. Yeah, she certainly could. Max was bigger than Wayne in every way, and he'd put money on it that this included cock size. Natasha's eyes would get all doe-eyed wide as she stared at his dick. He'd be ready to come, but he'd make himself wait.

She'd say something like, *Can I touch you?* and—

Max's phone pinged, shaking him out of his fantasy world.

Natasha: Goodnight

He looked up at the window, and she smiled and waved. He smiled back.

Max: I'll be thinking of you. In detail.

Natasha: Same ☺

The shade on her window came down, and Max slumped back into his seat. His cock was begging for attention. How the hell was he going to drive home with a raging hard-on?

He glanced around at the deserted side street. He was a dozen strokes away from coming. Fuck it. He was going all the way. Max grabbed a rag from the glove compartment and smirked. He had thought of a few reasons to put the little towel in the car, but this hadn't been one of them.

Leaning back in his seat, he fast-forwarded through his fantasy until he came to the part where she looked up at him and asked, *Can I taste?* Then she'd lick his tip, swirling her tongue around a few times before her lips closed around him. His balls tightened, and his hand moved hard and fast in a few last strokes. He grabbed the cloth and came hard into it, his hips thrusting. Max gulped in a few breaths of air. Goddamn, this woman wound him up for reasons he didn't even understand.

He glanced at the heap of his jeans next to his seat. The trip to Green Island was going to be interesting, and a hell of a lot of fun.

CHAPTER FIVE

WHEN MAX WALKED into the virtual conference room, the rest of the Blackmore Inc. team was already there. Derek Latu and Simon Rodriguez were sprawled in two of the seats behind the room's half-circle table, and a very real-looking image of Cameron Blackmore, the Sydney team's CEO, was on the large screen against the wall. Cameron's virtual half of the table, projected on the enormous screen on the wall, was from New York. The Sydney office's screen lined up with the New York office's table perfectly to complete a round conference table.

The whole setup had been Jackson McAllister's idea, from when she'd done PR work for the head office. She was the Sydney team's image consultant for a stint before Cam fell for her and chased her back to New York, where he was now working temporarily.

"How's the Big Apple?" asked Derek. "Jackson works, so I know you're not in bed all day."

The rest of the team chuckled.

"Cold as hell. Thank fuck we're leaving soon," said Cameron, smiling. "She's given her notice. We're going to take off for Paris soon. Not that it's any warmer there."

"You're getting on a plane again?" asked Simon. "Does Jackson really know what sitting next to you means?"

Max watched his friend carefully, waiting for the answer. Cameron had managed to keep his fear of flying well hidden from the public, but Max, Derek and Simon knew the lengths he had gone to in order to avoid travel over the years.

"She knows," said Cameron, his expression turning serious. "Let's get this meeting started. Surveillance update, Simon?"

Simon went through the growing list of clients their virtual security department was currently monitoring.

"You sure you're satisfied with more of a desk job going forward?" Cameron asked him. Simon had played a big role in developing this aspect of the team's services in recent months and would continue to oversee it.

"I'm using my degree and getting home for dinner every night," said Simon. "I'm satisfied."

Max let out a laugh and clapped Simon on the back. "We know you are, mate. We know."

Big grins came from Derek and Cameron, and Simon even cracked a smile.

"You're welcome for pushing you to take that job with Marianna," said Cameron.

"I've already thanked you a hundred times, asshole," rumbled Simon, but there was no malice in his voice.

He laced his fingers behind his head. "Sometimes I still can't believe she's here in Sydney with me."

Ever since Simon reunited with his first love when she came from Miami seeking protection, Max had seen a different side of his formerly stoic friend. The woman who'd been off-limits to Simon growing up was now his fiancée, and he actually looked…content. Derek had been married for a while, but now, Cameron and Simon head-over-ass in love?

That brand of happiness baffled Max. Sure, he could understand the appeal of having someone in his bed every night, but there were so many pressures that could wreak havoc on two people caught in a sex-induced haze. Life had a way of steering relationships south—as in Antarctic south—at least for the Jensen family. When his mother was still alive, the media storms surrounding his parents had pushed them to retreat to Western Australia permanently, and his brother…well, TJ was a lot like their father, and he just seemed to shut that part of his life off.

"Moving on," said Cameron. "Reconnaissance on the world summit in three weeks?"

Derek gave a run-down on his team's schedule, adding, "We've booked the final security walk-throughs and client meeting after Max returns from Green Island."

"I'll be back on Monday," said Max. "Henning is covering me and keeping an eye on Alya's ex-boyfriend's movements from the office."

Cameron frowned a little. "You sure you want to go on this job?"

"Why the hell wouldn't I want to?" he asked with a smirk. "Low-risk trip to a tropical paradise."

Natasha would be there for some bedroom paradise, too. Or maybe she liked it outdoors? He couldn't dream of more ideal workplace conditions if he tried.

The conference room was silent, and Max shook himself out of his wandering thoughts. He looked around the room slowly. All three men were watching him, and no one else was smiling. Derek rested his hand on Max's shoulder. "The Jensen Family Foundation dinner won't be easy next weekend. And you've got a lot of changes coming."

Max scowled. Goddamn, this was the last thing he wanted to think about right now. He had spent every day since he was eighteen making sure his family bullshit didn't run his life. There was no way he was going to start down that path now.

Which was why he'd continue to work for Blackmore Inc. for the foreseeable future. Of course, he'd need to dedicate a good chunk of his free time to fundraising, charity events and other activities for the foundation. At some point, he might even need to cut back a little on the number of assignments he took. But Max would never quit. He'd always want to keep this part of his life, where he'd earned his position on skills alone.

"It's not a problem," he said roughly.

"Someone else could go with Alya," said Derek.

Max frowned. "I dealt with my shit last year when my mother died, and I'll deal with it again next week. A few days on the beach won't change that."

The last thing Max wanted was to move back into the Jensen family world, where his easygoing nature didn't fit with his family's rigidity and stoicism. Where his every move was measured against his father's and grandfather's legacy. But his very last promise to his mother was that he'd take this position if his father asked, if her death was too much for him.

Frankly, when Max agreed, he hadn't actually expected that request to ever come, considering his father's well-established will of steel and unwillingness to show a hint of vulnerability. Yeah, his father had loved his mother, though he was more the taker than the giver in that relationship. Ironic that it took his mother's death to bend his father's will—when it was too late for her to appreciate it.

There were other issues that would come up when he headed the family foundation. Stepping into the Jensen family spotlight had the potential to play out just like his admission to Princeton. After years of falling short of family expectations, Max's father couldn't trust him to find a university that would take him on his own merits, so he had sweetened the deal behind Max's back. Price tag: a new graduate library with the Jensen name on it. That way, every single person who set foot on that campus knew Max didn't earn his place in the freshman class. The fact that his admission had cost a whole fucking library spoke for itself.

His father's vote of no confidence had made him doubt himself. Never, ever again. If Max had to take on everything that went with being president of the

Jensen Family Foundation, he would do it on his own terms. His mother's other hope—that Max and his father would finally reconcile—had been left unspoken. Even in her last weeks, his mother had known better than to ask for that.

But enough of that shit. For the next few days, he could concentrate on a job he had earned on merit and some downtime on an isolated island. Warm water, warm beaches, hot woman…

"Yeah, I can see why you don't want to give up an assignment like that," said Derek, stopping Max's schlong thoughts before they got any further.

Cameron smirked. "I'm sure there will be plenty of attractions for you to enjoy."

Max gave them all a smile, letting his reputation work to his advantage here. He certainly wasn't going to tell them that there was only one attraction on Green Island he was interested in. And he was finally getting private admission.

CHAPTER SIX

THE YACHT SLOWLY approached the Green Island dock, skimming through calm, cerulean waters. The ocean breeze blew through Natasha's hair, but it barely helped. It was hot as hell up in North Queensland, even out on the water in the shade of the boat's canopy. A bead of sweat trickled down her neck and disappeared into her tank top.

The engine cut, leaving only the sounds of water splashing against the sides of the boat and Natasha's own breaths. How had she never made this trip before? She had been meaning to come to the Great Barrier Reef since she and Alya moved to Australia three years ago, but she had familiar research sites on the Hawaiian reefs, so it was much easier to start experiments there. And Green Island wasn't cheap, so she couldn't just pop up here for an extended weekend.

The captain tied up the boat as Natasha tore her eyes from the green-blue waters and gazed at the little island. White sand, palm trees, just big enough to explore, small enough to feel remote, like nothing from the mainland could touch her. Paradise, for sure. It was no wonder *Tropical Bliss* was shooting their new branding campaign here.

The white beach that stretched along the shore of the island was empty of people, but as they pulled in she spotted a colorful row of beached kayaks, a sign that a resort lay somewhere in the tangle of palms. Max had timed their arrival ahead of the first ferry from Cairns. They'd stayed in the ocean-side city after flying from Sydney last night. It was early to be up on a Saturday but it was worth it. The day tourists weren't here, so the island was quiet, with only the resort staff and the other fashion shoot folks who had flown in. They had made it through the trip without even a hint of Alya's ex, as expected. Natasha let out a deep breath and glanced at Alya. Her sister leaned over the deck rail next to her, bundled in gauzy swathes of wraps and scarves, topped with a wide-brimmed hat. The only signs of stress were in her hands, fidgeting with the strap of her handbag.

Natasha brushed her fingers over her sister's. "It's official. We can relax now."

"I'm working on it," Alya said, the corners of her mouth turning up. "Max was right about this place. I can't see any way we could be caught unawares on this island."

Natasha said gently, "I'm sorry you have to think about this stuff in such detail."

Her sister sighed, her shoulders sinking a little. "It's probably time I stopped worrying so much, but I can't bring myself to just yet."

Nick Bancroft was the asshole responsible for that.

He'd used his charm, money and power to attain anything he wanted, and at one point that had been her big sister. Nick apparently believed that women didn't break up with him—that honor he reserved for himself—and his exes certainly didn't flee in the middle of the night.

That move had earned Alya some very unsettling threats. The restraining order on Nick had been so much harder to get than it should have been, and for a while, Natasha had begun to suspect what Alya believed from the beginning: that Nick Bancroft's influence kept him above the law. His obsessive and erratic behavior had resulted in their leaving Los Angeles and necessitated a security boost when Alya restarted her career on the other side of the world.

But Blackmore Inc. had influence, too, and in the end, money couldn't buy everything. Thank God. Now calls and surprise visits to Alya's workplace were violations of the court order, and even Nick couldn't talk his way around that. No more claiming that each encounter was a mistake or misunderstanding. Whatever Blackmore Inc. had done since their move to get Nick to back off, it had worked.

Despite the fact that Natasha had left behind her former academic community in California, she didn't regret moving here with her sister. They'd lived on a few different continents growing up—including Australia once. Home was wherever Alya was. That would never change.

"Blackmore Inc. has been a big help to me in moving past what happened in LA," said Alya. "And Max is here all weekend."

Natasha suspected the reassurance was as much for her benefit as for Alya's. Her sister still felt terrible about getting Natasha caught up in the mess with Nick. But she didn't mind that Max came along on various trips and events. Not at all.

Natasha took off her sunglasses and looked at her sister. "New rule. No Nick talk on Green Island."

Alya laughed. "You're right. New topic."

Natasha wiped her brow. Damn, she couldn't wait to get in the water. "Do these cabins have air-conditioning?"

"I hope so." Alya searched through her handbag and pulled out a brochure.

Her sister skimmed the little booklet while Natasha's interest wandered up to where Max was helping the captain unload their bags onto the dock. He was working, so she was free to gawk at him while he paid absolutely no attention to her. He was dressed in all black, his biceps stretching at the sleeves of his T-shirt, all muscles and tanned skin, and his thighs were outlined in his jeans. He had worn a blank expression on his face for most of the day, like he was immune to the sweltering heat and the amazing scenery, but as he'd climbed off the boat—giving her a nice view of his ass—he looked a little more relaxed. One step closer to the Max who had kissed her and then watched her strip through her bedroom window.

Most of the time, he exuded the kind of charm that echoed her mother's high-end world. Even without knowing the details of his background, it was clear Max came from money, both from the ease with which he moved through the functions he attended with Alya and from the implied confidence it took to reject that world. He, unlike most people, would always get a second chance. He had that in common with Nick, though somehow privilege didn't have the same asshole effects on Max.

But as soon as there was any hint of a threat, she got a glimpse of another side of him. Underneath his easygoing exterior was a man with laser-sharp focus and an iron will. Maybe this was the appeal of the high-end security business...because Lord knew he didn't need the money. One look at the tabloids—yeah, she occasionally peeked—suggested that Max took nothing seriously, but his résumé was filled with accomplishments that suggested the exact opposite.

Natasha had barely had to cyber-snoop to learn his story. Early years working for his family's ranching empire, graduating from Princeton with honors, starting position on a professional rugby team, principal at Blackmore Inc., the top security firm in the country—all accomplishments that couldn't be bought.

She admired his *fuck you* attitude toward all the expectations for perfection that she herself had buckled under.

"They have—" Alya looked up from her brochure, and her voice cut off. Natasha snapped her gaze away from Max and looked where her sister was pointing, but not quickly enough. Alya's mouth curved into a slow smiled.

"Soooo…" Her sister drew out the word suggestively. "Max."

"What about him?"

Alya wasn't deterred. Her smile grew as she waited. Okay, so it wasn't the first time her sister had caught her ogling Max, but like Natasha, Alya had also weathered enough of her mother's obsessive relationships to not mistake the stormy throes of lust for intimacy. Her mother's string of husbands had thrown the three Petrova women's lives into turmoil, moved them all over the globe, only to come to a calamitous end each time when the next budding starlet turned the man's head. Natasha didn't have to explain why Max was very bad news.

She sighed. "Max is the cotton candy of men."

Alya snorted. "Pink and fluffy?"

They both turned for a good look. The only hint of Max's more playful side right now was the dark blond hair that curled at the base of his neck. He stood, legs spread, in the middle of the dock waiting for them, his arms crossed. His mouth betrayed no hints of a smile, and his eyes were hidden behind dark glasses.

Nope, nothing pink and fluffy about him at all. Alya turned back and gave her a mischievous smile.

"Not exactly," said Natasha. "I was thinking light and delicious but bad for my health. There's a reason they only sell cotton candy at festivals. It's not for everyday consumption."

Alya tilted her head a little. Natasha couldn't read

her sister's expression behind those sunglasses, but she was pretty sure Alya was weighing just how far to push this discussion.

"I thought that while you're on holiday this week, you were easing up on all that pressure you put on yourself."

"I am," said Natasha. "And it's not pressure. It's sanity planning."

"But maybe it's festival time." Her sister's words were laced with amusement. She gestured out at the sparkling green ocean. "Just saying. A couple days of fun and escape, right?"

Natasha chuckled. "Mmm…maybe."

She wasn't ready to share her sexploration plans with Alya yet. Her sister made hooking up with Max sound so easy, so uncomplicated, but she couldn't for one moment forget the limits. The man was serious eye candy, and now Natasha was joining the ranks of women who would get a taste. One of many. She'd be offended for him if he gave any indication that he minded. Which was what made this time-limited plan work: clear boundaries.

Her sister took one last look at the brochure she was holding and stuffed it back into her handbag.

"The whole crew from the magazine is scheduled for a planning meeting this morning," said Alya. "Before too many boats come with the day tourists from Cairns, you'll have the reef to yourself to explore. You can try out your new bikini."

Natasha laughed. "I can't believe you bought that thing for me."

"What do you mean? You look fantastic in it." Her sister lowered her sunglasses and gave her a playful glare. "If I had those boobs, I wouldn't hide them."

Natasha rolled her eyes. "One loose string and there's no hiding anything. One of many reasons I'll be wearing a dive suit over it."

The captain called them over to the ladder and helped them out of the boat. Natasha grabbed the handle of her suitcase and pulled it over the uneven boards of the long dock that stretched out in front of her. The morning sun blazed down on her head, and she searched in her bag for something to cover up with.

"Looking for one of these?" her sister asked, pulling an extra sunhat out of her handbag and passing it to Natasha. "I'm so glad you came. We don't travel together as often anymore."

Natasha plopped the hat on her head. "Why didn't you invite Stewart? You could've taken the chance to get away as a couple."

Alya frowned. "I'm just not into him the way I should be. I'm starting to think I'm using him as a crutch, for comfort. Which is pretty harsh. For a little while, I actually considered taking this trip alone. No security." Natasha's steps slowed. Though she wanted her sister to feel unafraid, to go around without a bodyguard, that meant Max would disappear out of their lives. Out of her life. Natasha's gut gave an uncomfortable twist, and she frowned. She was getting way too many steps ahead.

Come on, brain. You're capable of a holiday, right?

* * *

The bright yellow ring around Natasha's snorkel peeked up above the calm waters, and her body skimmed the shimmering surface. Max watched her from the shade, leaning back, the sand warm under his fingers. The sun was high, and the last ferries were shuttling day tourists back to Cairns. The long jetty was mostly empty. Every other guest was on the other side of the island for the photoshoot. Only Natasha was in the water.

How long had he been sitting here, drifting in this sexual purgatory, watching her? Hard to tell, but after a long day, he couldn't think of a better way to unwind. Max had joined Alya for the two-hour planning meeting at the private resort they were staying at, which the magazine had fully booked. Now Alya had a couple hours of…well, the photographer had called it "walking through the concept with the stylist," whatever that meant. If he and Natasha were going to get down to business, now was the time. But an unfamiliar calm was spreading through him, and he wasn't quite sure what to make of it. Yes, the usual hot-naked-woman-in-his-near-future hum was going on, but for now, he was content to just sit back and watch. For now, that was enough. Strange.

Natasha dove under the rope of buoys that marked off the no-boat zone, then popped back up with a little spray of water from her snorkel. She was swimming straight for him, past the edge of the reef, to where the bottom turned white. Max brushed the sand from his hands and stood up. He wandered down the beach, the sun sparkling over the gentle waves. And from the middle of all this glimmer, Natasha emerged out of the water.

She stood up and lifted her mask. And, fuck, she looked good. The wet suit she wore hugged the curves of her hips, narrowing at the waist and filling out again over her breasts. She looked like a superheroine fantasy, the X-rated version—why the hell didn't someone make those kinds of movies? Max smiled. Natasha would definitely star in his own version of one of them.

She was twisting the water out of her long hair when she first caught sight of him. Her movements slowed, and her face lit up in an unguarded smile, like he was the most fascinating thing on the whole Great Barrier Reef. More enticing than fish. And it felt good.

"Hey, Max," she called. She glanced up and down the beach then toward the mainland. "How long have I been out?"

"Awhile. The magazine crew is on the other side of the island."

"I see." She was closer now, and her movements slowed as she met his gaze. Was she making the same calculations he'd made the minute he left Alya? He glanced down at his watch. Still plenty of time for fun.

Natasha bent down and pulled off her flippers, then she reached behind her back to unzip her wet suit. She peeled it down, revealing her shoulders, her arms…her tits. Fuck, yes, she was beautiful. The bikini was one of those barely there things that gave a perfect view of the plump roundness of her breasts on both sides. She pulled the wet suit down to her hips and let it hang there as she started for the shore. Water ran down her body, over her bare stomach, down her arms. Her pale skin glistened in the late-afternoon sun.

Max's dick twitched. Oh, yeah, he was finally, finally going to get a chance with this woman. Though staring at her chest wasn't really his A game for seduction. Max shoved his hands in his pockets and forced his gaze upward.

"See any fish sex while you were out?" he asked.

Natasha smiled. "Wouldn't you like to know?"

She strode up the shore, her gear in both hands.

"I would," he said. It was true. He was hoping to figure out what her area of expertise was all about. "Maybe you could take me out, show me around a bit."

She stopped right in front of him, staring at him with those gray eyes that sparkled with flecks of gold. A little crease formed between her eyebrows. Like she wasn't sure what to make of his suggestion.

"Seriously," he said. "I'd love for you to point out some of the creatures."

They stood, facing each other, close enough to touch. Her eyes had a hazy glow to them in the sunlight. He let his gaze wander down, pausing on her parted lips, on the tender hollow at the base of her neck where drips of water caught. Her hair settled in glossy ropes over her shoulders. There were so many places he wanted to kiss her right now.

Max leaned forward and brushed his lips against her cheek. "You look hot in that wet suit, by the way," he said, smiling. He tapped the mask in her hand. "Can I borrow that for a minute and get a peek under water?"

She didn't answer right away, just tilted her head to the side, taking him in. Finally, she gave him a little smile. "It would be more fun if you go get your own and we can look together."

"I just need a peek. I don't have one of these," he said, giving her wet suit a little tug, pulling her closer. If he leaned forward just a little...

She shook her head. "You won't need one. I just wore a wet suit to protect me from getting hurt on the reef, but we won't be diving. We'll stay on the surface just right around here." She gestured to the reef right along the shore.

He ran through that idea. Back in Natasha's apartment she had mentioned some shark she wanted to see that was common in this area. They wouldn't be seeing one of those today, would they? Not that he couldn't handle it, of course. He had surfed for years, which meant he had likely been close to a shark or two at some point, but Max much preferred going about his business without actually coming face-to-face with them. Hell, that went for plenty of things in life. The less he thought about some shit, the better. Though, next week, he'd be forced to change that approach. But not yet. He still had a couple of days on a beautiful tropical island before his life turned into something he no longer steered himself.

Back to the current issue.

"Any chance of seeing that shark you were talking about before?" he asked, keeping his voice casual.

Natasha shook her head. "I didn't see any over here. I think we have a better chance on the other side of the island, but you'd need a wet suit for that area."

"No worries." Max shrugged, like looking for the best area to swim with sharks was a regular topic of casual conversation. For Natasha, it probably was.

"There's a basket with water gear outside our cabin," she said. It gave him a small thrill that he and Natasha were staying in the same suite—of course, that was standard when he travelled with Alya, but still… "If you go get a mask and snorkel, we can have a quick look around."

Reluctantly, very reluctantly, he let go of her wet suit.

"Don't swim off on me, Aquawoman," he said, wagging his finger at her.

Natasha laughed and tossed her flippers onto the sand.

Max jogged through the forest along the boardwalk, turning off to the secluded area where a smattering of two-story beach cabins formed a circle around a swimming pool. He found the basket, dug out a mask and snorkel, and headed back to the beach.

She was sitting at the edge of the water, her wet suit still around her waist. Max walked along the shore toward her, where the water had cooled the sand. Natasha was looking the opposite way, out at the open ocean, her hair in a long mermaid tangle down her back, her curves on full display.

This woman was amazing. The tropical heat must have messed with his brain, because instead of steering them into the bedroom, where he could've been tasting and teasing that beautiful body, he had suggested getting back in the water.

Max slowed as he approached her. Natasha's arms were wrapped loosely around her knees, and her eyes were closed. She had left her flippers farther up the beach, by the trees, and her mask dangled from her hand. She looked so…relaxed. She never looked like this in Sydney.

He had been all for the idea of her coming along to Green Island for selfish reasons, of course. But looking at her now, just sitting with her feet in the ocean and the late afternoon sun on her face, he could feel her relief. Alya had been right to push her to come.

Max snuck up behind her, slowing as he approached, and tickled her under her arms. She laughed, squirming away.

"Not cool," she said, but she was smiling.

He sat down beside her so their knees just touched. He put on his mask and fitted the snorkel into his mouth.

"Ready," he said, the tube garbling his voice.

She sized him up. "You do know how to swim, right?"

He pulled the snorkel out of his mouth and gave her the best seductive smile he could manage with the mask pressing on the top half of his face. "Is this where my bad jokes about mouth-to-mouth come in? I have a few."

"Of course you do," Natasha said with a wry laugh. "I just want to know what I'm getting into. Do we need life jackets?"

He rubbed his chin, pretending to think. "I usually take a flotation device with me when I swim." She gave him a questioning look, so he let her think on that for just a moment longer before he added, "My surfboard."

She shook her head slowly, but her eyes sparkled with amusement. As he tried to rise, she shoved him a little so that he toppled over into the sand.

"Okay, hotshot," she said standing up. "Let's get in the water."

Natasha stood up and shimmied back into the top of her wet suit. Damn that was a nice visual, even if the process was going in the wrong direction. Max brushed the sand off his arms and stood up. Natasha fumbled behind her back for the long zipper strap, so he took a step closer and covered her hand with his.

"Let me get that for you," he said softly.

She stopped midreach, as his fingers brushed over her wrist. Then she lowered her hand.

He had never talked a woman into covering up before—it usually went the other way. But everything about her was different. He tucked in the material under the zipper, running his fingers up her warm skin. The sun was hot, but she shivered under his touch. Slowly, he pulled up the zipper and fastened the Velcro strap behind her neck.

He was so close to her, and the temptation to change his mind, to head back to the cabin right away, was strong. But that would come soon. Instead, he pressed his lips against her neck.

"Ready when you are," he whispered.

She laughed. "I'm sure you are."

Natasha started into the water, bending down to dip her mask and rinse it out.

"Make sure you drag your feet when you walk around here," she said. "The stingrays will move to avoid you as long as they know you're coming. You don't want to step on them."

Max's heart jumped at the word *stingray*. Of course, he knew there were occasional run-ins with these creatures, just like with the sharks, but he wasn't keen for a direct encounter.

"You mean the same kind of stingray that killed the crocodile bloke with a strike to the chest?" he asked. "What was his name?"

"Steve Irwin. And yes, that kind."

"Just checking."

Natasha didn't look bothered in the least bit, so neither was he. But, just to be safe, he followed her path. Tailing her gave him a nice view of her ass, too. They waded out, the sandy bottom massaging Max's feet, until they reached the edge of the reef. Natasha strapped on her mask and fitted her lips around the mouthpiece of her snorkel. Then she looked over at him.

"Let's go." Her voice was muffled, but she still managed to be sexy as hell. She lowered herself into the water and headed out into the endless ocean.

The water was balmy as he followed her out, warmer than the beaches back in Sydney where he and Simon surfed. And without the wind and waves, the water was a hell of a lot clearer. Which meant that instead of sitting on his board in blissful ignorance, he was about to get a close-up view of whatever was lingering just below him.

He sank into the water and looked around. Holy hell, it was amazing. There were fish everywhere, hundreds or even thousands, all in different shapes and colors that were brighter than what looked natural. Some kinds seemed to stick together in a formation, and others weren't team players. Like the long, red, snake-like thing with black and white spots that slithered by him. It looked like it could be poisonous, though it was currently minding its own business.

There seemed to be some sort of scrum action going on over to the left, and Natasha turned, swimming straight for it. But as they approached, the free-for-all broke up, leaving a maze of coral that looked like radioactive cauliflower. The bright blue sea stars he could identify, and those purple spiny creatures, well, he'd probably recognize their name if someone said it. But there was so much more. Like a clam thing that opened to reveal layers of deep pink petals that rippled inside. A few dirty jokes that would make Natasha smile came to mind, but they kept going.

She pointed to fish hiding in crevices or inside other marine life, and at one point, she stopped moving altogether to let a school of tiny, iridescent fish swim by. Slowly, she led them in a half-circle, making their way around the shallower spots on the reef until they were back at the edge of it, where the sandy bottom began.

Max stood up and lifted off his mask, and Natasha did the same. Then she turned to him and smiled.

And right there, Max's heart gave a mighty thump. The happiness on her was breathtaking. Water ran down her beautiful cheeks and the mask had left imprints all around her eyes. She looked glorious. Alive.

Why couldn't life be like this moment more often? He already knew there was no good answer to that. Beautiful moments had a way of coming then disappearing forever, so he swallowed and smiled back at her.

CHAPTER SEVEN

MAX SHOOK OUT his hair, water spraying off him like a shaggy dog as they headed up the beach.

"Now that was fun," he said. "And we didn't even get undressed."

Her smile widened. Okay, *this* was the Max she knew. She'd caught a glimpse of who he was under all that charm in the water, and the pure pleasure while exploring the reef was a new side of him. But he was still Max. Of course he was thinking about sex. "Do we still have time for that, too?" she asked.

He stretched his hands over his head, his arm muscles flexing. "Not sure. But I am definitely up for giving it a try."

He gave her body a slow, appreciative perusal, his gaze lingering on her breasts, which were currently being squeezed and flattened by her wet suit. But he didn't seem to be picky in this area.

"I didn't see any mating," he said conversationally. "Now I'm curious. How do they do it?"

She waved off his question with her hand. "It's really not very sexy. But I'm sure you can find videos."

"Hmm...videos." He grinned. "Thanks for the tour," he said, more seriously. "I loved it."

"You're welcome." She met his gaze, and the electric pull between them sizzled.

"What do you want to do next?" His voice came out lower, softer, leaving no question about what kind of plans he'd like to make.

A slow smile spread across her lips. "Go back to the cabin. Take off my wet suit. Get into the shower."

"You want any help with any of that?" he asked with mock seriousness. "Since I helped you zip up, I figured it only fair that I offer unzipping services, too."

She chuckled. "Very generous of you."

He took a step closer, and her laughter faded. Another step and her breath was a quick, sharp inhale. The sun sparkled through the drops of water on his eyelashes. Like he was magic.

Max leaned into her, his mouth close to her ear. "I'll start by carrying your gear."

Natasha bit her lip, but she couldn't hold back her smile. She had meant to get in the water for a bit, to enjoy the reef while no one else was splashing around. The cloudless days were perfect for diving, and she had lost track of time...until Max joined her. It felt good sharing her time in the water with him. Refreshing, actually.

Now, miracle of all miracles, fish were no longer the first thing on her mind. If she wanted to get this sex-ploration started, this was her window of opportunity. The heavy heat in Max's gaze, the way he leaned in, his mouth grazing her skin, suggested he was thinking exactly the same thing.

His hair was wet against her cheek as he nuzzled her neck. He smelled the ocean, of adventure, of temptation. Of Max. Natasha let out a soft sigh. Finally.

Though his hands were occupied with her gear, hers were free to explore, so she rested them on the hard muscles of his arms, exploring the planes and bulges with her fingers. There was so much she wanted to discover about him. She moved her hands higher, over his shoulders. Water dripped from his hair and ran down his neck. She traced one of the trails, first with her finger, and then with her mouth. His husky breaths came quicker in her ear. Just this little taste was getting her hot really, really fast.

Max lifted his head and met her gaze, his eyes heavy with desire.

God, he was breathtaking. If she were to select a match solely on baser characteristics like strength or sexual appeal, Max would be at the top of her list. Golden-blond hair hanging over his tanned forehead. Pronounced cheekbones, chiseled jaw. Her gear wasn't heavy, but his biceps flexed under the weight. She flashed to the image of those biceps flexing as he held himself over her.

"Back to the cabin?" she asked, her voice breathless.

"Definitely."

He gave her a soft kiss on her forehead and headed for the path, away from the beach. Natasha swallowed, her heart pounding, as she watched him.

Thank God Social Darwinism had long been debunked. Survival of the fittest didn't apply to everyday situations, and there was more to life than finding someone to get her pregnant and protect their offspring. She knew better than to choose a man based on physical prowess alone, and in case she was temporarily stunned by Max's blinding appeal, lured in by the promise of virility, birth control would save her from the pitfalls of sex with such an obvious winner.

But for now, none of that mattered. Time to put her analytical mind on pause and concentrate on her senses. Starting with touch.

Max took a few steps up the beach and then turned back toward her. He tipped his head to the side a bit. "You coming?"

Right. She had slowed to a stop and was just staring at him. Probably drooling.

"Just ogling you," she said, flashing him a smile.

Max laughed. "Then let's move faster."

Crunch. *Thump, thump.* Crunch. *Thump, thump.*

Each footstep in the coral sand cut through the pounding of her heart in her ears. Each footstep took her closer to the little cabin where she would finally discover what sex with Max Jensen was like. The thought was making her giddy.

He stepped aside to let her pass when they reached the boardwalk to the cabins.

"My turn to ogle," he whispered as she slipped past him.

The sultry air between them shifted. He walked close

behind her, close enough for his breaths to brush over her skin. She glanced over her shoulder, and he was no longer smiling.

What would this be like? These days were supposed to be about exploring her fantasies, things she might never explore again, but right now, all she could think of was one thing. Max naked. That alone was her fantasy.

The resort's pool area was still and empty. The palm trees rustled between the clusters of little white modern wooden cabins. Everything else was quiet, the pool in the center of the resort's little self-contained suites undisturbed. No one was here, and the erotic sound of Max's breaths rang in her ears. He wasn't touching her, but she was hyper-aware of him, so close behind.

Max dropped her flippers and mask in the basket, and she shimmied out of the bottom half of her wet suit. He leaned against the wall next to the door, his hands in his pockets. When she lifted her gaze to his, he flashed her a smile.

"Don't mind me," he said, his voice lazy and sensual as his gaze wandered down her body. "Just enjoying the afternoon view."

"Good to know," she said with a laugh.

Getting out of a wet suit wasn't the most graceful process, so she shut out Max's stare and concentrated on not falling over. Natasha tugged the last leg of the suit over her ankle and headed for the outdoor showers to rinse off. Max was impossible to ignore completely, so she took her time, letting the water cool her body. She had spent plenty of evenings sneaking glimpses at him over the years. He could be the one who stared this time.

She dried off with one of the towels stacked near the pool, hung up her wet suit and returned to the door of their cabin. "Ready?"

He gave a little nod and pushed off the building. The door clicked open, but he waited for her to enter. She wiped her feet on the rug just inside, and the door closed. Her breaths were coming faster, and a shiver ran through her that had nothing to do with being cold. This was it.

Slowly, Natasha raised her gaze. Max peeled off his sunglasses and laid them on the foyer table, but his eyes never left hers. He was staring at her with a kind of raw hunger that was new, different. He took a step toward her, a hot, intense fire alive inside his sky-blue eyes.

His hand was warm as he brushed it over her cheek and ran his thumb along her lips. His thumb moved lower, down her throat, over her collar bone. She was still wet, and his fingers glided over her skin, through the paths of water. He traced the edges of her bikini, slipping his fingers under the material. Natasha sucked in a breath. Her fingers trembled as she reached up to touch the smooth ridges of his stomach. He let out a soft groan.

"Let's move to my bedroom." His voice, smooth and deep, his gaze and his smile were all a trifecta of sexiness that hit her deep in the gut. It was no wonder that women fell all over themselves to get his attention.

She cleared her throat, trying to ignore the heart-stopping intimacy that was building around them. "Ready for some experimentation?"

Max nodded. "Always."

She followed him into his room and he threw a towel on the bed before sitting.

"You have any specific plans for us?" he asked.

Natasha sat down next to him, and he scooted closer. She cleared her throat, trying to concentrate. "How much time do you need for recovery?"

He raised his eyebrows. "You mean between rounds of sex?"

"Yes."

She was almost sure he was fighting a smile. "You know, I've never actually timed it."

He rested his hand on her thigh, caressing with slow explorations. Her eyes fluttered closed. His touch was warm, and her breath caught with each new movement.

"It varies," he continued, his voice a little rougher. "But I'm pretty sure it won't be long today." His smile was infectious, and she found herself smiling back.

"I'm just trying to get a sense of how much we have time for," she said, fighting to keep her voice even. Natasha took a steadying breath. This was indulgence with an expiration date. No danger in that. That sexy grin played on his lips again. Indulgence, personified.

"What exactly do you plan to do with me?" he asked slowly, his voice full of amusement. "What do you like?"

She shrugged and gave him a mischievous smile. "I'm not sure where to start."

He was probably looking for a more specific answer than *whatever gives me an orgasm*. Truthfully, she wasn't exactly sure what her full range of options were. That was why she was sitting here, across from the world's hottest guy, ready to get the sexploring started, to figure that out.

He shook his head slowly. "Tell me. I want details."

She bit her lip. "You go first. What do you like?"

Max's eyes were heavy with desire, and he smiled as he ticked off items on his long fingers. "I'd like blow jobs, going down on you and fucking you from behind, to begin with. Your turn."

The scenes Max alluded to rushed through her mind. Max's mouth between her legs. Or sucking him off. Or her on her hands and knees, looking over her shoulder as Max guided his cock into her. Yep, she liked those ideas.

She gave him a quick smile. "I like oral sex, too. I could definitely use your help on my technique, considering the fact Wayne turned down my blow job in favor of extra sleep."

Max's expression darkened. "I can't believe that had anything to do with you."

She blinked a couple times at his reaction. He sounded almost…angry. It happened so rarely that she wasn't sure what to do with it.

"It's okay," she said. "I'm over it."

Mostly.

Max took a long breath. "Natasha, you're incredible. Any guy who doesn't make you feel that way has no business being with you."

His eyes were bright and intense, and he looked so serious. The intimacy of his stare was doing crazy things to her heartbeat.

Natasha cleared her throat. "Have you ever done it in public?" *What the hell, Nat?* She'd scrambled to find a different subject and—well, she'd done that.

Natasha glanced up at Max. His eyes were wide.

"Goddamn," he said, shaking his head. "You're skipping the minor leagues and going straight for the championship game, aren't you?"

"Just because I'm not all…" she waved her hand in the air, searching for the right words "…out there doesn't mean I'm an innocent young thing. Seriously, growing up as Illana Petrova's daughter introduced me to plenty of things I couldn't unsee." She grimaced. Plenty of things. Including walking in on her mother's boyfriend fucking a much younger starlet on an empty film set one day. That had been followed by a lesson on how easy it was to get swept up in sex or fame with a man and mistake that for something deeper when he wasn't on the same page. Yeah, Natasha had had enough crazy to last her a lifetime.

Max was scowling now. Shit. How had they gotten into this territory so quickly?

"Look, I didn't mean for this to get all…" She paused. "Personal and talky. Let's move on."

Max looked a lot less relaxed now. He had stilled, and he was watching her, his expression much darker and, well, very un-Max-ish.

Natasha looked at her clock. "We only have one

hour and nineteen minutes left before Alya's shoot is over."

He nodded slowly, but he still didn't move. Where the hell was the man who took nothing seriously? Suddenly, the way they were sitting, every part of this, felt way too personal. Natasha bit her lip.

"Let's get started," she said quickly. "But I have a rule—no wasting sex time on the past."

Finally, a smile tugged at the corners of his mouth. "Fine. But I reserve the right to make rules, too."

CHAPTER EIGHT

"HEY," YELLED NATASHA, laughing as he grabbed her bare waist. "What are you doing?"

Max lifted her and rolled her on top of him as he fell back onto the bed. Natasha came down onto his chest, her warm, soft skin against his. He let out a little groan.

She squirmed, so he wrapped his hand around her ass and held her against him. Damn, she looked sexy as fuck right now, pressing down on him. She was trying to school her mouth into a serious line, but her eyes were alive with amusement. Laughter bubbled inside him as Max held her in place. Of course, his dick was loving this, too.

"Is this your idea of foreplay? Capturing me and not letting me go?" she asked breathlessly. Her voice was husky and low, suggesting that it was *her* idea of foreplay. Hell, just about everything with her felt like foreplay, but that wasn't why he'd done it.

"Maybe. We've all got our things, right?" He winked. "Or maybe I just wanted to make you laugh."

Her smile broke through, warm and happy, and her

whole body melted against his. "Success," she said softly.

Her elbows were by his sides, and she explored his chest with her fingertips. She sighed, as if she was perfectly content like this, mostly naked and on top of him. He certainly was.

Max gazed up at her. Back in Sydney, she had been clear that good sex was what she was after. But after listening to the comments about her ex-boyfriend and her mother, he had to wonder if this setup was a little more complicated for her.

He'd seen the moment the discussion got personal. If she didn't want to spill all her secrets, that was her choice. And now, as she hovered over him with that beautiful mouth just inches away, his brain was no longer doing its best thinking in this position. He was dying to taste those lips again. She had signed up for fun, and if he could keep her laughing, this would all go well.

Max rolled them both over so her legs were trapped under his. Her tiny bikini left miles of soft skin uncovered, and with each new position, a different part of his body met hers, making his cock harder. Long, blond hair, still damp, cascaded over her shoulders onto his bed. She squirmed under him, giving him little sounds of pleasure, and his eyes rolled back with pleasure. He was enjoying this way too much to let her free right away.

"Okay, you made me laugh," she said, breathless. "Now let's move on to the next part."

"What part is that?" he asked, his voice filled with feigned innocence.

She smiled playfully. "Blow jobs. Going down on me. Fucking me from behind." She said each word slowly, each a scorching-hot invitation from her plump lips. His cock jumped, and she flexed her hips in a slow, seductive grind against him.

The temptation to kiss her right now was overwhelming, so he leaned down and covered her mouth with his. Soft caresses of her lips. Velvety strokes of her tongue as she explored and he answered. They were there again, in that space where everything else fell away, and there was only touch and scent and the bone-deep ache to get closer to her. Damn. He could do this forever.

He nuzzled her neck and bit down gently, right at the base of her throat. She let out a little shriek, laughing, so he sucked and bit her again, this time a little harder. Yes, this kind of physical play was like a main-line to his cock. And all that wiggling was only making him harder. She moaned, and her breaths came in short pants on his skin.

Her other hand slid across his stomach, moving up and down. With each movement, her breasts pressed against his bare chest.

Max groaned. "You feel good."

She sighed, softening a little against him. "You do, too."

Max took a long inhale, breathing in her intoxicating scent. "You smell even better."

Natasha nodded against him. She brought her lips to his skin, tasting him. This was heaven.

"You ready to pick up where we left off back in Sydney?" he asked. "Against your kitchen table, when I was dying to take off that sweet little white dress of yours?"

"I imagined it in my bed that night. How it would be with you." Her teeth grazed his skin, dissolving all thoughts.

"Good. But first we need to get naked."

Max untangled his body from hers. He pushed up onto his arms, all rippling muscles and an amused smile, looking completely at ease with his raging erection. It was impossible not to stare. Now Natasha knew what it felt like to be on top of all those warm, hard muscles...

She sat up, her gaze fixed on the ties of his board shorts as he slowly untied them. But when the knot was free, he stopped.

He was watching her now, challenge in his gaze. The room was quiet, just the rustling of palm leaves through the window. A little flutter ran through her. She wasn't nervous, was she? She had stripped for him in her bedroom window, for God's sake. Though that had been less intimate, more of the red-light variety of entertainment. But their time in this little bedroom of the cabin was...well, a different kind of fun. Just moments ago, she had rolled around on the bed with him, losing herself in their kiss.

She took a breath, stood up and pulled at the strings around her neck, easing the bikini top slowly over her breasts. She pulled the strings around the back, and it came off. Max's smile grew wider.

"Your turn," she said.

"Sure." He eased his board shorts down over his cock, and, *oh, my*, Max was naked. And looking very alert. Just looking at him made it hard to breathe. All that…*man.*

He climbed onto the bed and propped a pillow against the headboard to lean on. He settled his hand on his cock and gave her a wide smile. "Keep going."

"Just waiting until you're comfortable," she said, her gaze on the fist that was making him extra content. He laughed, low and warm.

But as she reached for the ties of her bottoms, his eyes sparked hotter. She tugged the sides loose. He played with his cock as he watched her, unhurried, a smile playing at his lips. As she stepped out of them, he gave himself a stroke.

"I've been waiting for this since your little striptease back in Sydney," he said, his voice even lower. He shook his head slowly, smiling. "Goddamn."

She climbed onto the bed, and he guided her between his legs, facing away from him. He eased her back against his chest, skin against skin.

The position was somehow more intimate than sexual, despite his thick cock pressing against her back, and it got her thinking that there would be others after her, probably many others. Maybe he would even be serious about a woman someday. Maybe today would be a story he'd tell another woman when they discussed past sexual encounters.

Oooh, Nat, be careful.

Where was this idea coming from? It shouldn't bother her, but it did. They were just having a few days of fun. But with his sexy allure and easy charm, a guy like Max was so easy to fall for.

Ugh. Why couldn't she let go and enjoy herself for once?

Still, they were here on his bed. Even if these days on Green Island weren't leading anywhere, she wanted to keep them…private. It would be a lot easier to relax if she just put it out there.

"Can I ask a favor, Max? I'd like for the details of what happens here on the island to stay between us," she said softly. "Forever, I mean. Even when you're married to some princess in a foreign land—"

"That's not going to happen, Natasha," he interrupted.

"Fine. But wherever we end up, I'd like to have this island fling just for us."

His chest stopped its easy in and out rhythm. The hand that had been playing with her hair stilled. He didn't answer. What was going through his mind?

"I'm not embarrassed, Max," she added, turning to him. "That's not why I'm asking."

His blue eyes were dark and serious. In fact, she had never seen him look so serious. Then he reached for one of her hands and laced his fingers with hers.

"I can do that, Natasha," he said quietly. "I promise."

She bit her lip. "I did it again. I didn't mean to get so—"

"Personal?" The corners of his mouth quirked up. "Natasha, we're naked. My cock is a fucking rock right now, and we're about to get more intimate than we've ever been. How the hell is this not personal?"

She sighed. "You know what I mean. We're..."

She gestured for him to finish her sentence. He raised an eyebrow but didn't say anything. Why was he being so obtuse?

"We're exploring," he finally said, his breath in her hair. "What should we try first?"

CHAPTER NINE

NATASHA DIDN'T ANSWER right away. Good. Let her get used to this feeling that she could ask for anything, be open about her wants. That she could say what was on her mind. But Max could see this was hard for her.

She was a scientist, through and through. Natasha approached everything as an experiment, considering her methods and the variables. But good sex wasn't scientific. Sure, a big cock, some experimenting with angles and attention on a woman's responses all helped. But the mind was an enormous variable, unable to be controlled. Fantasies, past experiences, vulnerabilities—all these factors could turn good mechanics into hot sex…or not.

Their fingers were still laced together, but his other hand traced slow circles over her stomach, so soft and sexy. Goddamn, his dick was hard. Just sitting like this, with Natasha's body against his, touching her, breathing in her scent, was doing it for him.

"I have an idea," he said. "Let's play Choose Your Own Adventure. I'll make up a sex story about us, and you choose how it goes. Then we can switch if you want."

She nodded. Max slid his hand up her stomach, to the underside of her breasts, letting his fingers move along the lush curve of one, then the other. "An oral sex story," she said. "I did want to practice, after all."

Oh, yeah. This was definitely heading in a good direction.

"Let me think of one," he said softly.

Most of the women he'd slept with were turned on by his wealth and his athleticism. This wasn't just his ego talking—women had told him in various ways, cloaked in praise. Maybe that kind of story would work with Natasha. But there was something else, too. Despite the fact that she had hesitated at anything that felt personal, the scenes that were running through his head right now were exactly that. Real scenarios. Times when he had wanted to kiss her, to go down on her and yes, to see her on her knees, sucking his cock. *Oh, yeah.*

"Your dick is like a steel rod, Max," she said, a little breathless. "Are you playing Choose Your Own Adventure all by yourself right now?"

He laughed. "Just thinking through my choices. Ready?"

"Yes."

"Okay. Your first choice, do you want a story about after a rugby game, in the corner of the locker room, when I'm all worked up?"

Her breaths quickened, and she let out a soft moan. Yes, that would be hot for both of them.

"Or…" he continued slowly, drawing out the moment, "do you want a story about that night I brought you and Alya home and I almost kissed you?"

She whipped her head to face him. "You remember that?"

He gave her a pointed look. "I was the sober one."

Her eyes were wide, and she bit her lip. Yep, that definitely turned her on. He waited until, finally, she answered.

"That one," she said, her voice breathy.

"Good," he said, pulling her against him to settle between his legs. He started with slow caresses, running his hands up and down her sides. "It starts early in the night, when I pick you both up before the award ceremony, and I see you in that red dress with your tits on display for every goddamn man in that place to look at. And I have to remind myself all night not to look at them, not to think about how they would feel in my mouth when I sucked on them."

His hands moved to her breasts, cupping them, savoring the feel of finally touching them. He found her nipple with one of his hands rubbing his thumb over it as he continued with the story. "But instead of taking both you and Alya home, we drop Alya off at her boyfriend's. So when we get back to your apartment, it's just us."

"Mmm," Natasha whispered, nodding.

"This time, I don't say goodnight. This time, I kiss you, and I tell you how fucking hard my cock is from trying not to watch you all night. But you already knew that. You say you've been thinking about my cock all night, too. And where you want my mouth. You wore that dress just for me, so I wouldn't forget how I wanted this evening to end."

She moaned and moved against him. Max leaned down and kissed her on her neck. Then he moved his hand lower, down her stomach, at the crease of her legs. He explored her slowly, softly, touching her, listening to her breaths, taking in her reactions. His fingers found the tops of her thighs, and then, when he couldn't resist any longer, he dipped his fingers into her warm entrance. Oh, fuck, her pussy was wet and hot, and his cock surged at the slippery heat. Her moan came louder this time.

"Now here's your next choice," he whispered. "Do I go down on you first, or do you go down on me?"

She didn't hesitate. "I go down on you."

"Works for me." Max smiled. "So you move your hand down my stomach until you reach my cock. You take it in your hand and feel me. My tip, my balls, the length. Of course, you're impressed."

Natasha snorted. "Of course. And I say, *My God, Max, you're so big.*"

She drew the words out, her voice full of amusement, so he snaked his other hand to her waist and tickled her. She let out a yelp of laughter, squirming, sending more currents of lust through him.

He chuckled and bit her neck softly as she settled back against him. "You gonna let me tell my story?"

She nodded, still breathless. He moved his hand back

down, through her soft curls, just above her clit. He made slow, easy circles as the last remnants of laughter shifted to something hotter.

"Here's what you say to me. *Have you imagined my lips around your cock?* And fuck, yes, I have."

His fingers circled her clit as he spoke, and she moved her hips against his touch.

"Yes, Max." Never had he heard hotter words than the ones coming from Natasha's lips right now.

"Next choice, sweetheart," he whispered. "You want me standing up? Sitting down? Lying down?"

"You're sitting down on a chair. A kitchen chair," she said, her voice coming between soft pants. "And I'm on my knees."

"Oh, yeah," he bit out. He took a deep breath, getting his cock under control. "I take your hand, and we walk into your kitchen. I tell you I want to sit down because I'm so fucking worked up, so I pull out a chair."

"Mmm…" Natasha hummed with pleasure, and Max thrust his hips against her, gritting his teeth against the urge to do it again and again. But not yet.

"You kneel in front of me. And I say *You want to take it out? You want to suck me off?* And you say yes."

His voice was getting lower, rougher, and the need to satisfy them both was taking over. "You unzip my pants and pull down my boxers, and I sit in the chair and spread my legs. You look at my cock the way you look at everything, studying it, sizing it up, taking it in. And my hands are fisted by now because your mouth is so close to my dick that I can feel your breaths, and it's driving me fucking mad. But I wait."

She let out a moan. His fingers dipped down into the delicious wetness he was dying to taste.

"Now you have one last choice in this story. What do I say next?"

Oh, the sounds she was making, her raspy breaths and her little pants and moans. Goddamn, this was pushing his own limits.

"I could order you to suck my cock," he whispered in her ear. "I could tell you I like it hard and deep. I could take your hair in my hand and tell you I've been thinking about fucking your mouth all night. Giving you a mouthful."

She whimpered. Yeah, she liked that. But there was another option, one that he suspected might ring even truer. Her body was tense, taut. Like she was as enthralled with this story as he was. Time for option number two.

"Or I could look down at you, push the hair off your face," he said, running his tongue over her neck, tasting her, "and say, *You own me.*"

"Yes." The word was out of her mouth before she could think through what this choice revealed. Before she could weigh the risks of revealing this choice to Max. Because that was exactly what she wanted from that scene: to be the only one in the world he wanted at that moment.

But even that thought faded because Max was moving now. His hands flexed against her waist as he slipped out from behind her, moving with the urgency she had gotten a glimpse of back in her kitchen in Sydney.

"I'm so hard for you right now, sweetheart," he growled. "I want the real thing. I want you to sit on my face. I want to taste your pussy while you suck me off. You ready for that?"

Her body was answering in sparks and jolts.

"Hell, yes," she said with a giddy laugh.

Max lay on the bed, legs spread, knees bent, feet firmly planted on the bed.

"Climb on, sweetheart," he coaxed. His hands circled her thighs as she straddled his face. "This is going to feel so good."

She lowered herself onto her elbows, one on each side of his hips. Her heart pounded harder as she brushed a hand over the trail of hair that led to the thicker mass. His cock bobbed urgently, in case she needed a reminder of where she should be focusing.

Max had started his own exploring, as well, his fingers playing between her folds as if he were studying her just as carefully as she was studying him.

She licked his tip experimentally, and his hips bucked, giving her more than just a taste. His whole head went into her mouth, farther. She wrapped her lips around him and he pulled out with a harsh groan.

"Can I come in your mouth?" His voice was thick with lust. "I just want to know before we get too far."

She shuddered with pleasure as the idea took form in her mind, sharp and visceral. "Yes."

"Good. Put your hand around my cock so I don't choke you, because I'm going to want to move. And you can squeeze as hard as you'd like."

She shifted her weight onto one elbow and brought her other hand to his cock, running her palm over his wet head and moving it to the base. His hands tightened around her thighs, pulling her down onto his face.

"*Hell, yes*," he muttered, echoing her.

Then all thoughts disappeared except one: Max. His lips, his tongue, his fingers, all exploring, teasing, like there was nothing else on earth he wanted to do except feast on her. And that was exactly what he was doing right now, feasting. His mouth was hungry, and he sucked on her and licked her like she was the only thing that could satisfy him.

His cock throbbed urgently in her hand. He was doing crazy things to her with his tongue, making it hard to concentrate. She opened her mouth as another wave of blinding pleasure hit her. As she moaned, he thrust into her mouth.

"Yes," he growled, pulling her closer. "You make me so fucking hot, Natasha."

He swirled his tongue around her clit, over and over, as she lost herself further in the sensations. Her body quivered, and he sucked harder, sending her over the edge. She shook and came as he devoured her, drawing out her orgasm. Rolling waves of languid pleasure flooded her. She pulled back, releasing his erection from her mouth, and rested her head on his hip.

She sighed. "You're amazing, Max."

"I'm feeling pretty amazing right now," he said with a strangled laugh. "But I'm going to need to do something about this if you don't want to finish. Because staring at your pussy like this is only making it hotter."

Natasha considered the idea of watching Max jerk off in front of her. Watching his hand move up and down his cock, figuring out exactly what he liked. Her body certainly liked the idea.

But not this time. This time, she wanted to be the one to make him feel that way. "No, I want to finish."

"I was hoping you'd say that," he said. He palmed her ass and squeezed it. "Then stay just like you are. I like this view. A lot."

Natasha lifted her head and positioned herself with his cock right in front of her. Beautiful, sexy Max. She was trying not to think about her bare ass in his face, but it was hard to forget when his heavy breaths teased her, getting her going again. She reached for his erection, wrapping her hand around him once more, squeezing harder this time. His groan was heavy, tight. His story looped through her thoughts, weaving itself into each movement, each touch.

I could look down at you...and say you own me.

The tensing of his stomach muscles under her breasts, the hard grip of his hands around her thighs. In that moment, she felt it. She owned him. Natasha put her lips around his head and sucked. His hips bucked, but this time she was ready for it. She drew him in and out, matching the rhythm of his thrusts.

"Fuck," he roared. "I'm going to come."

He groaned and swore and came deep in her mouth. His big body flexed and shuddered under hers. Then came heavy groans of satisfaction mixed with a whisper of words too soft to understand. His hips slowed. His hands loosened around her thighs, stroking.

"Oh, Natasha," he said, his voice naked with wonder.

The words moved through her in soft flutters. These were aftereffects from the orgasm, from his breaths still teasing the length of her core, weren't they? This was by far the hottest experience of her life, so it was only natural that he was satisfied, too.

Gently, he lifted one of her thighs over to the side. "As much as I'm enjoying the view, you might be more comfortable up here, where the pillows are."

She pushed herself up lazily and shifted her legs under her. Max opened his arms, an invitation to lie with him. Natasha settled against him, resting her head on his shoulder. He wrapped his arms around her, and she closed her eyes, losing herself in the bliss of his warm embrace. The warm, hard muscles of his biceps against her back, her cheek in the hollow of his shoulder, just breathing him in. God, he smelled amazing. If she wasn't careful, she'd let herself lie here with him for the rest of the day.

"We definitely practiced oral sex," she said, reluctantly sitting up. "With thirteen minutes left for a shower."

CHAPTER TEN

By the time Max walked Alya back from the shoot, dusk was settling. The wind off the ocean found its way through the tangle of trees, warm and balmy. It was going to be a beautiful night.

Max changed for dinner and put in a quick call to Henning back at the Blackmore Inc. office. According to him, Alya's ex had eaten dinner in LA that evening, so he wasn't coming to Green Island anytime soon.

He sank down into one of the lounge chairs beside the pool outside their suite, waiting for Natasha and Alya to get dressed. The pool was empty, the still water sparkling in the evening sun, but a smattering of guests clustered on the deck. The models stood out, taller, shinier than the rest. A couple of them had given him the familiar once-over of women used to more than their fair share of attention. It was a look that said, *I'll take you*, like she was buying a bull for breeding. He knew that look because he had taken up the implied challenge more than a few times, just for a little fun. But the idea had lost its appeal, and it wasn't just because his magic wand had gotten its share of action earlier.

Even from a young age Max had been wary of this world, with its pecking order based on family name, looks and other things people were born with, though he had grown up with so many privileges shoved up his ass that he knew better than to complain. Ironically, it was his years at Princeton, a school that dripped with old money privileges, that got him started on a different path.

He had always excelled at physical sports, so he'd joined the school's rugby team. Growing up, he'd played on and off, mostly because it was as far from a gentleman's sport as he could find, just to mess with his father. But it wasn't until Princeton that he got serious about the game. The team quickly hooked him up with hot tutor Jessica, and for the first time he actually looked forward to a few hours of homework…and what came after. Yeah, he was a slow reader, but it turned out there were plenty of ways around that. He had always been a hard worker, but the results in anything that counted for the Jensen family hadn't been good enough. Jessica changed that. In fact, by sophomore year, he was making the honor roll. For the first time outside of the arena of sports, his position had been earned, not bought. And finally, finally it dawned on him that he wasn't as academically inept as everyone assumed—everyone including himself. He just had to find the right path.

Max's phone rang, bringing him back to the present. He glanced absently at the screen. Shit. Nalini Anderson, administrative assistant to the president of the Jensen Family Foundation. Which meant *his* future admin, the last person Max wanted to talk to right now.

It was nothing personal. Somehow she had managed to work harmoniously with gruff, abrupt, notoriously difficult Deacon Jensen for years, which was a tribute to her management skills, her people skills and her patience. But Max didn't want to think about that part of his future right now, not here on Green Island. This woman had a backbone of steel, though, and if she wanted to get in touch with him, she'd keep trying.

Max accepted the call. "Hi, Nalini. What can I do for you?"

"I'm sorry to bother you, Mr. Jensen," she said. "I understand you're working this weekend, and I'll make this quick. Your father felt this was urgent, and I wanted to give you enough time to make your decision about it."

Okay, this woman was good. She had gotten his attention.

"Thanks. Go ahead."

"You're only down for one person at next Saturday's fundraiser. No date."

Max scowled. There was a period back in his teens when his father had kept him away from women—all of them. And now Deacon Jensen was complaining that he didn't have a date? If his father thought Max's involvement with the foundation meant he could steer Max's life again…hell no.

"I'm not planning to take a date."

"I understand, Mr. Jensen," she said, and she sounded like she truly did. "I just want you to be aware that the partnership with the Martinelli Foundation has stirred up some talk about the connection between you and Francesca Martinelli. If you decide to go alone, the speculations will likely continue."

Damn. Max ran a hand through his hair. The Australian media already kept tabs on him, but it'd be worse when he stepped back into the Jensen family fold, where attending high-profile events and being in the public eye would be much more frequent. More critical, too, if the focus was no longer the lifestyles-of-the-rich-and-famous slant but, instead, something as serious as the cancer center. Max had thought he had another week before this circus started. Apparently not.

"You can get back to me on this," said Nalini. "Let me know how you want to handle it."

"Thanks," he said, and he meant it.

Max ran his hand through his hair once more, shaking his head. He hadn't even considered taking a date from the start. The casual nature of his usual list of possibilities made them out of the question for an event honoring his mother.

The only woman he would want there with him was Natasha. He hadn't considered asking her because of the public scrutiny that came with this kind of event. And he knew how much she hated it. Several months ago, when a photo of Cameron Blackmore coming out of a bar with Alya and Natasha on each arm had appeared on a gossip site, social media made it into something it wasn't. It was a long time before Natasha attended anything with Alya after that, and Max respected her choice.

However, the alternative Nalini had just presented, Max being publicly paired with Francesca, might hurt Natasha even more than keeping her away.

Could he ask Natasha to go? That would certainly make his night a hell of a lot better. It wasn't like she'd never attended a high-profile event, so she might consider it…if he could figure out how to keep the press away from her.

The irony of inviting Natasha didn't escape him. Max had spent a good portion of his adult life avoiding his father's path, determined not to make the same mistakes. But here he was, facing the similar crossroads: let go of the woman he wanted, risking the hurt she'd face alone, or pursue her, knowing that being with him came at a cost, too.

In his mother's case, the sacrifice had been her career as a jazz singer. His mother's refusals of his father's first two proposals were well-known, since they, like everything else the Jensens did, played out in the public eye. Max had dismissed his father's relentless pursuit of his mother as selfish, a motivation the opposite of love. But faced with a comparable situation, Max was beginning to understand that his father could have been driven by more than one emotion at the same time.

He looked up at the evening sky, streaked with wispy clouds. He could put this decision off for a little longer.

The door to the cabin opened, and Natasha walked out. Strings of little lights along the canopy of trees glim-

mered, giving her a hazy glow that stopped his breath.
She wore sandals and a green dress that tied behind her
neck, and her long, blond hair spilled over her bare shoulders. Her cheeks were flushed, and her lips, red...which,
of course, reminded him of where those lips had been
just a few hours ago. Her black-rimmed glasses were
the final touch. She had been wearing contact lenses
for most of the day, but it was nice to see that part of
her back in place.

"Alya will be right out," she said. "Her boyfriend
called."

Max stood up, drinking her in as he walked over.
The soft slope of her hips, the low cut of her dress, her
full breasts. "You look lovely, Natasha."

She gave him a wry smile. "This dress covers the
hickey on my neck."

She moved the strap of her dress down, exposing a
red patch. The place where he'd bitten and sucked on
her earlier. Damn.

Max rubbed the back of his neck. "Sorry about that."

"You sure you're sorry?" Her smile was warm, and
she didn't look upset at all.

Max relaxed a little. "Only if it hurt. But it's a good
look for you."

She looked so different right now in the fading sun.
There was something new in her gaze as they stood, facing each other, something softer. The island was working its magic—or maybe it was the orgasms he gave
her earlier. Goddamn, he could stand here for hours,
just looking at her.

His Blackmore Inc. brothers would love this. Derek would have some bullshit psychology explanation about his mother's depression and his need to keep women happy. Cameron would call it payback for mocking both him and Simon as they fell hard for the women they couldn't stay away from.

He shook himself out of that thought. This wasn't at all like what Cameron and Simon had gone through. He wasn't falling *in love* with Natasha after a day of sex. They were just having a hell of a lot of fun together.

"Are you on the clock tonight?" Natasha asked.

He shook his head. "Barring any unexpected action, like incoming boats or planes, I'm officially off duty."

She smiled. It was a sexy little smile, and he was almost sure dirty thoughts were forming. He hoped like hell they were for him.

"You lookin' for a good time tonight, ma'am?" He waggled his eyebrows at her. "We can sneak off into the bushes."

Before she could answer, Alya walked out of their suite. Natasha took a step back and straightened up. Interesting. She definitely hadn't told Alya about their little arrangement.

Max slipped his hands into his pockets. "You ladies ready for some dinner?"

Alya nodded, but she looked distracted. Max frowned. Was he missing something here? Was it about her ex?

"Anything wrong?" he asked gently.

She shook her head. "It's my current boyfriend, not

Nick. Though I might be turning Stewart into a crazy ex, too."

Alya's tone was wry, but Natasha's attention snapped to her sister, as if she had heard the same warning bells in that statement as Max had.

Natasha took a couple of quick steps to her sister's side. "You didn't turn anyone crazy. Nick did that all on his own, sweetheart."

Max nodded. "What happened?"

Alya sighed and leaned her head on Natasha's shoulder. "Nothing scary. Stewart's not the kidnapping type."

Natasha snorted. "Is there a kidnapping type?"

"I hope not. Because I'm starting to question my taste in men." Alya met Max's gaze, and her eyes widened. "Sorry, Max. I won't make kidnapping jokes. I'm not in any danger. Just the regular kind of relationship drama."

Max nodded, softening his stance.

Natasha gave her sister one last squeeze and tugged her toward the boardwalk. "What happened?"

Max let out a long breath and locked the cabin door. The danger level on this job was very low, but he was still ready for anything. Max walked far enough behind the two sisters to give them a little privacy.

They walked along the boardwalk that wound through the lush forest and turned off toward the island's only real restaurant. The evening sky glowed through the leaves of the tall palm trees, and birds called from deeper in the forest. They rounded a bend and the restaurant came into sight, lit with candles and little strings of lights.

The place was open, with just a roof over a patio, filled with square tables neatly set with glasses, linen napkins and white tablecloths. A swimming pool lay on one side of the patio, now glassy smooth, the deep blue water sparkling in the moonlight. On the far side, a generous buffet was set up along the wall of the building.

A good portion of the magazine staff was already at the restaurant, some perusing the buffet, others talking in small groups. As they entered into the glow of tiny lights, a man—definitely not a model—called Alya over to join his conversation.

Alya glanced at Natasha, then Max. "Will you two be fine on your own this evening? My agent told me I'm supposed to be networking."

"Go mingle," said Natasha, waving her sister off. "We'll be fine."

She squeezed her sister's hand and Alya walked away.

A smile tugged at the corners of Max's mouth. Oh, yeah, he was more than fine with alone time with Natasha. "So, about those bushes…"

"I'm hungry," Natasha interrupted, giving him side-eyes. "And not that kind of hungry."

But there was a flash of heat in her gaze, too. She definitely wasn't against the idea of slipping away.

The warm breeze rustled the trees overhead, and Max rested his hand on the curve of Natasha's back as they wove through the web of tables, over toward the buffet. The soft glow of the candles around them glittered in her hair and washed over her bare skin.

The closer they got to the buffet, the more crowded the place was. A little huddle of women fanned out as he passed, openly sizing him up appreciatively. He looked over at Natasha. Damn, she'd seen their looks. He got them pretty regularly from women, whether he encouraged them or not, but for the first time, it pissed him off. He was clearly walking with another woman.

Were they intentionally ignoring this detail, or had they assumed he wasn't with her? He didn't like either of those possibilities. Natasha's step faltered for a beat, but she straightened up and turned for the buffet. Good for her. Max scanned the restaurant, looking for a secluded place to sit, away from stares like this, but there was nothing.

By the time they reached the banquet table, her smile had returned. The spread was beautiful, full of fruits, cheeses, salads, maki rolls, some fish…things and other foods he didn't recognize. Max leaned over Natasha's shoulder to grab a plate, closer than he needed to.

"You think we were swimming around with any of these entrees earlier?" he asked.

She wrinkled her nose. "I doubt it."

"Let's get some food and find a spot of our own, away from here," he said gesturing out into the dark green tangle of trees.

"No bushes, Max," she said dryly. "Let's go to the beach."

"That definitely sounds sexier than the bushes," he

whispered in her ear as she picked up a bunch of grapes. That earned him a chuckle.

They loaded up their plates. Max nicked some silverware and napkins from a nearby table, shoving them in his pocket, and stopped at the dessert display for a few of the little chocolate squares, all arranged in the form of a manta ray. Waiters wandered through the groups of guests, carrying trays of champagne, and he grabbed two glasses for them before heading for Natasha, who had already started for the boardwalk.

The murmur of voices faded as Max followed Natasha off the patio, back into the trees. They walked along the path, turning away from their cabin, heading for the far side of the island.

"You'd think I'd be fine in that world after all the events with my mother and sister, but it still has a way of making me feel second-rate," she said quietly, not turning to face him. "Stupid, I know."

"Sweetheart, you are first-rate in every way." Max's urge to reach for her was thwarted by the plate and glasses he was currently juggling.

Natasha looked over at him with a small smile. "Thanks. I know I should have gotten over this kind of thing long ago. Everyone is beautiful in their own way, blah, blah, blah. But there really are people who are just strikingly beautiful, more than others. And those people happen to include my mother and my sister. And not me. Most of the time, I don't care."

For once, Max had no idea what to say. Where did he start? With the fact that he found her far more attractive than anyone else on that patio they had abandoned? The reasons were a mystery to him, and telling her this would sound insincere, like a consolation. His worry must have showed because she waved him off with her free hand.

"I'm fine, Max. Really. It doesn't bother me as much as it did growing up." She brushed his cheek, as if she was the one consoling him. "And there are definitely disadvantages to startling beauty. It's very hard for my sister to be taken seriously since everything is seen through the lens of her looks. You should hear her stories from her stint in nursing school. But sometimes it can be hard to walk in her world. Like tonight."

He nodded. "I don't think the high-profile life is easy for anyone. Each person's reasons might be a little different, but being in this world has a tendency to rub us all raw."

Natasha tilted her head to the side, as if she were thinking through that idea, figuring out what exactly it meant for him. She was quiet for a while.

"How did you get involved with Blackmore Inc.?"

"Cameron and I were roommates at Princeton," he said. "He needed help when he took over as CEO of the Australian division. His father hadn't left it in good shape. He brought me on for business strategy, but I wanted a piece of the on-the-ground action, too."

She raised an eyebrow. "And, of course, Max Jensen gets what he wants."

"Hell, no," he snorted. "I had to work my ass off to

train for it. I was in pretty good shape from rugby, but there was a lot I needed to learn."

"You like working hard, don't you?" she said. "Especially if it's something money can't buy."

He nodded slowly. "Yeah. I do."

The boardwalk came to an end at the beach. It was low tide, and a long stretch of flat, hard sand spread out for them to walk on. The ocean was quiet, and parts of the reef peeked out from the glassy water. The sun had sunk behind mainland mountains in the distance, and tiny dots of light glowed along the shoreline.

Natasha slowed at the edge of the water and kicked off her sandals. She sat next to them in the wet sand, her legs stretched out in front of her and her plate balanced on her lap. Max moved in behind her. He settled his thigh beside hers, just touching, and she was close enough that she could lean back against him if she wanted. He handed her one of the champagne glasses.

"To paradise," he said, and she tapped her glass against his and took a drink.

"This is what I love about the ocean," she said, gesturing to the view. "Nothing back there in the restaurant matters out here. No matter how beautiful or wealthy we are, no matter how much influence we have on land, in the water we're just mammals trying to swim and breathe, nothing more."

Max nodded slowly. The sentence was a little window into her, a gift, one he sensed she didn't give often. For all their differences, they weren't so unalike. As strange as it sounded, this was the same reason he loved playing rugby, because he knew that no matter how much influence his family name had, the rugby teams wouldn't have put him in the starting lineup unless he could play the game.

Natasha picked up a piece of a maki roll and popped it into her mouth. She was such a pleasure to watch, sandy feet, loose hair and red lips. That line of thought was going to give him a hard-on. Max scanned the empty beach. Could they get away with sex out here? He had slipped a condom in his pocket, just in case. Shit, he had a whole box of condoms back in his room and they hadn't even used one yet. And the trip would be over soon.

He frowned. They were just getting started, and this fling sure as hell didn't feel like it'd be done anytime soon. But his life was changing, and any woman he was with would not only be plagued by the media but would inevitably become frustrated by the restraints on his time. If rumors of infidelity didn't chip away at their relationship, unmet expectations and feeling second-best would. Wasn't that the case with his parents, until they'd retreated to Western Australia in search of privacy? His mother had been so gun-shy of the tabloids by that point that she didn't even return to Sydney for last-ditch cancer treatments. After watching his mother crumble under the weight of media pressure, he'd never put Natasha in that position. But that wouldn't start until after next Saturday's announcement. He just needed to broach the topic of the fundraiser with her.

"What comes next when we return to Sydney?" he asked.

Natasha shrugged. "I'm on holiday, but I'll probably start setting out my research plans for my new grant."

"And back to the dating scene?"

She sighed and took another sip of champagne. "I suppose. But I'm not really the casual sex type, and I don't make a very good girlfriend in most men's eyes."

"I'm not sure about that," said Max. He leaned forward and playfully nipped her shoulder. "I think a whole lot of men would disagree."

She laughed. "You're just thinking about sex."

"Of course I am." Yes, he was, but he was thinking about more, too. About the way she made him laugh. And about how magical it was to just sit here by the ocean with her, the moon reflecting off the water.

"But most of the day isn't spent in bed. And at some point, I find that men want extra services." She glanced over at him. "Not just the sexy kind. I mean the I'm-so-busy-can-you-just-help-run-my-life kind. And if that comes up, I can't even think about the M word."

"What M word?"

"*Marriage*," she said, then laughed. "What M word did you think I was talking about? *Max?*"

He snorted. "You said it. Not me."

She rolled her eyes and took another bite of a maki roll. Her smile faded. Was she thinking about Wayne or one of the other assholes she had dated? Max had plenty of faults, but he definitely wouldn't treat a girlfriend like his administrative assistant…though that could make for some fun bedroom play. Back to the point: if those were the kinds of men she was dating, then there was no reason not to extend their arrangement for a little longer after they left Green Island.

Max set his plate aside and took hers off her lap. He tugged her gently and gave her a suggestive smile. She took the hint, turning and climbing on top so she straddled him. Her dress was hitched high up her legs, and he ran his hands up the soft skin of her thighs.

She relaxed in his embrace. This was everything he could want. His blood was running south fast, and he had the urge to unzip, pull it out and ask her to ride him hard. Goddamn, it was hard to resist. But for now, he wanted her in his arms, just like this. He cupped her face and looked into her eyes. There was so much heat.

He wasn't ready to let Natasha go, but if this was temporary he wanted to leave her with something. That must have been why the next words came out of his mouth, so much more intimate than sex.

"I think any man with an ounce of sense wouldn't give a fuck about running errands or housework or any other thing like that. Not when he has someone like you," he said. "And outside the bedroom, every touch should be a reminder that he's the person in the room who makes you truly happy."

Right now, Max hoped like hell he was that man. And he had to figure out how the hell he was going to keep being that man for just a little longer.

CHAPTER ELEVEN

NATASHA'S HEART GAVE a leap, and she tried so hard to fight the swell of messy emotions his words stirred in her. Max's fingers lingered on her skin, and a shiver ran through her. His eyes were hot, intense, and there was no teasing smile on his lips. Something was happening between them, something more than just the sexy fun he had promised. She swallowed. Her breasts brushed against his shirt as she breathed, in and out, caught in this endless moment of intimacy. God, she could fall for Max so easily. Maybe she already had.

Max seemed to be doing some of his own contemplating.

She tilted her head, thinking through his words. "Does it work that way? That you can make someone happy?"

Max was quiet for a long time. "That sounds like a leading question," he finally said with a hint of a smile.

"Really, it's not," said Natasha. "It's just that I've always assumed it was the opposite with my mother."

"What do you mean?"

"The career she chose, the men she chose." She shook her head slowly. "It was all her doing. She made herself unhappy, and then, finally, she met her most recent husband and decided to make herself happy. But before that…" Natasha rolled her eyes.

"Even with your father?" asked Max after a while.

"Especially with my father," she said with a snort. "He's as volatile as my mother is. Thank God I was young when they split up. I don't think I could have handled the drama."

"What made things better?"

"She finally got out of the entertainment business," Natasha said. "No more secret affairs with directors, no younger actresses 'stealing' her roles, no tumultuous relationships with other self-involved actors."

His fingers made a trail up and down her arm. "Why did she leave?"

"One director told her in no uncertain terms that she was too old for lead roles." Natasha tamped down the memories of that day that threatened to take over. "But I'm actually grateful that asshole was so blunt. If he hadn't been, she'd still be scraping the bottom right now."

"Where is she now?"

"In Malibu. Barrett, her latest husband, is a lawyer for one of the studios," she said. "Nice guy, soft-spoken. Quite frankly, I thought she married him for the money, but they seem surprisingly happy together."

A crease formed between Max's eyebrows. "Maybe she just met the right person."

"Yes, that helped. But she probably wouldn't have noticed that right person if she was on the set of a movie.

She had to get herself away from the lure of stardom."
She was quiet for a while. "You know what drives me
crazy about it? It's like my mother still doesn't understand this. She'd never make the choice to leave acting
on her own. Why doesn't she see how much better her
life is without it?"

"Maybe she loved it. People want to choose with
their hearts, not their minds."

"Maybe." She sighed.

"But you want to do the opposite? Choose with your
mind?"

He reached up and tucked a stray lock of her hair
behind her ear. The hum of attraction between them
kicked up a few notches.

She met his gaze and held it, studying him. This was
getting very…intimate. Finally, she smiled. "We're supposed to be analyzing you, not me."

He chuckled. "But you're so much more interesting."

Natasha gave him a skeptical smile. "That's one way
of saying it."

"Natasha, I find you very interesting." His gaze was
warm, tender.

She waved off his comment. "It's the fish thing. Trust
me, it'll wear off."

Max shook his head. "I'm pretty sure I'd never tire
of listening to you talk about fish."

She stilled. This was dangerous territory. The *what-ifs*
and *maybes* of something more. It was the first step toward the cliffs of Illana Petrova insanity.

Natasha pulled away from the heat of his body.

"Thanks, but I'm pretty sure that after a few months you'd be running back to women who didn't bring up the surprising drops in the sea cucumber population at dinner parties."

Max shook his head. "Not a chance. I'd like nothing better than to be a part of that conversation."

She wasn't trying to put herself down, just insert a little dose of reality into this conversation. It was all theoretical, nothing to get worked up about, so she let it go. But there was something in his eyes as he looked at her. For a moment, he looked uncertain. Then his hands stopped, and he looked right at her.

"There's an event coming up next weekend. I'd like you to go with me."

She blinked at him. "What kind of event?"

Creases had formed between his eyebrows, deeper this time.

"A foundation dinner. For a charity." He seemed to be choosing his words carefully, and she was pretty sure she wasn't getting the whole picture.

"Just like that? You don't have another date lined up for it?"

He shook his head. "Wasn't planning on taking a date to this one. It's a family thing. But I'd love to hear you chat that room up with marine biology."

Natasha was still stuck on the word *family*. Even she knew he didn't get along with his notoriously surly father. Everyone in Australia knew it. More importantly, she knew instinctively that this subject was a no-fly zone in conversation, but now that he had opened the door on this topic, she pressed further. "What happened between you and your father?"

Max sighed. "Nothing monumental. Just the typical rebellious teen versus autocratic father thing. Which, apparently, I haven't outgrown."

The corners of his mouth turned up in the hint of a smile.

Now it was her turn to squeeze his hand. "You're not a sullen teenager, Max. Not even close."

"When I was a kid, I was the fuck-up younger brother. Which maybe you can imagine," he said, his smile curving into a smirk. "Too loud, too impulsive, too risky. My mother was the only one I was really close to."

"Your mother, the jazz singer your father very publicly fell in love with and whisked away to Western Australia?"

"Yep. And they stayed there all the way until the very end."

She sensed there was more to that comment, and she waited for more details but they didn't come. Maybe it was just as well that they didn't move into deeper territory. After all, this was just a sexy fling, even if it felt like... Well, she had no idea what this felt like.

Natasha bit her lip and pointed them onto safer terrain. "You're not going to tell me more about the dinner?"

"Why?" he asked, smiling a little. "Afraid it won't meet your standards?"

She raised her eyebrows in mock concern. "Aw, are you worried about meeting my standards?"

He tickled her sides, and she shrieked and squirmed in his arms. His cock was stiffening between them, and she rubbed against it, making them both moan. But as her breathing calmed, the original topic came back.

"Why are you inviting me, Max?" she asked.

"Beyond the possibility of getting laid afterwards?"

She rolled her eyes and tried to tickle him back, but it wasn't nearly as effective.

Then he looked away, out at the ocean, like he was really giving her question some thought. Finally, he said, "The flowers."

She blinked, her mind racing to make the connection. He must have seen her confusion because he added, "The flowers you sent after my mother died."

Those flowers. Of course. It wasn't that she had forgotten; it was the fact that he'd broached the subject at all that tripped her up. Natasha wouldn't have known about his mother's illness except that Max had let Alya know he would be out of touch for over a month, that someone else would be taking over any bodyguard duties she needed. Nothing else. Somehow, Natasha had known something big was happening. A few weeks later she'd read the news in the paper, so she sent flowers with a note.

You're not really a flowers kind of guy but I thought you might be this month. Natasha.

The next time she saw him, Max said nothing about his mother or the flowers. He had just been his usual, easygoing self. So she'd let it go.

"I should have said something before," he continued. "It meant a lot."

If she wanted more details about his family, this was her opening. "You and your mother were close?"

He nodded. "At least when I was younger. I didn't see her much after I left home. Not until near the end."

"Breast cancer, right?" she asked. "I saw her obituary."

"She was stage four when it was discovered, so it all happened pretty quickly. When she knew she didn't have much longer, she asked me to come. It was the least I could do," he said. "My mother gave up a lot for our family, and I wasn't the easiest kid."

The remorse in these words was doing funny things inside her. It must have shown on her face, because the corners of his mouth turned up, and he shook his head.

"Nope. Don't think it."

She let out an exasperated sigh. "You don't know what I'm thinking."

"I see that sympathy," he said with a wry smile. "But I'm the last person you should feel sorry for. I've been all over the world, graduated from an Ivy League school and played professional rugby. I have more than enough money, and…" His hands glided up her legs, around her ass, and he pulled her against his erection. "I even have a nice big cock, which you seem to appreciate."

She sighed. "Ah, the priorities of the male mind."

"If that's a priority list, I'll put big cock first." His delivery was so deadpan that she laughed, despite all the seriousness of their conversation.

He was doing it again. Teasing, making her laugh, steering her further away from any personal discussion about him. But maybe that was okay. Because they weren't together, and he seemed to be asking her to go to this function as a friend. Or some version of that.

"Max?"

"Yeah?" He was lazily stroking her thighs.

"I'll be your date for the dinner."

Max blinked at her in surprise. "You will?"

She nodded.

"It's not private," he said hesitantly.

"I gathered that."

"Thank you." He kissed her neck. "Thank you." He moved a halter strap aside and kissed the curve of her breast. His lips lingered on her skin, his hot breaths sending shivers through her.

"Are you going to give me a thank-you present?" she asked, rubbing against his cock.

He laughed. "You're lucky I brought a condom tonight. I don't think you want the kind of present that keeps on giving."

She pulled back. "You don't have an STD, do you?"

Max let out a whoop of laughter, his body shaking against hers. "Hell, no. I meant a-bun-in-the-oven kind of present."

She plopped her head onto his shoulder and laughed.

"I can't believe you just said that," said Max, poking her sides. Then he pulled her against him, flush with his body, and she rested her head on his warm chest. This was probably her best dinner date ever, despite the fact that the rest of her food was probably covered in sand at this point.

A burst of longing hit her, deep in her chest. Oh, he was so warm and sexy and fun, so Max.

She took a deep breath, resting her hands on his cheeks, the stubble of a day's worth of growth prickling her fingers. *Don't think, Nat. Just enjoy this before it disappears.*

"Okay," he said. "Thank-you present, coming up."

One of his hands moved up her back and tangled in her hair as he lowered his mouth to hers. His lips were soft, so achingly gentle. It was nothing like the explosively hot kiss in her kitchen, with its promise of other, dirtier things to come. This was a kiss just for this moment. He coaxed her mouth open, sucking on her bottom lip. She stroked his tongue with hers, and he responded. It was devastatingly intimate.

She lost herself in the kiss, her whole body coming alive as their mouths became one, promising, begging with hungry groans instead of words. Oh, she could kiss him all night long. Except they didn't have all night. Sooner or later, they had to get back to Alya. Natasha tried to get her mind to focus.

"Sex on a beach." Her lips brushed against his as she spoke. "I've had the drink, and it was just okay. Maybe the real thing is better?"

Max's smile pressed against her mouth. "I'm sure it is."

"You've never tried?"

He shook his head a little. "I'd think it could get… sandy."

"We could stand up. Over by the palm trees." She

pulled back a little and nodded to where the beach met the lush green of the island. "I'll hold on to a tree, and you can fuck me from behind."

His cock throbbed against her, and he groaned. Yes, that definitely turned him on, but he shook his head again. "No, I'd rather try it on the beach. It's more…" Max, who never hesitated, seemed to be choosing his words carefully. Finally, he said, "I think it'll be good like this."

Probably true, but she was pretty sure that wasn't what he'd wanted to say at first. She could think about that later. Instead, Natasha climbed off him and stood up, brushing the sand from her hands.

"We can sit on my dress," she said, standing in front of him.

He was staring up at her, his gaze hot. "I love that idea, especially if it involves you stripping for me."

She waved the comment away. "You've already seen that."

"Watching you undress could never get old," he said softly. It was the kind of comment he usually pulled off with a cheeky grin, but this time, his eyes were serious.

She stilled, digesting his words, reading into them before she could catch herself. But he didn't mean anything by it beyond attraction, so why did her chest squeeze at that admission? No, she would not ruin this night by searching for meanings that weren't there.

Max propped himself back on his arms and stretched out his legs, then crossed them at the ankles. The last glow of the evening bathed a hint of light on his face.

Natasha grabbed the hem of her dress and slid it up her thighs, over her hips and up her stomach, brushing her hands over her skin as she lifted. Max didn't move. Next, she freed her breasts as she pulled the dress over her head, leaving her naked, except for her panties.

Max's mouth was parted, and his gaze was fixed on her chest. "This whole night you weren't wearing a bra?" His voice came out a little choked.

She smiled. "The dress has built-in support."

"One more reason I love it."

She lifted an eyebrow. "What's the other reason? That it's easy to take off?"

Max chuckled. "That's another good reason." His smile faded. "I was just thinking it looks beautiful on you. You're beautiful, Natasha."

She had never felt so naked in her life. Natasha swallowed a lump in her throat. "Thank you."

The warm breeze caressed her skin as she turned for the ocean to shake the sand off her dress. Then she laid it carefully on the beach, the skirt spread to give them some room.

"You sit first," she said. "I'll straddle you. Then we can avoid sand in uncomfortable parts."

Who was this new version of her, planning and directing sexy situations with a guy? But it wasn't just any guy. It was Max, and after this afternoon together, everything felt so easy, so comfortable.

He stood up, brushing the sand off his hands. His cock jutted out impatiently as he unbuttoned his shirt and lowered his shorts. Then he put his hand out.

"Your panties?" Amusement danced in his eyes, and he added, "For a sand-free experience."

"Good idea."

She turned around, her back to him, and winked over her shoulder. Then she scooted out of her panties, sticking out her ass for a little extra fun. She dangled them from her finger, and he shoved them into the pocket of his shorts, his eyes still on her ass. Then he pulled out a condom and tore off the wrapper.

"I'll put that on for you," she said, taking it out of his hand. Their fingers brushed, sending a buzz of excitement through her.

Natasha crouched in front of him, his cock bobbing eagerly, so close to her mouth. So many possibilities, but she was determined to stick to her first plan. When her hands touched his skin, a little shudder ran through his body.

Max let out a tight laugh. "I'm so fucking turned on right now, you'd think I hadn't gotten action just a few hours ago. I can't believe how much I want you right now."

Her movements slowed, but she said nothing. She wanted him badly, too, probably more than she should. So she narrowed her focus to what was in front of her, running her fingers down his length, testing his girth, playing with his tip.

"Put it on, Natasha," he said, his voice darker. "I want to be inside you."

Slowly, she rolled the condom down his cock and

leaned back to admire her work. Max offered her a hand, and when she stood up, he didn't let her go.

She led them to the green dress, spread out on the white beach. He sat down first, leaving her standing with her bare pussy directly in front of him.

"Goddamn," he said softly. "Can I lick you?"

Natasha grinned. "I don't think my legs will hold out."

"Just once." His hands brushed over her ass, coaxing her closer.

"If you insist." The comment was meant to be dry and witty, but her voice came out breathy instead.

His tongue was hot and slick against her, short-circuiting her thoughts with an erotic jolt. Her legs almost buckled under her.

Natasha moaned. "I'm so ready."

"Then climb on, darlin'," he said, his hands still on her hips, steadying her.

She sank to her knees and reached between them for his thick erection. Positioning it, she lowered herself onto him. Slowly, inch by inch, the exquisite pleasure of his cock filled her. His eyes were steady on her the whole time, his face drawn in tight restraint as she took more and more of him. He was big, really big, and the overwhelming urge to move, to fuck, was already building as her body accommodated his size. She swiveled her hips and shimmied, taking more and more until, finally, she was sitting with his cock deep inside her.

"It's our first time," he said. His voice was serious, and his eyes were filled with wonder.

She nodded, unsure if she wanted to speak right now. Instead, she raised herself and came down, his hard length sinking into her again. Max groaned and lay back on her dress. The next time she lifted herself up, he grabbed her ass with both hands and brought her down on him, hard. Oh, God, this felt amazing. *He* felt amazing.

"You okay?" he asked gruffly.

She searched for her voice. "Much better than okay."

"Good."

The next time she slid down his cock, his hips bucked to meet hers.

"You feel so good," he rasped.

She was getting past the point of speaking, so she let the pleasure take over, rising up and coming down, stroke after stroke, each one harder, faster. His eyes stayed fixed on hers in silent challenge: *Look at me. Don't forget it's me who makes you feel this way.*

But she wasn't in any danger of forgetting.

"I'm close," she panted out.

"Touch yourself," he growled.

She slipped her hand between them and found her clit, swirling her fingers in all the wet heat, pushing her pleasure higher.

"Fuck, yes." His voice was wild.

His words sent her over the edge. A rush of ecstasy filled her as she came hard. Max's hands tightened around her hips as he lifted her, again and again, milking her pleasure until he roared, his whole body jerking under her.

Natasha collapsed onto his chest, heaving in breaths. Max's arms enveloped her, pulling her even closer. His heartbeat thumped in her ear, the leaves of the trees rustled and the water lapped onto the shore. Paradise. Beautiful, ethereal paradise.

Today had been absolutely perfect. She was on vacation with her sister, diving and relaxing on a tropical island, with a generous helping of sex with her first pick of men, Max Jensen. When had she had this much fun? Never. The pleasure of this day alone was well worth the coming heartache.

Because today had also made it clear that letting Max go would be hard. Maybe she'd even known from the beginning, deep down, that it would be like this. But she could be there for him on Saturday if he needed it. One more date with him wouldn't make a difference. She could handle it.

CHAPTER TWELVE

Natasha was left alone with her thoughts, and she was trying hard not to let those thoughts wander off the island. It wasn't working very well. Her view of the pool, after a morning full of wispy women and buffed and shaved men, was now empty. Everyone else was on the other side of the island at the photoshoot. Max had left to escort Alya, but he'd be back soon. It was Sunday, the last day of the shoot. Their last day together.

Natasha had probably laughed more in the hours she and Max had been alone together than during her entire relationship with Wayne. But that wasn't fair. Wayne was different—he made her think, pushed her to do better…well, at least it had started that way. They'd discussed journal articles, and he had helped her solve some of the stumbling blocks in her own research ideas, which had led to the grant that would be funding half of her salary next year.

Which was why she'd assumed that he'd be thrilled about the next step in her career. Yes, she'd known his most recent grant proposal hadn't gone through, but he was in a different field. This was what had stung the worst the night of her un-celebration dinner. Not that he'd encouraged her to see other people, but that his support ended the moment it looked like she might be a peer, not just a protégé.

Natasha frowned. She had devoted her life to a path that was the polar opposite of her mother's. And yet she had managed to hit that same sore point of betrayal. For her mother, each of her downward spirals had begun at the point when her career had begun to eclipse her partner's. For Natasha, it was the moment she realized that her relationship with Wayne had never been based on mutual respect, on equal footing.

She was pretty sure Max would never feel threatened by her accomplishments—that wasn't the issue. But if Wayne made her think, Max did the opposite: he made her feel things that made logical thoughts dissolve into lust-filled nonsense. Long-term, this would be a non-starter, but short-term? This could mean more of the kind of elusive, carefree fun that she was just starting to explore with Max.

As if she'd conjured him with her thoughts, she watched Max stride across the pool area toward her.

He stopped next to her lounge chair, so she moved her legs to the side, and he sat down, then ran a hand up her calf.

"Photoshoot going well for Alya so far?" she asked.

He grinned. "When I left, they had her lying on the beach, not far from where we were last night."

"Good thing you didn't leave that condom lying around," said Natasha.

"And let some poor sea creature find it?" he asked solemnly. "I wouldn't dare."

He was quiet, stroking her calf, looking out at the pool. This was their last time alone. Anything she wanted to do or know had to come now.

"Tell me more about next Saturday," she said.

He sighed. "The Jensen Family Foundation teamed up with the Martinelli Foundation to create a breast cancer research institute at the Sydney Memorial Hospital. It's the donor dinner, with a few quick speeches, dancing, an open bar." A hint of a smile quirked at the corner of his lips. "Shit like that is more fun if you have a couple drinks."

Natasha took a deep breath. If she wanted to ask more about his family, now was the time. "Are you on good terms with your family?"

"My grandma's a trip," he said. "You'll like her."

They both knew it wasn't his grandma she was referring to, so she waited. Like everyone else, she knew the basics. Max was third generation in a ranching family with more money than everyone else in Western Australia put together. Every country had its dynasties, and the Jensens were one of Australia's, partly because of their wealth and partly because of their mystique.

Max sighed. "The answer is no, Natasha. My father and I just aren't a good match. We never have been."

"What does that mean?" she asked gently.

"My father doesn't say much, and when he does, it's mostly to tell me what to do," he said with a wry smile. "My brother, TJ, doesn't say much, either, but he stopped telling me what to do once I got big enough to challenge him. So now we get along."

She heard a tangle of emotions in his voice. "It hasn't gotten better over the years, now that you live far away?"

"Somewhat. Though my father still had plenty to say about what the press printed about me." Max shrugged. "I don't give a shit about it unless it hurts someone else, though I suppose I'll have to change that now that I'll be heading up the foundation."

Natasha definitely understood what it felt like to not fit into the mold a parent had hoped for. Her own mother still couldn't grasp why she had pursued an academic career instead of something "easier"—and more lucrative—in entertainment.

Max was silent. He lifted her leg and rested it on his lap, holding it with his big, warm hand, his thumb caressing her calf slowly.

She thought the conversation might be over, but after a while, he spoke again. "When my mother was diagnosed with breast cancer, her depression got worse. My father—he didn't know what to do about it."

"What did you want him to do?"

"Help her. Make her happy."

She wrinkled her nose but said nothing. He seemed to understand her unspoken response anyway.

"I know," he said. "You don't believe in making other people happy."

She rested her hand on his. "Will it be hard to go?"

"It'll be a hell of a lot easier if you go with me," he said softly.

* * *

Inviting Natasha to come with him to the Jensen Family Foundation function was selfish. She had come to him this weekend for the best kind of fun, but every hour that this time-limited arrangement went on it seemed more and more like a mistake. It wasn't enough. Even during that first kiss in her apartment, when he had her up against the table, ready to fuck her right there, he had ignored the warning lights going off inside. And last night on the beach was…intense.

Maybe he should really come clean with her, tell her that his life was about to change, that, if his father's experience was any indication, any woman he was with would be put through the wringer, no matter how faithful he was. But they weren't together, and he could figure out how to hold off the press just for Saturday. And then he'd leave her alone.

It was his last day with her in paradise, and he didn't want to spend it talking about his family. Not when they could be doing other things… His dick usually provided him with the easiest distraction, and it didn't take much of a jump to get from *last day alone with Natasha* to *alone with Natasha*.

Yep, that did the trick.

Hell, he'd try sex in the pool with her right now if she wanted. Just thinking about it was enough to get his cock hard.

Wait. They had hours together. Enough time for some fun foreplay of the marine-life sort. Last night on the beach had been hot, with her on his lap, that lush body up against him. The beach, the ocean, the island, her laugh, her body that was so goddamn hard to ignore, her voice—all these pieces fit together to make something more. If this had to end, he wanted to enjoy every part of her. Make her laugh. Listen as she explained the nuances of fish relationships or whatever the hell she wanted to talk about. Just be the way they were together.

Natasha met his gaze and smiled. It was a real smile, soft and intimate, and it awakened every part of him. He'd had far too many "just sex" arrangements not to recognize that this was more than just sex. It had been more from the beginning. Her smile was full of pleasure, and it was just for him. He winced as the familiar warning sirens went off: *danger*. From their first kiss, he had suspected he was in danger of getting attached, but in that moment, he knew with no doubt that walking away from this fling would hurt like hell. He could deal with that. What gave him pause was Natasha's unguarded smile. Would she get hurt, too?

Still, he leaned over and ran his hand up her bare thigh again. Still, he looked into her eyes with something more than just lust.

But in a way, this was his warning to her. She could back away right now, get out from under the intensity of his gaze. She blinked up at him, her eyes wide and a little uncertain. He watched her soft, sweet throat as she swallowed. His heart pounded in his chest, but he forced himself to wait her out.

Finally, she broke the eye contact. "I've got another Choose Your Own Adventure idea," she said with a grin.

Max bit back a sigh of relief. No backing out. Later he'd worry about what all of this meant, but for a few hours today, it was just the two of them.

He leaned in farther, making slow circles on her thigh. "Tell me."

"Professor/student," she said. "Is that a scenario that turns you on?"

He quirked a brow, nodded, and she laughed as a flush crept up her neck. Embarrassment? Arousal? Or maybe both.

Max smiled. He could definitely get into this one. "I like it. In this story, are you the professor and I'm the student, or the other way around?"

"You're the professor, and you're blown away by my impressive knowledge about fish behavior." Natasha turned to him, her eyes sparkling. If there had been any trace of embarrassment when she broached the subject, it was gone now. "We talk after class about a paper you wrote about the behavior of reef sharks rereleased into the wild, and I point out some new possibilities for further studies. You're both intrigued by my ideas and turned on."

Max nodded slowly, intoxicated by the scent of her hair, the scent of her. Intrigued by her ideas and turned on? Hell, yes, he could do that, no role-playing involved. But she clearly had thought through this scenario in detail, and he was going to give her exactly what she wanted.

"What happens next?" he asked, his voice huskier.

"I come to your office after hours with an article about another fish with possible similar behaviors, one that you hadn't read," she said, her voice breathy. "It was a secondary finding in the article, easy to miss if—um, is this getting too detailed and science-y for you?"

"What? No." Max blinked down at her. "Why would you think that?"

Natasha frowned a little. "It's just that men tend to glaze over a little when I start talking about my research."

"That's your conclusion?" he asked. "A few assholes don't pay attention when you talk, and you think all men don't find you interesting?"

Natasha shrugged. "All people have parts that are more or less sexy." She perused the length of his body, a smile curving on her lips. "Well, everyone except you. You're hot, through and through."

Max's knee-jerk reaction to this comment was lewd, but he paused. Her comment was bothering him.

"Sorry, Natasha, but that's not how it works. We all come as package deals. And anyone who wants to unbundle the package, just choose some of the parts, doesn't know shit about people." He leaned a little closer and added, "Or about you."

She didn't answer right away. She was probably thinking about this, coming to her own conclusions, but then she smiled. "Did I just take all the sexy out of this moment?"

"Not even close." Max laughed. He turned around to straddle the lounge chair so he was facing her, with her legs resting on one of his. Then he reached forward and tickled her stomach.

"Stop!" she shrieked and wriggled away.

He stopped tickling but kept his hands on her waist. Just sitting next to Natasha was weakening his resolve to make this afternoon about more than sex.

And then he knew exactly what else they should be doing this afternoon.

"Before we get started playing out your scenario, I thought we could do a little reef exploring," he said.

Her eyes widened, as if that were the last thing she'd been expecting out of his mouth. A little crease formed between her eyebrows.

"You want to do that?" She grinned. "You don't have to go snorkeling to get me naked. I thought we already established that."

He chuckled. "I know."

But she still didn't look like she was convinced.

"I'm serious, Nat," he said. "I want to see some of that fish sex you've been talking about."

Natasha raised an eyebrow. "Fish sex instead of real sex?"

"We have four hours before the magazine shoot ends," he said. "While I'm flattered by your confidence in my stamina, I'm pretty sure four hours would push even my limits."

Natasha snorted, shaking her head.

"We have time for both. So let's go out."

He moved his hands lower, onto her hips, and smiled.

"Come on," he whispered. "There's tons of sexy stuff going on out there in the ocean, and we're missing it."

Her shoulders shook in a quiet laugh, but when she met his gaze, her eyes were warm and a little shy.

"How about we look for epaulette sharks?" she asked.

Um…sharks? Max frowned. "I thought people generally tried to avoid sharks when they went in the water."

Natasha just smiled. "Come on, Max. It'll be fun. You just need a pair of sturdy shoes."

Was she joking?

"I thought those things were called flippers," he said narrowing his eyes. "But who am I to correct the marine biologist?"

Natasha sighed in exasperation. "You want to be in charge of this outing?"

The corners of his mouth turned up. "Okay, I'm game. As long as this doesn't involve any strand-the-novice-in-shark-infested-waters humor."

She threw back her head and laughed. What the hell was so funny about all this?

"Shoes, seriously. In case you accidentally step somewhere sharp," she said. "And I promise I won't leave you alone with the sharks."

"All right," he said warily. He eyed her tank top and shorts. "You changing first?"

She shook her head.

"Nice," he said. "I like the wet T-shirt thing."

Natasha rolled her eyes and gave him a little push off the lounger. "Let's go."

Max headed for the cabin and changed into his suit and tennis shoes then met Natasha outside. She was still sitting on one of the pool deck chairs, now wearing sunglasses and a hat. Her gaze slid down his body, slowing at his bare chest. He waited, letting her get her fill. He knew he looked good. And after spending the morning trying to block out Natasha's luscious body in that red bikini she'd worn yesterday, he wouldn't mind flipping that dynamic. Maybe she'd—

"Um, you might want to put a shirt on," she said, interrupting that train of thought.

"I'm confident you can look without touching," he said, grinning. "But I'll let you know if I'm feeling violated."

He could see Natasha was fighting a smile. "For sunburn, Max."

Max waved off her comment. "I'm fine. I put on sunblock, though you're welcome to apply another layer. In any area."

She sighed and shook her head.

"At least sunglasses," she said.

"Aren't we using that stuff?" He gestured to the basket of masks, snorkels and other gear outside the cabin.

"Nope."

What the hell? Something was definitely going on. At her insistence, he grabbed his sunglasses and a shirt, and followed her down toward the beach.

They started along the trail that led out to the shore, where they had met up the day before. But when they hit the sand, she turned.

"We don't seem dressed for this," he said conversationally.

"You'll see."

They continued through the sand until they came to a row of sturdy-looking yellow kayaks.

"We'll take these," she said and headed up the beach to where the paddles lay.

Max looked down at the kayaks. More like oversized surf boards with a seat in the middle. The kind where their legs would be uncovered. He wasn't a small guy by any stretch, and it wouldn't take much of a nudge to tip him out of one of these. Into shark-infested waters.

"I've seen *Jaws*," he said casually. "And I'm pretty sure this little boat won't offer me much protection."

Natasha just laughed as she dragged the kayak down the beach. She looked completely at ease, and she had a hell of a lot more experience in this area than he did. Time to get his shit together and go look for sharks.

They slid the boats into the warm water, and Max climbed on, tottering a little before he found the center. Natasha paddled out toward the jetty, and he followed. The surface of the water was calm, almost glassy, and he rested his paddle to peer down at the reef. Fish of all colors and shapes swam under him, weaving through the bright coral. Slowly, they made their way around the island, under the jetty to the mainland side. The tide was low, and parts of the reef jutted out of the water.

"We're going there," she said, pointing at the exposed reef. "We'll probably have the best chance of seeing epaulette sharks right at the shallow edges."

Were they headed for some sort of drop-off point where the sharks gathered for unsuspecting prey? At least his kayak was red and not seal-belly gray... though red was the color of blood. She was right about one thing—flippers weren't the best choice for this viewing.

Max paddled through the roped-off snorkeling section and into a deeper patch with a sandy bottom. Right beyond them, the coral beds stretched off that side of the island, dark and glistening. Natasha stopped paddling, drifting right beside the exposed reef but not touching it. Max maneuvered his kayak just behind hers and looked down into the water. Sandy paths wove into the crevices between the coral. On these sandy paths, little things moved. The water stilled around them, giving him a better view of the fish that swam in and out of the channel.

"What are those fish called?" he asked, pointing at a yellow pair.

Natasha followed his gaze. "Those are longnose butterflyfish. But the one swimming there..." She pointed to another yellow fish just beyond the pair. "That one's a raccoon butterflyfish. See the difference in the black stripes?"

Yeah, he did.

"Hey, look," he said, pointing next to the raccoon butterflyfish. "Some creature took a dump in here. Pretty big. Is it shark shit?"

Natasha looked where he was pointing. "That's a sea cucumber, Max. It's alive. And they're not dangerous."

His eyes met hers, and she started to laugh. A rush of tenderness swells inside him as her eyes glittered with warmth and humor. It felt so good to do just about anything with her. They were nowhere near the bedroom, but every moment together made the attraction between them grow.

"You sure this is shark territory?" he said. "I know I'm not the scientist here, but I'm pretty sure they need deeper water to sneak up on their prey. The reef is really shallow here."

She *tsked* at him over her shoulder. "Patience, Max."

The hot sun blazed down on him. It was probably good he'd covered up because the heat was intense.

They paddled farther along on the reef. Some of the channels were deeper, so he kept a lookout on both sides for approaching sharks. Natasha slowed as they came to one of the crevices, looking into clear water.

Max looked, too, but there was nothing but sand. "Is this when you tell me that the shark is invisible?"

Natasha laughed. "No. I thought I saw an eel. But if we see a shark, it'll be around here, too."

"Come on, Nat," he said. "What's going on?"

"The sharks we're looking for are small," she said with a wink.

Max eyed her skeptically. "How small are we talking about?"

Natasha held out her hands. The space between them was less than the length of two rugby balls.

"You're kidding," he said. "A mini-shark?"

"An epaulette shark," she corrected. Then she gave

him a wide smile. "But wait until you hear what it does. It walks."

Her excitement was infectious. "On its fins?"

"Yes! Exactly," she said. "Crazy, right?"

Max might have found that fact interesting on its own, but the joy and excitement in Natasha's voice raised it another few notches. Before he met her, Max had never thought much about fish beyond his own menu preferences, but it was the way she lit up when talking about marine life that had him hanging on to every detail. Yes, he teased her a little about it, but more than anything else, he admired it. There was something so pure, so uncalculated about her passion for fish, of all things.

"Does this thing look like a shark?" he asked. "Will I recognize it?"

"The shape is similar to other sharks, but it's spotted," she said. "Big spots."

He pressed his lips together. *Just ask the question, you wanker.*

Max cleared his throat. "Is it, um, known for biting humans?"

A grin spread across her face. "It's not dangerous, Max."

Some of the tension left his shoulders, and he cleared his throat. "Just checking."

He was almost sure she smothered a laugh as she turned to paddle away. They floated along the edge of the reef, peering into the channels of water.

"Low tide is a great time to see some of these species up close without disturbing them. I would have taken you diving, but the shallow water is full of different stingers, so you'd need full gear. Underwater it's even better." She pointed down at a bright sea star draped over a small piece of coral. "Check out this guy."

Max leaned over the side of the kayak to get a better look. "How do they work? I don't see the eyes or mouth."

"They don't have eyes. And their version of a mouth is underneath."

"Huh," he said, studying it. "What does sea star sex look like?"

Natasha snorted. "It's not sexy. We can watch a video later if you want to."

"I like videos," he said, the corners of his mouth tugging up.

Her kayak was next to his, and he was dying to get closer to her. The sounds of the shore, the palms, the breeze, the lapping of water on the coral, all mingled with her breaths, shorter, faster, as if she, too, was taking in the gentle friction between their bodies. He wanted this woman.

She bit her lip and smiled. "If that's your thing. I'm not judging."

Max threw back his head and laughed. When he looked at her again, Natasha's smile was full and glorious. She looked so happy. And his heart, his breaths, expanded in the glow of her happiness.

"Why fish, Natasha?" he asked.

She tilted her head to the side, her hair falling over her shoulders in sexy waves. "What do you mean?"

"Your parents are both actors, and your sister is a model. How the hell did you get interested in all this?"

She shrugged. "I first got into biology because I love patterns. I love that even some of the craziest behaviors make sense if you look hard enough. Though the more I look, the crazier—"

Suddenly, she put her hand on his leg, as if to still him.

"There it is," she hissed. "An epaulette shark. Don't move."

She pointed just up the channel they were hovering over. And there, swimming toward them, was a little…shark. Yeah, it did look like a shark if he set aside the size. Pointy nose, dorsal fin and it had a few other fins, too.

"Watch its bottom fins," she whispered. "It uses them to walk on the reef."

They watched in silence as the shark slowly swam up the channel, oblivious to its audience. Max looked at Natasha, her long hair cascading over her shoulders, sunglasses propped on her head, her eyes filled with wonder and amazement as she studied the shark. The water lapped against the rocks, and a warm breeze cut through the heat of the sun, rippling the water. This moment. He wanted to stay right here forever, in the hot sun, with her hand on him like it was the most natural thing in the world.

Natasha's gaze followed the shark's path between

the ridges of exposed reef. Then she met his eyes, and her smile was open and free. She patted him on the leg and straightened up.

"You survived your first shark sighting," she said, amusement sparkling on her face. "I told you I wouldn't leave you alone with them."

CHAPTER THIRTEEN

NATASHA'S SHOES SANK into the sand as she started across the beach, back to the cluster of cabins where they were staying. Max walked next to her, close, his hand brushing against hers or lingering on the small of her back every so often. Thank goodness he had put on his shirt. Even an epaulette shark sighting wouldn't be enough to distract her from the glistening muscles that rippled down his chest. The dusting of hair, the trail that disappeared into his suit. It was all so intimate, so…there.

Oh, no, was she falling for him? It was like he had his own gravitational field, pulling in women who got too close. Even her, who knew better. Life would be so much easier if she were a shark. She'd mate with Max and then her little brain would forget all about him soon after he moved on. Instead, she was stuck with a human brain that wasn't going to forget Max. Especially not after last night on the beach.

Warning signals were flashing in her annoyingly hyperactive brain, and not for the first time. *Get out now. Don't wait until it's too late. You'll turn into a crazy woman.*

But she already knew she wasn't backing out of their last day on the island together. Not when she knew that, no matter who she dated, he'd never be as fun as Max. Or as hot. If this was her chance with him, she was going to take full advantage of it. If she could just resist the temptation to make this more than it was going to be, she might still be able to walk away.

They headed across the beach and cut onto the path that wove through the plants and palm trees toward the cabin. Max's hand brushed the small of her back, and then he reached around and pinched her ass. Natasha yelped and jumped away.

"What was that for?" she asked, laughing.

Max lifted his sunglasses and gave her a mock-serious glare. "You knew I was nervous about the whole shark thing, and you let me think the worst."

She suppressed another laugh. "Maybe."

He dove for her and tickled her. Then, before she could get away, he wrapped his arms around her waist and nuzzled her neck. "You enjoyed it."

"Okay, maybe I did," she said, grinning. "It was fun to feel like I had the advantage for once."

He gave her a searching look, his smile fading. After another beat his expression shifted into something that looked a lot like determination. Max laced his fingers with hers and led the way around the pool, back to their suite. Silently, he opened the door and headed for his bedroom. She followed, and as soon as he shut his door, he slowed to a stop. He turned so they were face-to-face, his hands on her arms, his intense gaze fixed on her. He walked her backward until she was against the cool wood of the door, his sun-warmed body brushing against hers.

He bent over and kissed her neck, her jaw. Every breath, every quiet groan sent another jolt of edgy pleasure through her. Then he pulled back and looked right into her eyes.

"I'm very into this, Natasha," he whispered, his lips so close to hers. "Every part of it. I don't want any misunderstanding about that."

The electric pull jumped and sparked between them, and his gaze dipped lower, to her mouth. Her breath caught in her throat. All day she had suppressed the urge to touch him, to explore, to feel his weight against her. It was so good to be with him on the reef, just laughing, touching, talking. But all that time, tension and want for Max brewed deliciously inside. And they hadn't even taken off their clothes.

Now she wanted more. She wanted a taste of what they would be like together if he wasn't Max Jensen, the press's favorite wealthy playboy.

She kept her gaze steady and lifted her hands to his face. His eyes grew hot as she guided his mouth to hers. His warm lips brushed against hers, soft, almost reverent in their touch. She sighed. His mouth met hers again, and she kissed him back, tasting his bottom lip, then his top.

A deep rumble came from him, and then they were really kissing. Hungry, needy kisses, searching, finding, looking for more. He eased her back onto the bed and climbed over her, breathless gasps mingling together. His palms came to her cheeks, and he tilted his head, kissing her, stroking her neck, her sides. His cock was hard on her stomach, and she moved against him, loving the intensity of his arousal. Strong hands lifted her so she could straddle him, her clit against his erection. He groaned and thrust, and the hot burst of pleasure rushed through her. She tilted her hips and ground against him. She nipped at his lips, and he answered with strokes of his tongue. So hungry. So good.

That thought was enough to stop her. Natasha pulled back, shaking off that wild magic that tingled through her. Her fingers and toes and breasts—every part of her begged not to stop. But finally, her brain had caught up with her. She brought her hands to his face and held him a few inches away.

He opened his mouth as if to speak, then closed it again. Finally, he sighed.

"This isn't how it usually feels for me. This feels like…something more."

His expression was so serious, so intense. His hand was on her cheek, coaxing her eyes to his, as if he were daring her to look away. The electric pull between them was sparking again. Natasha still could steel herself against the power of Max's charm…couldn't she? But now that those warning lights had turned on, it was impossible to ignore them. She could recognize that road to crazy from a mile away. And she had already started down it. Which wasn't supposed to happen after a couple days of sex and fun.

"We don't have a package deal, Max," she said, keeping her voice steady. "This is à la carte, remember?"

Natasha wasn't even sure what they were negotiating, but her feelings about him were shifting, something that wasn't what she'd bargained for.

"What if I'm interested in some items not listed on the à la carte menu?" he asked with a hint of frustration.

Her heart sped up, pumping unwanted hope through her. Still, she shook her head. "It doesn't work that way."

Max's expression turned darker, so un-Max-like. "I wouldn't do anything to hurt you."

He clearly had more to say, but for once, the words didn't flow out of his mouth. Leave it to her to provoke the world's most easygoing man.

Or maybe it wasn't that. Because the more she looked into Max's eyes, the more that explanation felt like an excuse. Maybe he was just letting her see more of him this time, even that intensity, that drive that he kept so expertly cloaked beneath his good-natured exterior. She mentally squirmed under Max's gaze but was determined not to look away.

His gaze softened, and she saw more. Something profound and aching, something she had no words for. He was struggling, too. Her chest tightened. She drew in a shaky breath, fighting the deep ache of tenderness she felt for him. It was too much.

Finally, he bowed his head, and when he looked back up at her there was something new in his eyes. Understanding? She swallowed the lump in her throat.

He nuzzled her on the neck, tickling her with the stubble on his jaw until she smiled.

"You want to stop?" he asked.

His cock was still hard against her, reminding her of one of many reasons she was here with this man.

She smiled a little. "Hell, no."

Physical memories from the beach yesterday flashed through her. His voice rumbling in her ear. The hard muscles of his chest. His arms around her, his thick cock inside her. She let out a hum of pleasure as some of the heaviness between them dissolved.

He nuzzled her once more and pushed up onto his knees. The muscles across his chest rippled and flexed. "I think it's time to get naked."

He undid the laces of his board shorts and stuck his hand inside them. A satisfied groan came from his mouth. Damn, she could watch him all day long. Or she could get naked and do more than watch.

Natasha shed her clothes. Max reached into his bag and pulled out a condom, tossing it onto the bed. Then he was right behind her, his hands on her hips, his hard length between her legs.

"Oh, yes, Max," she whispered, a shudder of pleasure coursing through her. "More."

"On your hands and knees, sweetheart," he whispered.

Max never let go of her as she turned around on the bed. He ran his hand down her back, over her ass, around her hips and between her legs. He teased her clit and slipped two fingers inside her. Waves of pleasure radiated through her as she moved against his hand.

"Last night, in my bed, I imagined looking at you like this," he said, his voice lower. "First, you'd take out my cock and ride me, just like you did on the beach, and I'd watch your beautiful tits bounce as you moved up and down. And then, when you were out of breath, I'd turn you over and fuck you just like this."

His fingers were teasing her, but it was his words that really got her going.

"I want that, Max."

"I'm so worked up right now," he rasped. "And you feel so ready."

"I am," she said, losing herself in the pleasure.

His hand left her, and she turned her head to watch as he tore off the wrapper from the condom and rolled it down his glistening cock. His face was twisted with pleasure. Then he looked up at her, right into her eyes. He held her gaze, his expression stormy. He opened his mouth but hesitated, as if he was debating whether to speak.

He swallowed, then positioned his cock against her. "This is my wet dream, Natasha. You are my dream. That's not going to change."

Before she had a chance to think further about his words, he sank inside her in one, slow thrust that took her breath away.

Fuck, this was so good, so right. Max clenched his jaw, teetering on the edge of control, willing himself not to give in to the overwhelming urge to come. Just burying his cock deep inside the delicious warmth of Natasha's pussy was more than he could bear. Just hearing her gasp and sigh and moan as he filled her would push him over the edge if he wasn't careful.

His balls were tingling, aching for that satisfying slap of contact at each hard thrust, but he resisted. Max had resigned himself to his never-ending need for this woman. He had long passed the point of stopping before he got in too deep.

But the vulnerability on her face as he said he wouldn't hurt her had twisted hard in his gut. Still, he had pushed her further.

You are my dream. That's not going to change.

The truth, despite the fact that he was on a path that she had spent her life trying to avoid. But instead of slowing this down, making sure she understood, he was burying it in sex.

He should have called it off, but he hadn't. He had passed by all the warning signs and sunk balls-deep inside her again. Max would like to blame his insatiable cock, but that would be a lie. He wanted her to laugh. He wanted her to tell him about whatever went on in her mind—sex, fish, her worries, her past. Everything. He wanted her to let herself *want*. But now, after a few days together, he wanted even more than that. He wanted to be the only man to give her these things.

He wanted to take back every limit they had made about this weekend.

If she wouldn't let him, at least he could show her

what it was like for a man to want all of her, not just parts. He could show her what it felt like to have a man worship her.

Max eased his fingers from her hips and explored the soft skin of her waist, her back, her arms. He gathered the long strands of her hair and moved them over one shoulder. Then he lowered himself over her, his hands on the bed beside hers, his chest skimming her back. He pressed a kiss on her shoulder blade.

"You feeling good, sweetheart?" he asked, his lips brushing against her skin.

"Better than good."

"Even for à la carte customers, I aim to satisfy," he said.

She laughed, but her voice sounded shaky.

Then he started to move. His legs were longer than hers, long enough that straddling hers, he could experiment with angles a little, figure out what made her body hum. And then he found it. Her breaths turned to moans, deep and loud with every thrust. Yes, he could do this for her, give her what she wanted.

"Do you feel how hard you make me?" he growled in her ear. "Everything about you turns me on, Natasha. Everything."

"Oh, Max," she moaned. "This is so good. I want—"

Max slowed, waiting for the end of the sentence. What did she want? Was it about sex, or was it more? But she didn't finish. Instead, her body moved and hummed under his, and he found his way deeper inside her, over and over. And still he wanted more. Deep down, he was a selfish bastard, and he wanted it all with this woman.

"Lay your head down," he rasped. "Let me in deeper. Give me more of you."

"Always." Her voiced mingled with her breaths. She came down onto her elbows, lying on her cheek, her ass still up in the air. Her eyes were closed, her mouth parted, gasping, as if she were on the brink of ecstasy. Even if this had to end, this moment was theirs. Real.

"Oh, baby, I want you," he groaned, his hips moving faster. "Natasha."

She cried out as he spoke her name, meeting each thrust, gasping, saying his name over and over. She came, clenching around his cock, setting off bursts of pleasure through him. He needed to come, and this time he wasn't going to stop that urge.

His body went rigid as his cock went off. Max dropped down to his elbows and let go, sinking his teeth into the tender slope of her neck. Her pussy tightened again as she bucked beneath him, wailing, "Yes, Max, yes," the words branding into him as the waves of pleasure shot through him. There was nothing else except Natasha.

Slowly, the rest of the world came into focus. The rustle of the palm trees, the squawks of birds, the soft lull of the ocean.

He lifted his mouth from her shoulder and looked down at the red bite mark.

"Shit," he muttered. "I bit you again. Hard."

"Hard enough that the whole island probably heard me," she whispered. "It was amazing."

He kissed the spot, then turned her over to study her face. Her gray eyes were still a little unfocused, and a languid smile played at her lips, but her forehead wrinkled a little. Was she turning over his words in her mind, just like he was?

Then she smiled up at him as if there was nothing more that she needed in the world. Just him. And it was so goddamn tempting to believe it. To push aside all the reasons to the contrary and promise that he was the one for her.

She blinked up at him, her smile fading. Natasha lifted her hand and stroked his cheek, and he closed his eyes and let everything else fade away except her touch. She stroked his jaw, her hand moving back and forth over the stubble. Her fingers trembled as they moved over his lips. When he opened his eyes again, she was staring up at him with a crease running across her brow, as if she were studying him. Memorizing him.

"How long until the boat comes?" asked Alya, rolling her suitcase to the bedroom door.

Natasha looked up from the pile of clothes in front of her and glanced at her watch. "A little more than thirty minutes."

"I'll be by the pool if you need me."

Natasha blinked up at her sister. "You're already packed?"

"Yep. You'd be packed, too, if you hadn't been staring at your suitcase for the last twenty minutes." Her sister looked out their door, in the direction of the other bedroom. "Is everything okay between you and Max?"

Natasha frowned. "Why wouldn't it be?"

Her sister shrugged. "Your mind is somewhere else, and he just seems a little…subdued. For Max."

"We're fine. Nothing's changed." That was the problem. Everything felt different now, but nothing had really changed. She would return to Sydney, pretending that Max had not turned her entire world upside down on Green Island. She bit her lip and looked down at her half-packed suitcase before Alya could read any more into her expression. "I'll be out in a bit."

Alya didn't leave. She stood by the door, her eyes still fixed on Natasha, as if she had more to say. Natasha turned away, shoving shirts and socks into her suitcase, and a few moments later her sister's footsteps shuffled out. At the sound of the door, her shoulders slumped.

God, she was a mess. Earlier, neither of them had said a word as she'd slowly pulled her clothes on, but his touch had been gentle, soothing.

After just a few days in paradise, Max had succeeded in slipping through every protection she had built around herself, and the crazy want for him was building up in her. Was she falling in love with Max Jensen, Australia's notorious heartbreaker, all Illana Petrova style? God, no. She couldn't be.

What she needed was time. Time to think this through rationally.

So after she left his bedroom for the last time, she'd avoided him for the rest of the afternoon, spending time in the water. When she'd come back, Max and Alya had returned from the final shoot. Soon they would leave Green Island behind. This would all make more sense when real life resumed on Monday.

Natasha unplugged her phone and looked at it for the first time since she had arrived. Sixteen missed calls from Wayne. Sixteen messages. Natasha raised an eyebrow. An unprecedented effort by him. A few days ago, she might have called him back. But right now, she didn't even care. All she could think about was Max. She shoved her phone into the side pocket of her bag and grabbed another handful of clothes.

Natasha didn't hear Max enter, but all at once she felt him there, behind her. She turned around slowly. The scruff, the board shorts, the tousled blond hair—that Max was gone. In his place was the clean-shaven man, dressed in black, all hard muscles and intense gaze. His blue eyes were dark and stormy, and tension radiated in his every move. His jaw ticked as he stared down at her.

"I need to pack, Max," she said, hoping he'd take the hint and leave.

Of course, he didn't. He just stared down at her.

"I knew this could hurt you, and I still did it."

"You knew it could hurt me? Not you?"

He looked annoyed. "You're missing the point. This isn't about whether or not *I* get hurt."

"Of course it's not," she said lightly. "You're Max Jensen, the most easygoing bachelor in the whole country. You'd just let it roll off you and move on."

For a moment, the hurt on his face was so raw that

she felt sick to her stomach. Oh, God, what was she doing? Hurting him intentionally? Even as she spoke these words, she'd known they weren't true. He just acted like everything rolled off him, and she was using it against him. This whole conversation was a bad idea.

Natasha took a deep breath. "I didn't mean that, Max. I know it's not true, and I'm sorry. I think we should end this conversation before I say anything else I regret."

She turned away, back to her suitcase, but Max didn't leave. He came closer, squatting down beside her. His breaths rang in her ears, and his scent was everywhere. She closed her eyes, unable to stop the want flooding through her. God, she would probably never get over this man. No more events with Alya. She'd have to just keep her distance.

His warm hand glided over her bare arm, and she braced herself against the bolt of desire that coursed through her. He must have felt her reaction because he let go.

"*Shit*," he muttered. She opened her eyes, and he was so close, his face twisted with frustration. Her heart squeezed in her chest.

He held up his hands. "Please, let me finish." Heat flared in his gaze, and his voice lowered as he spoke these last words.

Natasha bit her lip, nodded and his gaze jumped down to her mouth and stayed there for an extra beat. When his eyes met hers again, the flames burst higher.

The tidal wave of emotions was building in her, the feelings that weren't supposed to come with a quick fling. After spending years constructing her life to avoid her mother's path, somehow she had ended up here anyway.

"I know how you feel about who I am and what it means to be a Jensen, but that doesn't stop me from wanting you anyway," he said, his voice low.

She blinked up at him, too stunned to get words out. That was how he saw their situation? Red warning lights were flashing in her brain. She squeezed her eyes shut, resisting the overpowering urge to do something stupid and rash, searching for other reasons that they could never be more than a fling. "It's not just that. I've seen how you feel about monogamy."

Max winced. He opened his mouth to speak but hesitated. Then he leaned closer, so they were almost touching.

"Let's make this clear. I have no problem with monogamy," he said, his voice low. "I just don't see the point unless it's someone I'm serious about."

"You're looking for someone serious but you're sleeping around?" she asked, not bothering to hide her incredulity. "Hmm…"

He gritted his teeth. "I'm thinking that I've found someone I could be serious about. But she doesn't want me, exactly as I am."

That was a direct hit, and the words shook the foundation of her entire adult life. It was the truth, and spoken so plainly, it sounded awful. When she distilled all her hesitations, she didn't want him because she was afraid of his high-profile position, something he was born into, something he didn't control. And he knew it. Yeah, he slept around, but the same prying eyes would have torn into his life even if he didn't—Alya's own battle with the media during her career had taught her that much. Natasha sucked in a shaky breath as he brought his hand to her cheek.

"What would you have preferred, Natasha?" he asked quietly. "I expressed my interest three years ago, and you didn't want anything to do with me. Were you expecting celibacy?"

She shook her head slowly. She hadn't exactly been celibate, either. But the larger question was this: Could she really put herself out there, take a chance on a connection forged through a few days of sexcapades? That chance had to be carefully weighed against the very high probability she'd be analyzed, scrutinized, and she knew exactly where that would lead.

"I don't even know what we're talking about anymore," she said quietly. "Sneaking around for more sex until we get caught? Dating?"

He stroked her cheek but didn't answer.

"I was the ugly duckling sister," she said. How did those words still have the power to hurt her? This was the last thing she wanted to talk about, but it was better that Max understood.

"Thirteen is a tough age to see that in print. And I had a mother who agonized over everything that was written about her, so, of course, I believed it mattered. As did most of the kids I went to school with." Natasha swallowed, pushing herself to continue. "At first,

I tried to hide myself, and then I tried to fix myself, to be someone different. Even when I finally decided that I wasn't going to care anymore, sometimes I still found myself wondering, do people still see me as the ugly duckling?"

She had told this story to Wayne, too, but saying it to Max, the man who made her feel both beautiful and vulnerable, was different. Harder.

"Coming to Australia wasn't just good for Alya. It was a fresh start for me, too. I didn't realize how much I needed it until I arrived." Natasha straightened up. "I can't go through that again, Max. Even if I'm not an ugly duckling anymore, the media always finds something."

She took a deep breath and looked at him. Hurt was etched into his beautiful features, and there was so much worry and fear in his eyes. Still, he said nothing. His touch was gentle, and his gaze never left her.

"Max and Nat?" Alya's voice came from the front door. "It's time to go. We have to catch the boat."

The tension in the room shifted instantly. This was really coming to an end. Max got to his feet. His eyes met hers for one last moment before he turned and walked out the door.

CHAPTER FOURTEEN

NATASHA TOOK A sip of her coffee and cringed. It was cold and bitter. How long had she been sitting here at the kitchen table, staring at the wall, replaying scenes from Green Island…in graphic detail? Too long. She was on holiday, free to do whatever she wanted, and she was spending it on porn-worthy Max memories. And other ones, too: in the water, on the beach, just being together, laughing with him. Natasha sighed. She hated just how much she ached for him,

In a few days she would see him again. Talk to him, touch him, maybe even dance with him. And have one more night of amazing sex, of course. He would make her laugh. And he would make her feel like she was the only woman he wanted. And then what? God, she wasn't going to chase after him, was she?

She doesn't want me exactly as I am.

Max's accusation ran through her head. But, no, it wasn't quite true. She *shouldn't* want to be with him, and yet, after a few days apart, she still did. What made that accusation uncomfortable was that it had echoes of the ugly duckling incident: she had felt rejected for things she had no control over.

Natasha bit her lip. Still, as fantastic as Max was, she was still reasonably sure that there were two kinds of men: manageable and crazy-making. If common sense wasn't enough to convince her to avoid the latter, she had her mother's husbands, number two and number three, to drive home the point. Both had been Max-like—gorgeous, charming playboys. And they both took her mother straight to Crazyville. All that jealousy, staring at the tabloid photos of her husband with other women. Then late-night screaming matches when he came home. But when her mother finally broke away from husband number two, she climbed right back on that crazy bus for husband number three.

Natasha had already felt twinges of jealousy when Max had appeared in the tabloids, kissing his latest fling. Did he look at that woman with the same mix of heat and warmth? Did he make her laugh with the same sexy humor? If all these little stirrings of jealousy had prickled her before Green Island, it would be worse now, whatever their future was together.

Still, Natasha couldn't let go of the possibility that a relationship with Max might be different. Or maybe this was just wishful thinking. At least, it had felt that way on Green Island. But that was so far away from the world Max Jensen, grandson of Deacon Jensen, Sr., moved through.

Alya's footsteps echoed from the hall, and her sister appeared in the doorway.

"Late night?" Natasha asked.

Alya nodded, slumping into her usual chair. She took a sip of Natasha's coffee, cringing as she swallowed.

"Sorry. Should have warned you I've been staring at that cup for a while," said Natasha, taking back the mug. "What happened to you?"

"Couldn't sleep. Stewart came by for his things after you went to bed," she said. "I should have broken up with him a long time ago."

Natasha shrugged. "I get it. You don't like being on your own."

Alya frowned. "That's about the worst reason to stay with a guy I can think of. And I'm done with that." Her sister took a deep breath. "For the last few years, I've built my whole life around a fear. That ends today."

"Wow." The corners of Natasha's mouth tugged up for the first time that morning. "No wonder you couldn't sleep."

Alya smiled and grabbed Natasha's coffee cup, heading for the counter. Pulling two new mugs from the shelves, she poured them each a fresh cup from the pot and returned to the table. Natasha took a sip and sighed. Yeah, coffee tasted much better hot.

She studied her sister. Beyond the puffiness resulting from her recent breakup, Alya's eyes had a new glimmer of determination. Had she shifted from frightened to angry? Angry at Nick for what he'd put her through and angry at herself for spending three years worrying about it?

"So, what's your plan?"

"Still deciding," Alya said. "But for starters, no man in my life for a long time, until I'm no longer using a relationship as a defensive strategy."

"If you want to live on your own at some point, let me know," said Natasha.

Alya wrinkled her brow. "I love living with you, but I think I'd be okay living alone, too. I'm not going to stop using Blackmore Inc.'s services right away. I might occasionally need Max and their IT guy. Henning is very…thorough."

Her voice faded out, and the creases between Alya's eyes deepened. A look crossed her face that Natasha didn't recognize. It wasn't fear, not at all. Something else. But it disappeared almost immediately, before Natasha could make sense of it.

She raked her hands through the tangles in her hair and pushed it over her shoulder. Her sister looked over at her, as if she was going to say something, but her gaze snapped down to Natasha's neck.

"That's a hickey!" Alya's eyes were wide.

"It's, um…yeah." Shit. She'd forgotten about that. She wasn't going to lie to her sister, but right now, Max was the last topic she wanted to discuss.

"From who?" But Natasha could see the realization flicker in Alya's eyes before the question had left her mouth. "You and Max? For real?"

Natasha rolled her eyes. "Is there a way for me to get a hickey that's not 'for real'?"

Alya's eyes brightened as she shook her head slowly. "I could tell something was going on when you two snuck off at dinner that night on Green Island, but I can't believe I missed that it really happened."

"I wore halter tops to cover it, if that makes you feel better."

Alya snorted out a laugh. "Not the hickey. I mean you and Max. You two have been hot for each other forever. I've been waiting for the moment of indulgence to come along."

"Yeah, indulgence," Natasha muttered.

"More than that. You two are great together."

Natasha frowned. "We're not together."

"What? You *have* to be." Alya wrinkled her forehead.

Natasha shook her head. "I'm pretty sure I'm right about this one."

"Really? Because I was sure that once you two got it going—"

"Nope." Natasha's answer came quickly. She had gone over this too many times already.

Alya's eyes widened. She paused, tilting her head, really looking. "Why not, Nat?"

Natasha bit her lip. This was her sister, after all, the only constant in her childhood whirlwind of international moves, foreign languages and her mother's new boyfriends. It was the reason Alya had chosen modeling over college in the first place. The money meant that she and Natasha could live on their own, outside of their mother's chaos. Alya had to understand why she couldn't go there again.

"This is Max. He's just so…" She waved her hand

in the air, searching for the right word. "So much. So out there. It would be the ugly duckling thing all over again. It wouldn't end well for me."

"You are *not* an ugly duckling, Nat, and you never were." The force of her sister's voice startled her. "That photo was taken when you were coming out of the orthodontist's office right after getting braces. Damn. You were thirteen, and those tabloids and gossip sites would say anything to get a reaction. You're letting *that* stop you from even considering Max?"

"It's not just that," Natasha said quietly. "I'm already falling for him. After one weekend."

Alya took her hand. "Natasha, he's crazy about you. He has been for a lot longer than these last few days. He tries not to make it too obvious, but I see it when he's not on the job."

Alya was offering evidence. Reassurance. Did Natasha want to know more, to fan the fires of this attraction to Max higher? She couldn't resist.

"All right, Alya. I'll bite," she said. "How do you know he's crazy about me?"

"Just the way he pays attention to every detail about you." Alya squeezed her hand. "Remember that last night when you were out with Wayne? When I mentioned you sounded upset on the phone, he was ready to go out and look for you."

The tingle of hope inside was spreading too fast to squash it. "Why didn't you say something?"

"Because I was worried, too," Alya said with a snort. "The man does have a reputation."

Natasha sighed. "Yes, he certainly does."

"But, Nat, we were on an island with a group of women and men hired specifically for their good looks and allure, and he had no interest in anyone but you. One of the women—Maxine, with the curly blond hair—even asked me if I was with him. I said no and then watched to see how it would play out. She tried more than once to flirt with him when he walked me to the shoot site, and he gave her no encouragement. None at all."

Natasha had no trouble remembering the looks the women had given Max.

Her sister's eyes were serious. "He's different with you."

Natasha frowned. "But even if that's true, think of what I'm putting myself out there for. Public scrutiny."

"You're right. And there will always be speculation about Max's life, no matter how he lives it."

Alya said this in such a matter-of-fact voice that Natasha blew out a hiss of frustration. How could her sister pretend that it didn't matter when she knew how badly it could go?

"And what happens when it ends?"

"What happens if it doesn't?"

Natasha buried her face in her hands. Why was her sister being so dense about this? "I can't fall for Max. I don't trust myself. You saw how women can't stay away from him. I'm going to be just like our mother, drowning in my own jealousy and suspicions. I've been so careful, and…"

Alya jumped in before she could finish her sentence.

"And you ended up with Wayne, who can't put his big ego aside for one night to celebrate your grant."

Alya was right. Was Wayne really the better option? The kitchen was silent, and Alya's gaze was still fixed on her.

Finally, her sister sighed. "Max wants you exactly as you are. I think we both know that. What could be more important than that?"

Natasha swallowed. "In our larger-than-life family I'm just the ordinary daughter with a minor obsession with fish."

"Nat—"

Her sister tried to interrupt, probably to refute that statement, but Natasha held up her hand.

"The novelty will wear off at some point. I don't want to be just another woman he blows through."

It was hard to speak those words aloud. Was this her real fear—that she'd give all of herself to him, and he'd decide that she was nothing special? That she wasn't enough?

"You don't know what will happen. Isn't that the risk of every relationship?" Alya reached across the table and squeezed Natasha's hand. "You just have to decide if Max is worth the risk."

Max leaned back in the leather office chair and scrubbed his hands over his eyes. Goddamn, this was a mess, and in the three days since they'd returned from Green Island he still hadn't figured out how to fix it.

Now that they were back in Sydney, the fling with

Natasha was supposed to be over. Natasha was supposed to be enjoying her holiday, and Max was supposed to return to work and whatever the fuck he wanted to do.

Except what he wanted to do was to talk to Natasha, be with her, naked or clothed. Yeah, naked was preferable, and Max was almost sure that she'd be more than happy with that choice, too. That wasn't the problem. Once they were alone, all the problems faded, and all that mattered were the good things. Very, very good things.

And, once again, he was thinking with his dick. Not in front of anyone this time, but doing it in his office when he had a shit-ton of work to do wasn't much better.

No matter what he did or what Natasha wanted, everything had changed the moment they left Green Island. Because as they'd walked along the jetty for the last time, it was clear that Max could no longer work with Alya, and it had nothing to do with his new role as president of the Jensen Family Foundation. It had been a challenge to keep his attention off Natasha in the past, but now it was impossible. Thank fuck the risks level had been low—he'd gotten the Petrova sisters through the trip without incident.

But if he no longer worked with Alya, his path wouldn't cross with Natasha unless she wanted them to. Now it all came down to Saturday.

Max propped his feet on his desk, on top of the reports he was supposed to finish this morning. But all he had thought about since he woke up was Natasha. He was so caught up over this woman. All his accomplishments were earned through his ability to block out every distraction and methodically go after exactly what he wanted. He had chosen each of his goals because they were objective measures, unable to be bought with the money and privilege he was born into.

Except it was becoming clear that all his experience of pursuing goals was no help when it came to figuring out what to do about Natasha. Years of going after other women for a little fun gave no insight into what to do now, either, when he truly cared about the outcome. In the past, he had given every woman an objective risk assessment and pulled out if the risk was too high. But with Natasha, the risks were exponentially higher, and he still couldn't let her go.

At the very top of his list of risks was convincing her that a relationship with him wouldn't hurt her. Because it was a promise he knew he couldn't keep.

"Max?"

Derek's voice brought him out of his thoughts. Max looked up and gave him a grunt of acknowledgment.

"You look like shit, mate," said Derek casually, settling into one of the armchairs in front of Max's desk.

Max shrugged. "I met with Alya, told her it was best if I handed her security needs over to someone else at Blackmore Inc. She's determined to be less dependent on security, so the timing is good."

"Who are you thinking of as a replacement?"

"Henning's the obvious choice."

Derek frowned. "Really? He knows every detail of her situation, and his undercover work with the Australian Federal Police speaks for itself. But I thought he refused to do any on-the-ground work now after what happened in that last bust. That's why he's in IT."

"Yeah, that's what he says," said Max. "But I have a feeling he wouldn't turn down an assignment with Alya."

"Okay." Derek gave a slow nod. "Did you talk to Natasha?"

Max gave a humorless snort of laughter. "She left the apartment because she found out I was coming over. I don't know what the fuck kind of planet that's a good sign on, but I'm certainly not living there."

"So ask her out," said Derek. "I can't believe I'm having this conversation with you, Max. If she were any other woman, you'd just come straight with her."

Max huffed out a breath. "It's complicated."

Derek nodded. "That's all the more reason to ask her out. Because you're never complicated when it comes to women."

"She's my date on Saturday," he added quietly.

"Saturday?" Derek narrowed his eyes. "You mean this Saturday, the anniversary of your mother's death, which you'll be spending in the same room as your father and brother?"

"Yeah, that one," Max muttered.

"Ah, good choice. You really know how to sweep a woman off her feet."

"Fuck you," growled Max. "It was the best option I had. She'll know what my life is like now. Because it's only going to get worse."

Derek clapped him on the back. "Okay, bro. Not sure what the hell you're thinking here."

"Fucked if I know."

His friend was quiet, and his expression softened, the way it did when he talked about his wife, Laurie. "Is it time for us to have a sappy follow-your-heart talk?"

Derek was probably Max's closest friend—one of the only people he could actually have this conversation with. When Max's mother's prognosis had gone from bad to worse, it had been Derek who convinced him to take a few months off and be with her. That asking for such a long stretch of leave wasn't abusing his privilege and didn't come from a sense of entitlement. That his love for his mother was worth the same as anyone else's, that he was doing it for his mother as much as he was for himself.

If anyone understood why this was making him crazy, it was Derek.

"Christ, Derek," he grumbled. "It's not *my* heart that I'm thinking about. I don't want to break her heart, and I'm not sure I can be the person she wants to fall in love with."

"Why don't you let her make her own decision about whether or not you'll make her happy?"

"I think she already did," he said flatly. "She ran in the other direction. Literally."

"But she's going to your mother's event."

"As far as I know," Max said, frowning. "I just can't bring myself to tell her that the pressure is only going to get worse. The fact that I didn't tell her shows how low I'll stoop just to see her again."

Derek chuckled. "Sounds like you could be falling in love, my friend. Welcome to the club."

CHAPTER FIFTEEN

"IT CAN'T BE TRUE," said Alya, staring down at Friday morning's newspaper over Natasha's shoulder. "It's all speculation."

Natasha's glasses were fogging from the steam that rose from her sister's coffee cup, which dangled precariously over Natasha's pajama-clad arm.

She swallowed, rereading the headline for the hundredth time that morning: Powerhouse Couple Seals the Deal. Underneath the headline, Max's easy grin beamed at her, his arm slung over the shoulder of Francesca Martinelli. The embrace in the photo looked more like that of friends, but that hadn't stopped the reporter from including rumors about their personal history. Because of course Max probably had an intimate history with this beautiful woman. The effect of the article hadn't worn off. Every single time she looked at it, the nausea hit her hard. But no matter how many times the bile crept up her throat, Natasha couldn't stop looking at it. The two of them were so perfectly beautiful together.

Alya yanked the newspaper out of her hand. "Don't

keep looking at this crap, Natasha. All we know is that the foundation she heads gave money to the breast cancer clinic that the Jensen Family Foundation is setting up."

"We also know that they were probably a couple a few years ago," said Natasha, her eyes still on the newspaper, crumpled in Alya's hand. "Why is he in the photo and not his father?"

"Natasha?"

It took a moment to realize that Alya was waiting for her attention. Slowly, Natasha lifted her gaze. Her sister's eyes were full of sympathy. Natasha sighed. "What is it?"

"You don't really believe that Max would so carelessly brush you aside like that, do you?"

"We've made no commitments to each other. He's not tied to me in any way." She winced at her own words. Even she didn't buy this argument.

"Really?" Alya frowned. "You truly think Max would do that?"

Natasha took off her glasses and massaged her temples. Finally, she shook her head. No, she didn't. Everything she knew about Max told her he was careful about hurting anyone. So why did she still feel like throwing up?

"Just talk to him about it," Alya said softly. "Call him."

Natasha took a deep breath. "Maybe you're right. But I need to calm down a little first."

She eyed the newspaper once more, but Alya hid

it behind her back. "Nope. I'm getting this out of our apartment."

Her sister headed off to her room, presumably to get dressed, and Natasha flopped back onto the sofa. She propped her legs on the arm and covered her face with a pillow. What the hell had she gotten herself into? The larger-than-life man, the media speculations, the jealousy—she was firmly in Illana Petrova territory. But even with years of watching her mother's dramas unfold, she couldn't just get herself to be logical and rational about the article. It was doing crazy things to her insides.

This was Max Jensen, a man whose family had captured the nation's interest over and over. And probably always would. This wouldn't be the last time she'd read speculations about who he was with, and any relationship with him would be publicly dissected. Natasha knew exactly what she would be signing up for.

If she called him right now, she'd regret it. Everything in her ached to fight back, to make him see why this wasn't fair to her, to sever all ties with him—anything to get out from under the jealousy and inadequacy that were seething through her. Feelings she had left behind when she'd moved to Australia. And tomorrow she was his date to the foundation dinner. She threw another pillow over her head and squeezed her eyes shut.

"I'm going out to recycle the newspaper," called Alya from the hall. "I'll stop at the bakery to pick up something buttery and sugary, too."

"Thanks," Natasha mumbled from under the pillows.

The front door creaked open, and Alya said something too softly to hear.

"What?" Natasha called.

Her sister didn't answer, and the door closed. Natasha took a couple deep breaths, but her *serenity now* moment was interrupted by footsteps.

"Forget something?" she called to her sister.

"Nope."

The deep, male voice startled her, but she knew exactly who it was. She sat up, the cushion slipping onto the floor. "Max?" She pushed her hair out of her eyes. "What are you doing here?"

"I've been standing outside your door for a while, debating whether to knock, and then your sister made the decision for me," he grumbled. He stopped in front of her, and she blinked up at him.

"You don't look so good," she said. His hair was standing up on one side, and the dark circles under his eyes suggested he hadn't been sleeping well.

Max ran his hand through his hair and gave an exasperated sigh. "Thanks. You look hot as ever."

"Don't say—"

But he cut her off before she could finish.

"This is exactly why I didn't want to be involved with my family," he said, his words tumbling out. "The press release was supposed to raise awareness for the charity. I never would have agreed to it if I'd known…"

He let the last word linger in the air as he shook his head. Then he squatted down in front of her, resting his hands on her legs. Her heart gave a traitorous leap. He was so close, and his blue eyes were intense and serious.

"You know it's not true," he said softly. "I would never do that to you."

She blew out a breath. "No, you wouldn't. Not like that. Not on purpose."

"Thank fuck," he muttered. He brought his hands to her cheeks and pressed his lips against hers. It was the softest, the gentlest of kisses, and he stayed like that, eyes closed, breathing against her.

"I've missed you these last few days," he whispered.

She bit her lip. "I missed you, too."

"Please come with me to the fundraiser tomorrow." His words came out forcefully, and he huffed out a breath.

Natasha frowned. "This is shaping up to be my worst nightmare, Max."

"I know, Nat."

"I don't want to deal with…this." She gestured between them helplessly. "The drama, the public humiliation."

"No," he said, and he leaned forward to kiss her. "I won't let it be like that."

"Not on purpose." All the problems faded away as he touched her, smoothed her hair, took her bottom lip between his. God, she loved kissing this man. It was hard to stop once she started.

"I'll make sure you're protected," he said. "No photos of you published, no photos with Francesca or anyone else that could set off suspicions."

Another kiss, and another. Her heart was thumping madly, and her body ached for more. It felt so good, but she pulled back. "What are you doing?"

"Reminding you of why you want to say yes."

She chuckled. It was, in fact, a very good reminder. "What am I walking into, Max?" she asked softly.

"The breast cancer clinic is for my mother, her legacy," he said quietly, his eyes so sad and serious. "I have to be a part of that."

Natasha nodded. "Of course you want to be there tomorrow, Max."

Max shook his head impatiently. "I'm not just attending the event." He sat back on his heels and rubbed the back of his neck. "This is my future, Natasha. I'm going to be the president of the Jensen Family Foundation, which means I'm the face of it, too. All that PR bullshit. Which was why that photo with Francesca happened."

She stilled. The situation had just managed to get worse. And he was still asking her to step into this with him.

"And if I go, I'll be a part of that?" she asked.

"No, not if you don't want to," he said. "You'll be there because there's no one else I'd want to go with. And this is our family's function, so I can control what members of the press come and what photos they're allowed to publish. But after this one, things will probably change."

She wrinkled her forehead. "And you're inviting me so I can witness that?"

He shook his head. "No. I'm inviting you because it'll

be a hard day, and having you there will make it a lot better. Maybe that makes me selfish, but I'm feeling a little desperate right now." He rested his hand on her thigh, moving it up and down slowly. "I want you with me."

She tried to contain a swell of hope as he ran his other hand through her hair, down her neck, over her shoulder. He leaned closer, so his mouth was almost touching hers.

"I've been thinking a lot about my new position this week. I'm going to have the attention of the media, and what matters is what I do with it. I can use it for something good," he said. "But that goes for you, too. If the media spotlight points your way, you can deflect it toward something you care about—a cause, an organization, whatever."

He was talking about more than just Saturday's event. He was asking her to consider beyond Saturday, to try something more. Her gut reaction was to argue that things were different for him and her, that being the woman who took him off the market, with the possibility of being publicly labeled as inadequate, wasn't the same as being known as Australia's beloved playboy. But Max already knew it wasn't the same. He was asking her to look at it differently, to look at what she could do with it instead of what it did to her.

"I'll consider it," she said softly. "I'm still making up my mind about Saturday."

The intensity of his gaze didn't let up. The man in front of her was pretty much the opposite of laid-back Max.

"You attend evenings like this with Alya," he said, pressing her. "Why is this different?"

"Alya is my sister. I know she'd never—" Natasha stopped, midsentence. *She'd never what?* It took a minute to sort out the rest of her thought. Her sister would never do anything at Natasha's expense. Alya would always protect her, the way Natasha would always be there for her sister. The way their mother hadn't. Illana Petrova had been too far down the rabbit hole of her own drama to have time for a thirteen-year-old's insecurities. "She'd never leave me exposed."

Max seemed to be hanging onto every word she said. He nodded slowly. The living room was quiet, just the sounds of Max's breathing, the slide of his fingers over her pajamas and the thump of her heart.

"No matter what happens between us, I would never leave you exposed," he said, breaking the silence. "Please trust me on that."

She looked into his beautiful blue eyes, so achingly serious. Maybe, just maybe, she could trust this man.

"Can I get back to reminding you why this is all worth your while?" he asked, his lips brushing against her neck.

She took a deep breath and nodded. God, she still wanted him, no matter what crazy thoughts or hang-ups scrolled through her head. "My sister will be back soon."

"Does that mean yes, please, move faster?"

She smiled and shook her head. "It means let's go to my room."

* * *

Holy hell.

Max was in Natasha's room, with its carefully organized shelves and her neatly made bed. White walls, sparsely decorated with a cluster of photos. One of Alya and her as kids. One on a beach with friends or colleagues, diving gear off to the side. One with another group of friends, piled in a car... There were so many parts of Natasha's life he didn't know about, so many things he wanted to know. There was also a photo of a couple, and Max recognized the woman: her mother. Was that her father, too? Under the photo arrangement was a low shelf, filled with thick novels. He pulled one out. Science fiction—at least it appeared to be from the cover. Was that what she liked to read?

Beyond the photos and the books, there wasn't much else in the room beyond the basics. A desk with nothing but a single framed picture on it. This was Natasha's sanctuary, where everything was kept in its place. The glimpse at her orderly room hit him like a punch in the gut. He was turning her orderly life upside down. Of course she was wary of him. Hell, even he was wary of the kind of chaos he could wreak on her life.

He wandered across the wooden floor to the window where Natasha had stood that first night and stripped for him. He lifted a row of the blinds and peeked out at the street below. Down in his truck that first night, he had jacked off imagining a blow job from her. Not once wondering what she was imagining upstairs.

Natasha closed her bedroom door and leaned against it. "You okay, Max?"

"Of course." He turned around and took her in. Her hair hung in messy waves around her face, and her pajama top was a little askew. Beautiful as ever. And no bra. Max sighed. Horny thoughts once again, though with Natasha, they were mixed up with other feelings now.

He crossed the room and stopped in front of her. Her cheeks were flushed, and her breath caught as he slipped his hand around the back of her neck.

"Remember that first night?" he asked.

She raised an eyebrow. "You mean the red-light district show I gave you?"

"Yeah, that one." He smiled. "Did that night have a happy ending for you, too?"

Natasha chuckled. "Yep."

"What did you imagine?"

A new flush crept up her cheeks, and she swallowed, her delicate throat quivering.

"Nothing exciting. I just imagined plain old sex with you, nothing more. Right here against the door, actually."

He brushed his fingers over her pulse, throbbing at the base of her neck, then kissed her forehead. That was what she wanted.

"Boring, right?" she added with a wry smile.

He shook his head. "Not at all." He pressed his lips against hers. Heaven. That was what this was right now.

He kissed her again. "Was I gentle? Or rough? Or something else?"

Just standing here, touching her, breathing in her scent was making his dick hard. He had been aching for her every day and every night since they left Green Island. Talking about this was going to drive him insane, but it was time to put himself aside.

"Not gentle or rough. Just…" Natasha bit her lip. "Just the way we were when we kissed in the kitchen. Like that."

He nodded. "It was good, wasn't it? You want to pick up right from there?"

"We're not there anymore, Max."

Max kissed her jaw and nipped at her neck. "This will be better than where we were. I promise."

She laughed and held his face in her hands, bringing his mouth to hers again. He met her soft gray eyes, and her smile faded.

"I'm trying." Her voice was so husky and serious.

I'm falling in love with you. Derek had been right, and he wanted to tell her. But not now. He needed to give her a chance to think about what he had said. Give her a chance to think about a future that they shaped together, not the pressures that could shape them.

Max fingered the buttons of her pajama top. One by one, he slowly unfastened them. The shirt slipped down over her shoulders revealing the tops of her breasts.

"Jesus," he muttered. "I could spend the whole day getting off with your beautiful tits."

Her breath caught. Then she smiled a slow, sexy

smile. "I feel the same about many of your parts." She reached between them and put her hand on his cock.

He groaned. Fuck, it felt good. And he wanted her to feel just as good right now.

"Hold that thought, darling," he said, moving her hand to his waist. "Let's go a little slower."

His hands skimmed over the curve of her hips, and he bent down and took a mouthful of one plump breast. Her skin was soft. He could have sworn he still tasted the ocean on her skin, but maybe it was just her. He sucked experimentally, swirling his tongue over her nipple, and she shivered and moaned. He did it again, and her fingers flexed hard into the muscles of his torso. He kissed a trail to her other breast and opened his mouth for another taste. Natasha arched into him and breathed out his name.

He wanted this woman, and his dick throbbed, begging for attention. He kissed a trail up to her neck, to her ear. But when he looked down, it was her. Natasha. The woman he teased, who made him laugh, who came on to him and stripped for him in her bedroom window. This time, it was for real.

"Natasha," he groaned, cupping her face.

Her eyes softened as she stared up at him. His lips crashed against hers, starved for so long, so achingly hungry. Her arms wrapped around his neck, pulled him to her. She opened for him, licking, biting, and he responded, searching for more of her. The magic pulled between them. Her lips were so soft and salty-sweet, and he took the bottom one between his teeth. Fuck, he had to be careful or he would devour her. He caressed her mouth with his tongue, teasing, showing her how it would be if she gave him a chance. He traced a line down her stomach, slipping his hand into her pajama bottoms.

His fingers reached the warm, wet heat and then he found her clit. Yeah, he definitely found it, by the way she was twisting and panting and breathing his name. Max's brain stuttered as the urge for more stepped up another notch. Her cries stirred a deep rumble in his chest.

Too many clothes. He wanted to sink deep inside her, to hear her moan, to feel her shudder. But he couldn't get himself to let go of her. Max took a deep breath and released her.

Her forehead wrinkled in confusion. "Why are we stopping?"

"Just give me a second," he groaned.

After a few more breaths, he pulled his wallet from his back pocket and found a condom. The wallet dropped to the floor, then the wrapper, and he unzipped himself and finally, finally let his aching cock free. Slowly, he rolled on the condom.

His entire body was tingling, and his cock was fighting to shut out every thought except one: sink deep into her sweet heat. But not yet. "It's so good between us, Natasha. That's not going to change."

He lifted his hand to her cheek and waited until her eyes met his. She hesitated, and when she finally blinked up at him, her eyes were filled with wonder.

As if she was searching just as hard to make sense of this as he was. Then the wonder in her eyes turned to molten heat. This was happening, right now.

She tugged down her pajama bottoms, and they fell to the floor. Her eyes narrowed with lust.

"Hold on, sweetheart."

He lifted her. Natasha's legs opened around him, positioning herself over his rock-hard erection. He leaned forward, pressing her back against the door, his face buried in her hair. Slowly, he lowered her, inch by inch. Her breaths came faster in sharp pants. Heat, so much warmth, calling him.

"I'm going to drown in you, Max," she whispered.

"Then we'll go down together. I'm right there with you," he said. "I promise."

Fuck, she was going to drive him insane. He was done with slow. He was done with holding back. With one hard thrust, he buried himself deep. Her teeth sank into his shoulder, and he let out a groan of deep satisfaction. *Yes.*

"You can bite me as hard as you want to," he said, teeth gritted. "It makes my cock even harder."

Before she could react, he moved his hips, pulling out and coming in. Natasha tilted her head back and moaned. He held her up against the door, her soft ass in his hands, drove into her, again and again. Her nails dug into his biceps, his muscles strained from lifting her, from the relentless thrusts, and his balls tingled with the promise of ecstasy. His whole body was alive. This was so goddamn perfect.

Natasha's moans turned to cries, and she clawed at his back, pulling herself closer. The still-functioning parts of his mind warred between the need to come and the even deeper need to wait for her.

"*Max.*"

His name. The sweetest sound he had ever heard. Her body shuddered, and her teeth clamped down on the tense muscles of his shoulder once more. She clenched around him, and her orgasm set him off. Something primal took over. He roared and thrust and came with his cock deep inside her as white-hot pleasure shot through him, over and over.

Nothing else. Just Natasha.

Rational thoughts trickled in. Like how he was going to collapse soon.

Slowly, he pulled out and rested his forehead against the door. He pressed his lips against her damp hair and took a deep breath of her salty scent. She unwrapped her legs from his hips in shaky movements, and he kept one hand on her ass to make sure she didn't fall.

She said nothing.

He shifted and slid his hand to the back of her neck. But when he looked down for a kiss, her eyes were wide. Her lips parted, but nothing came out. Like this was all too much. Like her well-ordered life wouldn't survive this kind of shake-up. Like she had no idea what to do with what had just happened.

Well, neither did he.

He leaned forward and brushed his lips against hers. She stared at him for another beat. Then, slowly, she

closed her mouth, and the shock dissolved from her face.
A hint of a smile tugged at her lips.

"That was a pretty good reminder," she said.

He chuckled. "Did I convince you?"

"I guess," she said with a shrug, her voice teasing.
Then she kissed him. "I'll be there for you tomorrow
night."

CHAPTER SIXTEEN

NATASHA STEPPED OUT of the sleek black town car, and the driver shut the door behind her.

"Mr. Jensen will be out to meet you in a moment," the man said before heading back for the driver's door. He climbed in, started the car again and rolled away, leaving Natasha in front of the Prince Henry Centre.

More cars pulled in, and well-dressed couples were making their way into the building. Floor-length gowns, tuxedos, the works. Natasha pushed her glasses up her nose and frowned. She had chosen the dress, gauzy sea-green and flowing, because it was her favorite. It was supposed to be a *this is the real me* statement, but standing next to the red carpet entrance, she was clearly underdressed. Probably an accurate *this is the real me* statement, actually.

Natasha fiddled with her wrap. She had spent most of the fifteen-minute car ride trying not to overanalyze Max's last-minute switch in plans. His reason for sending a car instead of picking her up himself didn't change anything.

Because he wanted her here with him. This past

week had only added to her curiosity about Max's relationship with his family, but today wasn't about her.

The warm ocean breeze curled around her bare skin.
Natasha tugged at her wrap again, and when she looked
up, he was there, walking out the door. And he was
looking for her—Natasha Petrova, lover of fish and
logic and rules, the plain Jane to the breathtaking beauty
of both her sister and her mother. Max Jensen, the most
spectacular man in the world, was looking for *her*. Her
heart beat with giddy hope, and this time, instead of
tamping it down, she let that hope flow through her.

Her sister's words came back to her. *You just have
to decide whether Max is worth the risk.* Yes, he was.
That decision was easier than she'd thought it would
be. The other question—how would she handle being
next to Max as he took the spotlight?—that was harder.

Please trust me...

His plea had stayed with her. Whatever happened
tonight, she did trust him. But he couldn't control everything.

Max continued to scan the area, and his face lit up
when he saw her coming toward him. Natasha's stomach flipped, and her heart pattered faster.

She bit that man yesterday. *Bit him.* Coming down
after that mind-blowing orgasm, she had stared at the
red teeth marks on his shoulder. Not that Max seemed
to mind her teeth on him.

But the man in front of her tonight was a different
Max Jensen. As he closed the space between them,
it was clear he wasn't at ease. Not even close. Lines

creased his forehead, and his whole body radiated tension, as if he were on full alert. He didn't even say hello. He came straight for her and wrapped his arms around her, holding her tightly against him. He kissed her head and stroked her hair.

"Thank you for coming, Natasha," he whispered. "I'm so sorry I couldn't pick you up. I needed to talk to Francesca and some other donors about you and me, about why I needed to be careful about photos today."

He kissed her again and then let her go, his hands lingering on her bare skin.

"You okay, Max?"

He nodded. "Much better now that you're here."

The lines across his forehead eased as he looked down at her. He rested a large, warm hand on her cheek as his eyes blazed into hers.

"I wish I could have stayed at your place longer yesterday," he said. "If it wasn't for tonight, I would have."

"It's okay," she said.

His fingers trailed down her neck, over her shoulders, down her arm until he found her hand. He laced his fingers with hers.

Now that he was touching her again, looking at her, into her with those clear blue eyes, the longing of this week hit her hard. He was reminding her of all the things she had tried to put behind her since they'd left Green Island. That warm, open smile that came so easily. His voice, low and intimate. The weight of his body as he moved against her. Her cheeks flushed as this last image flashed through her in graphic detail.

Later.

Because they were no longer alone on a tropical island. They were outside a high-profile fundraiser for the Jensen Family Foundation.

Max's smiled faded, and he bent down to brush his lips over hers. Once. Twice. Then he looked into her eyes with an intensity that made her breath catch.

"You look beautiful." He ran his fingers over the strap of her dress. "Ocean green. I love it."

These last words came out soft and slow. He opened his mouth again, and she was almost sure he was on the verge of saying something momentous. But then he sighed and muttered something to himself that sounded a lot like, *bad timing, asshole.*

Then, for the first time that day, he gave her that familiar, playful grin. "You ready to meet the illustrious Deacon Jensen, Jr. and his better-behaved son, TJ?"

She took a deep breath. "Probably not. But I'm ready to walk in there with you."

"That's enough." He kissed her again. "Just having you here is enough."

Then he tugged her hand, starting toward the central courtyard between two buildings. Her heart sped up as they came closer. Natasha attended high-profile functions with Alya, but this was different. It was personal, Max's world.

Her heels clacked against the stone, echoing between the buildings. The structures were angular and modern, and the courtyard was unadorned except for a few benches with a view of the dunes and the ocean in the distance, the water was quiet, peaceful.

She didn't even realize she'd slowed to a stop until Max's lips brushed her cheek. "You like this place? There's a great view from the windows inside."

He tipped his chin to indicate where another couple was entering through heavy wooden doors. From inside, a slow, sexy jazz number played.

His mother's music. Natasha looked up at Max's clenched jaw. It must be. Even without the conflicts between him and his father, hearing his mother's voice today, on the anniversary of her death, would be painful.

"Is this your—?"

He nodded before she could finish the question, so she squeezed his hand, and they walked in. The stage and dance floor came first, with the setup for a band in the corner. Glass balls of all sizes hung everywhere from the ceiling, glittering in the light of the dozens of candles on each of the round tables. The sun sparkled over the ocean at the far end, through the groups of guests talking, drinking from champagne flutes.

But she couldn't properly take in any of the details because her attention was fixed on Deacon Jensen, Jr., just a few feet ahead, who was currently staring her down.

Natasha had seen photos of Max's father before—everyone in Australia had. And Deacon Jensen, through his clashes with the press, had made it known he didn't like that. Though, to be fair, Natasha wasn't sure she'd do well with the kinds of privacy invasions the Jensen family endured.

She had seen Max's father's scowl on the front pages often enough, and yet until this moment it had never once crossed her mind just how similar father and son were. Same height, same light blue eyes, same jaw, same golden skin, though Deacon Jensen, Jr.'s had clearly seen more days in the unrelenting sun. The two probably had had the same build at some point, but Max's father was wirier, his hair a little grayer.

The man stared at Natasha with the kind of intensity that she had seen glimpses of in Max. But where Max's eyes sparkled with attraction and warmth, Deacon Jensen's gaze ran cold.

Max released her hand. Natasha's breath caught in a moment of panic. Was Max leaving her alone with this man? He had promised. She grabbed for him again, but as her hand brushed against him, his arm slipped around her waist, bringing her in closer. She found her breath. Natasha was here to support Max, not to impress his notoriously surly father.

Deacon Jensen's eyes flicked back to Max as they came closer.

"Your welcome speech begins in ten minutes, Maxwell," he said, his voice sharp. "You just walked out."

To Max's credit, he showed no signs of distress.

"Natasha, meet Deacon Jensen," he said smoothly, then turned to his father. "This is Natasha Petrova."

His father's stare lingered on Max for an extra beat, and then he turned to Natasha. He studied her, his face betraying no emotion. What would it be like to have this man as a father? A fierce defensiveness for Max grew as she met his father's gaze and held it.

Then, Deacon Jensen defied all her expectations. The man smiled at her. A real smile. His whole face lit up, much in the way Max's did, and he extended his hand.

"I apologize, Natasha," he said. "Clearly, my manners have deteriorated since my wife passed, and even before that I was a little rough around the edges. But I'm happy to meet you."

She shook his hand. "Thank you. This is a beautiful tribute to your wife."

Deacon Jensen looked from Max to her and back to Max. There was a glimmer of emotion in his eyes. "She would have loved to be here right now."

Natasha looked up at Max, getting his attention. He blinked down at her, shaking off whatever thoughts were behind his hostile stare.

"Let me show you to our table and introduce you to my brother," he said gruffly. "I want to make sure you're comfortable before I speak."

The evening had surpassed all Max's expectations, though, admittedly, they were low, as always, when his father was in attendance. The crowd seemed receptive to his speech, and Natasha was actually enjoying herself.

His father had given him hell all day about bringing a date, clearly expecting Max to have invited some just-for-fun woman to get under his father's skin. True,

Max had pulled that kind of shit in the past, but the fact that Deacon assumed he'd do that at an event for his deceased mother had made him mad as hell. But the moment his father met Natasha, everything shifted. Well, that was how Max felt about her, too. Now he just needed to figure out a way to convince her to trust him further, trust in what they had together.

Most of his public duties had ended for the evening. He had spoken about his mother's battle with breast cancer and laid out the priorities of the hospital's new research and treatment center. He and Natasha had made their way around the room, shaking hands and thanking friends and donors. She looked surprisingly comfortable in this role. He had sent a car at the last minute instead of going himself so that he could double-check that everyone—photographers, organizers, and his family—understood she was off-limits. But she'd insisted on staying by his side for most of the night.

He shoved his hands in his pockets, watching her from across the room as she talked to TJ. They were standing by the windows that looked out over the ocean, and she was pointing at something along the coast. Her hair covered some of the open back of her dress, but not all, and he couldn't take his eyes off her bare, creamy skin. Back on Green Island, he had kissed her there, run his hand down her naked back while his cock was buried deep inside her. Max checked his watch. When the hell was this evening over?

This woman could even make conversation with his brother, which was saying a lot, considering how little came out of his brother's mouth under any circumstances. In fact, TJ looked very interested in whatever she was saying right now. Max gritted his teeth, biting back the urge to go over there and remind his brother that Natasha was here with him—and was going home with him, if Max had any say in the matter.

"She cares about you, Max. I could see it right away."

Max hadn't noticed his father approach, and now it was too late to dodge him completely.

"Yeah, well, the feeling's mutual," Max grumbled.

His father gave him a look that said, *So don't fuck it up.* But then his expression softened. "I can see that, too. Your mother would have liked her."

Max said nothing. Instead, he focused his gaze on the way Natasha's hair glittered in the candlelight.

"Your speech was compelling," said his father. "Thank you."

"You pushed me into this position," said Max dryly. "I'm not sure a thanks is in order."

Max pulled his gaze away from Natasha, and to his complete surprise, his father's mouth twitched up into a crooked smile. A new record of two smiles in one day.

"I was giving you a good reason to step up and take your place," he said.

"I'm doing it for Mum's sake."

Across the room, Natasha was still talking to TJ. Was his brother making a move on her? Hell, no.

"I need to check on Natasha," he said, not even glancing in his father's direction.

"Son, hear me out." Something about the word *son*

kept Max in place. How many years had it been since his father had used that term? Not since he had been a boy had he felt like Deacon Jensen, Jr.'s son, and he had been pretty sure the feeling was mutual. But the way his father said it put a crack in the wall that had stood between them.

Max shoved his hands deeper into the pockets of his pants. "I'm listening."

"From the beginning, this was for you, Max," he said, gesturing to the room. "The cancer center, everything. Your mother wanted you to be the one to carry on her legacy. She was afraid—" His father's voice broke, startling Max out of his Natasha-induced stupor. His gaze jerked over to his father, and he froze. There were so few times in his life that Deacon Jensen, Jr. had ever showed visible emotion. His father's jaw twitched as he opened his mouth to speak again. "Your mother was afraid you'd split from the family forever. I promised her I wouldn't let that happen."

Max took an unsteady breath. His mother hadn't asked him to promise that, but she had asked his father.

"Why didn't you do more for her in the end?" said Max.

His father flinched. "Maybe it wasn't enough, and Lord knows I'm not an easy man. But I tried to help her the best way I knew how."

"How can you say that? She left everything for you. She left her career and Sydney for a station in the middle of Western Australia," said Max, not hiding any of his bitterness. "I know, she always said she wanted to leave Sydney, too, but even at the end? The best place for another round of chemo was here."

Pain shattered the stoic composure of his father's face. He opened his mouth, hesitating, as if he were debating whether or not to speak. His father, who never hesitated. Finally, he took a deep breath. "Max, your mother absolutely insisted on staying at the station. It wasn't my choice."

Max blinked, taking in his father's words.

"I respected her wishes," he said softly. "It was the hardest thing I've ever done, Max. But the chances the doctors gave her weren't worth it for her. Not compared to the trade-offs."

"You could have begged her," Max said, shaking his head slowly.

"I could have." The loss was written all over his father's face, but he continued. "Max, your mother didn't want to spend her last months feeling so awful that she couldn't spend time with her family. She wanted us to spend the time together, not focusing on false hope."

"She never said that to me," said Max.

"Because she didn't want to spend the time she had left debating it. And the truth is that her last month, when you came home, was one of the best of our lives. Both of ours. Even though you barely spoke to me." The affection in his father's gaze was surprising.

"How the hell can you say that? All those years you rode me so hard, like I was the fuck-up of the family. Like you couldn't wait for me to move far away."

His father blinked at him, and then his face broke out into a smile, warm and genuine. "Max, you were a fucking pain in the ass as a teenager. You didn't listen for shit to me and you fought with your brother nonstop. Of course I rode you hard."

Then his father had the nerve to laugh. "If I hadn't taken your car away, you would have gotten half the town pregnant. Instead, you got yourself into Princeton."

"We both know that I got into Princeton because of the library you donated," muttered Max. "No one on campus missed that."

The amusement on his father's face disappeared.

"No, Max. I didn't make that donation until after you were admitted," he said slowly. "Look, I know our family name carries weight, and it's impossible to know how much just being a Jensen influenced your ticket in the door, at Princeton or anywhere else. But it's what you do with that ticket that counts. And you proved that you belonged there beyond a doubt."

His father looked at him with…pride? The ground was shifting under Max's feet. He glanced across the room, at Natasha, who was still chatting with TJ. Damn, he wanted to be next to her right now.

His father put his hand on Max's shoulder. "I'm telling you this because I see the way you look at this woman, and I see the way she looks at you. This is your route to happiness. What are you waiting for?"

Natasha's head turned, and she met his gaze. Her smile was warm and full. Was there love in that expression, too? Time to find out.

"Nothing," he said. "I'm not waiting for anything."

His father chuckled. "Good. Just watch your temper with your brother."

* * *

"Your father let Max spend the night in jail?" Natasha gaped at TJ.

TJ laughed. "The police were all friends with my father, and Max was too drunk to know the difference that night. My father thought Max might learn something from the experience."

Natasha rolled her eyes. "I doubt that."

"Me, too. He—" TJ stopped midsentence, just as Max's hand slipped possessively around her waist.

"She's my date, TJ," Max grumbled.

TJ gave his brother a good-natured shrug. "You're the one who left her alone." He kissed Natasha on the cheek. "Let me know if you want to hear more stories."

She smiled. "Thanks. I'll be in touch."

TJ walked away, leaving her with a surly looking Max.

"You trying to make me jealous?" he said. His tone was only half-joking.

Natasha rolled her eyes. "I'm trying to be friendly to your brother. He had some interesting stories about your teenage years."

Max snorted. "I'll bet."

The whole night he had been a little on edge, and from across the room, the conversation with his father had looked tense. She turned to face him. "How are things with your father?"

He brushed his lips over hers. His hand moved lower, over the top of her ass, as he pulled her closer. "Better than expected."

She slipped her hands under his jacket and rested her

cheek on his chest, letting her mind drift. No *what-ifs*, no rules, no pressure, just the sizzling warmth of his body against hers. The evening sun was long gone, and the candlelight glowed and flickered against the glass of the windows. Over the din of conversation, the band was now playing, a slow, seductive number.

"Want to dance?" she asked.

"With you? Always." He smiled and settled his hand on the curve of her waist. Their bodies pressed together, moving, teasing.

Natasha glanced across the room at the dance floor. "Here?"

Max nodded, and a slow smile spread across his lips. "No one's paying attention to us. Which means no one will notice when I slip my hand under your dress."

She laughed. "Classy, Max."

She laid her head on his chest again, and he pressed a kiss into her hair.

"You seem to be handling this scene well," he said.

"You were right," she said. "I don't feel exposed here when I'm with you."

He squeezed her against his chest, and her heart thumped harder.

"Have I told you how much I've missed you this week?" he whispered. "So much."

Such simple words, but they filled her with a bright burst of happiness. Oh, this man. She was falling in love with Max Jensen, a notorious heartbreaker, right in the middle of a public event, for everyone to see. The idea should've been frightening, but it wasn't. But this didn't have to mean she was following in her mother's footsteps. She trusted Max would protect her privacy, no matter where their relationship went. That was what made the difference.

"I've missed you, too," she said.

He sighed, and then his chest rumbled, pleasure dancing in his eyes. "All of me? Or just certain parts?"

She pulled back a little and met his gaze. "The whole package."

Slowly, all traces of amusement faded, and what was left was a burning intensity, the side of him he so reluctantly let show. The raw ache in his eyes was almost unbearable, but she didn't look away.

"You sure about that?" he asked, his voice rough.

Natasha nodded. "I'm scared of what being a part of your life might mean for me."

His jaw tightened, and he looked away. "I know that, sweetheart."

She took a deep breath. "But I'm not going to let that stop me from falling in love with you."

Their slow sway came to a stop. The words were out in the world, floating in the air around them, coloring everything. He still wasn't looking at her. His throat bobbed as he swallowed, and the pulse at the base of his neck ticked fast.

Natasha straightened up. She was going to handle this with dignity, however it went. "I want to be with you. I want more."

She didn't get any more words out before his hands cupped her cheeks. His eyes were on hers, searing her, stopping the words. His gaze flicked down to her mouth, still parted, midsentence.

"Natasha Petrova, I want everything. All the parts of you you're offering. Especially if it involves more of those sex-filled days on tiny tropical islands."

She smiled, but then his lips met hers with an aching hunger that rushed through her. They were kissing. Thank God they were kissing again. She slid her hands into his hair and pulled him closer. Yes, she was drowning in this all-consuming desire, so familiar now, and so achingly good.

"I want you, Natasha," he said. "I've been after you since the first time you told me off, three years ago, and after those days together on Green Island, I only want more."

"Me, too," she said, standing on her toes for another kiss.

They stared at each other, moving slowly to the music.

He brushed a hand over her cheek. "But I'm not a fun ride all day, every day. I can be a hardheaded asshole, as you might have noticed with my father tonight. I spent a lot of my teenage years that way."

She wrinkled her brow at him. "That's part of what makes you *you*, Max. You really think I still want the à la carte menu, not the whole package?"

He smirked at her word choice. "I know you like the whole package, baby."

Natasha rolled her eyes, trying to hold back her smile. "Terrible line, Max."

Natasha rested her cheek on his chest again, letting

it all sink in. This man had given his heart to her long ago, and she was pretty sure she had done the same on Green Island. Yes, he did have the power to drive her crazy, but she trusted him not to abuse that power. Besides, she was starting to believe the feeling was mutual.

Natasha closed her eyes. He pulled her closer, his body pressed against hers as the slow, sexy jazz played.

"I like this place, too," he murmured in her ear. "Far away from the city with an amazing view of the ocean."

She nodded. It was perfect. In fact, everything about this moment was perfect, really.

"When we get married, I think we should do it here." The words came out in the same easy tone, as if this were the most natural thing to talk about, five minutes into a relationship.

Natasha's eyes snapped open. She came to a full stop and pulled away, gaping up at him.

"What?" she choked out.

Max's eyes glittered with warmth and humor, and his lips curved up in a mischievous grin. "What's the matter? You afraid of the M word?"

"No, but…" She bit her lip and frowned. "You can't just throw it out at the beginning."

His eyes glimmered, and then his smile grew wider and he shrugged. "I figured I'd get it out there right away. Three years of lust and fantasies about you is doing crazy things to my brain."

Natasha smiled a little. "Okay, maybe I've been lusting after you for just as long."

"Good to know." He coaxed her head back down, so

her cheek pressed against his chest. They swayed to the music for a bit. God, he smelled heavenly.

"I've been thinking," he said after a while. "Are there any fish species that are monogamous?"

She nodded against him. "Sure. Some butterflyfish form lifelong pairs, for example."

"I would love to hear more about those butterflyfish, Natasha," he said.

Natasha lifted her head to study his expression, checking for signs of interest. His smile was warm and genuine, and his eyes weren't glazing over. In fact, he looked like he was waiting for her to continue. Well, he was asking for fish talk, so it was time to take him at his word.

"Actually, I find monogamous basslets even more fascinating," she said, grinning up at him. "They pair bond, but they're simultaneous hermaphrodites."

Max drew his eyebrows together. "Really?"

She nodded. "Really."

He was quiet for a moment, and he looked deep in thought. Finally, he grinned. "I don't think those videos would be very sexy."

Natasha laughed and shook her head. "Me, neither."

"But, please, go on," he said, stroking her back. "Tell me more about monogamous basslets."

And so she did.

EPILOGUE

Two months later

"I THOUGHT YOU said we were going someplace special," said Natasha as Max put his car into Park.

"We are."

She looked up at the facade of her and Alya's downtown apartment building. "My place?"

"There are plenty of special things that have happened there." Max winked at her, and there was a spark of desire in his eyes. "I can give you details if you need help remembering."

"Are we going to reenact that first night when I stripped for you?" she asked, laughing.

"I really like that idea, Natasha." His voice got a little husky when he whispered her name. "But I had something else in mind first."

All evening Max had been quiet. Odd, especially for him. He seemed almost…nervous. Which was completely out of character. But the way he kissed her so gently, the way he held her hand—he hadn't stopped touching her since he'd picked her up from work. She was almost sure this special thing wasn't bad, at least, it didn't feel that way. But what the hell were they doing here?

Max came around the car and opened the door for her. "Let's go up."

They walked in and crossed the lobby, heading for the elevator.

"I forgot to ask—how was the meeting with your father?"

Max shrugged. "Decent. I half-expected him to still try to steer things, but he was surprisingly hands-off about the decisions I'd made when it came to funding priorities."

Natasha searched his face for the tell-tale hardening of his jaw when he spoke about his father, but it wasn't there. Things were definitely improving.

"And did you finish up your schedule?" he asked.

She nodded. "I think so. I figured out a way to fit in both the research trip and the conference I'm presenting at and still be at the foundation's gala."

Max found her hand and squeezed it. "You don't have to go to the gala."

"I want to," she said, returning the squeeze. "I want to be there for you."

They stopped at the elevators. Max punched her floor number then turned to her. He pressed his hands to her cheeks and kissed her softly. "I really hope you like this."

"Should I be nervous?"

He shook his head slowly. "No. But I'm nervous as hell."

"You're killing me, Max," she said. "Does Alya know?"

He nodded.

"Before me?"

He soothed her, his hands moving up and down her arms. "You'll see. I wanted to make it a surprise."

It couldn't be an engagement. They hadn't been together very long, and he knew she wanted to take it slow. So what could he surprise her with in her own apartment? If it were something small, like jewelry, he'd more likely have given it to her at dinner. None of this made sense.

"I'm completely stumped," she said, frowning. "Just a clue?"

Max nuzzled her cheek with his whiskery one. "This is fun. I should keep secrets from you more often. I didn't realize how much it got under your skin."

"Maybe I just need to rethink my waiting strategy," she said. "Maybe I just need to distract myself."

She coaxed him closer and pressed her lips to his, but before she got further, the elevator came to a stop and opened at her floor.

"We'll get to that soon, too," he said, amusement in his voice. They stepped out of the elevator, and she turned toward her apartment, but he caught her hand and shook his head. "This way." He nodded in the other direction, down the hall.

Now she was really confused. They were in her building but not going to her apartment? But she followed him. He led her to the last door, then he turned to her.

"This is the surprise," he said, and stuck a key in the lock.

Natasha blinked, trying to register what was going on.

"Still haven't figured it out?" he asked, his voice serious.

Natasha shook her head slowly.

"I bought this apartment," he said quietly. "Here, down the hall from you and Alya."

"You...bought it?"

He studied her face for an extra beat, his forehead creasing. "I've been looking for one anywhere in the building for a while. So I was really excited when something on your floor came on the market."

She was still having a hard time registering this information, but she wanted to ease the worry in his eyes. She reached for his hand and squeezed. Slowly, his uncertainty disappeared.

"So I can sneak over in the middle of the night?" she asked, smiling a little. "In my pajamas?"

Max shook his head. "I'm hoping there will be no sneaking. I'm hoping this means we'll be spending a lot more time together."

"You bought this apartment just to be closer to me?" she whispered.

He nodded, squeezing her hand in return. "I know your career is a priority, and I have a lot going on. I thought this would be a way for us to spend more time together. I mentioned the idea to Alya when I saw the listing, and she thought you'd be thrilled. But let me know if you're not ready for this. I don't have to move in and can easily rent it out."

Natasha blinked at him, still trying to get her head around it. He had bought an apartment down the hall, so they could be together.

"Of course, your sister was thrilled to have this fine specimen of a bodyguard down the hall from her." He gestured to himself with a cocky smile. Then he leaned over and pressed his lips into her hair. "But, more importantly, I didn't want you to have to choose between your career and us, or your sister and us."

Her mind had come to a full stop. She looked up at this amazing man staring at her. How had she ever doubted that they could make it together? She shifted to face him and ran her hands over the hard muscles of his chest. She cupped his jaw, coaxing him down for a kiss, whisky warm and seductive.

"I'm hoping these last few months have shown you that we can carve out our own life. And I'm ready to start that life now," he whispered.

"Me, too, Max," she said. "I'm ready."

She rested her hand on top of his, her fingers around the key to the apartment, too. She turned it, and the door swung open, the afternoon light shining across the bare floors. The place was gorgeous. While Alya and her apartment faced other high-rises, Max's new place had a view of the Sydney Harbour. But the part she liked best ran along the far wall: a newly installed aquarium, still empty. She was almost sure he had put it there for her. Natasha walked over to it and touched the glass.

Max followed close behind. His lips pressed against her hair. "I didn't want to fill it with fish until I consulted you."

"Thank you, Max," she said quietly, her words catching in her throat.

She turned to him, and she couldn't stop smiling. He kissed her and then winked suggestively. "If you feel like you need to keep the fish under close watch, you could even move down the hall. Just to make sure they're well cared for."

She smiled, letting the surge of love flow through her. *Oh, Max.* This was more than she had ever expected. And she was happier than she had ever thought she could be.

"One step at a time," she said, kissing him back. "Let's start by christening the rooms."

* * * * *

COMING SOON!

We really hope you enjoyed reading this book. If you're looking for more romance, be sure to head to the shops when new books are available on

Thursday 27th June

To see which titles are coming soon, please visit

millsandboon.co.uk/nextmonth